**"I have some advice for you, Detective."**

"You can call me Waco."

"No one's going to talk to you," Ella said. "You look like the law."

"I *am* the law."

"I rest my case. It's too dangerous for you here."

He laughed. "Too dangerous for *me*? Are you serious? We'll be lucky if we get out of this town alive."

"If you're trying to scare me—"

He swore and raked a hand through his hair in frustration as she climbed in and slammed the pickup door. She pulled out and headed back in the direction they'd come.

He watched her go for a moment, debating what to do. Follow her? She hadn't seemed to have gotten any information from the owner of the bar, and yet she was leaving? Why was he having trouble believing this?

Because he thought he knew Ella after such a short length of time?

**B.J. Daniels** is a *New York Times* and *USA TODAY* bestselling author. She wrote her first book after a career as an award-winning newspaper journalist and author of thirty-seven published short stories. She lives in Montana with her husband, Parker, and three springer spaniels. When not writing, she quilts, boats and plays tennis. Contact her at bjdaniels.com, on Facebook or on Twitter, @bjdanielsauthor.

## Books by B.J. Daniels

### Harlequin Intrigue

#### *Cardwell Ranch: Montana Legacy*

*Steel Resolve*
*Iron Will*
*Ambush Before Sunrise*
*Double Action Deputy*
*Trouble in Big Timber*
*Cold Case at Cardwell Ranch*

Visit the Author Profile page at Harlequin.com.

New York Times and *USA TODAY* Bestselling Author

# B.J. DANIELS

## COLD CASE AT CARDWELL RANCH

## &

## BOOTS AND BULLETS

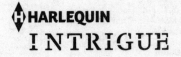

HARLEQUIN
INTRIGUE

# HARLEQUIN®
# INTRIGUE®

ISBN-13: 978-1-335-90968-8

Cold Case at Cardwell Ranch & Boots and Bullets

Copyright © 2021 by Harlequin Books S.A.

Cold Case at Cardwell Ranch
Copyright © 2021 by Barbara Heinlein

Boots and Bullets
First published in 2010. This edition published in 2021.
Copyright © 2010 by Barbara Heinlein

This edition published by arrangement with Harlequin Books S.A.

For questions and comments about the quality of this book,
please contact us at CustomerService@Harlequin.com.

Harlequin Enterprises ULC
22 Adelaide St. West, 40th Floor
Toronto, Ontario M5H 4E3, Canada
www.Harlequin.com

**Printed in Lithuania**

MIX
Paper from
responsible sources
FSC® C021394

# CONTENTS

# COLD CASE AT CARDWELL RANCH

This book is dedicated to all the cowgirls out there.

# Chapter 1

The wind whipped around him, kicking up dust and threatening to send his Stetson flying. Cold-case detective Waco Johnson cautiously approached the weatherworn boards that had blown off the opening of the old abandoned well.

The Montana landscape was riddled with places like this one, abandoned homesteads slowly disappearing along with those who had worked this land.

He hesitated a few feet from the hole, feeling a chill even on this warm Montana summer afternoon. Nearby, overgrown weeds and bushes enveloped the original homestead dwelling, choking off any light. Only one blank dusty window peered out at him from the dark gloom inside. Closer, pine trees swayed, boughs emitting a lonely moan as they cast long, jittery shadows over the century-old cemetery with its sun-bleached stone markers on the rise next to the house. A rusted metal gate creaked restlessly in the wind, a grating sound that made his teeth ache.

It added to his anxiety about what he was about to find. Or why being here nudged at a memory he couldn't quite grasp.

He glanced toward the shadowed gaping hole of the old well for a moment before pulling his flashlight from his coat pocket and edging closer.

The weathered boards that had once covered the opening had rotted away over time. Weeds had grown up around the base. He could see where someone had trampled the growth at one edge to look inside. The anonymous caller who'd reported seeing something at the bottom of the well? That begged the question: How had the caller even seen the abandoned well's opening, given the overgrowth?

Waco knelt at the rim and peered into the blackness below. As the beam of his flashlight swept across the dust-dried well bottom, his pulse kicked up a beat. Bones. Animals, he knew, frequently fell into wells on abandoned homesteads. More often than not, it was their bones that dotted the rocky dry bottom.

Shielding his eyes from the swirling dust storm, Waco leaned farther over the opening. The wind howled around him, but he hardly heard or felt it as his flashlight's beam moved slowly over the bottom of the well—and stopped short.

A human skull.

He rocked back on his haunches, pulled out his phone and made the call. The bones were definitely human, just as the anonymous caller had said. How long had the remains been down there? No way to tell until he could get the coroner involved. He made another call, this one to the state medical examiner's office, as a dust devil whirled across the desolate landscape toward him.

He tugged the brim of his Stetson down against the

blowing dirt, and Waco's gaze skimmed the wind-scoured hillside as his mind raced. That darn memory teased at him until it finally wedged its way into his thoughts.

He felt a chill as he remembered. His grandfather, an old-timey marshal, had told him a story about remains being found in an abandoned well on a homestead in the Gallatin Canyon near Big Sky. Waco couldn't remember specifics, except that it had been a murder and it had been on the Cardwell property, one of the more well-known ranches in the canyon.

While more than fifty miles from where Waco was now standing, and a good fifteen years ago, he found it interesting that another body had gone into a well. He rubbed the back of his neck. There was always something eerie about abandoned homesteads—even when there weren't human remains lying at the bottom of an old well. But right now, he felt a little spooked even as he told himself there couldn't be any connection between the two cases.

Standing, he walked back to his patrol SUV and slipped in behind the wheel and out of the wind. Taking out his phone again, he called up the Cardwell Ranch case. The story had gone national, so there was an abundance of information online. As he read through the stories, he felt a familiar prickling at the nape of his neck.

Waco didn't know how much time had passed when he looked up to see a Division of Criminal Investigation van tear up the dirt road toward him. Behind it, storm clouds blackened the horizon. This part of Montana felt as far away from civilization as he could get. But in truth, it was only a few miles north of the Gallatin Valley and the city of Bozeman, one of the fastest-growing areas of the state.

He liked that there were still places that time seemed to have forgotten in Montana. Places where a person could spend a day without seeing another person. Places developers hadn't yet discovered. Waco often found himself in those places because that was where a person could get rid of a body.

As the DCI van pulled up next to his SUV, he climbed out and felt that familiar prickling again.

His instincts told him that the person in the bottom of this particular well hadn't accidentally fallen in. If he didn't have an old murder case on his hands, then his name wasn't Waco Johnson.

# Chapter 2

Ella Cardwell sat at the large kitchen table in the main house on Cardwell Ranch as she had done for almost thirty years. She tried to listen to her mother and aunt Dana discuss the ranch garden and what they would be canning over the next few weeks.

But a tomboy who preferred being outside with the critters, Ella had never been interested in what went on inside the ranch house. Since college, she'd made her living wrangling with her cousins, Brick and Angus. Until recently. Both had fallen in love and settled down, leaving her at loose ends.

She'd returned to the ranch, where there was always plenty of work to be done, and moved into one of the small cabins on the mountain overlooking the spread. This morning she was waiting for her cousin to pick her up. The two were driving south to buy a new bull—and Angus was late.

Ella noticed that her mother didn't seem to be paying

any more attention to the canning plan than she was. Stacy Cardwell was staring out the kitchen window, as if a world away.

It was a look Ella had seen all her life. Her mother had secrets. Even at a young age, Ella'd sensed something dark in her mother's past. When she was older, Ella had tried to get her to talk about it. But Stacy had always brushed off her concerns and questions, denying anything had ever been wrong.

Her mother had brought her to Cardwell Ranch when she was a baby. Ella had never known her father. The ranch and her extended family were all she'd ever known. Over the years, her mother had occasional relationships with a man, but none that had led to marriage. Not that Stacy hadn't been married before. Her mother's apparent wild years weren't something the family talked about.

Just as they didn't talk about Stacy's disappearances for days at a time. No one knew where she went or why she'd left. Aunt Dana always said that Stacy just needed to get away sometimes.

"Not away from you, Ella," her aunt would say and hug her. "You're my sister's world. But we all need to escape once in a while." Except that Aunt Dana never had run away from the ranch or her children.

Ella suspected that her mother was feeling restless again. She'd always sensed it long before it happened. She knew what it meant. Stacy was about to disappear, never warning anyone or even telling Ella where she'd been once she eventually returned.

"Ella?"

She realized Aunt Dana had asked her something. "Sorry?"

Her aunt smiled. "I just heard Angus honk. He must be

anxious to go pick up that bull. Didn't you say you were going with him?"

She shot up from the table, nearly tipping over her coffee cup.

"I'll take care of that. You better get going." Dana laughed. "Have fun."

Ella shot a look at her mother, wondering if she would be there when Ella got back. After a lifetime of worrying about her mother and her dark secrets, she reminded herself that Stacy had always come back. Why would this time be any different?

At loose ends waiting to hear something from the DCI investigators, Waco headed for Gallatin Gateway at the mouth of the canyon. "Gateway," as the locals had called it since 1917, had gotten its name from the Milwaukee Railroad when the town had become an entryway to Yellowstone Park.

The anonymous call about the bones in the well had come from a phone at the local bar in the town. It had been bothering Waco that the caller had refused to give a name. That brought up even more questions about how the person had happened to just stumble upon the bones in the well and recognized them as human remains. It made him think that maybe the caller had known the body was down there. Otherwise, why not leave a name?

Waco had listened to the recorded 9-1-1 call. The voice had been so well muffled that it had been difficult to tell if the caller had been male or female. The call had been short and to the point, a lot of bar noise in the background. "I saw some human bones in an old well on the Hanover place near Maudlow." That was the extent of it. The operator had tried to get a name but the caller'd disconnected.

When she'd called back, no one seemed to know who had used the bar's landline because it was Saturday night and the place had been packed.

Waco drove into the small community originally started by the family who owned the sawmill, and parked in front of the bar. While there was a school, a bar, and at one time a service station and a place that made cheese, Gateway had never really taken off.

He entered the dimly lit tavern and talked to the bartender. He learned that there were two landline phones on the premises—one behind the bar, the other in the office at the back. No, the office wasn't normally locked during business hours. No, the bartender couldn't remember if anyone had used the phone behind the bar.

Leaving with the names of the servers who'd been working that night, Waco was driving back to Bozeman when he got the call from the state medical examiner telling him to come to the morgue.

He'd wanted the best, so he'd asked for Henrietta "Hitch" Roberts the moment he'd seen the skull at the bottom of the well. He'd worked with her before on a lot of the cold cases in rural areas that barely had a coroner, let alone a medical examiner. It just surprised him that she'd arrived so quickly—not that she'd gone right to work. That was Hitch.

As he walked into the Gallatin County morgue, she shot him a narrowed green-eyed look.

"I hope you don't mind that I asked for you," he said, holding up his hands as if in surrender. "And, yes, I did pull a few strings to get you. But I should have known, after your last rough case and what's going on with your personal life, that maybe you weren't up to this one."

Hitch laughed and shook her head. "You aren't really using reverse psychology on me, are you, Waco?"

"If that didn't work, I was not above using flattery if necessary," he answered tongue in cheek. "Seriously, Hitch, I need you on this one. But I don't want to put you in a spot with your new family." He paused briefly before getting right to the point. "DCI drop off everything from the well?"

"As soon as I got the call, I went out to the site to have a look for myself. But, yes, they delivered the obvious pieces of evidence. They are still sorting through the dirt and debris, but the main discoveries are here. Lucky for you, I've already found something that might interest you."

"Great." He nodded at the large, beautiful diamond engagement ring on her finger. "By the way, when is the wedding?" He'd heard that she was engaged to Ford Cardwell, a cousin of the Cardwell Ranch Cardwells. Soon they would be her new family.

"Christmas."

"Good for you. You seem happy."

"I am. Now, do you want to hear about what I've discovered?"

He chuckled. "Marriage isn't going to change you, is it?"

That was another thing Waco loved about working with Hitch. Once she got her teeth into a case, she didn't let go until she got answers. Waco was the same way, so it was no wonder the two of them worked well together.

He took a breath and stepped deeper into the room. With his job, he'd become familiar with a lot of morgues around the state. They all had that sterilized smell with just enough of some underlying scent to make most people queasy. Not that it seemed to bother Hitch as she motioned him over to a long metal table covered with human bones.

There was no one quite like Hitch, he thought as he watched her pick up the skull in her gloved hands and inspect it for a moment. Hitch was a petite brunette with keen green eyes. Her long curly hair was pulled into its usual bun at the base of her neck. It occurred to Waco that he'd never seen her wear her hair down on the job. Because, he knew, like always, her focus was on her work, not her physical attributes. This was a woman who loved what she did and it showed.

"You said there is something interesting about this one?" Waco asked anxiously. He needed to know if his instincts were right. If so, he had a killer to catch and enough time had already been lost. He suspected that whoever's bones these were had possibly died years ago. Not that the "when" concerned him as much as the fact that someone might have gotten away with murder all this time.

"Patience, grasshopper," Hitch said and went into medical-examiner mode. "The remains are male, midfifties," she said, carefully setting down the skull and picking up a leg bone. "Average height, six-one. Average weight, one eighty-five. Walked with a slight limp," she noted. "An old tibia break that didn't heal right, which tells me he didn't have it properly seen to by a doctor for whatever reason. He wore glasses, nearsighted." She looked up as if anticipating his surprise. "The glasses were found in the bottom of the well. Black plastic, no-nonsense frames."

"Nice job. Now just give me a cause of death."

Hitch shook her head. "You'd love a bullet hole in the skull, wouldn't you? Even better, an old pistol that had been tossed into the well after him?"

Waco admitted that he would. "So what are you telling me? This guy just stumbled into the well, died, and that was that?" he asked, wondering why she'd said there was something interesting. More to the point, why he'd been so sure it had been a homicide.

"It could have been an accident," Hitch said. "Just not in this case. If you look at the lower cranium—"

"Remember, speak English."

She smiled. "What I'm saying is that someone bashed him in the back of the head." She picked up the skull again and turned it under the overhead lamplight. "See these tiny fractures?"

Waco nodded. "Couldn't those have been caused by the fall into the well?"

Hitch was shaking her head. "If it had been any other part of the skull, maybe. But not this low, just above the spine. This man was hit with something that made a distinct pattern in the fracture."

"Something like what? A chunk of wood?"

"Something more narrow. More like a tire iron."

"Was it enough to kill him?"

Hitch gave him an impatient look.

"Wait—are you saying he didn't die right away?"

"If the blow didn't kill him eventually, then the fall into the well and being trapped down there certainly would have," she said. "But he was alive for a period of time before he succumbed to his injuries."

Waco rubbed his neck, the prickles stretching across his shoulders and down his arms. "So someone hit him with an object like a tire iron in the low part of the back of his skull, then knocked him into the well."

"It's one theory."

"Well, we know that they didn't go for help." He thought again of the Cardwell Ranch case. "Any idea how long he's been in the well?"

"I'd say just over thirty years."

"You can call it that close?" Hitch only smiled at him. "Any way to get DNA to identify the remains?" he asked.

"With bones that old, probably not. But, fortunately, we don't have to." Hitch reached into a plastic bag and pulled out something brown, dried and shriveled. For a moment, Waco thought it was a dead animal. "He had this leather wallet on him when he went into the well." The ME grinned. "Inside, I found his Montana state-issued driver's license tucked in a plastic sleeve. Luckily the well was dry. Even the money in his wallet is intact."

"You're enjoying dragging this out, aren't you," he said, understanding how Hitch had been so certain about his age and weight and the rest.

"His name is Marvin Hanover, and if the wedding ring found at the site is any indication, he was married." Hitch produced another plastic bag. "The ring's engraved. 'With all my love, Stacy.'"

*"Stacy?"*

Hitch gave him a look he'd come to know well. "Stacy is also the name Marvin carved into a sandstone rock at the bottom of the well before he died."

Waco was about to let out an expletive before he caught himself. *"He named his killer?"*

"Or he planned to leave her a message and didn't live long enough to write it." She handed him a photo taken at the bottom of the well by a crime-scene tech. It showed the crudely carved *Stacy* followed by smaller letters that hadn't been dug as deep in the stone.

Waco stared at the photo. "It looks like *Stacy don't...* But 'Stacy don't' what?"

"'Don't forget me'?" Hitch suggested.

"Or how about 'don't leave me here'?" Waco said.

"What makes this case interesting, and also a problem as far as my being involved, is that Stacy *Cardwell* Hanover was still married to him when Marvin disappeared and—I suspect—went into the well. Coincidentally, as you know, I'm about to marry into the Cardwell family."

Waco stared at her, goose bumps rippling over his skin. "Stacy..." He could hardly speak. "So there is a connection."

"I already checked. She wasn't living on the ranch at the time her husband disappeared," Hitch said. "I looked up the date of their marriage."

"So did I," he said. "The marriage took place before the body was found in the well at Cardwell Ranch. So she would have known about that case. Three months later, Stacy reported her husband missing. She and her brothers were in a legal battle over the Cardwell Ranch at the time."

Hitch nodded. "So she would have known about the body in the well on the old Cardwell homestead." The remains of a young woman had been found at the bottom of the well. She'd been shot in the head, but apparently only wounded. She'd tried to scratch her way out after being left there to die.

Waco swore under his breath. No wonder the case had stuck in his mind after his grandfather had told him about it.

"Don't tell him those stories," his mother had chastised her father at the time. "You'll give him nightmares—or, worse, he'll grow up and want to be like you."

He hadn't gotten nightmares, but he had grown up to become a lawman. It was his grandfather's stories that he hadn't been able to forget. Waco's love of history had proved to be effective at solving cold cases. He partly put it down to his good memory skills when it came to crimes. That and his inability to give up on something once he felt that prickling on the back of his neck.

He still couldn't believe it. The cases had felt similar, but damn if there wasn't a connection between them—

just not the one he'd expected. "I'm sorry for bringing you in on this case," he said to Hitch. "I figured it might be a copycat 'body dump in an old well' kind of case. I had no idea it might involve someone from your future family."

"Stacy is my fiancé's father's cousin. I've barely met her, so I'm not worried. I can notify the family for you or do anything else you need done. If it gets too close to home, I'll bow out."

He nodded. "Sorry." He could tell she'd hate to have to walk away from this one.

"It sounds like it could turn into a really interesting case."

"What can you tell me about Stacy?"

She shrugged. "She's been living on the ranch since her daughter, Ella, was born—almost twenty-seven years now," Hitch said. "She doesn't have a record, and from what I know, she babysat all the Cardwell-Savage kids. She now helps with the cooking, canning and gardening. Not really murderer material."

"You know that's not an indication," he said.

"I know, but just because there was a similar case on the family ranch doesn't mean she did this. That old case got a lot of media attention. It could have given anyone the idea."

Hitch was clutching at straws and they both knew it as he pulled out his phone and called the ranch. He couldn't wait to talk to Stacy Cardwell, the former Mrs. Marvin Hanover.

Early the next morning, Ella buttoned her jean jacket as she left her cabin on the mountainside overlooking the main ranch house. She stopped on her large porch overlooking the ranch. She and Angus had gotten back late from picking up the new bull. All the lights had been out, including her mother's, so while she hadn't been tired, she'd gone up to her cabin alone and read late into the night.

This morning she'd awakened to sunshine and the scent of pine coming in her open window. The early Montana summer day still had a bite to it this deep in the Gallatin Canyon, though, not that she noticed. She'd awakened to birds singing—but also a bad feeling that she'd had since yesterday.

She needed to check on the new foal before heading to the main house for breakfast with Aunt Dana and her mother. The two should be busy at work canning by now. Yet she'd stopped on the porch to look out across the valley, trying to shake the anxious feeling that her mother hadn't shown up to can this morning.

As she headed for her mother's cabin through the shimmering pines, Ella caught glimpses of Big Sky in the distance. The resort town would soon be busting at the seams with tourists for the summer season. She'd noticed that traffic along Highway 191 had already picked up. Locals joked that the area had only two seasons: summer tourists and winter tourists. The only break was a few weeks in the fall before it snowed and in early spring when the snow melted and the skiing was no longer any good.

Here on Cardwell Ranch, though, only a slight hum of traffic could occasionally be heard through the trees. This morning she could hear the murmur of the river below her, the sigh of the pine boughs in the breeze and an occasional meadowlark's song. The state bird sounded quite cheerful. Normally that would have put a smile on her face.

She loved living on the ranch, working with the rest of the family. While her mother had always liked cooking in the kitchen with her sister or helping out in the garden or with the kids, from a young age, Ella had taken care of the horses and helped round up the cattle. She'd made a good living as a wrangler, traveling all over the state and beyond with her Savage cousins Angus and Brick.

But now Angus and his wife, Jinx, lived on the ranch. Brick and his fiancée, Mo, would be building a place on the spread, both of them in law enforcement rather than ranching. It had surprised Ella when her cousins had settled down so quickly. She knew it was because both had finally met women who were their equals. Love had struck them hard and fast.

She'd never had that kind of luck when it came to men and love. Not that she had been looking. With branding over, the family would soon be rounding up the cows and calves and herding them to the land high in the mountains for the summer. It was one of her favorite times of the year, now that the snow had melted enough in the peaks to let them access the grazing lands.

Ella was content here, so it was no wonder she didn't care that she hadn't met anyone who made her heart pound. But her mother had never been settled here, she thought, realizing why she'd hesitated on her porch this morning. She'd tried her mother's cell first thing this morning, but it had gone straight to voice mail. If her mother was in the kitchen busy canning with Aunt Dana, she had probably turned off her phone.

Still, Ella couldn't shake the feeling that her mother wasn't there...

Aunt Dana answered on the third ring. Ella could almost feel the warmth of the kitchen in her aunt's voice. By now, there would be canning pots boiling on the stove, as well as a cake or cookies baking in the oven. She could practically breathe in the scents.

"Is Mom there?" Ella asked, already knowing the answer deep in her chest where worry made her ache.

"No. I was going to call, but I decided to let her sleep. She's been running tired lately. Are you headed down? I've got corn cakes and bacon for you."

"In a minute." Ella disconnected as she continued across the mountain. Hers and her mother's cabins were two of a half dozen perched above the ranch.

As she neared her mother's place, she tried to understand why she'd been so worried about her mom lately. Since Ella had come back to the ranch after a wrangling job in Wyoming, her mother had been distant. Stacy swore she was fine, but Ella didn't believe it. She sensed it was something much deeper and darker. And that was what worried her. She knew her mother's mood swings better than anyone. Not that she could say she knew her mother any more than she knew the woman's well-guarded secret past.

Reaching her mother's cabin, she climbed the steps to the porch and stopped to listen. Maybe Stacy really had slept in this morning. From here, Ella could catch glimpses of the Gallatin River, the water a clear pale green rushing over granite boulders as it cut through the narrow canyon. Pines soared toward the massive blue sky overhead, broken only by granite cliffs that glistened gold in the sunlight. The smell of pine and the river wafted through the crisp, clean air.

Ella heard no movement from within the cabin. She tapped at the door. When she got no answer, she knocked harder. Still no answer.

Opening the door, she called, "Mom?"

The cabin had a hollow feel.

She stepped deeper inside, a chill moving through her. The place felt empty. She went toward her mother's bedroom. The door was ajar. "Mom?" Pushing it open, she saw that the bed had been made.

Out of the corner of her eye, she noticed the open closet doors and the empty hangers. Her stomach dropped. Even before she checked, she knew her mother's suitcases wouldn't be there. Stacy was gone.

# *Chapter 3*

Dana Cardwell Savage had known something was wrong even before her niece walked into the kitchen. First, Stacy not showing up to help can. Then the phone call from Ella inquiring about her mother. One look at the young woman and she knew it was bad.

Ella was a lot like her mother in that she kept things to herself, minding her own counsel. Even as a young girl, Ella, with her beautiful green eyes like the river and her long blond hair like summer wheat, had always been the quiet, pensive one. Calm waters ran deep.

But it was more than that. Ella saw and felt things that others missed. Because of that, her niece had always worried about her mother—even when it appeared that Stacy had changed.

"I'm sure there is no reason for concern," Dana said, knowing she was trying to convince herself as much as Ella. "You know your mother."

When Dana had gotten up this morning, she'd noticed that one of the ranch pickups was gone. She hadn't thought much about it since anyone on the ranch could have taken it. Ella had also apparently noticed. "Stacy's probably just taking a break like she usually does."

"Haven't you ever wondered where she goes on these so-called breaks?" Ella asked with a sigh.

"Of course. I would ask all those years ago after she came back to the ranch with you, but you know Stacy... I had hoped by now..." Dana shook her head. She'd never understood her sister from the time they were little. They were so different. Stacy had always hated the ranch and couldn't wait to leave it, marrying when she was very young, divorcing, marrying again...

But when she'd come home with baby Ella and settled in, she'd seemed to be happy for a while. Dana had thought her sister had gotten all that wildness out of her system after Ella's birth. Unfortunately, now, even at the age of sixty-four, Stacy still took off without notice, returning days later and refusing to talk about it.

Dana continued slicing the early-season strawberries for jam. She'd gotten up before daylight to get the job started. Her sister had promised to help, so she'd been surprised when she hadn't shown up. Stacy was usually up before anyone.

"It's different this time," Ella said. "She took all her clothes. I don't think she's coming back."

Dana set down the knife. "That can't be true. She always comes back," she said, hoping it was true for Ella's sake. Learning that her sister had packed up everything and simply left came as a shock. But hadn't she often worried that Stacy might do something like that? Just out of the blue. Like this time. Should they be worried?

"She didn't say or do anything yesterday that seemed odd at the time?" Ella asked.

Dana frowned. "Stacy did get a phone call late in the afternoon. Not on her cell but on the ranch landline. I answered it. The man asked for Stacy Cardwell. I asked who was calling, thinking it was probably an annoying sales call." She hesitated. "He introduced himself as cold-case homicide detective Waco Johnson. I thought he was probably calling for a donation. He asked if Stacy was available and I handed over the phone."

"A cold-case homicide detective wanted to talk to her?" Ella asked, disbelieving that Dana hadn't thought that might be important.

"I honestly thought it was about the law-enforcement yearly fundraiser," Dana said in her defense. But now she wondered why she hadn't thought more of it. "I had a batch of cookies going in the oven and the timer went off, so I left your mother and returned to the kitchen."

"Did you see her after that?"

Dana shook her head. "I looked into the living room after I set the cookies to cooling and she was gone."

"So you have no idea what the detective wanted with her."

"No. But like I said—"

"What was the detective's name again?"

Dana repeated it, feeling stricken. She was surprised she even remembered his name, the way her memory had been going lately. Most calls from law enforcement were for her husband, Hud, the marshal. They were either work-related or inquiries about how he was doing after his heart attack and whether he'd retired yet.

She wanted to argue that a homicide detective wouldn't have any reason to call Stacy, let alone make her go on the run. But even as she thought it, Dana felt her heart drop. Stacy had run, taking everything but her daughter with her.

Ella had her cell phone out. "You don't remember where the detective said he was calling from, do you?"

Dana looked out the window for a moment, seeing past the pines to Lone Peak Mountain. She'd believed the call wasn't about anything important. She hadn't even mentioned it to Hud. Because while he said he was fine and had returned to being marshal part-time until his retirement date, which he kept moving farther out, she hadn't wanted to bother him.

Had Stacy been surprised? Scared? Had she reacted at all? Dana couldn't recall even a change in her sister's expression as she'd taken the phone. Dana had been busy, as usual. She hadn't thought any more about it—until now.

Strawberry juice ran down her arm. She wiped it away with a paper towel and picked up her knife to continue cutting the sweet ripe fruit. This jam needed to be canned, and right now she was thankful for the task. Not that it would keep her mind off Stacy. What was a cold-case homicide detective doing calling her sister?

Dana mentally kicked herself for not paying more attention. She should have been there when Stacy had hung up to ask what was going on.

"I'm sorry. He might have said Missoula, but I honestly can't remember. Ella…" she said, slicing the last strawberry. She then put down the knife and rinsed the sticky juice off her hands before drying them on her apron. "I'm sure your mother's fine. She's done this many times before and has always come back after a few days."

Her niece didn't look any more convinced than Dana herself was.

* * *

Ella tried to reassure her aunt that it wasn't her fault. No one could predict anything Stacy might do.

"I would say wait until your mother contacts us," Dana said, "but I can see that you're too anxious for that." As her aunt lowered herself into one of the kitchen chairs, Ella began calling around the state, trying to find cold-case homicide detective Waco Johnson. The kitchen was warm with the scent of strawberries and heavy with a worried tension.

As she placed one call after another without results, Ella looked around the kitchen. Some of her favorite memories had been made here, surrounded by family and friends over the years. This room had often echoed with laughter. Tears had also been shed here and wiped away with the corner of an apron, followed by hugs and reassurances.

Ella pulled out a chair and joined her aunt, knowing that major decisions had been made at this table and that she was about to make one. She'd tried her mother's number again and again; it had gone straight to voice mail. She'd given her mother the morning to contact them, hoping she was wrong.

Her mother had left her no choice.

She'd started with the Missoula Police Department, then the county sheriff's office, then worked her way through the state, starting with the larger cities. She was beginning to think that maybe the man who'd called wasn't even a homicide detective. That there'd been some sort of mistake. That Waco Johnson didn't exist. With a name like that…

She hit pay dirt in Butte.

"Waco?" the woman who answered at the sheriff's department said with a laugh. "He's on cold cases now and hardly ever in the office. If you leave your number—"

"I'm returning his call, but I've misplaced his cell phone number. He said it was important and to call him as soon as possible."

Silence. Then, "I'll tell you what. Give me your name and number. I'll call him to see if he still is interested in talking with you."

"Stacy Cardwell," she said automatically and gave the woman her cell phone number. If the call had been important, then Waco Johnson would get right back to her.

As she hung up, she glanced at her aunt. "If it was nothing, he won't call."

Ella was trying to sell herself on that point—and the idea that her mother had just needed a break from the ranch and wasn't in trouble—when her phone rang.

For a moment, she hoped it was Stacy. But, of course, it wasn't. It was cold-case homicide detective Waco Johnson calling her back. The moment she heard his low, deep voice, she knew he was as anxious to talk to her mother as Ella was. And that meant only one thing.

Whatever trouble her mother was in, it was serious.

# Chapter 4

*"Stacy Cardwell?"* Waco asked, trying to keep the surprise out of his voice. The woman who answered his call wasn't the same one he'd talked to yesterday who'd promised to call him this morning—when she wasn't so busy. She'd given him her cell phone number. But when he'd tried it, it had gone straight to voice mail.

No, the voice on the other end of the line was much too young to be Stacy Cardwell.

"I'm her daughter, Ella."

That made more sense, for sure. "May I speak to Stacy?"

"I thought you spoke with her yesterday," Ella said.

He chuckled softly. "She must have accidentally disconnected after she gave me her cell phone number and promised to call me back this morning."

"So you haven't heard from her?"

"No, but if she's there, please tell her it is very important that I speak with her."

He heard the hesitation in the young woman's voice before she spoke. "I need to know why you're interested in talking to her."

He groaned inwardly. Nothing like a protective daughter. "I'm sorry, but that's between your mother and me."

"It's personal?" His slight hesitation didn't go unnoticed. "It's official police business?"

"Look, if you put your mother on the line—"

"I can't do that. She isn't here."

"When do you expect her back?" he asked, unable to shake the feeling that had his nerves on edge.

"I'm not sure."

He was wondering how Cardwell's daughter even knew about his call. "Did she tell you I had called?"

"No, I haven't seen her. My aunt Dana told me and I tracked you down."

He felt a small thrill ripple through his blood. "Are you at Cardwell Ranch now? I'd love to talk to you. And your aunt, Dana Cardwell Savage, if she's around. I can be there in thirty minutes."

"I doubt we could be of much help to you," Ella said. "Maybe if you could tell me what this is about…"

"It's about one of your mother's former husbands, Marvin Hanover. Your mother reported him missing thirty-one years ago. His remains have been found. I'll see you in thirty minutes at Cardwell Ranch."

There was a long moment of silence before the young woman said, "We'll be waiting for you."

Ella couldn't breathe for a moment. Remains had been found. A cold-case homicide detective wanted to talk to her mother and her mother had taken off. This wasn't one of her mother's short escapes. She'd taken all of her clothes. Ella had known that this time was different. Stacy was on the run. Wherever she'd gone, she wouldn't be coming back. Except in handcuffs.

She'd heard whispered stories about what a wild woman her mother had been in her younger days. Not just quickie marriages and divorces, but missing money and devious plots. Ella had even heard that Stacy had been responsible for Dana and Hud breaking up all those years ago—before they'd gotten back together.

Everyone liked to say that Stacy had changed, that she'd put all of that behind her. Ella had hoped that was true, and maybe it was. But now she feared that her mother's past had just come back to haunt her.

"What did he say?" Aunt Dana asked, looking as worried as Ella felt.

"He said Mom's wanted for questioning in the murder of her husband Marvin Hanover." That wasn't exactly what he'd said. But she knew it was the case. "Did you know him?"

Dana shook her head. "It was her shortest marriage, I believe. Just months. She and I weren't really talking around that time."

"Evidently, he'd gone missing, but his remains have turned up," Ella said, feeling sick to her stomach. "What do you know about him?"

Dana sighed. "Marvin was a lot older than Stacy. He had grown children, two or three, I believe. One of them stopped by looking for her after Marvin went missing. I just remember that the woman was really rude. Apparently she thought that Stacy had gotten away with some of her deceased mother's jewelry and some money."

Dana lowered her head to her hands. "I had really hoped her younger, wild days were over. She'd seemed so changed when she brought you here. All these years, she's helped me here on the ranch." She raised her head. "Stacy's done a lot of things she shouldn't have, but she could never kill anyone."

Ella nodded, even though she feared there was a side to her mother that none of them wanted to acknowledge—but might be forced to face soon.

It had been years since Waco had been through the Gallatin Canyon. His family had taken a trip to Yellowstone Park when he was a boy and gone this way. He'd forgotten how beautiful the canyon was with the Gallatin River carving its way through the cliffs and pines, and mountains soaring up around it.

He used the patrol SUV's navigation system for directions to the Cardwell Ranch. Not that he couldn't have asked just about anyone how to get there. Everyone around here knew the Cardwells and Savages, especially with Hudson Savage still being marshal. Waco had made a point of learning everything he could after talking to Ella Cardwell.

Hud's son Brick was now a deputy, and Brick's fiancée, Maureen, had been hired on as a deputy. Rumor had it, she was a shoo-in for marshal when Hud retired. After Hud's recent heart attack, it probably wouldn't be long.

Waco figured it was just a matter of time before Hud got wind of the cold-case investigation—if he hadn't already heard. In the meantime, Waco hoped to learn as much as he could without any interference. He knew how protective families could be. As marshal, and Stacy Cardwell's brother-in-law, Hud Savage could be a problem. Hitch had told him how fierce and protective Dana Cardwell Savage could be when it came to her family. The family would quickly close ranks to protect Stacy. He'd already gathered as much from the tone of Stacy's daughter's voice on the phone.

He knew he was walking into a grizzly den. The thought made him smile. If there was one thing he loved, it was a challenge. He couldn't wait to meet this formidable family, especially the daughter, Ella. What was it he'd detected in her voice that had him intrigued? He had no doubt that she would do whatever it took to protect her mother. While he admired that, it wouldn't stop him from finding Stacy.

At the turnoff to the ranch, he slowed and pulled off onto the ranch road. He caught a glimpse of the roof of the house, and a large red barn behind it, as he crossed the bridge over the river. A dozen horses raced along the pasture fence line, the wind blowing back their manes. He put down his window and let the summer air with its scents of green grasses and pine trees rush in.

As he pulled into the yard in front of the two-story ranch house, two women stepped out. He knew at once he was looking at Dana Cardwell Savage and Ella Cardwell. Dana, in her sixties, had grayed, but there was strength in her slim body and life-etched face that he'd seen in other ranch women. She was a woman to be reckoned with.

Waco took in the younger woman and smiled to himself as he cut the engine and exited his SUV. Ella Cardwell was a surprise. Her long blond hair was plaited to one side of her beautifully carved face. She was no more than five-five, yet she had a presence that made her seem just as strong and self-assured as her aunt.

As he approached the porch steps, he felt the young woman's emerald green gaze on him and knew that he'd just met his match. He would need to tread carefully with her. If he hoped to get any help from Ella Cardwell, it was going to be a battle.

But then again, he did love a good fight.

Ella watched the man slowly remove his Stetson and look up at her. His blue eyes seemed to nail her to the porch floor. He was much younger than she'd expected—and handsome in a way that caught her off guard. She tried not to show her surprise or react to the intensity of his gaze. When he spoke, his voice had a low, deep rumble to it that quickened her pulse at the same time it put her on alert.

"Afternoon, ladies," he said, tilting his dark head slightly as he nodded first to her aunt and then to her. His hair was longer than most lawmen she knew. He also didn't wear any kind of uniform. He was dressed in jeans and a green-checked shirt, the sleeves rolled up to expose muscled and tanned forearms.

Having always been able to pick up a sense of a person immediately, Ella found herself struggling to get a feel for this man other than the obvious. He was too handsome for his own good. His hips slim, his legs long, his shoulders broad and just as muscular as the rest of his body. There was determination in his stance and those blue eyes seemed to see clear to her soul.

"You have some kind of identification?" she asked, not letting her voice betray how off balance the man threw her.

He gave her a slow smile before reaching into his back pocket and pulling out a badge. His long legs closed the distance between them until he was standing on the lower porch step in front of her, eye to eye.

She took the badge. As she looked at it, she could feel him watching her with a concentration that would have made her nervous if she had let it. "Detective Johnson," she said and handed back the badge.

His warm, dry fingers brushed hers, making her gaze leap to his as she felt the jolt. She saw amusement and challenge in all that blue and warned herself to watch this man very carefully.

"Would you like some lemonade, Detective?" Dana asked. "I just made a fresh batch."

"I'd love some. But, please, call me Waco."

"If you'd like to have a seat," Dana said after she and Ella escorted the detective into the house. "I'll get the lemonade." She started toward the kitchen, but he insisted on coming with her.

"If you don't mind, I'd prefer talking in here," he said. "You have a wonderful kitchen. It reminds me of my grandmother's."

When Dana offered him a chair, he sat at the table and stretched out his long legs, reminding her of a young Hud Savage. Ella took a seat across from him, leaving the head of the table free for her. She could feel how wary her niece was of the man.

Dana poured the three of them a tall, frosty glass of lemonade each and tried to remain calm. She kept telling herself that there was nothing to worry about even as concern bloomed in her mind.

The detective looked around the kitchen, she noticed, taking it all in while also taking the measure of not just her but Ella, as well. She wondered if she should talk to him or if she should call Hud to join them.

"Can you tell us what this is about?" she asked after taking her seat at the table. Ella had filled her in earlier, but Dana wanted to hear it straight from the detective.

Waco cleared his throat. "Are you aware that one of your sister's husbands disappeared some years ago? Maybe you knew him. Marvin Hanover?"

Dana shook her head. "I know that my sister was married a couple of times. She's two years older than me. But I don't recall her ever mentioning that name."

"This marriage didn't last long. In fact, it was only for a few months. Your sister got the marriage annulled, saying that her husband had abandoned her," the detective said.

Dana glanced at Ella, wondering what she thought of the information and the detective. She'd always trusted Ella's instincts when it came to people. But nothing in her niece's expression gave her any indication of how she was feeling about the man.

"Why are you asking about this now?" Ella inquired, getting to the heart of it.

That was so like Ella, Dana thought.

"As I told you on the phone, Marvin Hanover has turned up." The detective seemed to hesitate, his gaze going from Ella to Dana and back again. "His remains have been found. The coroner has evidence suggesting that he was murdered."

"And you think this might interest my mother? As you said, it was years ago that my mother was married to him—"

"Almost thirty-one."

"—for only a few months."

Waco smiled and Dana felt her heart skip before he said to Ella, "Marvin never abandoned your mother. He never left town. His remains were recently discovered on some property once owned by his family—at the bottom of an old well—and we believe they'd been there for more than thirty years."

Dana couldn't help the gasp that escaped her lips. She felt the detective's gaze shift to her and her heart fell. Not again. Not another body in a well. She fought to keep her expression from showing the emotions suddenly roiling inside her. She'd been here before.

"I believe some remains were found in one of the old wells here at the ranch years ago," Waco said, his gaze never straying from her face. "It was back when your siblings were trying to take the ranch away from you, isn't that right?"

Dana had no doubt that he knew exactly when it was. Back when her mother, Mary Cardwell, had died and they hadn't been able to find her most recent will, leaving the ranch to Dana. Back when Hud had just returned to Big Sky to take the marshal job and steal her heart again. Back when she'd been at war with Stacy and her brothers, Jordan and Clay. They'd been determined to force her to sell Cardwell Ranch and give up the family legacy—all for money. Her siblings had only been interested in splitting up the profits. If she hadn't found her mother's will when she had...

"As it turned out, the death of the young woman in the well had nothing to do with our family," Dana said, surprised how calm she sounded.

"No," Waco said, nodding. "But the timing is interesting. Your sister, Stacy, was thirty-three. She'd married Marvin right before the remains turned up in your well here on the ranch." He hesitated for a moment. "Marvin allegedly disappeared after that—after the discovery of the body in your well. Not long after, your sister got an annulment on the grounds of abandonment."

Dana could have heard a pin drop in the kitchen. She didn't dare look at Ella, let alone speak.

"You have to admit, the timing is interesting. Now your sister's former husband's remains have been found in a similar abandoned homestead well," the detective continued. "I'm afraid, this time, it *is* connected to your family."

# Chapter 5

Waco studied the two women. They both hid their reactions well. It would seem that these two didn't know where Stacy had gone or when she'd be back. He didn't think either of them would lie outright to an officer of the law—not when one of them was married to a marshal.

"You can see why I want to talk to Stacy. When did you say you expect her back?"

"We didn't. I believe we already told you that we don't know," Ella said.

He nodded. "She's taken off, hasn't she?"

"I'm sure she's just gone for a few days," Dana said and sent a silent message to her niece that she couldn't miss. Stacy had taken off after his call. That alone made her look guilty and they all knew it.

"Any idea where she might have gone?" Waco asked, guessing that, again, they didn't know. They both shook their heads and avoided his gaze. "It isn't anywhere she normally goes, I take it?" he asked when neither answered. "I see." He did see. He saw what he'd expected. They would try to protect Stacy even if she returned or called to let them know where she was. If they were telling the truth, which he thought they were, then Stacy had hightailed it out of Dodge soon after his call without telling anyone.

He picked up his lemonade and drained half the glass. "This is very good. Thank you." He glanced around the kitchen for a moment before adding, "I'm going to be staying in the area for a few days. Can you suggest a place?"

"There are some cabins just down the road toward West Yellowstone," Dana said. "Riverside Resort. The cabins are right on the water. You might like those."

He noticed that she hadn't looked at her niece as she'd said it. Clearly, she didn't like the fact that he wasn't leaving town. Finishing off his lemonade, he put down his glass and rose.

"I would appreciate you letting me know when you hear from Stacy. It will save me from tracking her down. And I should probably warn you—I don't give up easily." He sighed. "Actually, I never give up. It's a personality flaw." He picked up his Stetson and turned the brim in his fingers for a moment. "We'll be talking again soon." Dana started to get to her feet. "Please, don't get up. I can show myself out."

He gave them each a nod and strode from the room, knowing he wouldn't be hearing from either of them. He was going to have to find Stacy Cardwell on his own.

Ella looked at her aunt as she listened to the detective drive away. She hadn't moved from her spot at the table. She'd hardly breathed.

"It probably isn't as bad as it sounds," Dana said, but Ella had noticed the way her aunt had dropped back into her chair as if relieved to have the man gone as much as she was.

"My mother really never told you anything about Marvin Hanover?" she asked her aunt.

Dana shook her head. "Stacy and I were hardly speaking at the time, other than to argue about the ranch. She'd already been married at least one time by then..."

"I don't know what to do," Ella admitted. "It's bad enough that my mother took off the moment she heard that a detective wanted to talk to her about the man's death." She could see that even Dana was having a hard time coming up with something positive to say. With a sigh, Ella pushed herself up from the table. "The longer she stays away, the worse it will look. I have to find her before he does."

"Why don't we talk to Hud first?"

"Are you sure you want to involve him in this?" She could tell that her aunt didn't want to involve him any more than Ella did. Otherwise, wouldn't she have mentioned that a cold-case homicide detective had called looking for Stacy?

"He'll be upset if he finds out we kept this from him," Dana said. "The detective will probably go to him anyway. But maybe not for a while."

Ella smiled at her. "That will give me some time to find Mom and get her back here, if possible. Anyway, there's nothing Uncle Hud can do," she said. "Unless he knows where my mother's gone." She studied her aunt for a moment. "Unless you do." She watched Dana swallow, eyes lowered.

"There might be one place," her aunt said as she lifted her gaze. "There's a woman Stacy knew in high school. I think they've kept in touch. The woman called her a few months ago. She lives in Gardiner. Her name is Nora Cline.

I don't have any more information than that, I'm afraid. You could call her."

She shook her head. "If my mother is there, I don't want her knowing I'm on my way."

"You're assuming Stacy's running from the law."

Ella let out a bark of a laugh. "That's exactly what she's doing, and I think we can both guess why."

Her aunt shook her head adamantly. "Stacy has had her problems with men over the years, but she wouldn't…" Dana's gaze met hers. "You can't really think that she's capable of murder."

Ella figured Dana knew her sister as well as anyone. Look how Stacy had reacted to the phone call. She'd acted impulsively. It used to be her go-to reaction—especially when she was in trouble, from what Ella had heard. She gave her aunt a hug. "I'll call when I know something."

Waco drove down the road to a pull-off where he could see anyone coming out of Cardwell Ranch. He was no fool. He'd known that Dana had been trying to get rid of him by sending him to a motel miles from the ranch.

He didn't have to wait long before a pickup came roaring out and turned north toward Bozeman. He saw a flash of blond plaited hair and grinned. Just as he'd been betting with himself, it was Ella Cardwell.

He started his truck. Unless he missed his guess, she was going after her mother.

Waco had learned early on in his career to follow his instincts. It had gotten him far. Right now, his instincts told him that the daughter would go after Stacy Cardwell. Either Ella had an idea where she might be, or, like him, she was looking for her.

He was about to find out. His cell phone rang. It was

Hitch. He picked up as he started down 191, going after the pickup that had come from the ranch.

"Just checking in with you. I'm going to notify the family."

He smiled. "Great."

"I thought I'd stop by," Hitch said, making his smile grow even wider. She couldn't resist an interesting case.

"Good idea. Let me know how it goes since I'm in the process of following the suspect's daughter, hoping she'll lead me to Stacy."

"Stacy is…gone?"

"On the run, I'm betting."

Hitch sighed. "Okay. After I notify the next of kin, I'll probably step back from this case. Unless you need my help for anything." Clearly, this case had gotten under her skin, too.

He chuckled as he disconnected, keeping the pickup in sight as Ella continued down the canyon to where it opened into the Gallatin Valley. He found himself thinking about the young ranch woman in the vehicle ahead of him. He'd always been a pretty good judge of character. He'd seen intelligence in her eyes, strength and determination—all things that would make her keep whatever she learned from him. If she could, Ella would try to save her mother.

But did Stacy need saving? That was the question. Given the time frame of the Cardwell Ranch remains found in the well and Stacy's missing husband ending up in one, it looked suspicious. Add to that the fact that Stacy had taken off after his call—a telling sign. The woman had something to hide. He just had to find out if it was murder.

# *Chapter 6*

When Mercedes "Mercy" Hanover Davis heard the news, she let out a bloodcurdling scream that set all the dogs in the neighborhood barking.

Hitch was used to dealing with a wide range of emotions when faced with delivering bad news. As coroner when she'd started, and now medical examiner, she was often the one who notified the next of kin that a loved one had died. She'd caught fainters before they hit the floor, administered to those in shock and consoled the heartbroken who'd dissolved into tears.

But Mercy's scream, followed by a string of oaths, was a new one for her. The woman beat the wall with her fists for a moment before she turned to Hitch and demanded, "What about his money? What about my father's money?"

For a moment, Hitch could only stare at her open-mouthed as she tried not to judge. She'd offered to let the family know about Marvin's remains being found since

Waco's number one suspect was a runner he needed to track down. At least, that was her excuse. Everything about this case was interesting and getting more so by the moment.

Now, standing in the doorway of the youngest daughter's apartment, Hitch reminded herself that everyone handled grief differently. "Your father's *money*?" That was definitely not the question she'd been expecting.

"Yes," Mercy snapped before going off again on another tirade. She was a buxom woman in her mid- to late-fifties with a tangle of brown hair and small, color-matched eyes. Right now, her mouth appeared too large for her face.

Since the door had opened, all Hitch had been able to inform Mercy of was that her father's remains had been found. Nothing else. Now she asked, "Are you interested in knowing where he was found or how long—?"

"You said *remains*. You didn't say *body*. So I assume he's been dead for a long time. Let me make a wild guess. More than thirty years. Duh. That's when he disappeared. That's when that woman killed him. We all knew she'd only married him for his money. She'd said he'd abandoned her. Ha!"

Hitch knew the woman was referring to Stacy Cardwell. She'd been disappointed to hear from Waco that Stacy had taken off after his call. She hadn't spoken to Ford yet today. She suspected not all of the family knew what was going on.

After she notified the rest of the Hanover family, she had to let this case go. It wouldn't be easy, though. Jewelry? Money? "I will be informing your brother and sister after I leave here," Hitch said.

Mercy made an impatient gesture. "Don't bother. I'll tell them. But this won't come as a surprise. What I want to know is if you found the money with his remains, or if that woman got away with not only murder—but also the rest of my father's fortune and my mother's jewelry."

* * *

Waco followed Ella into Bozeman. She sped through the bustling city and got on the interstate heading east. He followed at a distance far enough that he didn't think she would spot a tail and wondered where they were headed. His hope was that she would take him straight to Stacy. It would certainly save him a lot of time, and yet he didn't mind the chase. Just as long as it ended with him solving the crime and bringing justice to the dead man in the well.

His phone rang. He quickly accepted the call on the hands-free Bluetooth. "Hey, Hitch."

"Thought you'd want to hear what happened when I let Mercy Hanover Davis know."

He laughed as she told him, not surprised. "From what I've found out about the deceased, Marvin Hanover had been a loathsome, though wealthy, bastard. Someone probably would have killed him eventually anyway. But the money and jewelry issue is interesting."

Marvin had been considerably older than Stacy and wasn't known for his good looks. Waco made a mental note to find out what had happened to his estate. With Stacy annulling the marriage, he doubted she'd gotten much, if anything.

He was looking forward to talking to her, curious why anyone would settle for anything less than love. Did money really make the difference? Or had it been about security? Either way, it was a bad deal. Not that true love—if it even existed—was easy to find. He knew that firsthand.

"I'm going to notify the rest of the next of kin," Hitch said. "Can't wait to see what kind of reaction I get from them."

As he disconnected, Waco smiled. He and Ella had left the lush valley surrounded by pine-studded mountains to cross the Bozeman Pass. The highway had been cut through the mountains along a creek. As he topped out and dropped off the pass, he saw the blink of the right-hand signal on the pickup far ahead of him.

Ella was exiting the interstate at Livingston. As he followed her, he wondered if this town was where she would lead him to Stacy. But she turned right again, this time heading south through Paradise Valley toward Gardiner and Yellowstone Park.

He felt his pulse quicken at the thought of finally coming face-to-face with Stacy Cardwell. If anyone knew exactly how her husband had ended up at the bottom of that abandoned well, he had a feeling it would be her.

But then he thought of Ella. How well did she know her mother? What would it do to her if she found out that her mother was a killer? Was she ready to have her heart broken?

He couldn't help but wonder where this case was going to take not just him but Ella, as well. Not that it mattered. He was buckled in for the ride. He hoped Ella was, too, because if the prickling at the back of his neck was any indication, things were going to get ugly and soon.

Mercy stood at the window, watching the medical examiner leave. She hugged herself, suddenly aware that she was shaking all over. Her father was dead. His remains had been found. And maybe the money and jewels would be found.

She felt a surge of anger and righteousness. Now Stacy Cardwell would be arrested and go to prison for her crimes.

That thought gave her little comfort. What about the money? Had Stacy taken it, spent it all? Was it gone? Or was it still wherever her father had hidden it? Was there still hope?

She pulled out her phone and called her brother.

"Lionel," she said before he could hang up. "The old man's remains have been found." For a moment, she thought she hadn't spoken quickly enough. It was unusual for her brother to even take her call, given the animosity between them. Even stranger that he seemed to still be on the line.

"Who told you that?"

"The medical examiner was just here. I'm sure she's on the way over to tell you and Angeline. Maybe you should prepare her. I wouldn't want this to kill her."

Lionel made a dismissive sound. "We've all suspected that he was dead for years. I really doubt Angeline is going to keel over at the news. Maybe it would be a blessing if she did."

Mercy cringed even though she'd never been close to her older sister. "That's pretty cold even for you, Lionel."

"You aren't taking care of her and watching her slowly die each day," he snapped.

"What happens now?" Mercy asked, cutting to the real purpose of her call.

"I have no idea. I have to go." With that, he hung up.

She stared at her phone before angrily calling her boyfriend. He answered on the third ring.

"He's really dead," she said into the phone without preamble.

"Who's dead?" Trevor didn't sound all that interested.

"My father. They found his remains. Now they will finally arrest Stacy Cardwell and we'll find out about the money before it's too late. I'm sure it's too late to find my mother's jewels."

"I thought you said Stacy Cardwell didn't have the money or the jewels."

"She hasn't lived like she has it, but maybe she's been

sitting on it all this time in her cabin at the ranch." Even as she said that, Mercy knew it didn't make much sense. Who would sit on a fortune all these years?

"So have the police arrested her yet?"

"I don't know. Maybe. It should be in the news soon, I would imagine."

"How are things at the house with your brother and sister?" Trevor asked.

"Do you even have to ask? Lionel won't do anything, and Angeline is too sick to do anything. Someone in this family needs to find that money."

"I have to go," Trevor said. "Talk to you later." And, like Lionel, he, too, was gone.

Mercy felt a sense of desperation as she put her phone away. But what could they do other than wait to see what the police did about this?

She told herself that there was hope for the first time in a long time. Their father's inheritance had run out. There wasn't much to sell off anymore except the house—in spite of the fear their father's fortune was hidden somewhere inside it.

Mercy scoffed at that. They'd all searched the house, even opened some of the walls. The money hadn't been there.

She tried to hold out hope that Stacy would reveal everything she knew to save herself.

Mercy grabbed her purse, no longer worried about running up more credit-card debt. Her father had taken his secret and his money to his grave. Until now. She had a good feeling that being broke was behind her. It made her want to go shopping.

Ella parked in front of the small stone house just off the main highway into Gardiner. She'd found the address online. What had struck her was the fact that she'd never heard her mother ever mention Nora Cline. As far as she'd been able to tell, her mother had no close friends—at least, none that Ella had ever met. Stacy had seemed content on the ranch with her sister and daughter.

Now it made her wonder if her mother had a secret life— one she'd lived in the wee hours of the night. Or maybe on those mysterious days when she'd disappeared.

Ella feared that her mother's secrets were about to come out. How devastating would they be for not just her but the entire family?

Sitting in front of the small house in Gardiner, she watched the windows for a moment, waiting for the front curtain to move. It didn't. The ranch pickup her mother had taken was nowhere to be seen. But maybe it was hiding in the old garage behind the house—just as her mother was hiding inside this house.

The curtains still hadn't moved. As she got out, she could hear the sound of traffic and the squawk of a crow in a nearby pine tree. The crow watched her with glittering dark eyes as she walked up to the front door and knocked.

From inside the house, she heard movement. A moment later, the door opened. The woman standing in the doorway looked vaguely familiar, as if they had crossed paths before. About the same age as her mother, Nora Cline looked to be in her midsixties, with laugh lines around her warm brown eyes and her mouth. Her gray hair was pulled back in a ponytail. She wore a bright-colored caftan that floated around her bare feet. She looked like a person who was comfortable with the woman she'd become. Ella had to wonder if her mother would ever be.

She glanced past Nora into the small house. It was decorated in bright colors, much like the woman, from the paintings and posters on the walls to the furnishings. "Is Stacy here?"

Nora blinked. "Stacy *Cardwell*?"

"My mother," she said, meeting Nora's gaze.

"Ella! Of course. I should have recognized you. But I haven't seen you since you were a child. Come in." She stepped aside to let her enter, but Ella stayed where she was.

"I need to speak to my mother."

"I'm sorry. She isn't here." Nora was frowning, squinting into the bright summer day outside. A steady stream of tourists could be heard from one street over since the entrance to Yellowstone was just across the Gardner River. "Did she tell you she would be here?"

Ella studied the woman, wondering why it had been so many years since she'd seen her mother's friend. She couldn't remember her mother ever bringing anyone to the ranch. When Stacy disappeared for days at a time, was that when she visited her friend? Did she have other friends she kept even more secret than Nora? "When was the last time you saw her?"

Nora seemed to give that some thought. "It's been a while. Has something happened?"

Ella didn't know how much she wanted to tell her. "If she should show up here, would you give me a call? It's very important. Also, I'd appreciate it if you didn't mention the call to my mother."

Nora looked uncomfortable. "Stacy is an old friend. I wouldn't want to keep anything from her."

She liked the woman's sense of loyalty. "I'm afraid my mother is in trouble." She realized she'd have to be more honest with Nora. "Did she ever tell you anything about her past? Something she only confided in you? It's really important, or I wouldn't be here."

Nora shook her head, her expression one of sympathy. "She said she'd done some things she'd regretted, but haven't we all?"

"I was thinking along the lines of one big regret."

The woman met her gaze and hesitated. "She never told me, but…I got the feeling that there was something she didn't want to come out because of you. So I know she wouldn't want you to—"

"No." Ella shook her head. "It's too late for that. There is a homicide detective looking for her. When he called, she ran."

Nora's eyes widened. *"Homicide?"*

"Let me give you my number. She might call you, and if she does…" Ella looked up at the woman. "If you know my mother, then you know she has an impulsive side that comes out when she feels backed against a wall."

Nora nodded and pulled out her phone so they could exchange numbers. Ella did the same.

From down the street, Waco watched the interaction. He couldn't hear what was being said, but he could read a lot into the fact that Ella hadn't bothered to go inside the house. Stacy Cardwell wasn't there.

The discussion looked serious. He had no doubt that Ella was looking for her mother. To tell her the homicide cop wasn't giving up?

He was pretty sure Stacy had figured that out on her own. It was why she'd taken off. So why was Ella looking for her? To warn her. No, to help her.

He thought about what he'd glimpsed in the young woman's amazing green eyes. He knew that kind of determination well. But he'd also seen a need to protect her mother as if Ella had been covering for her for years. He wondered how much Ella knew.

While he found it admirable and even touching, he didn't see what the daughter could do to help her mother—especially if Stacy was guilty. He felt bad about that, but it was part of the job.

Ella finished her conversation and headed for her pickup, after the cell phone number exchange. What had the woman told her? Something that had Ella moving again.

Waco considered sticking around and questioning the woman in the brightly colored caftan who now stood in the doorway watching Ella drive away. But he thought he had a better chance if he stayed with Stacy's daughter.

He followed her all the way back to Bozeman. When she stopped at a grocery store along Main Street, he couldn't find a parking place and was forced to drive around the block. There seemed to be more traffic than usual even for Bozeman.

His cell phone rang while he was caught in another red light. He saw that it was one of the investigators from the crime lab and quickly picked up.

"I sent a preliminary report of our findings in the well," Bradley said. "But we just found something in the dirt taken from the well that we've been sifting through."

He held his breath, hoping whatever it was would break this case wide open.

Dana was too restless even to bake after Ella left. She'd paced the floor, debating if she should call her husband or wait until he came home for lunch to tell him. This was something she'd decided she couldn't keep from him. More than likely, the homicide detective would contact him anyway—if he hadn't already, she told herself.

Finally, unable to sit still, she'd decided to head up the mountainside to Stacy's cabin. She didn't figure that she would find anything; after all, Ella had already looked. But she knew her sister. Maybe there was a clue as to where she had gone that Ella wouldn't have recognized.

For years, Dana hadn't butted into Stacy's business. Yes, her sister took off every few months and didn't return for days without any explanation. Dana had given her room and hadn't questioned her after the first few times. All of them living on the ranch together, she knew, didn't offer a lot of privacy. And she'd wanted to give Stacy space, which she'd apparently needed. But the homicide detective's visit had changed that. If Dana could help find her sister, she had to try.

The breeze swayed the pines as she walked up the mountainside. There was nothing like summer in the canyon. The sky overhead was a robin's-egg blue, with only a few white puffs of clouds floating above the high peaks still capped with snow. She could smell the pines and the river. It was a smell that had always grounded her.

Years ago, they'd built a series of cabins on the side of the mountain above the main ranch house for guests and family. Stacy had moved into one of them when she'd returned to the ranch when Ella was but a baby. At the time, Dana had thought it was temporary. She and Hud had offered Stacy land to build her own house on, but she'd refused.

"This cabin is perfect for one person," her sister had argued. When Ella was grown, she'd moved out of her mother's cabin into one of her own for those times she was home on the ranch. So, for years, Stacy had lived alone.

"It's so small," Dana had countered.

"I don't need more room," her sister had said. "I'm fine

where I am. Anyway, it makes it easier for me to just come down the mountainside in the morning to help with the cooking and baking." Before that, she'd helped with all the children, both theirs and the cousins' kids who loved spending time on the ranch.

Dana had often wanted to ask her sister if she was happy, but she'd held her tongue. Stacy was so hard to read. She'd seemed content, which had surprised Dana. Growing up, there'd been so much restlessness in her older sister. Wasn't that why Stacy had run off and gotten married the first time at such a young age?

Their mother used to say that Stacy would be the death of her. By then, Mary Cardwell had been divorced from her husband Angus. She'd done her best with Stacy, but had always felt she hadn't given her oldest daughter enough love, enough attention, enough discipline. She'd blamed herself for the way Stacy had turned out.

But when Stacy had come home years later, after their mother's death, Dana had seen a change in her. Stacy had baby Ella and had stayed on to help with Dana's four children. Their brother Jordan had also returned to the ranch, reuniting them all. Now Jordan lived with his wife, Liza, and their children in a home they'd built on the ranch.

Dana loved having her family so close. The only one who didn't live on the ranch was her brother Clay. He lived in California, where he was involved in making movies, and only got home occasionally.

As she reached Stacy's cabin, Dana slowed, reminding herself how blessed she was to have had her sister here all these years. She couldn't lose her now.

Like most doors on the ranch, this one wasn't locked. She turned the knob and let the door slowly swing open.

She heard a sound from deep inside the cabin.

"Stacy," she called, flushed with instant relief. She had returned. No doubt her sister had realized how foolish it had been to run. Stacy must have driven in along the road that ran behind the cabins, hoping no one would be the wiser about her leaving—and coming back—the way she had.

"Stacy!" Dana called out louder as she stepped inside. The shadow-filled cabin felt cool even though it was past noon on a bright sunny day. The large pines sheltered the cabins, providing privacy as well as shade.

Dana stopped in the middle of the living room as she realized that whatever she'd heard, it had stopped. Had she only imagined the sound? She stared at the normally neat-as-a-pin cabin in shock. It looked as if a whirlwind had come through. Drawers stood open, even the cushions on the couch had been flung aside, as if someone had been searching for something.

Had Ella done this? She wouldn't have left such a mess. Dana's heart began to pound. But if Ella hadn't—

She jumped as the door she'd left wide open behind her caught the breeze and slammed shut. Startled, she tried to laugh off her sudden fear. But her laugh sounded hollow. "Stacy?"

Surely her sister had heard her. Was it possible she was in the shower? As Dana stepped toward the back bedroom where she'd heard the sound coming from, she saw that the door was partially closed. Did she just see movement behind it?

"Stacy?" She hated the way her voice broke. "Stacy!"

She was almost to the room when the door flew open. A dark figure filled the doorway an instant before rushing at her, knocking her down, as he fled.

Dana lay on the floor, dazed and gasping for air. She heard what sounded like a motorcycle start up behind the cabin. Her heart felt as if it would pound out of her chest at the sudden shock. She tried to move. It took her a moment to realize that she wasn't badly hurt—just her ego bruised and battered.

Sitting up, she pulled out her cell phone and called her husband.

# Chapter 7

On the way back from Gardiner, Ella remembered that her aunt had mentioned they were out of lemons. She stopped at the market on Main Street in Bozeman, wondering if she was still being followed by the detective as she went into the store.

When she came back out to her pickup, she couldn't see him. But there was a woman with a wild head of brown curly hair and wearing a leopard-spotted poncho leaning against her truck.

"Can I help you?" Ella asked and then realized she'd seen the woman before. An old memory nudged at her.

"You're her kid, right? Ella Cardwell. You don't look like her."

"I'm sorry?"

"I'm Mercy Hanover Davis. Your mother used to be married to my father."

Ella nodded, taking in the woman as she wondered what

she wanted. It had been years since she'd seen Mercy Hanover, but the woman hadn't changed all that much. Like today, she'd been waiting by their vehicle then, too.

Only years ago, she'd been angry and much scarier. "Where's our money?" she'd demanded of Ella's mother.

"I don't know what you're talking about," her mother had answered.

"Like hell you don't, Stacy. You think we don't know what you've done?" The woman's laugh had scared Ella more than her anger. "What did you do with him?"

"If you don't leave me alone, I'm going to call the police."

The woman had laughed harder. "Sure you are."

Stacy had shoved the woman away, and she and Ella had gotten into their pickup and driven away.

When Ella had asked who the stranger was, her mother had said she was some poor demented person who was confused. Stacy had claimed that she'd never seen Mercy Hanover before.

Ella knew better now. She decided to wait Mercy out even though she was anxious to hear what the woman had to say.

"We should have coffee." Mercy looked around, spotted a coffee shop. "You drink coffee, don't you?"

Ella was anxious to find her mother, but so far, her attempts had come to a dead end. "Why not?"

Neither of them said anything as they walked the short distance to the coffee shop.

"I'm buying," Mercy said once inside. "What do you want?"

"Just plain coffee."

The woman gave her a disbelieving look, as if buying plain coffee at a coffee shop was a total waste of money.

"Whatever." She stepped up to the counter and ordered a caramel mocha latte and a plain cup of coffee.

Ella took a seat out of the way. There were only a few people in the shop this late in the day, a man and a woman, and two women. All were looking at their phones.

Mercy returned, handing her a coffee before lowering herself into the chair opposite her.

"Thanks," Ella said and took a sip. It was hot and not nearly as good as her aunt Dana's.

Given the circumstances, Ella offered her condolences to Mercy. To which Mercy grunted in response.

"You're not much of a talker, huh?" Mercy said, studying her over the rim of her cup as she took a sip and then put the latte down. "Not much like your mother."

"I suspect you have something on your mind?"

Mercy bristled. "I just thought we should get to know each other."

"Why?"

"We're almost family. Your mother was married to my father."

"That's a bit of a stretch family-wise, don't you think?"

Mercy looked surprised for a moment but then laughed. "Maybe you're more like your mother than I thought. So let's get right to it. Where's your mother?"

"Why do you care?"

The woman sighed. "You aren't going to make this easy, are you?"

Ella leaned forward. "What do you want with Stacy?" She'd called her mother Stacy when she was little because all the other kids did. Also, sometimes it was hard to think of the woman as a mother. Like right now, when she was missing and possibly wanted for murder.

"What your mother took from me. My father and his

money—not in that order. She also stole my mother's jewelry before she left."

"My mother doesn't have your money or jewelry, and we know where your father is. We just don't know how he got there," Ella said. "But since your concern seems to be money and jewelry over the loss of life, I'd say my mother isn't the only suspect in his murder."

Mercy sat back with a look of almost admiration. "You're smart."

"And not easily intimidated," Ella said.

That got a smile out of the woman. "No, you're not. Look, I know your mother ran the moment my father's remains were found. What does that tell you?"

"That the law and your family would be after her—no matter her innocence."

Mercy laughed. "Honey, your mother is far from innocent. She ran because she's guilty." Ella said nothing. The woman leaned toward her. "My father was a bastard. I wouldn't blame your mother for killing him. But we need that money."

"I don't know anything about any money."

Sitting back, Mercy said, "Maybe she already spent it."

Ella shook her head. "My mother and I have never had any money. After I was born, she brought me to Cardwell Ranch and went to work with the rest of the family. Does that sound like a woman with any money?"

Mercy eyed her sharply. "How old are you?"

"Almost twenty-eight."

"That wouldn't have given her much time to spend the money." The woman sighed. "If your mother doesn't have the money, then who does?"

Hitch parked in front of the huge old three-story mansion. Faded letters on the mailbox spelled out the name Hanover. In its day, this place must have been something, she thought. The massive edifice, perched above the Gallatin River, had a view of the valley.

But its age had begun to show. More modern, more expensive houses had sprung up in the valley, eclipsing the Hanover house. It now looked like a place that trick-or-treating kids would avoid.

When Mercy Davis had demanded to know what had happened to her father's fortune, Hitch had thought the woman was exaggerating. But maybe the man really had had a fortune at some point. Had Stacy gotten away with it? Maybe, since this place looked as if it was in need of repair and no one had done anything about it. Could the family no longer afford it?

Hitch walked up many steps to the wide porch with its towering stone pillars and raised the lion's-head knocker on the large wooden door. She'd barely brought it down when the door flew open and she found herself staring at a man in his early sixties. He was wearing slacks, slippers and a velvet smoking jacket. Hitch felt as if she had stepped back in time.

His hair had grayed at his temples, frown lines wrinkled his forehead, appearing to be permanent, and his mouth was set in a grim line. He looked enough like his younger sister Mercy that she knew he had to be Lionel Hanover, the eldest of Marvin's offspring.

"I'm State Medical Examiner Roberts," she said. "Lionel Hanover?" He gave her a distracted nod. He seemed to be more interested in looking down the road behind her than at her. "I'm afraid I have some bad news—"

"I know. Mercy called. Is that all?"

She was taken aback by his abruptness, as well as his complete lack of interest regarding his father's death. "Do you have any questions?" she asked almost tentatively, still standing outside with the door open. She reminded herself that he had probably let out any emotion he'd had about the news after Mercy's call. And it had been thirty years since his father had disappeared.

She quickly did the math. Lionel, the oldest, would have been in his early thirties when his father died. His sister Angeline would have been a few years younger than Lionel, and Mercy would have been in her midtwenties. Not children by any means.

That, she realized, meant Stacy had been the age of Marvin's offspring while Marvin had been the age Lionel was now.

A woman appeared from the shadows deep within the house, her wheelchair squeaking as she rolled into view. "Is this her?" asked a faint, hoarse voice.

Lionel didn't bother to turn. "I'm handling this, Angeline."

Hitch blinked as the woman wheeled herself into a shaft of light behind him. Her hair was black with a streak of white like a cartoon vamp. She was thin to the point of emaciation and, from the pallor of her skin, not in good health.

"My sister is ill," Lionel said.

"I'm not ill," Angeline snapped. "I'm dying. But I'm not dead yet." The woman turned her narrowed eyes on Hitch. "So, what are you going to do about my father's death?" she demanded, her dark gaze seeming to pin Hitch to the floor.

"Cold-case homicide detective Waco Johnson is handling the investigation," Hitch told the two of them. "I'm sure he'll be contacting you."

"Murder?" Angeline croaked and then erupted in a coughing bout.

"The medical examiner just said that a cold-case *homicide* detective would be contacting us, Angeline. So, of course it was murder." Lionel looked past Hitch to the street. A buzzing sound filled the air, growing louder and louder.

Hitch turned to see a dark-clad figure come roaring up on a motorcycle and park behind the state SUV where she'd left it. As the rider removed his helmet, she saw blond hair that dropped to the man's shoulders. He looked up the hillside toward the gaping front door and Hitch standing there. His smile was filled not with merriment but with spite.

When she turned back, Lionel's face was pinched in anger. "Thank you for letting us know, Miss…"

"Roberts," she said in the same clipped tone he'd used with her.

"Is that Trevor?" Angeline asked. "Is Mercy with him?" She didn't sound as if either's arrival was welcome.

Lionel started to close the door in Hitch's face. As he moved, he said over his shoulder, "Just Trevor, and I'm in no mood to deal with him right now."

The door slammed.

Hitch turned to look down at the road. Mercy's boyfriend? Mercy was midfifties, but the man standing by the motorcycle appeared younger—at least from this distance. As she descended the steps, she could feel his gaze on her. It wasn't until she reached his level that she saw that Trevor was quite a bit younger than Mercy. Hitch would guess a good ten years.

Trevor gave her an insolent look as he flipped his long hair back. "You the undertaker?" he asked with a smirk.

"State medical examiner."

"Isn't that the same thing?"

"I'm an investigator as well as a coroner."

His eyes widened a little. "So you cut up people? Cool."

Yes, cool. "I suppose you heard about Marvin Hanover," she said, wondering if anyone would mourn the man's death.

"Marv?" He shrugged. "Never met him. Mercy said someone snuffed him, but from what I've heard about him, he probably deserved it." His eyes gleamed. "Is it true that now they're going to be rich again?"

"I wouldn't know about that." She glanced back at the house. "They seem to be doing all right."

Trevor laughed. "Looks can be deceiving. The house is about all they have left. Pretty soon they won't even have furniture to sit on, but they still act like they're better than the rest of us." He started to turn toward the house when Lionel called down from the porch to say that Mercy wasn't there and closed the door again.

Trevor hesitated. "I had some news for them, but if they're not interested…" He grinned. "It will be nice to see Lionel eat crow." He laughed and swung a leg over his bike before starting the noisy motor and taking off.

*To see Lionel eat crow?* Hitch had no idea what he meant by that and, at the moment, didn't care.

Once in her SUV, she headed back to Bozeman. On the way, she'd called Waco to fill him in. Her job was done and yet she felt the pull of the case. Left with so many questions, she itched to find the answers. She likely had some time before being called in on another case and wished there was some way she could help with this one. Waco had his hands full and the DCI part of the investigation was pretty much over until he turned up more evidence—and found Stacy in the hope of getting to the truth.

Her cell phone rang. She didn't recognize the number or the name. Did she know someone named Jane Frazer?

She picked up with a simple "Hello?"

"Henrietta Roberts?"

"Yes?"

"I'm Jane Frazer. I thought you might be contacting me."

"I'm sorry," Hitch said. "What is this in regard to?"

"The death of my father, Marvin Hanover."

"*Your* father? I wasn't aware that—"

"That he had another daughter?" Jane let out a bitter snicker. "It would be just like Mercy and Angeline to completely forget me, but I would have thought Lionel might mention my name.

"I'm the product of an affair Marvin had with my mother. When my mother was killed in a hit and run, he moved me into his home. I spent time with the three of them. I knew there was no love lost for me, but it would have been nice if they'd thought to let me know about our father."

"I'm sure they're probably not thinking clearly," Hitch said, wondering why she was covering for them. "This has to have come as a shock to all of you."

Jane laughed. "You've met them. Did they appear any more shocked than I am? Nor am I surprised someone killed Marvin."

Hitch noticed that Jane hadn't immediately pointed a finger at Stacy Cardwell.

"Marvin and my mother were engaged when she died. Who knows if my mother would have actually gone through with a wedding? My father...well, he was a difficult man. But he had his...allure when it came to women, if you know what I mean."

Hitch thought she did. "Was this after Marvin's first wife died?"

"Only months after *her* tragic accident," Jane chortled cynically. "For years I was convinced that Marvin had killed his first wife as well as my mother. I still wouldn't be surprised. I expected him to kill his third wife. So I was shocked to hear that someone had killed him instead."

Hitch was trying to put all this information together, but Jane Frazer had added a whole new dimension to the family tree. "I would love to sit down and talk with you. From your area code, you live in Idaho?"

"Not far from the Montana border. If you want to know about Marvin and that family of his, then I'm your girl," Jane said.

Hitch knew she couldn't walk away. Not yet. "When would be a good time?"

Mercy hadn't wanted to believe Ella Cardwell, but she did after their talk in the coffee shop. The daughter didn't know where her mother was. She also didn't know anything about the money.

Her cell phone rang. She saw that it was Trevor and picked up.

"I have something you might want to see," he told her.

Since he was her boyfriend, and also her drug source, she brightened. "I'm on my way to my apartment. Am I going to like it?"

"See you in a few." He disconnected.

Fifteen minutes later she heard his motorcycle pull up out front. As he came in the door, he glanced over his shoulder as if afraid he'd been followed. Whatever he had must be good.

Mercy couldn't help her excitement. "So?" she said, holding out her hand.

He reached into his pocket and laid three photographs on her open palm.

She stared at them, trying not to be disappointed. "I thought... What are these?"

"I broke into Stacy Cardwell's cabin. I didn't find any money, but I found these in some photo albums hidden in a space in the wall behind the closet."

She glanced at the snapshots, still unimpressed. All she'd really heard was that Trevor hadn't found any money. Nor had he brought drugs.

"I think it might be a clue," he said excitedly. "I was going to show them to your family, but they weren't interested in seeing me. Their loss."

Mercy looked more closely at the photos. They were old, the clothing out of style, the shots not even that well composed. But she did recognize the much younger Stacy.

"How are these helpful?" she asked him.

"I don't know." She heard his disappointment. "I thought you might have some idea. They have to be important, right? Why else would she hide them?"

Mercy looked again at the photos. She didn't want to tell him, but breaking into Stacy's cabin had been a bonehead idea. Worse was thinking that these old photos were important. The least he could have done was taken something of value.

"I'll have to give this some thought," Mercy said, dropping the snapshots on the coffee table. "You don't have anything to smoke on you, do you?"

Trevor looked crestfallen for a moment. "I have a little weed."

She brightened, the photos forgotten as she snuggled up against him. She hoped her brother wouldn't hear about what Trevor had done. Lionel had enough problems with her young boyfriend.

# *Chapter 8*

Marshal Hud Savage swore as he watched his wife rub the side of her thigh she'd landed on. "Are you sure you're all right?" he asked again after she finished telling him everything that had happened.

They were sitting on the porch swing in front of Stacy's cabin. Inside, several crime-scene techs were searching for evidence that could be used to locate the person who'd not only ransacked the place, but also knocked Dana down when he'd escaped.

"I'm fine." She sounded more embarrassed than hurt. He could be glad of that. "I'll be black-and-blue tomorrow, but fortunately, nothing was broken."

Hud shook his head. "Can you describe the man?"

"There wasn't time to get a good look at him. He was wearing a hoodie. I only got a glimpse of his face. Maybe forties. Brown eyes. Long blond hair. He smelled of exhaust fumes."

Hud chuckled. She made a better witness than most detectives he'd come across.

"Oh, and there was something jingling in his pocket when he moved," Dana said. "He was just under six feet, slimly built. And he was wearing boots. I remember the sound they made on the wood floor. Biker boots, because after he left, I heard a motorcycle start up behind the cabin. That would explain the exhaust fumes I smelled on him."

Hud couldn't help but smile at his wife. "Is that all?"

"I think so. No, he also was wearing gloves."

So that meant no fingerprints. "You have no idea what he was looking for in Stacy's cabin?" The whole place had been vandalized. Full drawers dumped on the floor, containers pulled from the closet added to the pile.

"That's what's odd. If he hadn't taken the photos, I'd think he was there to steal something of value," Dana said. They'd discovered several old photo albums on the floor. Empty spaces on a few of the pages indicated that some of the photos were missing.

"I've never seen those photo albums before," Dana said. "I can't imagine the young man broke in to take photographs. Can you?"

He couldn't.

"Is it likely this has something to do with why that homicide detective is so anxious to talk to Stacy about her ex-husband's death?"

Hud wished he knew. Stacy was missing. Someone had ransacked her cabin. The intruder had knocked Dana down as he'd escaped. What bothered him most was how bad things might get before this was over.

"What do you know about this former husband of hers? Marvin Hanover?"

"Nothing, really. I never met him. He was a lot older

than Stacy. She'd been married a couple of times by then. She was living in Bozeman at the time, I think. Mother and I hardly ever heard from her back then. I never really knew who she'd married or divorced," Dana said. "It wasn't like she ever brought them to the ranch. I vaguely remember her mentioning someone named Emery. That's it. She could have already been married maybe a couple of times by the time she married Marvin. That's probably why she didn't tell us about him, let alone about the marriage and annulment."

"Dana, you need to be ready for the worst. You know Stacy. She could have killed the man. She could have known about the body that had been thrown down the well on the ranch."

Dana glared at her husband. "I refuse to believe it. Everyone knew about the remains found in our well. Disposing of a body in an old well would be an obvious choice to a lot of people who might have wanted to get rid of someone."

Hud had to laugh. "Remind me to stay away from old wells." Rising from the swing, he said, "You think you can walk back to the house?"

She rose, wincing but clearly trying to hide it. "Stop treating me like an old woman." Stepping past him, she started down the mountain path.

Hud followed. In his years of law enforcement, if he'd learned anything, it was that most people were capable of murder. Some people more than others, Stacy being one of those people. When backed into a corner, people did whatever they had to do to survive. Before she'd had Ella, Stacy had proved over the years that she was a survivor—even if it meant breaking the law.

"You really should have told me the minute this homicide detective called," he said to his wife's back as they descended the mountain. "Now Ella's gone looking for her?" He groaned. "What am I going to do with the women in this family?"

Dana stopped and turned to look at him. He saw the fear and worry in her expression. Family meant everything to her. He put his arms around her and pulled her close.

"Do what you always do," she said, her voice thick with emotion. "Protect us, Hudson Savage. Don't put a BOLO out on her. Not yet, please."

He wanted to argue but instead he kissed the top of her head, holding her tighter. He didn't know what he would do without Dana. She was his life. He hated to tell her that the cold-case homicide detective had probably already issued a BOLO for Stacy. If he hadn't, he would soon.

"Ella was asking me about Stacy's past," his wife said as she stepped out of his arms and they walked together the rest of the way to the house. "I didn't know what to tell her because I don't know. I've never wanted to know."

Stacy had attracted trouble much of her life. Some of it she'd brought to the ranch. It appeared she had again. "Don't worry," he told her. "Stacy will turn up." He just hoped it would be alive and not under arrest.

In the meantime, he had to find out everything he could about Stacy's past and Marvin Hanover and his murder.

Waco couldn't wait to hear what had been discovered in the bottom of the well. "What did they find?" he asked the DCI agent at the other end of the phone line. He'd worked with Bradley before and knew he was thorough.

But right now, he also had something else on his mind. Ella Cardwell. He'd followed her to the grocery store and circled the block. He'd almost circled the block for a third time when the vehicle in front of him stalled. Ella certainly seemed to be taking her time at the store, which was either a ruse or she was headed back to the ranch with a pickup full of groceries and no longer in search of her mother.

"It's a key," Bradley said.

"A key?" Waco echoed with disappointment. "A car key, safe-deposit key…?"

"Larger than a normal key. Odd shape. Definitely not a key to a car or house. Of course, we have no idea how long it's been down there or if it even belonged to the deceased. But from the look of it, the key's been down there for years."

"I'm going to want to see it," Waco said as another call came in. "Can you get it to me at General Delivery in Big Sky?" he asked before disconnecting.

"I just finished notifying the rest of Marvin's family," Hitch told him.

He listened as she described her reception at the Hanover house, her impressions of Lionel and Angeline, as well as Mercy's boyfriend, Trevor.

"The surprise was another daughter by another mother," Hitch told him. "Jane Frazer. I'm on my way to talk to her."

"Thanks. I appreciate your help on this one," Waco said as the man in the car in front of him finally got the vehicle running again.

"I'll be off this case as soon as I talk to Jane."

"Just don't stick your neck out too far. I wouldn't want you on the wrong side of your soon-to-be relatives before you even get to the altar. Or worse."

"There is one thing Jane told me on the phone that might interest you," Hitch said. "Her mother was killed when she was young. Jane ended up living with Marvin and his other children. None of them mentioned her to me."

"Interesting."

"That's not the interesting part. Marvin's wife and fiancée died in accidents. I just looked it up on my phone. Wife number one fell down the stairs, broke her neck. Almost-wife number two, Jane's mother, was killed in a hit and run."

Waco let out a low whistle.

"So it is rather amazing that Stacy Cardwell Hanover is still alive."

He grunted at that. "Maybe only because she killed him before he could kill her." Waco hadn't considered what might have happened at the edge of that well before Marvin went into it. "What if he took her out there to throw her down the well, but she pushed him instead?"

"Interesting since both the wife's and fiancée's deaths were considered suspicious," Hitch said. "Jane said when she was young, she suspected her father had killed them both. She said she thought he would kill Stacy, too, and was surprised that someone got to him first."

"Let me know what Jane has to say," Waco said as he came around the block and saw Ella pulling back onto Main. "By the way, DCI found a key in the well. I haven't seen it yet, but they're sending it to me."

"The key to Marvin Hanover's heart?"

"Hopefully, the key to this case," he said. "Oh, looks like Stacy's daughter is headed back to the ranch. I don't believe she knows where her mother is," he said with a sigh. "A dead end. At least, temporarily. Thanks for the update on the family and taking care of the notifications. You're the best. If you weren't already spoken for—"

"You'd run like the devil was chasing you if any woman seriously showed an interest in you," she said, laughing. "Save your sweet talk for someone who cares. I'd be interested to see what you make of the family. Just…be careful. I picked up on some real animosity."

"You're worried about me? I knew you had a soft spot for me, Hitch."

"Just between my ears," she said and disconnected.

Ella didn't know what to make of her encounter with Mercy Hanover Davis. But apparently she and the detective weren't the only ones looking for Stacy. She couldn't help her disappointment in not finding her mother, but she wasn't going to let that stop her.

She drove home, anxious to see if Stacy might have called the ranch. At the main house, she found Dana and Hud in the kitchen. What she overheard as she walked in shocked her. An intruder had knocked down her aunt?

"You're sure you're all right?" Ella asked after hearing what had happened at her mother's cabin. She could see that her aunt was more scared about her sister than before and trying hard not to show it.

"I'm fine," Dana insisted. "You and Hud don't have to worry about me."

The marshal snorted at that and said he had to get back to the office. "Can you stay out of trouble until I get home?" he asked his wife before he kissed her goodbye.

"I'll do my best," Dana promised, smiling as she watched him leave. Then she quickly turned to Ella. "Any luck finding her?"

Ella shook her head. She hadn't learned anything from Nora Cline except that Stacy kept secrets—even from her secret friend.

After being sure that her aunt really was all right, she walked up to the cabins, going straight to her mother's. The marshal had cleared it after the forensics team had finished. Her uncle had said the intruder had apparently been wearing gloves, so he hadn't left any fingerprints.

Ella set about cleaning up the mess. Her aunt had mentioned that the intruder might have taken some photos. Dana said she had never seen the photo albums before. Ella realized that neither had she.

Taking them to a chair, she began to go through them, wondering why her mother had never shown her these albums. She'd never seen them before or any of the photos. Nor did she recognize any of the people in the snapshots—except for her mother.

When and where had these been taken? There were photographs of her mother when she was much younger, possibly in her late twenties or early thirties, with people Ella didn't know.

It felt strange, seeing her mother so young—before Ella'd been born. From the photos, it was clear that Stacy had known these people well. So where had the shots been taken? Not on the ranch or in the canyon, from what she could see.

She found her mother's magnifying glass. Stacy had been complaining that printed instructions were either getting smaller and smaller, or her eyesight was getting worse. As she studied the photos, Ella noted that they were from different years, different decades, given the clothing. Each year, each decade, there was her mother—often with the same people. The people aged the deeper she got in the album—just as her mother did.

Ella had an idea, gathered up the photo albums and took them to her cabin. Taking out her own albums from the same time period, she compared the photos of herself as a child on the ranch with her mother and family, and realized that she'd stumbled onto something.

There was a photo of her mother in a favorite summer dress that Ella remembered—and there she was in the exact same dress in one of her mother's photographs from her secret albums with the mystery people.

With a shock, she realized this had to be where her mother disappeared to for days at a time over the years—and it could be where she had gone now. Her mother had two separate lives; she'd been coexisting all these years. A secret life away from Cardwell Ranch.

Why couldn't Stacy tell them about this place, these people? Why keep it a secret when this other life obviously meant something to her? She wouldn't have kept the photos otherwise. It made no sense—just like her mother's moods.

Where was this place that her mother had gone to year after year before Ella was born? She scoured the photos again, looking for something in the background that would give her a clue as to where they'd been taken. If she could find the place, she had a feeling she would find her mother.

Her hand holding the magnifying glass stopped on what appeared to be a sign, barely distinguishable in the background. A bar? Ella looked for other similar photographs until she found one with a more legible portion of the sign. She wrote down the letters she could see and searched for more until at last she looked at what she had written. Hell and Gone Bar.

Her heart beat faster. So where was this place? Recognizing some of the license plates on cars in the background, she noted Montana plates from different years and decades. There were enough Montana tags, she thought excitedly, that the town had to be in the state.

Going to her phone, she thumbed in the words *Hell and Gone Bar.* She blinked as an older article came up on the screen. The story was about a place in Montana with a photo that made it look like a ghost town. Was anyone left?

It appeared that at least a few businesses were still operating when the photo had been taken.

Removing a couple of the snapshots of Stacy and her friends from her mother's album, people who appeared to have families of their own, Ella pocketed them. If there was anything left in Hell and Gone, Montana, she thought, she would go there. Her instincts told her that it was also where she would find her mother.

But as she thought it, she realized that she wasn't the only one with photos from this other place, this other time. Whoever had broken in had taken some of the older snapshots. By now, the intruder could have also figured out where Stacy had gone.

# Chapter 9

Jane Frazer was a surprise. Hitch put the woman who answered the door somewhere around forty-five. An attractive brunette with wide gray eyes, she wore a suit and heels, explaining she had been called into her office earlier and had only just returned.

"You're a doctor of psychology," Hitch said once they were seated in her neat, modern living room.

"I blame the Hanovers for that. Spending time in that house would make anyone crazy." Jane laughed. "I shouldn't have said that. It's not polite to use the word *crazy* anymore. Unfortunately, *dysfunctional* just doesn't cover families like Marvin's. I was fourteen when my mother died. Fortunately, a maiden aunt of mine came and rescued me."

Hitch was delighted to get this kind of insight into the family dynamics and said as much to the doctor.

"Oh, my view is too biased to be clinical," the woman admitted. "So, what exactly do you want to know?"

"I'm curious. Your text with your address said that you would meet with me, but only if I didn't let anyone in the Hanover family know where you were."

Jane raised a brow. "When I tell you what I know about Marvin, I think you'll understand. I haven't been around his offspring in years, but I would suspect the apple doesn't fall far from the tree. Marvin was a very dangerous man."

"You said you thought at one point that he'd killed his first wife and your mother. Do you still feel that way?"

Jane nodded.

"Any idea who killed him?" Hitch asked.

If Jane was shocked by such a direct approach, she didn't show it. "Any number of people."

"Family members?"

"Definitely. They all hated him. The only reason they put up with him at all was because of the money."

"So I've gathered, but what kind of money are we talking?"

The doctor shrugged. "Apparently, a fortune. He'd inherited it from his father, who had made the money in shady deals back East before moving to Montana. Marvin's father is the one who built the house. Have you seen it?"

Hitch nodded.

"Like his father, Marvin didn't trust banks. At least, that was his story. I suspect the money hadn't gone into the bank because it would then be traceable and—even worse—taxable. The story was that the bulk of his fortune was hidden somewhere in that maze of a house—and Marvin was the only one who knew where. Believe me, everyone in the family tried to find it, myself included. It was this delicious mystery." She chuckled. "As far as I know, he never revealed where it was. He had this key he wore around his neck and guarded with his life."

A key? Like the one Waco said had been found in the bottom of the well? "Like to a safe-deposit box?"

Jane shook her head. "It was larger and odd-shaped. More like to a building or a steel door somewhere."

"What was your first thought when you heard about Marvin's remains being found in the old homestead's abandoned well?" Hitch asked.

"Someone found a way to get that key and now has his fortune." She smiled. "Once they start spending the dough, you'll have your killer."

"And if they didn't get the key?"

Jane frowned and seemed to give that some thought. "How disappointing. Unless, of course, the killer just wanted Marvin dead."

"Stacy Cardwell?"

"She wasn't the only woman who wanted him dead. There was another woman before Stacy, but just for a short time. Her name is Lorraine Baxter. She's in a county nursing home now. I can give you the information, but she has mild dementia. If you can catch her on a good day, she'll probably be happy to tell you why she had every reason to want to see Marvin at the bottom of a well. Or then again, she might not," Jane said with a chuckle.

Hitch thanked her and left.

Once behind the wheel, she called Waco. His phone went to voice mail. She left him a message highlighting what she'd learned and giving him Jane Frazer's phone number and address. "She's expecting your call. You might want to talk to a girlfriend he had between her mother and Stacy. Her name is Lorraine Baxter. From what I heard, she might have had reason to want Marvin dead. But so did the rest of his family members, according to Jane." She left the name of the nursing home in Livingston.

She'd gotten only a few blocks along when her cell phone rang. Seeing it was her fiancé calling, Hitch was already smiling when she picked up. "Hey," she said into the phone.

"Hey. You working?"

"Actually, I just finished."

"Good," Ford said. "Mind going to dinner at the ranch? Dana's got a giant pot roast on. I think she just needs the company tonight," he added. "I suppose you heard."

"I got called in on the case, but once I realized who the deceased was, I pretty much just notified the relatives. I'm now leaving it to the investigator, cold-case homicide detective Waco Johnson. I'm sure he'll be talking to everyone in the family." Silence filled the line for so long, she thought they'd been disconnected. "Ford?"

"Sorry, I was just closing the gate here on the ranch. I wasn't referring to a case, but maybe I was. Dana was up in Stacy's cabin earlier. There was an intruder. He knocked her down on his way out."

"Is she all right?" Hitch asked quickly.

"Just bruised. I'm sensing it's connected to this case you mentioned."

"I would imagine," she said. "What is Stacy to you?"

"My dad's cousin. Does that make her a second cousin? I don't know. Still close enough that I'm glad you aren't involved. Must be hard for you, though."

She laughed. "It is an interesting case, but like I said, I'm stepping away. Is that why you called?"

"No, actually. I just called about dinner. Dana is getting the whole family together. It's what she does when there's trouble. Can you make it?"

Hitch glanced at the time. "I probably won't make dinner, but I'll definitely make dessert. I'll meet you there."

Waco got Hitch's message and decided to swing by the nursing home. He had hired a private investigator to watch Cardwell Ranch and follow Ella if she left again.

In the meantime, all he could do was keep investigating Marvin Hanover's death without Stacy. She would eventually have to show up.

Unless someone got to her before he found her.

The notion had come from out of nowhere. Could she have run because she was in danger? From Marvin's family? Or from someone else?

Lone Pine View turned out to be an assisted-living facility in Paradise Valley. It looked and felt more like a resort, he thought as he got out of his patrol SUV and entered the ultramodern facility.

Lorraine Baxter wasn't in her room. He was directed to the tennis courts, where he saw two fiftysomething women in great shape in the middle of a vigorous game of singles. Lorraine, it turned out, was the attractive redhead who tromped the other woman in the last set. She was still breathing hard when Waco walked up to her.

"Nice game," he said, recalling what Jane had told Hitch about Lorraine having mild dementia. He wondered what this place cost a month and what a person had to do to get in here. If Lorraine had gotten in because of her dementia, he had to question how bad it was. She sure hadn't had any trouble remembering the tennis score.

He introduced himself, getting no more than a serene eyebrow lift at the word *homicide*. "I'd like to ask you a few questions about Marvin Hanover."

Lorraine motioned to a patio with brightly colored umbrellas and comfortable-looking outdoor furniture. Two women appeared to be having tea at one of the far tables, but other than that, they had the place to themselves.

"I'm not sure how helpful I can be," Lorraine said.

"Because of your dementia?"

She smiled. "Because it's been so long since I dated Marvin, let alone was engaged to him—neither for very long."

"Who broke it off?" he asked.

A waiter appeared at the table. "Would you like something, Detective?" Lorraine asked. "They serve alcoholic beverages."

He wondered if she thought all cops drank. At least she hadn't suggested doughnuts. "I'm on duty, but thanks anyway."

"Then I'll take a sparkling water and a gin and tonic with lime." The waiter nodded and left. "I'm sorry. You asked who broke it off. Actually, it was mutual." She shrugged.

"You knew about his other fiancée and his wife's death?"

With a chuckle, she nodded. "Terrible accidents. Poor Marvin."

Poor Marvin? Waco stared at her until the waiter brought her drinks and left again. "From what I've heard about Mr. Hanover…well, he wasn't well-liked."

"Really? I found him delightful." Smiling, she glanced around the facility.

He took a wild guess. "Marvin is putting you up here?"

"Why, yes, he is, even in death," Lorraine said.

"I hate to even ask how much—"

"Wise not to," she said. "It's mind-boggling what they charge. But it is a nice place, wouldn't you say?"

"I'd say. But what I really want to know is how it is that Marvin is paying for it—'even in death'?"

She gave him an innocent look. "Well, when we mutually agreed to part ways, Marvin insisted on taking care of me for the rest of my life." She blinked her blue eyes and Waco got a glimpse of the young, beautiful woman who'd conned Marvin Hanover into taking care of her.

Waco let out a low whistle. "Neat trick, if you can pull it off. What did you have on him? It would have to be something big with enough evidence to put him away for life—if it ever came out." All he got from the attractive redhead was another blink of eyelashes and that knowing smile. "Does his family know?"

She chuckled. "I doubt it, since I'm still alive."

He realized she wasn't joking. "You think they would have killed you years ago if they knew how much this was costing their father?"

"In a heartbeat. So let's keep it between us. Even with my insurance, that bunch is so unstable, I wouldn't trust them to have good judgment. Anyway, that's not why you're here. You want to know who killed him. You don't have to look any farther than that house of vipers. They all hated him, desperately wanted his money and couldn't wait for him to die."

"What about you? He could have changed his mind after he met Stacy Cardwell and wanted out of the deal he made with you."

"Our deal was ironclad," Lorraine said as she touched a diamond tennis bracelet at her wrist. "There was no getting out of it. And if I die of anything but natural causes before I'm eighty… Well, he wouldn't want me to do that and besmirch the family name. Marvin worried about his legacy."

"So, just to be clear, you didn't want him dead?" Waco asked.

"I didn't care one way or the other," she said, draining her sparkling water before reaching for her gin and tonic.

"But I have to admit, I haven't missed him. Not that I had any contact with him after he married Stacy. I admired her for holding out for marriage—even knowing what happened to the others."

"Maybe she thought she would make out like a bandit the same way you did," he suggested. "I understand his first wife's jewelry disappeared at some point."

Lorraine's laugh was bright as sunshine. "Really? How sad. Marvin wanted me to have it." She shrugged.

Waco shook his head. "You must have had proof that he killed his first wife and his fiancée."

Lorraine didn't admit it. But she also didn't deny it. "I got lucky. But I don't think things went as well for Stacy."

Waco didn't think so, either. So why had she married him? He watched the woman finish her drink as quickly as she had her water.

"I need to go change," Lorraine said, excusing herself. "I have a massage soon. I hope I answered all of your questions."

"You did."


He was almost to the Gallatin Canyon when he noticed that Hitch had left him a second message. He listened to it, hearing the worry in her voice. She passed along Jane Frazer's concerns that Lorraine might be in danger. He told himself that Lorraine was fine, but still placed the call.

When the redhead came on the line, he could hear dinner music in the background. "I thought you should know that Marvin's daughter Jane Frazer is worried that you might be in danger." He waited for a reply.

Not getting one, he continued. "She'd had a visit from the medical examiner about her father's remains being found.

They discussed Marvin and his...women. Your name and your location came up. That's how I found you."

"I'm sorry—what is it you're trying to tell me?" He could hear the soft clinking of cutlery and the murmur of voices. It sounded like she was in a five-star restaurant.

"Your life could be in danger."

"Oh, Detective, that is very sweet of you to think of me, but as you noticed when you arrived here, I live in a gated community surrounded by staff and other residents. I'm not worried. Also, I still have my...insurance policy, so I'm fine."

"Marvin's dead, so that insurance policy might not be worth the paper it's printed on."

Lorraine laughed. "It wasn't just Marvin, Detective. At least one of his...offspring was also involved in helping him terminate those two relationships."

"That is the sort of evidence I'd like to see."

"You didn't hear it from me. But thank you so much for your concern." She hung up.

He sat for a moment mumbling under his breath. People often thought they were safe because a community was gated. Or because they had incriminating evidence as so-called insurance. He shook his head. Maybe Lorraine Baxter was right and there was no cause for concern.

One thing kept coming up time and again—a common denominator. The Hanover heirs. Were they as dangerous as he was being led to believe?

It was time he found out.

# *Chapter 10*

The last thing Ella needed right now was a family dinner. But she knew her aunt. Dana needed to get everyone together. It was her strength in times of crisis. If this wasn't a crisis, then Ella didn't know what was.

Before coming in to dinner, Ella had noticed a vehicle in the distance, the same one she'd seen there earlier. Waco Johnson or someone he'd hired to watch the ranch?

Dana had seated them all in the huge dining room. Pot roast, corn, potatoes and green beans from last year's garden were passed around the table, along with a slab of fresh sweet butter and honey to go with corn bread piping hot from the oven. There was apple pie for dessert or Dana's favorite chocolate cake. Her aunt believed food was love and that all of them seated around the table together would make whatever was happening better.

But Ella had her doubts. She wondered what Stacy was doing right now. There still hadn't been any word from her.

The ranch was being watched by a homicide detective, and tomorrow Ella was headed for Hell and Gone with only a prayer's hope of finding her mother.

After helping her aunts with the dishes, Ella escaped to a corner of the living room. She heard the front door open and saw Hitch enter. Ford rushed to his fiancée. Earlier, when Ella had gone down to the barn to check on the new foal, she'd heard Ford on the phone, leaving Hitch a message. He'd said, "I know you're probably still working, but if you get a chance, give me a call. Just getting a little worried about you." Ella wondered what case Hitch was working that had him worried—surely not Marvin Hanover's murder.

She could see that Ford was relieved and happy to see his fiancée. Everyone in the family had accepted Hitch, it appeared. Ella was withholding judgment until she got to know the medical examiner better.

When Ford went to retrieve the piece of pie Dana had saved for her, Hitch approached Ella. "I was hoping you would be here," the young woman said quietly. "I heard you've gone looking for your mother."

Ella knew there was no keeping secrets in this family—unless you were Stacy Cardwell. She said nothing and waited since Hitch seemed to feel uncomfortable talking about it.

"It's gotten more dangerous," Hitch said quietly.

"My mother—"

"As far as I know, she's fine. But when I spoke with Waco—"

"You two are on a first-name basis?" Of course they were. Ella wasn't sure why that annoyed her. Lines had been drawn in the sand. Hitch was on the wrong side if she was with Waco.

"We've worked together for several years now," Hitch said.

Ella studied the woman. "Are you working on a case with him right now?"

"If you're asking about the homicide case involving your mother—"

"We don't know that it involves my mother," she interrupted.

"I just meant—"

"Waco's after my mother."

Hitch looked uneasy. "Waco is interviewing everyone who was closely associated with Marvin Hanover. He's just following standard procedure."

"Spare me the administrative lesson. My uncle is a marshal. I grew up with standard procedure," Ella snapped.

"Then you know I can't talk about it."

Ella took a breath. "But you can tell me what kind of lawman Waco is."

For a moment, Hitch looked as if she wasn't going to comment. "He's good at his job. He's thorough, but he's fair. He's...likable." Ella quirked a brow. "But he won't stop until he gets to the truth."

"I'm curious just how close the two of you are," Ella said, hating that she'd actually voiced the words out loud.

Hitch seemed surprised. "If you're asking what I think you are, Waco and I are just friends. That's all."

"You two never dated?"

The other woman smiled. "No. He's never been interested in me as anything more than a coworker."

"What about you?" Ella knew she should stop. She could see Ford headed their way.

"Sorry, not my type—not that there is anything wrong with him for someone..." Hitch's smile broadened. "More like you, maybe."

Ford walked up with a small plate and a slice of apple pie. He put his arm around his fiancée. "Dana insists you come into the kitchen. She's made you a dinner plate."

Ella felt Hitch's gaze shift to her.

"Please, just be careful," the medical examiner said, a knowing look in her eye.

Was she referring to the murder case? Or Waco?

Ella could have mentally kicked herself. She'd sounded jealous of Hitch and Waco, when that wasn't what she'd been getting at in the least. She felt a knot form in her stomach as she watched Hitch and Ford head to the kitchen. She told herself that this strange feeling had nothing to do with her and Waco, but Waco Johnson and Hitch Roberts and where—and if—the woman fit into this family.

The Hanover house was exactly as Hitch had described it. Waco had called and Lionel had said they would be waiting for him. After he parked and walked up to the large front door, it had opened and he'd gotten his first look at Lionel and Angeline. Like her description of the house, Hitch had done a great job sizing up two of Marvin's offspring.

He'd gone through a list of preliminary questions about Marvin and about their relationship with their father, and was just getting to Stacy Cardwell Hanover when the younger sister arrived.

Mercy burst in, the sound of her voice racing her into the room only seconds before she appeared. While Lionel and Angeline were dull as dust and about as forthcoming as rocks, Mercy was a turbocharged gust of fresh air.

The robust fiftysomething woman with her wild curly brown hair and small granitelike eyes stormed over to him. "Well?" Mercy demanded.

He pretended he didn't know what she was talking about

as Lionel tried to shut his sister up and Angeline wheeled herself to the bar to pour herself some wine. Hitch had said that the woman was ill and apparently dying. Waco wondered if she was on any kind of medication and yet still drinking wine.

"What have they been telling you?" Mercy looked from Lionel to Angeline and back. "Don't believe anything they say."

Lionel groaned. "Mercy, this is not the time for—"

"They hated our father as much as I did. Maybe more."

"I'm going to do my best to find his killer and give you a little peace," Waco said.

Mercy howled at that. "You think finding his killer will give us peace? We already know who killed him. What we want is the money," the woman said, ignoring her brother's attempts to silence her.

"What money?" Waco asked, hoping he looked genuinely confused.

Mercy flung her hands in the air. "Our father's fortune. Of course, they didn't tell you. He wore a key on a chain around his neck. Tell me you have the key."

"I have the key." The room suddenly went deathly quiet. Mercy was staring at him, as was Angeline. Lionel was frowning at him.

"You have the key?" Mercy repeated. "Then give it to us."

"I'm afraid it's evidence in a murder investigation," Waco said, and the woman erupted with a string of curses. "You'll get it back when the investigation is over."

Mercy swore again. "How long is that going to take?"

"Let the man do his job," Lionel said before Waco could answer. "Have you talked to Stacy?" he asked.

"She's definitely on my list," Waco said.

Mercy shot a look at her brother. "Is he serious?" She swung her gaze back at him like a scythe. "Stacy Cardwell murdered our father. Why wouldn't you have already talked to her?"

"We haven't established that Stacy killed anyone," Waco said. "Tell me this. Why did your father marry Stacy?"

Mercy gave him a disbelieving look. "She was young, she was somewhat pretty, I suppose, and she was easier than an Easy-Bake Oven."

"He wanted another son," Angeline said in a hoarse whisper as she picked up her full glass of wine and straightened the quilt on her lap. "No offense, Lionel, but you know it's true. He would have given anything—and I mean anything—for another son."

Lionel looked down at the expensive worn rug at his feet. Waco noticed it was threadbare like the furniture. The light in this room was dim, but he began to see how outdated everything was. Was the family hurting for money? It would appear so.

"None of our father's offspring at the time met his expectations," Lionel snarled. "But I see no reason to air our dirty laundry with—"

"Our father would have married anyone he could get pregnant with a son," Mercy said, cutting him off. "Since the bitch said she was pregnant—"

"Wait!" Waco said in surprise. "Stacy was pregnant?"

"No, she *wasn't* pregnant," Mercy snapped as she shrugged off her jacket and dropped into a chair by the fire. "She lied to him so he'd give her the money he'd promised her."

"In all fairness, Stacy said she miscarried the baby after the marriage. At least, that's what she told us. Then, when our father disappeared, she got an annulment," Lionel said.

"If anything, she got rid of the baby—if she'd ever been pregnant to begin with," Mercy said. "Why keep it if it wasn't going to make her any more money?"

Waco was having trouble keeping up. "Your father paid her?"

"Ten thousand dollars to prove that she was having a son," Angeline said.

"So she was pregnant?" Waco asked, trying to fit the odd-shaped pieces together.

"He believed her, but who knows if it was even true?" Mercy said. "Stacy had an ultrasound photo in her purse that supposedly he accidentally found. But I suspect she planted it there, knowing he was so jealous and suspicious, he often searched her purse."

"What my sister is saying," Lionel added, "is that we aren't certain the photo was necessarily hers."

"But she didn't have any trouble taking the reward he gave her," Mercy piped up. "Ten thousand dollars. Apparently, that's what a son was going for back then."

"I'm sorry—I'm confused." Waco held up his hand.

"It was a boy, so Stacy's work was done," Lionel declared with obvious disgust. "Once the baby was born, he planned to divorce Stacy and raise his son himself."

Waco couldn't believe what he was hearing. "And Stacy was good with this?"

Mercy laughed. "There never was a baby. It was all a lie. You know she used someone else's ultrasound. She just wanted that ten grand he'd promised her. Once she had it, she must have realized she couldn't keep up the lie, so she killed him."

"I think she killed him because he caught her in the lie," Angeline said, her weak voice cracking as she slurred her words. "That's why we never believed that he had abandoned her. When he disappeared, we knew he had to be dead."

Mercy nodded in agreement. "*Daddy* would have wanted his money back and threatened to take it out of her hide."

Waco thought they might be right. From what he'd learned so far about Stacy Cardwell, the story might actually fit. She had used men for money before and she'd also been questioned in a police investigation about stolen money from a fundraiser event.

"She wouldn't have had to kill him," he said, realizing it was true. "She had the reward money. Why not just take off? He would have had a hard time getting his money back once he realized he'd been cheated."

"You didn't know my father," Lionel said. "He would have tracked her down to the ends of the earth. He would have gotten his money back one way or another. If he didn't kill her, he would have made her wish she was dead."

"He sounds delightful." The words slipped out before Waco could stop them. "So maybe he did find out the truth and Stacy killed him in self-defense."

Mercy groaned. "Who cares? When he disappeared, we all thought he took the money and ran. But now that we know he was murdered… If Stacy didn't get the money my father kept hidden all those years, then where is it?"

Waco didn't have an answer for her.

It was getting late. He was about to stand to leave when the boyfriend Hitch had told him about entered just in time to hear Mercy's question.

"Yeah, where is this fortune?" Trevor said in a mocking tone. "'Bout time someone produced it or I'm going to start wondering if the whole thing was just a way to keep you all in line." The cocky young man looked to Waco.

"You must be Trevor," he said.

"You've heard about me." The man smiled. "You the cop who found him at the bottom of the well?" Waco nodded. "So someone iced him, huh?" Glancing at the family, he said, "Someone in this room?" His laugh had a knife edge to it.

"Must you, Trevor?" Lionel said, shooting a displeased look at Mercy.

"You'll be notified as to when you can take possession of your father's remains," Waco told the others in the room.

"And the key," Mercy added quickly.

"That and the rest of his belongings found with him," Waco said.

"You can keep his bones," she said. "It isn't like we're going to pay for a funeral for him. Not after thirty years. Not after…" She waved her hand through the air. "As far as I'm concerned, you can keep him."

Lionel rose. "Let me see you out."

At the front door, the oldest Hanover offspring apologized for his family. "This has all come as a shock."

Waco didn't point out that they didn't seem shocked, just angry. When he'd run preliminaries on each of them, he'd found that not one of them had a job, let alone a career. Had they all been sitting around for the past thirty years, waiting for their father's money to turn up?

He'd wondered how they lived until he'd done a little investigating. He'd found ads on Craigslist where they'd been selling off their father's holdings over the years. Stocks, bonds, land. Even antique house furnishings when things had begun to turn lean. It explained the condition of the entire house.

Glancing back as he made his way to his SUV, he questioned the timing of the anonymous call. Why had the bones turned up now? He thought about the recording. Any one of the family members could have called from the Gallatin Gateway bar down the road from the house. The caller's voice had sounded hoarse. Because they'd lowered their voice to disguise it?

The big question: Had one of them made the call because they were running out of money and hoped the investigation would turn up the dough? Or the key?

Waco had felt a sick kind of desperation in that room. Marvin Hanover's children appeared to have run out of possessions to sell. If they didn't get their hands on the money soon…

What would they do? he wondered. What had one of them or more than one done thirty years ago when their father had tried to make a new family with a new wife?

Waco couldn't shake the feeling that the killer he was searching for might have been in that very room.

# *Chapter 11*

It was late when Ella returned to her cabin and researched everything she could find on Waco Johnson, Henrietta "Hitch" Roberts and the Hell and Gone Bar. Not surprisingly, everything Hitch had told her about Waco seemed to be true. He had an amazing record for solving cold cases. That should have relieved her, but it didn't.

As for Hitch, she had excelled as state medical examiner, was well respected and solved a huge percentage of her cases. What Ella could find about the woman proved that Hitch was much like Waco in her dogged determination to stay on a case until the very end. Ella knew that was true from what had happened with Ford. Hitch had refused to give up. Ella wondered if that wasn't part of the reason Ford had fallen for her. That and the fact that she was beautiful and smart and had saved his life.

Researching the history of the Hell and Gone Bar turned out not to be as hard as she'd thought it would be. She found that the place was named after what had once been an old mining town in the middle of Montana, miles from anything else. Ella had never heard of it—or the bar's owner, a woman named Helen Mandeville. But the article she'd first stumbled on had painted quite a picture of the bar and what was left of the town.

"It's one of those bars that you know right away when you walk in is dangerous, with dangerous characters," the travel writer had written. "I was told that more than half of the people who frequent the bar have at least one outstanding warrant. It's a true example of how the Wild West is still alive in middle-of-nowhere Montana."

Ella was sure it was the same place in her mother's photographs. But why would Stacy go there?

"The bar had once been the true center of this small mining town, aptly named Hell and Gone, Montana," the author continued. "Now the town is little more than a wide spot on a two-lane, miles from any other community, the iron ore that had given it birth having run out long ago."

"If it wasn't for the bar, Hell and Gone would have dried up and blown away years ago," the bar owner had been quoted as saying.

What about this place had drawn Stacy all these years?

Ella had always suspected there was a secret man in her mother's life. A man so unacceptable that Stacy hadn't dared bring him to the ranch. Instead, she'd sneak off a few days here and there to be with him. Was that the case?

Early the next morning, she called Nora Cline, hoping the woman was an early riser like her mother. Nora answered on the second ring, sounding wide-awake.

"Have you ever heard of a place called Hell and Gone?" The woman's silence made Ella realize that she had. "My mother must have mentioned it."

"Jokingly, one time when we had too much to drink," Nora said. "Are you telling me it's an actual place?"

"Apparently. What did she say about it?"

"I'm trying to remember. I can't even remember what we were talking about. Life, I suppose. She said she'd been to Hell and Gone, and then laughed. Then she began to cry. We'd had way too much to drink that night. What she said after that didn't make a lot of sense. But I got the impression there was some man in her life she hadn't been able to get over."

"Is it possible he's in Hell and Gone?" Ella asked.

"If it's a real place, then that would make sense," Nora said. "But you shouldn't go alone. If your mother is in trouble, it might be dangerous."

"I won't be going alone," Ella said, thinking of Waco Johnson. "I'll have a homicide detective following me."

Waco was up before the sun after a restless night. Everything he'd learned since seeing the bones in the bottom of the well and meeting the Hanover family had haunted his dreams. The PI he'd hired to watch the ranch had let him know that Ella hadn't gone anywhere. Yet. Waco didn't believe for a moment that she'd given up on finding her mother.

As soon as the post office opened, he stopped to see if his package had arrived. It had. Inside the padded manila envelope was a key in an evidence bag. The key looked old and much larger than he'd expected. He had no idea what it might belong to. He wondered if Stacy knew. But first he'd have to find her.

He still believed that Ella would take him to her. All his instincts told him that she would keep searching until she found her. So he wasn't surprised this morning, when he relieved the PI, that he didn't have to wait long before he saw the woman's pickup coming out of the ranch.

He smiled to himself as he watched her turn onto Highway 191 and head north. Where were they going today? He couldn't wait to find out. He'd sensed that she was like him. Once Ella got her teeth into something, she didn't let go.

She went straight at the Four Corners instead of turning right and heading into Bozeman. She made a beeline for I-90 and then headed west.

Waco settled in, keeping a few vehicles between them. He had a lot to mull over. Everything he'd learned about Stacy so far had led him to believe that she was quite capable of murder—especially given what he now knew about Marvin Hanover. She might even get a reduced sentence for killing the bastard.

But what about the money? *If* there really was a fortune somewhere. This key might hold the answer. If someone hadn't already gotten to it and spent every dime. From what Waco knew of Stacy Cardwell, she had left the marriage with ten thousand dollars, which had lasted only until she'd given birth to her daughter a few years later.

When she'd returned to Cardwell Ranch, she'd had a baby to raise. Was that why she'd returned to the ranch and never left? If she'd killed Marvin, then she obviously hadn't gotten the key. Why not?

The key was a puzzle. How had it ended up at the bottom of the well with Marvin if that was what the killer was after? If he'd kept it around his neck, why hadn't the killer taken it before knocking him into the well? Or had the killer tried to take it and failed. But if the killer knew the key was at the bottom of the well, wouldn't he or she have tried to climb down there to retrieve it over the years?

He had too many questions. He suspected Stacy had a lot of those answers.

Ahead, he saw Ella turn north off the interstate. With luck, it wouldn't be long now.

Marshal Hud Savage had seen the worry in his wife's eyes. Her sister had put her through hell, but for years had been relatively stable. Except for those times when Stacy would disappear. Dana, fine with not knowing where her sister went, had begged him not to interfere.

Now he wished he had. Maybe then he'd have some clue as to how much trouble his sister-in-law was in. Stacy had had a few scrapes with the law, but nothing that landed her in jail or even resulted in a record. Her marriages, though, had been recorded, starting with her first to a man named Emery Gordon.

It didn't take long to find Emery and his home overlooking Bozeman. Hud knew he was clutching at straws interviewing Stacy's husbands. But he had to start somewhere. Stacy had been divorced from Emery for years. Still, as he stood on the man's front stoop, he could only hope that Gordon might know where she went when she disappeared.

Emery, then twenty-six, had married seventeen-year-old Stacy. On her marriage certificate it stated that she was twenty-one—no doubt she'd used a fake ID she'd picked up somewhere. Hud wondered why she'd been in such a hurry to marry—let alone to marry Emery at such a young age—except for the fact that the man must have been a way out. Also, Emery's family had money.

Hud rang the doorbell and heard the chimes echo inside the house to a classical song he couldn't quite put his finger on. He'd grown up on Western boot-scootin' music.

A woman opened the door, complete with uniform. "May I help you?"

"I'd like to speak with Emery Gordon, please," the marshal said, flashing his badge.

The woman's eyes momentarily widened before she nodded and said, "Please, come this way." She led him into a den. "Mr. Gordon will be right with you. Please have a seat."

Hud thanked her, looking around the well-appointed room without sitting. A few moments later, a man some years older than Hud came into the room and apologized for making him wait.

Like his home, Emery Gordon was dressed impeccably. While Hud doubted anyone had ever called the man handsome, he wore his age well.

"Can I offer you something to drink, Marshal?"

He declined. "I need to ask you about Stacy."

"Stacy?" Emery seemed surprised as he motioned to the set of leather chairs. "Please, have a seat, although this probably won't take long. Stacy and I were married less than a year many years ago."

They sat. The chairs were angled so that they almost faced each other. The den was warm and smelled rich with leather and the faint hint of bourbon.

"If you don't mind, why did the marriage last such a short time?" Hud asked. "I know she lied about her age when the two of you eloped." He suspected she'd lied about a whole lot more. He was uncomfortable with such personal questions and wouldn't have been surprised if the man told him it was none of his business.

But if Emery Gordon was offended, he didn't show it. "I don't mind at all. Stacy is your sister-in-law?" Hud nodded. "Do you mind telling me why you're inquiring about something that happened so long ago?"

"Stacy is missing. I'm trying to find her, which means prying into her past for answers." He didn't want to tell the man that she was wanted for questioning in the murder of one of her other husbands. He feared all that would come out soon enough—probably in the newspapers when she was arrested.

"I see. Then what I have to tell you shouldn't come as a surprise. She swept me off my feet. She had a way about her..." Emery seemed lost in the past. He shook himself back to the present. "The truth is, she married me for my money. When she found out that most of it was tied up in a trust that I couldn't touch until I was forty-five, she bailed and took what money she could. I'd like to say that I regretted the time I had with her." Emery smiled. "I can't. Even eight months with Stacy was worth the expense, the embarrassment and the painful lesson she taught me."

"I'm sorry. I hated to bring it up, but I was hoping you might know where she went next."

Emery laughed. "To whom, you mean? You're welcome to talk to him. At the time, he was my best friend. Now he's Congressman Todd Bellingham. He lives outside of Helena."

"Stacy..." Hud wasn't sure how to form the question.

"Todd didn't marry her, but it still almost cost him his marriage and our friendship. He might not want to talk about it."

Hud had taken off his Stetson and balanced it on his knee. Now he picked it up by the brim and rose. "Thank you for your candor."

"Not at all," Emery said, rising, as well. "You've brought back some interesting memories, some I actually cherish. Stacy was a wild child back then. I thought I'd heard that she'd changed. Doesn't she have a daughter?"

"Yes. Ella, who's a beautiful, smart, capable young woman with a good head on her shoulders. Nothing like her mother," Hud said, thankful for that.

"I hope you find Stacy." For a moment, Emery looked genuinely worried that something bad had happened to her.

"Me, too," Hud said, more worried than Emery Gordon could know—and not just about Stacy.

Ella had no idea what she was getting into. But he knew she was determined to track down her mother. Hud suspected that if Stacy had killed Marvin Hanover, then she'd gone to someone from her past whom she thought could help her. Someone dangerous. And Ella was headed straight for it.

Hours later, Ella looked around the wide-open, sage-covered country. She'd driven a narrow two-lane north for miles, reminding her just how large Montana really was. With each mile, the population counts had dropped considerably. Cows had given way to coyotes as the land became more inhospitable, the highways even more narrow and less traveled. What was a bar doing out here in such an isolated place?

She knew the answer to that. Want to disappear? Go to Hell and Gone Bar. That was what the writer of the article had suggested. And her mother might have done just that.

Buildings began to take shape on the edge of the horizon. The closer she got, she saw what little remained of the once-thriving mining town. Ella slowed on the edge of the community. The few remaining structures looked abandoned.

As she drove slowly through the town, she saw that the hotel still stood, its sign hanging by one hinge. Across the worn stretch of narrow pavement, she could see a neon beer sign glowing in a window and an almost-indistinguishable hand-printed faded sign that read Hell and Gone. That was the only indication that there was a bar inside. That and the four pickups parked out front. None of the trucks had the Cardwell Ranch logo on the side, although Ella couldn't be sure her mother was even still driving the ranch pickup.

A few empty building lots beyond the hotel, there was an abandoned Texaco station, its serve-yourself gas pumps rusting away. Past that, nothing but a dark ribbon of pavement forged its way through more sagebrush before disappearing in the distance.

After the town ended abruptly, she turned around and drove back through it, even more slowly. Across from the bar she noticed a tiny general store with dust-coated windows. Hand-printed signs in the window advertised sandwiches, mineral rocks and muck boots.

But Ella was more interested in the bar and its owner, Helen Mandeville. She took the first street past it and drove around the block. There were some small older houses, most in desperate need of repair and paint. But directly behind the bar on the dirt street, she spotted an attached house that appeared to have been painted in the past decade. There were flowers in the front yard. The house looked so out of place among the other buildings around it, Ella knew it had to belong to the bar's owner.

She kept driving, aware that Waco was right behind her in his SUV. Detective Waco Johnson had been following her for miles. She hadn't even bothered to try to lose him—not that she was sure she could. Now that she was here, she wasn't that sorry to see him still with her, given that this town looked like the kind of place where a person on the run would come—and disappear whether she wanted to or not.

But if Ella wanted to find her mother, she worried that

no one in this town would talk to her with a cop on her tail. Getting rid of him could be a problem.

She pulled in and parked next to one of the pickups in front of the bar. Was her mother here? Because of some lost love? Or was she simply on the run from her past mistakes, especially this big one? Ella couldn't imagine her mother in this town for any reason—other than knowing she could hide here and no one would give her up, especially to the cops.

But then, that would mean Stacy had good reason to fear the law, wouldn't it?

Waco was at the point that he thought Ella Cardwell was merely taking him on a long wild-goose chase when he'd spotted buildings on the horizon. Way ahead of him, he saw her brake lights. He'd thought she'd only slowed for what appeared to be some sort of dying town.

But then she'd driven through it and turned around and headed back. By the time he'd reached the edge of town, she was parking her truck next to four others in front of what appeared to be a bar.

He slowed. She hadn't tried to lose him. He watched her park and get out of her truck. By the time he pulled in, she was headed for the weathered, discolored wood door next to the neon beer sign.

She didn't seem like the sort who suddenly needed a drink. Nor did this look like the kind of place a young woman alone would choose to enter for a beverage. He could see the broken beer bottles and other garbage on each side of the front door. Everything about the place looked rough, he thought as he shut off his engine and got out. It was definitely the kind of place an officer of the law should avoid—especially one alone with little chance of getting any backup.

But all that aside, including the fact that Ella wasn't going to appreciate him being there, he couldn't let her go in there alone. The heavy weathered door groaned as he pushed it open. He was instantly hit with the smell of stale beer, old grease and floor cleaner. He caught sight of someone standing at a grill behind the bar, a spatula in his hand. He heard the sizzle of meat frying on the griddle and the clank of pool balls knocking together, followed by hard-core cussing in the back. Over all of it, country twang poured from the old jukebox.

Waco blinked in the cavern-like darkness as the door closed behind him with a solid thud. Ella was standing only a few feet inside. A half dozen men of varying ages had turned on their bar stools to stare at her. Another four were at the pool table, their game momentarily suspended as they took in the strangers who'd just walked in.

All of the men were staring at Ella, except for the ones who were leering. She'd definitely caught everyone's attention. Another song began on the jukebox to the sizzle of whatever was near burning on the grill. Otherwise, the place had now fallen drop-dead quiet as the four men in the back leaned on their pool sticks and stared.

Waco only had a few seconds to decide what to do. He stepped up behind Ella and said loud enough for the men to hear, "Honey, let's sit in a booth." There were several sorry-looking booths against the wall to their left.

At the sound of his voice, she started and half turned, making him realize that she hadn't noticed him enter behind her. He took her arm before she could resist. "What would you like to drink?"

They were here now—best to act as normal as possible.

These were the kinds of bars that a fight could break out in at a moment's notice—and usually for no good reason other than the patrons were drunk and bored. Between him and Ella, Waco feared he'd given them an even better reason.

She glared at him but let him lead her over to the booth. "Bottle of beer. I don't need a glass," she said, those green eyes snapping as they telegraphed anger to cover what he suspected might be just a little relief at not being alone in this place.

"Wise decision," he said quietly. This wasn't the cleanest establishment he'd ever been in. Walking over to the bar, he nodded at the men sitting along the row of stools. They were now staring at him with way too much distrust.

The bartender, a heavyset man with an out-of-control beard, took his time coming down the length of the bar. "You lost?" he asked quietly. The pool game had resumed with a lot of loud ball smacking followed by even louder curses.

Waco spotted several baseball bats behind the bar. He had no doubt there was probably a sawed-off shotgun back there, as well. This was the middle of Montana, miles from anything. Justice here was meted out as necessary on an individual basis.

"Two bottles of beer. Whatever you have handy." Ella hadn't stopped here because she was thirsty. Unless he missed his guess, she'd come here looking for her mother. That alone gave him pause. Why would she think Stacy would be here, of all places?

That worried him. If it were the case, then Ella wouldn't want to leave until she'd gotten what she'd come for. That fact was going to make this excursion a whole lot trickier. Because if Stacy Cardwell was here, which he had to doubt, he knew these people weren't going to give her up easily.

There would be no demanding answers here. Waco knew his badge would be useless—worse than useless. It would be a liability, and he wasn't in the mood to have the stuffing kicked out of him—let alone to end up in a shallow grave out back.

"You want these to go?" the bartender asked, glancing from Waco to Ella and back.

The open-container law aside, Waco didn't think Ella was planning on leaving that soon. "Here."

"Suit yourself." The bartender walked back down the bar to open a cooler and pull out two bottles of beer.

Waco got the feeling that not many tourists found their way here. If they did, he'd bet they sped up and kept right on going.

The men at the bar were watching him, except for the ones still leering at Ella. He cursed under his breath. Did she have any idea what she'd walked them both into?

# *Chapter 12*

Stacy's second conquest attempt had a home on Canyon Ferry Lake outside Helena. Hud had tried calling Todd Bellingham's residence first, only to get a recording. He'd headed for the lake, arriving in the afternoon. The sun shimmered off the surface of the water as he pulled in, parked and exited his SUV. The day was warm, the scent of the water rising up to meet him, along with shrieks of laughter from the other side of the house.

As he rounded the front of the house overlooking the lake, he could see a group of teenagers frolicking in a cacophony of spray and high-pitched shrieks at the water's edge.

"Grandkids," a distinguished gray-haired man said from a lounge chair on the patio as the marshal approached. "I tell people they're what keeps me young, but the truth is, they wear me out." He chuckled. "Marshal Hudson Savage, right?" he asked as he started to rise from the chair.

"Please, don't get up," Hud said quickly. Clearly, Emery

Gordon had called to let Todd know he was coming. "And it's Hud."

"Then join me, Hud." Todd Bellingham motioned to the chair next to him. The man glanced back through the wall of windows into the house and made a motion with his hand. "I'm having iced tea. Have a glass with me?"

"Thanks. That sounds good," Hud said as he took the lounge chair in the shade. The view of the lake and the mountains on the other side was spectacular. Gold had been found in those mountains over a century ago, one area said to be the richest place on earth. It was no wonder that Montana had first been known as the Treasure State.

A woman appeared with a tray. "This is my wife, Nancy. Marshal Hudson Savage," Todd said by way of introduction.

The woman smiled as she left the tray. "Nice to meet you, Marshal."

"You, too," he said as she exited quickly, as if sensing this wasn't a social visit.

Below them on the mountainside, the group of teenagers had apparently exhausted themselves for the moment. The girls had plopped down to sun on the beach while the boys had climbed into a wakeboard boat and turned on the music. It blared for a moment before one of them glanced up at the house and then quickly turned it down.

"What can I do for you, Marshal?" Todd asked after they had both sipped their tea.

"I'm here about Stacy Cardwell Gordon." He didn't think it came as a surprise, given that Todd had been expecting him.

The congressman nodded slowly, his gaze on the lake. "I understand you spoke with Emery, her first husband." When Hud said nothing, Todd continued. "I was young and foolish and Stacy... Well, she was Stacy." He glanced at the marshal, then back at the lake. "Why the interest after all this time?"

"Stacy's missing and she's wanted for questioning in a homicide investigation."

Todd shook his head. "Homicide." He didn't sound surprised. "I'm sorry to hear that. I liked Stacy."

"You were married when you began seeing her," Hud said, keeping his voice down.

"I was and so was she. It almost cost me my marriage." He didn't sound sorry about that. "I almost let it." He looked over at Hud. "I was in love with her."

"What happened?"

Todd chortled. "I didn't have enough money. My future at that time didn't look great. I was working for my father at the car dealership, hating it and kind of feeling at loose ends. I would eventually inherit the business, but it wasn't quickly enough for Stacy. She wanted…more."

"More as in whom exactly?"

The man smiled over at him. "You do know Stacy, huh. His name was Marvin Hanover, a wealthy man from Gateway who apparently came from old money. She'd caught his eye and vice versa. And that was that."

Hud thought about it for a moment as below them, on the shore, the teenage boys called the girls from their towels spread on the sand into the boat. He watched them speed away, the boat's wide wake sending water droplets into the air.

"When was the last time you saw Stacy?" he asked after finishing his drink.

Todd frowned. "Just before she married Marvin. I tried to talk her out of it." He laughed. "Like I said, I was young and foolish."

"When was the last time you saw Marvin Hanover?"

"I never met the man." The congressman smiled. "If you

think I killed him for her..." He chuckled at that. "A man can only be so young and foolish and survive."

"Did Stacy ask you to kill him?"

Todd Bellingham only smiled before draining his tea. "I hope you find her before...well, before anything happens to Stacy. I still think about her sometimes." His gaze took on a faraway look. "I've wondered how different my life would be if I had stopped her from leaving me." He turned to look at Hud. "Or how different hers would be now."

Ella felt her skin crawl as she looked away from the leering men at the bar to check her phone. Her phone showed that she didn't have a strong connection. She should have expected it might be sketchy out here. Not that she'd thought she'd have a call from her mother. But she might have to make a call for help—and not just for her. Waco wasn't safe here; that much was clear.

She saw that she had voice messages from both her aunt and uncle. She didn't listen to them, knowing Dana and Hud were worried about her and anxious to know where she'd gone.

As the detective returned with two bottles of beer, she pocketed her phone and hoped he didn't see that her hand was trembling.

Ella had been warned that this was a rough bar. And yet, when she'd walked in, her feet had frozen to the floor just inside the door as she'd felt the suspicion, the mistrust, the menacing vibrations. She'd stared at the faces of the men, hoping to recognize at least one of them from her mother's photos. She hadn't.

Over the years as a wrangler, she'd been in dangerous situations with horses and cattle, but she'd always been in her own element, one she knew well, and had felt confident in her abilities to get herself out of trouble. Walking in here, though, when she'd looked into the faces of those men, she'd known she was out of her depth.

Waco set a beer in front of her and slid into the opposite side of the booth. He met and held her gaze as he lifted his bottle in a salute that told her he was as wary of what might happen next as she was. "The bartender wouldn't take my money. I suspect another beer will be out of the question."

She knew what he was trying to tell her. She lifted her beer to her lips but hardly tasted it. The two of them were still being watched. At the pool table, two of the players were arguing loudly.

The detective took a swig and set down his bottle, leaning toward her as he spoke. "I think we should leave."

Ella knew he was right, but she'd come here to get answers. She wasn't leaving without them. Her mother had been coming to this place for years. All her instincts told her that, now on the run, Stacy had come here again. "You know where the door is," she said with more bravado than she felt.

He chuckled. "If you think I'm leaving you here alone…" But his look said he was tempted just to show her what a fool she was.

Out of the corner of her eye, she saw a door open at the back of the bar. A woman with dyed red hair entered with an air of ownership. No one paid her any mind as she stepped behind the bar and opened a large old-fashioned cash register.

Another song came on the jukebox as a fight broke out at the pool table. The woman behind the bar picked up a glass and hurled it at the two scuffling in the back. The glass hit the wall and shattered, loud as a gunshot. The two stopped in midmotion.

"Lou, Puck, you've been warned. Outside. I've had enough of the two of you," the woman said in a deep, gravelly voice as brash as her hair color. She turned to the bartender. "They don't leave? Throw them out and don't let them back in. Best clean up that glass before some fool cuts his leg off."

Lou and Puck were still in a brawlers hold. For a moment, they glared at each other, and then the larger of the two shoved the smaller one aside and left. The smaller man looked to the bar and the woman. "Come on, Helen," he said with a groan. "You know it weren't me that started it."

She motioned toward the back door and then turned, freezing for a moment as her gaze lit on Ella and then Waco. Her movements were slow and deliberate as she asked the bartender what they'd ordered. Then she scribbled something down and walked the length of the bar, coming around the end and heading straight for their booth.

Ella sat a little straighter. She recognized the woman even though her hair hadn't been red in the old photos. Helen had aged over the years and now had to be pushing seventy, maybe more. As she reached them, Ella swallowed the lump in her throat. This was her chance to ask about her mother.

"What are you doing here?" Helen's quiet words were directed at her. In the older woman's hand was what looked like a bill for the beers. Guess they would be charged after all.

"I need to talk to you about my mother, Stacy Cardwell," Ella said, keeping her voice low since she could feel all the attention in the room focused on the three of them.

"I don't know anyone by that name. You need to leave. Now." Helen had started to turn away when Ella grabbed her slim wrist. She looked down at the hand stopping her before looking up at Ella.

The look in the woman's eyes made her flinch inside, but Ella didn't let go. "I'm not leaving until I find my mother. I know she comes here," Ella said just as firmly as the older woman had spoken. "I suspect she's here now."

"You've made a mistake," the woman whispered. "You don't belong here."

"And my mother does?"

Helen's gaze shifted to Waco as she reached down and gently peeled Ella's fingers from her wrist. "You brought a cop?"

"He's looking for her, too," Ella said. "We're *not* together."

The woman swung her gaze back to Ella. For a moment, she thought she caught a glimpse of kindness in the woman's faded eyes. "Leave now. While you can." With that, she wadded up their bill and dropped it in front of Ella before turning and walking back to the bar.

"What are you all lookin' at?" Helen demanded of the men at the bar in a raspy bark. They all turned away from Ella and Waco as the woman took her spot behind the bar again.

Ella surreptitiously pocketed the wadded bill and got to her feet. Waco rose, as well, and reached for his wallet to leave a twenty on the table.

As they walked out, she could feel eyes on her. But only one set felt as if it was boring a hole into her back. How had she ever thought she'd seen kindness in those eyes?

"You thought your mother was here?" Waco demanded once outside as he followed Ella to her pickup. She started to climb inside the truck, but he stopped her with a hand on her arm. "Why would you think that?"

She sighed and shook off his hold. "I had my reasons. I'm going home, in case you want to follow me all the way back."

"You're not leaving," he said after a split second. "I already know you better than that."

"You don't know me at all," she snapped.

"I wish you were smart enough to turn your pickup around and hightail it out of here as quickly as possible. That would be my advice—not that you'd take it. If there is one thing I know, it's that this is getting dangerous and you're just stubborn enough to think that by staying around here you're going to get some answers."

Ella mugged a face at him. "Believe what you will." She started to get into her pickup but stopped to look back at him. "I have some advice for you, Detective."

"You can call me Waco."

"You're the one who should hightail it out of here. No one's going to talk to *you*," Ella said. "You look like the law."

"I *am* the law."

"I rest my case. It's too dangerous for you here."

He laughed. "Too dangerous for *me*? Are you serious? We'll be lucky if we get out of this town alive."

"If you're trying to scare me—"

He swore and passed a hand through his hair in frustration as she climbed in and slammed the pickup door. As the motor roared to life, he swore again and stepped back before she had a chance to run over his toes. Did she really think he was going to buy her story about leaving?

But as she pulled out, she headed in the direction they'd come. He watched her go, for a moment debating what to do. Follow her? She hadn't seemed to have gotten any information from the owner of the bar and yet she was leaving? Why was he having trouble believing this? Because he thought he knew Ella after such a short length of time?

A man came out of the bar and glanced after Ella as he climbed into his pickup and started to take off in the same direction Ella had gone.

Waco let out another curse as he hurried to his SUV. Once behind the wheel and racing after Ella and the man, he glanced back at the bar's front door. Another man stood there, watching them leave before turning his gaze on Waco.

Waco floored the SUV and quickly passed the older pickup, putting himself between Ella and the male driver hunched over the wheel of the old-model truck. As he drove after Ella, he recalled the way Helen had wadded up their bill and thrown it at Ella. He'd seen the woman write something on it before coming over to them. Was it possible she had written a message on it?

Ahead of him, he could see that Ella appeared to be driving out of town—just as she'd said she was going to do. So why didn't he believe her? Just as she'd told the woman at the bar, Ella wouldn't leave until she got the information she needed.

He shook his head in both frustration and admiration. Ella reminded him of himself. Stubborn to a fault and just as crazy cagey. He just hoped she didn't get herself killed, because as capable and strong as she was, she wasn't trained for this kind of dirty business.

Glancing in his rearview mirror, he saw that the pickup from town was gaining on them. He'd known it wasn't going to be easy to get out of there alive.

# *Chapter 13*

$A$s Ella drove, she dug the bill Helen had thrown down in front of her from her pocket. She flattened it out and read what was written on it. Just as she'd suspected, the woman had sent her a message.

She felt her pulse jump. That meant Helen had known who she was before the bar owner had come over to the booth—just as she'd suspected. Had her mother shown her photographs of Ella over the years?

She stared at the scrawled words.

*Go home before you hurt your mother more than you know.*

Her heart thundered against her ribs. She'd found her mother. Or at least found someone who knew her mother. But then what? How could she hurt her mother more? Stacy already had a homicide detective after her. More to the point, could Ella trust Helen, a woman she didn't know?

Her hope was that she could talk her mother into returning to the ranch—at least until she was arrested for murder. It wouldn't be easy. Worse, she had Waco Johnson dogging her every step, she thought, glancing in her rearview mirror to see his SUV not far behind. The detective wasn't giving up any more than Ella was.

She wondered how she could get rid of him so she could double back. Maybe if she could convince him that she was returning to the ranch and then somehow lose him... In the meantime, she had to act as if she really had given up.

Her cell phone rang. She figured it was Waco and let it ring a second time before she saw that it was her mother.

"Mom?" she said quickly, taking the call.

Silence, then Stacy's quiet voice. "I thought I'd better call you and let you know that I'm all right. I just need a little time to myself and I'll come home. I don't want you to worry."

For a moment, it was such a relief to hear her mother's voice, to know that she was all right, that Ella didn't respond.

"I hope everything is all right at the ranch," her mother was saying. "Tell Dana that I'll be back soon to help with the canning."

Ella was gripping the phone, trying to control a jumble of mixed emotions. Her mother was pretending that she didn't know Ella'd been in town. "Helen called you," Ella said into the phone, her words clipped. "Did she also tell you that I'm not leaving here until I see you?"

"Ella, I don't know what—"

"I found your photo albums, Mother. I know. That's why I'm here. Right now I'm trying to lose the cold-case homicide detective who is as determined to talk to you as I am. Then I'm coming back and staying as long as it takes.

You can't run from this anymore. The truth has caught up to you."

"You don't understand."

"You can explain it all to me back at the bar or wherever it is that you stay when you're in Hell and Gone."

"I had my reasons for what I did." Her mother was crying now.

"For keeping the place and your life there from everyone, including me? Or for killing Marvin Hanover?"

"No, you can't believe—"

"I don't know what to believe." Ella heard the pain in her voice. She hadn't realized how hurt she was about her mother's secret life.

As she glanced again in her rearview mirror, she feared that her mother wasn't the only one who wanted to keep the past a secret. The truck from the bar was coming up fast behind the detective's SUV.

What she saw next made her let out a cry. By the time she got her truck stopped, her mother had disconnected.

Waco had seen the pickup's driver make his move. He'd known it was only a matter of time, so he'd been ready. The front of the older-model truck slammed into the back of his SUV, but not hard enough to drive him off the road. He kept going, maintaining his speed, waiting to see what the driver would do next.

Ahead of him, he saw Ella's brake lights, and he swore. The last thing he needed was for her to stop now. Worse, he realized, was for her to turn around in the middle of the road and come back. But damn if that didn't look like what she was planning.

This time, the pickup smacked the back of his SUV with more speed and force, jarring Waco and making the vehicle shudder. The pickup's driver was really starting to tick him off. He got the SUV under control and released his shotgun from the rack between the seats. This was going to get ugly, and the worst part was that it appeared Ella was determined to be in the middle of it. She was in the process of turning around and heading back this way. If he didn't do something quickly...

Hitting his brakes, he turned the wheel hard to the left. The SUV teetered for a moment, wanting to roll, just before he got it under control. The driver of the pickup hadn't anticipated the move. Waco saw the man lay on his brakes as the patrol SUV was suddenly sitting sideways on the highway in front of him.

Instinctively, the driver turned hard to the right, going off the road in a cloud of dirt. Waco grabbed his shotgun and jumped out. The pickup had come to rest wheel-well deep in the sagebrush and dirt thirty yards off the highway.

As Waco started to leave the highway, the man jumped out, fired off two wild shots with a handgun in his direction and then ran off across the expanse. Waco considered going after the guy, but only for a moment as Ella came racing up in her pickup.

Ella got her truck stopped and jumped out. Waco Johnson stood at the edge of the road, shotgun dangling from one large hand, his Stetson cocked back as he looked at her.

She'd known the man in the pickup was going to run Waco off the road. Maybe even kill him. When she'd seen the driver get out of his stuck pickup with a gun and start firing...

"Are you all right?" Ella asked as she tried to still her racing heart after watching the pickup driver repeatedly crash into the back of the detective's SUV. She'd feared that the man was going to kill Waco—even before he started shooting. That was when she'd realized he wouldn't be here if it wasn't for her. She didn't want his blood on her hands.

"I'm fine. I thought you were going home?" he asked in that deep, low voice of his. It warmed her in a way that made her feel vulnerable, which was the last thing she wanted right now. Yet her heart was still hammering from what had happened. What *could* have happened.

"You knew I wasn't leaving." She hesitated, surprised that she was about to give up the information even as she said it. "I just heard from my mother."

His gaze sharpened. "That so? She have anything interesting to say?"

"Just what you would expect. She wants me to go home and pretend that I never came here."

Waco nodded. "I would imagine that's about the same thing Helen wrote on our bar bill?"

So he'd seen that, had he? "She said that if I stayed here, I would end up hurting my mother more than I could know."

"Your mother is wanted for questioning in a murder investigation," he said. "What could you do that would hurt her worse?"

"That's what I said."

"So she's here." He didn't sound happy about that as he looked from Ella to the shotgun in his hand before heading back to his SUV. He deposited the shotgun in the rig and looked over the hood to see that she was still standing there. "I'm assuming we're going back to Hell and Gone?"

"What about the man who was trying to kill you?" she asked.

"I think I recognize him from a drug case I was working in Butte. He probably thinks I'm here to take him in."

Waco shrugged. "At least he can't shoot worth sh— Worth a damn."

"I suppose there's no way I can convince you to leave?"

He seemed to give it some thought before he shook his head. "It wouldn't be chivalrous of me to leave you here alone, even if my reason for being here wasn't to take your mother back for questioning."

"She didn't kill Marvin Hanover." Ella had hoped to put more conviction into her words.

Waco shrugged. "Maybe not. But you should know that he didn't die right away. He scratched your mother's name into the rock wall at the bottom of the well. If his intent was to name his killer...well, then he did."

Waco regretted his words as all the color drained from Ella's face. She wanted to believe the best of her mother. He hadn't wanted to take that away from her. "I'm sorry."

She quickly recovered, but he could still see fear in her green eyes. Of course, her mother would be a suspect, given that Stacy had been married to Marvin when he disappeared. But she hadn't known about the writing on the wall, the one thing that could get Stacy convicted of murder.

The sun hung low in the sky, painting them with a golden patina. He looked at Ella and felt something snap inside him. Damn, but the woman was beautiful. Not just beautiful. Smart, sexy—the whole package. The thought struck him like a crowbar upside his head. A man would have to be a fool not to have noticed.

He'd noticed, but it hadn't hit him at a primal level before. Now that it had, there was no going back, he realized.

"What?" Ella asked, frowning at him.

He stared at her, hoping he hadn't said the words out loud.

"You were saying something about the hotel?" she asked.

Hotel. "Given all the traffic backed up with my SUV sideways in the highway, I suppose we should move our rigs, huh."

She gave him a blank look since there was no traffic. "Sarcasm? Really?"

Without another word, Ella turned and walked back to her pickup. He watched her climb in behind the wheel before he climbed behind his. Starting the motor, he pulled to the side of the road and let her lead the way back into Hell and Gone. That revelation about Ella had come with an ache like nothing he'd ever felt. He wanted to protect her at the same time he wanted to ravish her.

Waco shook his head, telling himself that he needed food. It had been a long day and this case was driving him a little crazy. Worse, just the sight of the sorry excuse for a town on the horizon filled him with worry. How was he going to keep Ella safe? Worse still, he didn't know how to deal with this mix of feelings. *Nothing good will come of this*, he thought.

Yet he had no choice but to stick to Ella. Stacy Cardwell was here. Unfortunately, so were some dangerous people. He'd thought he'd recognized the man who'd left the bar earlier to watch them leave. Another fugitive from justice. This one from an assault case Waco had worked on.

The sun had sunk behind some mountains in the distance by the time he parked in front of the hotel and waited for Ella to get out of her pickup.

With nightfall coming on, both he and Ella were stuck in Hell and Gone. Just the two of them in this old hotel tonight. And that meant they were both in serious danger for a whole lot of reasons.

# Chapter 14

Helen Mandeville heard about what had happened outside of town. She'd known there would be trouble the moment she'd seen the two sitting in the booth at the bar. The one was obviously a cop. The other... Well, she'd recognized Ella from photos Stacy had shown her over the years.

She'd always known that Ella would show up here one day. It had just been a matter of time. She'd told Stacy, but of course Stacy hadn't listened.

"What would you have me do?" Stacy had cried.

"Tell the truth."

"You know I can't do that."

"Who are you really protecting? Stacy, did you do something back then, something that will bring the law down on us?" Helen had asked, and Stacy had assured her that there was nothing to worry about.

Except the law was here—and Ella.

After the two had left, she'd warned everyone at the bar

to leave them be. "That one's a cop or my name is Sweetie Pie," one of her customers said. Everyone but Helen had laughed. "He's looking for someone."

"Just stay clear of him," Helen had told them. "He's not interested in taking any of you in."

"How do you know that?" another man demanded.

"I know. He won't be around long." She'd expected that to be the end of it as she'd taken last night's money out of the cash register and returned to her house behind the bar. But she should have known some fool would go after them.

Shaking her head, Helen hoped it wouldn't bring more cops down on them. She turned on her police scanner. It squawked a few times, then fell silent. It was quiet enough that Helen realized she wasn't alone. She turned to face the man standing in her doorway. "You heard?"

"Ray Archer never had the sense God gave a hamster," Huck said with a rueful shake of his head. He still had a thick head of blond hair, although it had started to gray at the temples. Her hair had grayed years ago. She could barely remember her natural color before that, making her aware of how many years had passed. Nor was Huck that strapping handsome young man who'd wandered in off the road too long ago to count. Not that she was the woman she'd been, either. But her pulse still quickened at just the sight of him, and he seemed genuinely fond of her.

"What are you going to do?" he asked.

They all expected Helen to keep them safe, like she was the mother hen of this chicken coop. She was getting too old for this, she thought. "Nothing." She raised her chin and straightened her back. The years had been good to her. When her ex had keeled over and left her the bar, she'd thought it was a trick or bad joke. He'd never given her anything but grief.

But the place had turned out to be a gold mine. As the only bar for miles around, she'd had no competition. Raking in the cash for years and investing it wisely, she'd known that the day would come when she'd need it. Helen had a bad feeling that day had come.

It wasn't as if she hadn't been thinking recently that it was time for a change. She'd seen too much over those years. Mostly, she was just tired of it. Well past the age of retirement, she had enough money to make the rest of her life cushy somewhere else. Maybe Arizona. Maybe Florida. Maybe some island in the middle of the ocean.

Helen brought the subject up, saying as much to Huck, only to have him roll his eyes.

"You'd go crazy within a week. You need the drama. Not to mention the fact that you'd miss us."

Helen met his gaze. "You could come with me."

He grinned, reminding her of the first time she'd laid eyes on him. He'd walked into the bar, all cocky and cute, and she'd felt her heart float like batter in hot grease. She realized that not much had changed. Except now he was one of her bartenders as well as her lover. "If you're propositioning me..." He said it in that sexy way he had, especially late at night when the two of them were curled up in her big bed.

"I'm serious, Huck."

He shook his head slowly. "You're talking leaving Montana. I'm not sure I can do that. I'm not sure you can, either. There's no place like this. You know that, don't you? Damn, woman, when's the last time you drove in traffic?"

Helen nodded, seeing that if she left, she'd be going alone. She wasn't surprised. It hurt, but she understood. Roots ran deep here. She would have a hard time pulling Huck from this place and replanting him even in Arizona, let alone Florida. Maybe he was right. Maybe neither of them would fit anywhere but here—in the middle of nowhere with a bunch of other misfits.

"That couple who came into the bar…" He let the question hang in the air. "They're looking for Stacy, aren't they?" He didn't give her a chance to answer before he let out an oath. "I figured as much. You tell the girl where to find her?"

Helen shook her head. "You know I couldn't do that. But she's Stacy's daughter, and with what happened outside of town just now…"

"She and the cop will be hanging around for a while," he said and met her gaze. "She's going to find out. Maybe it would be better if you—"

The scanner squawked again. "It would be better if Stacy Cardwell had never come here, but she did." Helen thought of the girl who'd had a flat tire outside of town and how she'd felt sorry for her. She'd hired her to work in the bar temporarily, but then one thing had led to another.

"What are you going to do?" Huck asked.

"Deal with it like I always have until I leave. And then it will be yours, problems and all."

"I'm going to miss you," he said softly, stepping closer to take her in his arms.

She leaned into his still-strong body. Not as much as she was going to miss him, she thought.

Ella parked in front of the hotel and saw Waco do the same. It was clear that he would be doggin' her until he found her mother. She couldn't see any way around it at this point.

With a sigh, she reached over to the passenger seat for her backpack and climbed out. There was no getting away from him—at least for the moment. She hoped her mother would contact her again. On the way into town, she'd tried her mom's number. The call had gone straight to voice mail.

But as she looked around what was left of this town, she knew Stacy was here somewhere. She'd find her, somehow. Hopefully, before Waco did. After what he'd told her about the name scratched in the old well, her mom would be going in for questioning, probably handcuffed in the back of his patrol SUV.

Waco was already out of his SUV as she started toward the front of the hotel. He hurried to open the door for her. "After you," he said with a slight bow, making her roll her eyes.

The musty smell hit her first. It reminded her of antiques shops her aunt Dana had taken her to in Butte on a girls' trip. Stacy had stayed in the car, saying she didn't like old things. That had made Dana laugh and say under her breath, "Except for rich old men."

Ella thought of that now. Marvin Hanover had been one of those older men. Not so funny now, given the way that marriage had ended.

An elderly man behind the reception desk eyed them suspiciously as they approached. Ella got the feeling he'd come from the back when he'd heard them pull in. Or maybe he'd been expecting them. As few guests as she suspected this hotel registered in a month, she couldn't see him standing there all that time.

"We need a couple of rooms," Waco said and pulled out his wallet.

"I'll be paying for my own," Ella said without looking at the cop.

The elderly man behind the counter eyed them. "We only take cash. Forty dollars a room."

Forty dollars, from the looks of this place, was highway robbery. But given where they were, they had little choice. Waco threw two twenties on the counter.

The old man's watery gaze shifted to Ella.

"Do you have change?" she asked as she set down a fifty, glad she'd thought to bring cash.

Grumbling, the old man pulled out a cash box, rummaged around in it for a few moments and handed her ten worn dollar bills. Then, putting the cash box back under the counter, he turned and took keys from two of the small cubbies on the wall.

He held out two old-fashioned keys, each attached to a faded plastic orange disk. "Rooms 2 and 4 upstairs. Bathroom is down the hall. The lock's broken, so knock before entering." His gaze sparked for a moment as if he thought the two would be sharing more than the bathroom before the night was over.

Ella snatched a key from the man's hand and, with her backpack slung over her shoulder, started for the stairs. She heard Waco on the creaky steps behind her, his tread heavy and slow. She could feel his gaze warming her backside and wished she'd let him go first. Earlier, he'd looked at her...funny. She shook off the thought. The detective was too single-minded to even think about anything but finding Stacy.

The wooden landing groaned under her footfalls, making her hope the whole place didn't cave in before she could get out of town. She'd taken the number two key and now stopped to insert it into the lock. Out of the corner of her eye, she watched Waco stop at the next door down.

From what she could tell, the place was deserted. They were the only guests. She thought about the bathroom door lock that didn't work and groaned inwardly. Right now she would love a shower, but wasn't up to even seeing how awful the unlockable bathroom might be. She didn't have high hopes as she pushed open the hotel room door and saw the marred chest of drawers and the sagging double bed with its worn cover and dust-coated window behind it.

"It ain't the Ritz," Waco said with a chuckle from next door as he took in his own room. "Let's hope we aren't here long. Hey," he said to her before she could disappear into her room. "If you need me, just pound on the wall. Not too hard, though. I'm sure it's thin."

She said nothing as she entered the room and closed the door behind her. Immediately, she rushed to the window, hoping it opened. It didn't. But there was a hole in the glass where it appeared a rock might have entered and that let in some fresh air. She opened the dusty dark drapes all the way to let the night and air in and looked down on the side street.

A man stood below. His hair was dark, curling at his neck. When he looked up in her direction, she felt a start. She stepped back from the window. What was there about the man that had given her a jolt? She'd only gotten a glimpse of him, but he looked familiar. Had he been one of the men in her mother's photo albums?

Sliding the backpack off, she set it on the creaky wooden chair next to the bed, already debating how to slip out later without Waco following her.

# *Chapter 15*

Waco listened to Ella moving around in her hotel room next door. He realized that he'd been so busy trying to keep her alive—and himself, as well—that he'd forgotten his main objective. He needed to find Stacy before someone else did—especially her daughter.

Why was he convinced that Stacy Cardwell's trouble was more than just running from the law? Maybe even more than murder? He had no idea. Just a gut feeling he couldn't shake. Coming here made him all the more worried that they would find her too late.

He opened the door to his room and stepped to Ella's. Tapping, he said, "It's me." Like that would open doors for him with her. "I'm hungry."

There was nothing but silence behind the door. If he hadn't known better, he would think she'd already given him the slip. A floorboard creaked on the other side of the door a moment before it opened.

He grinned at her. "I thought food might be something we could agree on."

Grudgingly, she smiled. "I have my doubts about finding anything to eat in this town, but I'm willing to try. I'm starving."

"My kind of woman," he said with a laugh. Seeing her expression, he quickly added, "Sorry. Just an expression."

They went down the stairs and out into the twilight. Fortunately, the small shop next door hadn't closed yet. A bell jangled over the front door as he opened it and let Ella lead the way. Narrow aisles cut through tall rows of food staples, clothes and gifts. He didn't see the rocks until they made their way to the checkout counter off to one side of the store. A box of ordinary-looking rocks were marked $1.00 each.

The elderly woman standing behind the counter didn't seem at all surprised to see them. Word around town probably spread on the ceaseless wind that now rattled the front windows. Behind the counter, he spotted the milkshake machine and a microwave. On the wall was a sign that listed microwavable sandwiches.

Waco glanced over at Ella. "Name your poison." They both went for the ham-and-cheese grill and chocolate shakes.

"You can sit up there by the window or take it back to your room," the clerk said, pointing to a couple of small tables at the front of the store. "I'll bring it to you when it's ready."

"My kind of woman, huh?" Ella asked when they were seated. "What exactly is your kind of woman?"

"It's just an expression."

"Uh-huh," she said, holding his gaze with her steely green one. "So you don't have a woman in your life."

He laughed, seeing that she was enjoying giving him

a hard time. He felt a spark between the two of them that should have surprised him, but didn't. He held that gaze, feeling the heat of it.

"I suppose there's a man in yours." He realized that he really wanted to know. But their sandwiches arrived straight from the microwave and the moment was lost.

Heat rose from the sandwiches, the steam making them impossible to unwrap. She seemed relieved to have the diversion. They looked at each other in terror as they peeled back the wrap and ate greedily as if neither of them had had a meal for hours.

Waco suspected it was true of Ella since she hadn't stopped for anything that he'd seen other than gas. He knew it was true for him. When the milkshakes arrived, he and Ella slowed a little on their sandwiches.

She seemed to relax, considering where she was and why. He wondered if she thought staying around here was a good idea in any way. The man who'd chased them out of town was the perfect example of how dangerous it could get. Waco figured the others back at the bar shared the man's feelings. These people didn't like strangers. Especially strangers who asked a lot of questions. In such an isolated spot in the state, these people were used to handling their own problems. He and Ella were problems.

"I suppose you wouldn't want my advice," he said and saw the glint in her green eyes. Still, he plowed ahead. "Whatever your mother might have been doing here—if she even came here—"

"She's here."

"As I was saying, people in some parts of this state don't like *anyone* asking a lot of questions. They might not even know your mother. Just on general principle, they aren't going to cooperate. So continuing to ask questions could be really bad for your health."

Ella smiled at him. "Has anyone ever taken your advice?"

He chewed at his cheek as he studied her for a moment. He couldn't help smiling. Everything about this young woman was refreshing. She intrigued him and he couldn't remember a woman who had ever interested him more. The problem was how to keep her alive. "I suspect you get your stubbornness from your—"

"Whole family. But if you're asking if my mother is stubborn…" Ella frowned and he saw a crack in her composure. "No more stubborn than me, I'd say, but then again…" She looked away, her eyes shiny. "Before you showed up, I would have said I knew my mother."

"But now?"

She shook her head. "I'm not sure I ever knew her. That's why I'm determined to find her and get some answers. No matter where it takes me. Or who I have to deal with." She narrowed her eyes at him. "Even you."

"Even if it gets you killed?" Her green eyes flared. Before she could speak, he raised both hands in surrender. "Sorry, it's an occupational hazard, trying to keep people alive."

"That and dispensing advice?"

He gave her a nod in acknowledgment of her jab. "Can I ask why you're so certain your mother is here? Did she tell you on the phone—?"

"No. She pretended that she didn't know where I was, but I'm sure Helen told her I was in town." She seemed to hesitate. He could tell something was on her mind, something she had been debating telling him.

"Someone ransacked my mother's cabin back on the

ranch. My aunt stumbled onto the man. He'd been going through my mother's photographs. He took several, knocking my aunt down as he left. She's all right," Ella said before he could ask.

"All he took were *photographs*?" He was surprised at that and the fact that she'd shared this information with him. She seemed a little surprised that she had, too. "Any idea what he wanted with them?"

Ella shook her head. "I didn't even know Stacy had an album of older prints hidden in her closet."

He saw her swallow and caught the flicker of pain. How many more of Stacy's secrets would come out before this was over? Some worse than hiding a photo album of old snapshots in her closet, he figured.

Waco didn't know what to say. He had no doubt that she was strong and determined and capable. But still, she was out of her league, and he had a feeling that she knew it. Unfortunately, that wasn't going to stop her.

"Whatever the reason someone took the photos…" Again she hesitated, her eyes coming up to his and locking. "It's how I found this place. That's how I know she's here. It's… where she comes."

He stared at her. "This is where your mother comes when?"

Ella pulled her gaze away to stare out the window. With the descending night, darkness had settled among the buildings of the town, making the place look even more desolate, if that were possible. "My mother has always disappeared for a few days every few months. I never knew where she went—until I looked through the albums." Her eyes came back to his. "She came here. Apparently, she has been living a secret life for years when she comes here."

He looked out the store window at the dark, dying town. "Why?"

"That I don't know," Ella said with a shake of her head. "Evidently, she knows these people well, especially Helen, and they know her. Helen recognized me, so I would assume my mother has shown her photographs of me over the years. The thing is, whoever broke into my mother's cabin and took the photos must have realized they were important. He could come up with the same conclusion I had and show up here."

Waco had no idea what to make of this. "Do you have any relatives up this way?" She shook her head. "Helen is older than your mother." But he supposed they could be friends from way back. "You've never met her before today?" Again she shook her head.

"I think maybe my mother comes here because of a man she wanted to keep secret." He raised a brow at that. "Okay, I shared with you," Ella said. "Now you tell me about the key."

He didn't think he'd reacted, but he must have, because she smiled knowingly. "How did you hear about the key?" he asked.

"Mercy Hanover Davis. She wondered if my mother had it. It would explain why someone ransacked my mother's cabin. So?"

"Sounds like you know as much as I do."

She laughed, an enchanting sound he thought he could get used to. "Was the key in the bottom of the well?"

"It was, but I have no idea what it belongs to. Did Mercy mention—?" She was already shaking her head and looking disappointed.

"She mentioned money."

Waco nodded. "Yes—apparently, that is what is at the forefront of the entire family's minds these days."

"My mother doesn't have it, nor any of their mother's jewelry."

That he already knew from Lorraine. "She hasn't spent the money if she does have it," he said, giving her that much.

"I can't imagine the money is here. Can you?" she asked and looked away. She did have the most amazing green eyes.

"No," he said. "Only a fool would hide a fortune in a den of thieves."

"So at least we agree on that. Any idea how much money we're talking about?"

Waco shook his head. "The family said a fortune, but that's all relative, isn't it?" He could see the wheels turning as Ella looked across the street at the bar again. He hated to think what she planned to do next. "Can I ask one favor?" He rushed on before she could tell him he was owed no favors from her. "If you decide to go back to the bar, take me with you. I'll try not to look so much like the law, if that would help."

"Good luck with that," she said and took a couple of slurps of her milkshake.

The cold chocolate ice cream clung to her lips for a moment before her tongue came out to whip it away. Those lips… He dragged his gaze away, tucking just the thought of kissing those lips away, as well.

Waco had more important things to be thinking about, like keeping this cowgirl alive. They were both chasing a woman Ella wanted to believe was innocent while his gut told him Stacy Cardwell could very well be a cold-blooded killer.

They eyed each other across the table in a standoff until she sighed. "Helen won't talk with you here."

"You're assuming she'll talk to you at all. I have the option of taking her in for questioning."

"Good luck with that." Ella's gaze didn't waver. "While you're getting beat up, I can cry and get her sympathy."

He laughed as he watched her take another sip of her milkshake. "You already have mine."

She looked up sharply, and he saw that the last thing she wanted from him was sympathy. Pushing away her nearly empty glass, she rose. "Looks like neither of us is going to get the opportunity to talk to her."

He followed her glance as it shifted to the front window. Helen came out of the bar and quickly climbed into the passenger side of a Jeep. The driver took off, leaving Waco little doubt where they were headed. He wasn't sure he could catch up to them. Still, he had to try. Ella was already heading for the door.

"Let's take my SUV. It's faster," he said, knowing that if they didn't go together, she would try to catch Helen in her pickup.

As they pushed out the door, he electronically opened the doors to the patrol SUV. Ella hesitated only a second before jumping in. He swung behind the wheel, started the engine and went after the set of red taillights disappearing in the distance.

# Chapter 16

The sky was black except for the pinpoints of light from the vehicle ahead of them. Ella glanced at the speedometer. One hundred and ten and gaining on the Jeep in the distance.

She took in the strong angles of Waco's face in the light from the dash, questioning what had possessed her to jump into his SUV to begin with. It had all happened so fast. She'd let those moments of intimacy in the store make her think for an instant that they were on the same side. They weren't. Their reasons for finding her mom were miles apart. Now here she was. With him. Chasing after Helen and whomever was driving that Jeep.

"I don't know why I let you talk me into coming with you," she said.

He shot her a quick glance. "Because we're in this together?"

"We're not in this together."

Waco seemed to concentrate on the road ahead and the

taillights way in front of them without looking at her. "But we should be," he said. "We both want the same thing."

"I highly doubt that," she said, watching him gain on the Jeep. The detective had been right about one thing, though. His patrol SUV was faster than her pickup.

Ella felt a surge of adrenaline. Earlier, she'd felt exhausted after the long day on the road. Her body ached as if she'd driven all over the very large state of Montana. The food had helped, but her conversations with Waco had affected her in other ways. Being around the man had been both intoxicating and exhausting as they'd parried. She'd felt herself sinking deeper and deeper into the quagmire that was her mother's past life, as if all Stacy's mistakes were now about to come to a head.

Now she felt the exhilaration of the chase. Helen was leading them to Stacy. It seemed too easy. What if it was a trap? Why else would Helen get into the Jeep right across the street from the hotel? Did Helen really think they wouldn't give chase? That they wouldn't be able to catch the Jeep?

"I just had a thought," she said as Waco kept the pedal to the metal. She didn't get a chance to raise her suspicions before he spoke.

"Seems too easy, right? Helen is either taking us to your mother or we're racing into a trap. Or—"

Ahead, the taillights blinked out.

Ella braced herself as Waco hit the brakes. The Jeep had disappeared into the darkness.

Waco stared out at the blackness. There was no light. Not from the sky now shrouded in low clouds or from any houses in the distance, because there didn't seem to be any. He felt as if he'd driven into a black hole the moment the taillights had disappeared.

He'd thrown on his brakes, worried that the Jeep had stopped in the middle of the road, the driver turning off the lights. He didn't want to rear-end the Jeep and kill them all. Especially at the speed he'd been going.

"There!" Ella cried, pointing to her left. "I see the taillights."

He did, too, then. The Jeep had turned off onto a narrow dirt road that Waco had almost missed. As the taillights disappeared over a rise, he turned off his headlights and followed. The road was straight enough and there was just enough light to see where he was going if he kept his speed down.

Even as dark as the night was, Waco could see that they were now headed up into the mountains.

"Do you think she's going to my mother?" Ella asked, voicing the concern he'd had himself. "Or just getting us out of town so they can kill us?"

He shot her a look and shrugged. "It could be a trap, but I think Helen definitely wanted us to follow her." Now that they had, he was having his own concerns about where they were being led. He shouldn't have taken Ella. But the alternative would have meant she'd have raced out here in her pickup—alone. She was safer with him. At least, he hoped that was true.

The road left behind the sagebrush to climb into the mountains. The black skeletal shapes of pine trees on each side of the road made it easier to stay in the tracks of what was now little more than a Jeep trail. But Waco didn't dare take his eyes off the narrow dirt road for long.

Wherever they were headed, his gut told him they would find Stacy Cardwell, dead or alive.

Ella stared after the taillights down the road. The low clouds parted for a moment. Ahead, she could barely make out the contours of the mountains, black silhouettes against a midnight blue sky.

Where were they headed? To her mother? She wondered why all the secrecy, why her mother was hiding out—possibly in the mountains ahead—and why here with these people instead of at home on the ranch.

Ella had to believe it wasn't a trap. Helen was taking her to Stacy. She was putting an end to this. For the first time, Ella wondered what she would say when she saw her mother. She had so many questions. The biggest one was why she had run after the call from the homicide detective and what a dead ex-husband had to do with any of this. But then there was the anger about her mother's secret life.

She sat back and tried not to think about it as they continued toward the mountains. Would whatever was up ahead explain why her mother had been acting strangely long before Marvin Hanover's body had turned up at the bottom of a well? If it was a man, had he been pressuring her to run away with him until her mom finally had?

The road narrowed further. The dark shape of the mountains loomed over them as Waco turned up another path through dense pines. She saw pine trees and rocky bluffs as the patrol SUV bucked and groaned its way up the narrow rough road.

Ella's pulse pounded in her ears. Was Helen leading her to Stacy? Or did the bar owner know she was being followed and was leading them up into the mountains to finish this yet another way? Hadn't her mother always said that some secrets were better left buried?

Waco had been forced to back way off once the Jeep began to climb up into the mountain. He caught only glimpses of the taillights through the pines as the road switchbacked upward. It was much darker in the pines, the dirt road becoming precarious.

He feared he might lose the Jeep, except he had no choice but to hang back. He had to gear down and drive slowly or use his brakes, turning on his brake lights, which he feared would alert them that they were still being followed. Unless they already knew he and Ella were behind them—as per their plan.

As the road surface worsened, his nerves grew even more taut. He finally pulled off onto one of the old logging roads and parked, killing his engine. "Stay here," he said as he heard her pop her door open. He turned to her. "Ella, don't make me lock you in the back."

She climbed out as if she hadn't heard him and started up the road. Since he wasn't going to arrest her, he grabbed what he needed and followed her up the mountain.

He hadn't gone far when he realized he could no longer hear the sound of the Jeep's engine. The driver had stopped.

Waco hoped he wouldn't need backup. Not that it could reach him in time even if he called for it. Not that it stopped him as he headed up the mountain. Ella kept pace, her expression determined. Like her, he suspected Stacy Cardwell was up here.

What worried him, though, was who might be with her and what they would do. As the two of them came around a bend in the road, he spotted the Jeep parked in front of a small rustic cabin set back in the trees. Light glowed from the front window. He caught sight of shadows inside.

But he also caught sight of a figure moving along the edge of the cabin—on the outside.

Ella's breath caught at the sight of the cabin in the woods. Her mother was in there. She felt it. She shivered in anticipation, but also from the chill. It was July in Montana, but cold up here in the mountains.

She stared at the cabin and the glow of the lamp burning inside, and took a breath as she tried to still her anger. She took a step toward it, but Waco grabbed her arm and tugged her back, out of sight of the cabin.

"Listen," he whispered as he pulled her close. "We can't just go walking in there. You understand that, right?"

She hadn't thought of anything but confronting her mother about all her lies and secrets. Every step up the mountain had made her more angry at Stacy's deception all these years. And for what? Some man?

"You have to let me handle this my way," he said, holding her gaze in the darkness. They were so close, she could smell chocolate shake on his breath. His grip on her arm tightened. "The other option is me handcuffing you to one of these trees. We do this my way."

Ella nodded, realizing that he meant it. She'd come so far to find her mother, and now that she was sure that she had, she didn't want to spend another minute handcuffed with her arms around a tree.

"There's someone outside the cabin," Waco whispered. "I need to take care of him first. Then we enter. I go in first, so you don't get shot. That means you stay behind me the whole way. Agreed?"

Ella had no choice. If she even hesitated… "Agreed." He studied her for a few more moments. "I swear," she said and got a grudging ghost of a smile out of him. "I'm behind you all the way."

They started again toward the cabin. She saw movement. A man with an ax standing next to a woodpile. The man froze for an instant as if sensing them.

But before he could raise the ax, let alone swing it, Waco

had taken him down and cuffed him. When the man had tried to yell a warning to whomever was inside, Waco stuffed the man's bandanna into his mouth.

She watched him pull the man to his feet and steer him toward the steps into the cabin.

"I'd like to see my mother alone," she said behind him.

"Fat chance," he said as they ascended the steps. Reaching around the man, Waco opened the door, throwing it wide and shoving the man inside. The man stumbled and fell to the floor.

Ella was right behind the detective when she saw her mother sitting in a chair at the table. Stacy looked up. Then their gazes met and her mother's eyes quickly filled with tears.

They'd barely gotten in the door when Waco barked, "Everyone stay where you are and don't move. I'm Detective Waco Johnson. So everyone just settle down."

The man sprawled on the floor was struggling to get up, but he stopped as Stacy, who'd been sitting at the table, got up, rushed to the man on the floor and dropped to her knees beside him.

Ella was so shocked that she couldn't move, couldn't speak.

As Helen came into the room, holding what appeared to be a glass of water, and stopped in the small kitchen doorway, Waco asked, "Is anyone else here?" Helen shook her head and pushed open the door to the only other room not in view—the bathroom. It was empty.

"Take off his handcuffs," Stacy demanded from the floor where she was next to the cuffed man. When the detective didn't move, she shot him a narrowed look. "Unless Jeremiah is under arrest, take off his handcuffs."

"Only if he doesn't cause any trouble," Waco said. "Otherwise, I will arrest him."

"He won't cause any trouble," Stacy said.

Ella stared at her mother, who seemed to have aged since the last time she'd seen her. She watched her comfort the man she'd called Jeremiah as Waco removed the handcuffs. Jeremiah glared at Waco as he rubbed his wrists. Ella got the impression it wasn't the first time he'd been cuffed, but her gaze quickly shifted to her mother.

She stared at her mother as if looking at a stranger. All this concern for this man? Where was Stacy's concern for her family that she was putting through all this worry?

Her mother rose and started to take a step in her direction, but Ella shook her head and Stacy froze, looking uncertain.

"What is going on?" Ella said as she found her voice. "No more lies. No more secrets. What are you doing here with these people?"

Her mother wrung her hands for a moment, tears filling her eyes again. "I'm so sorry, Ellie. It's...complicated."

She could barely look at her mother. "Sorry doesn't cut it. Not anymore. And I'm sure it's complicated or you wouldn't be here."

Stacy seemed to cringe at the look Ella was giving her.

"Don't talk to her like that," Jeremiah said, his voice sharp-edged as he stood and put an arm around Stacy's shoulders.

Ella swung her gaze to him, surprised, now that she got a good look at him, that he wasn't much older than she was. When she met his pale blue eyes, she felt a jolt. There was something strangely familiar about him. Even stronger was the feeling that she'd met him before. Had her mother brought her here when she was younger?

He appeared to be in his late twenties or early thirties, with a head of curly sandy-blond hair and blue eyes. His expression was surly. Clearly, he resented Ella's being there.

"Who are you?" she demanded. "You can't be my mother's boyfriend. She always goes for rich men twice her age." The poisoned arrow hit its mark. Stacy winced as if in pain and stumbled to the chair to sit again.

"Please, Ella," she said. "Don't take your anger out on Jeremiah. It's me you're upset with, not him."

Helen cleared her throat. "Maybe Jeremiah and I should step outside and let you—"

"No one is leaving," Waco said.

Ella felt Jeremiah's hard gaze. "Why are *you* here with a cop?" he demanded.

Ella spun on him, flipping her long blond braid over her shoulder as she tried to keep her temper in check. "I'm here to see *my* mother. The question is, who are you and why is this your business?"

Jeremiah glared at her as a tense silence filled the room. "She's my mother, too."

# *Chapter 17*

Waco turned to Ella. She looked as if the floor had dropped out from under her. Jeremiah was her *brother*? He thought about what he'd learned from his visit to the Hanovers. Marvin Hanover had wanted a son. His daughter Mercy believed that Stacy had lied about being pregnant. What if she hadn't?

His mind was whirling. He could well imagine how Ella's was spinning. She hadn't moved. Hadn't even looked as if she had taken a breath. Her green eyes had darkened as all the color had drained from her face. The room had gone deathly silent.

He watched her slowly turn to look at her mother. Stacy was crying softly as she pleaded silently with her daughter. She seemed to be begging for Ella's understanding.

Helen went to Stacy, shooing Jeremiah away. He moved to stand with his back against the wall, scowling at Ella in defiance.

"Is it true?" Waco asked Stacy.

She nodded distractedly, her gaze refusing to leave Ella's face.

"I'm so sorry," Stacy said. "I can explain, if you just give me a chance."

"What is there to explain?" Jeremiah demanded. "She knows it's true, and pretty soon the rest of the family will, too."

"It should have been done a long time ago—just as I've said so many times before," Helen said.

Stacy could only cry and nod.

Ella had taken the initial shock like a blow. But she recovered quickly, because the moment Jeremiah had said he was Stacy's son, she'd known it was true. The eyes. The feeling that she knew this stranger. Still, she hadn't been able to speak for a moment as her thoughts went wild. She didn't want to believe it. It would mean that her mother hadn't just kept her son a secret. She'd hidden him from the rest of the family. She'd hidden a brother from Ella.

She realized that Jeremiah had spoken and was now staring at her.

"You know it's true, don't you?" he said.

Ella dragged her eyes from him to look again at her mother. "I don't understand."

"What's there to understand?" Helen snapped. "Your mother had a son before you were born. She had her reasons for leaving him with me."

"Her *reasons*?" Ella echoed. "What mother has her reasons for leaving her son with a stranger and never telling her family—including her daughter—about him?"

"I wasn't a stranger," Helen said. "I was a good friend."

Ella shook her head. "Such a good friend that my mother kept you a secret all these years, as well?"

Helen's cheeks flamed, anger glinting in her eyes for a moment before she lowered her regard. "Like I said, your mother had her reasons."

"It was the only way I could have him in my life," Stacy said.

"You could have brought him to the ranch," Ella declared, her voice breaking. "You didn't have to keep him a secret along with all your other secret friends. You could have let me grow up with a brother."

"I couldn't do that. You don't understand," Stacy said.

"I think I do," Waco said.

Ella had almost forgotten that he was in the room. She turned to look at him, as did everyone else.

"It was because of his father," the detective said. "You didn't want Marvin to know about his son because he planned to take him away from you once he was born."

"Not just Marvin," Stacy conceded, her voice stronger now. "His entire family. You don't know what they are capable of, but I do. When I heard about your call, I knew I had to get to Jeremiah."

Ella hated how much it hurt that her mother hadn't reached out to her after Waco's call. Instead, she'd gone running to her secret son.

"I figured Marvin was dead or you wouldn't be calling," her mother was saying. "That meant an investigation." She looked at Waco. "That's why I had to come here. I had to warn everyone, especially my son."

Jeremiah cursed under his breath. "She was just protecting me," he said, as if it needed to be said. "Now you come here with your cop friend—"

"He isn't my friend," Ella said automatically. She was

still trying to make sense out of this. "So Marvin Hanover is his father?" she asked her mother.

Stacy nodded. "I'm not sure how much you know about him."

"According to the family, he paid you ten thousand dollars when you proved to him you were having a son," Waco said.

Jeremiah's jaw tightened, lips clamped.

Ella's gaze shifted to her mother.

"I'm not proud of that." Stacy looked down at her hands in her lap. "I thought I could go through with it, being married to him. But after seeing what kind of man he really was, once I found myself pregnant, I knew I couldn't turn a child over to him. Yes, he was demanding that I walk away after I gave birth. I'd done my duty, he'd said. He was kicking me out and taking my son. So…yes, I took the money. I needed it to get out of there before my son was born. I would have done anything to keep Marvin from getting his hands on my child."

"Does that anything include killing your son's father?" Waco asked and motioned Jeremiah back as he started to launch himself off the wall in defense of his mother.

"I didn't kill Marvin," Stacy said. "I swear it." She looked pleadingly at Ella and then turned to smile at her son. "I just wanted Jeremiah to be safe."

Ella followed her gaze. She'd always been the only child—at least, where her mother was concerned, she'd thought. Being raised around her cousins, she hadn't felt that way. But she'd thought there had always been a bond between her mother and herself.

Now she wondered if she would ever come to grips with this secret of her mother's—and having a brother, let alone this one. He seemed as wild and untamed as this place where he'd grown up. Even as she thought it, she saw some of herself in him. She, too, wanted to defend her mother.

"I'm sorry, Jeremiah," she said to him, realizing that while she'd been raised on the ranch, he'd been raised here with strangers.

Her half brother shot her a withering look. "Don't feel sorry for me. I'm fine. We're not doing any brotherly-sisterly bonding, all right? You brought a *cop* here."

"She didn't *bring* me." Waco ground the words out. "I've been tailing her, knowing eventually she would lead me to Stacy, because she's one determined, strong young woman who cares about her mother."

Jeremiah actually looked chastised by the detective's words. Ella was surprised by them herself and grudgingly grateful.

Stacy said, "Please. I'll tell you everything."

Ella doubted that and wondered if Waco did, too, but she said nothing. Her body had burned hot with anger and fear, then icy cold with shock and hurt, and finally with relief that her mother was all right. At least for the moment. The day had been long, and exhaustion tugged at her.

"You're going to have to come back with me to Bozeman for questioning," Waco said to Stacy. "Jeremiah, as well."

"You don't understand," Stacy cried. "If Marvin's family finds out about my son, they will *kill* him."

"Why would they do that?" Waco demanded.

"Because Marvin knew I was pregnant. He told me he was changing his will and leaving everything to our son."

"If he really is Marvin's son."

Stacy grimaced. "So the family told you that he wanted a DNA test done even before my son was born? I'm sure they told you that's why I killed him, so it would never come out that I'd lied. Jeremiah *is* Marvin's son. At any time, he could have come forward and claimed what is rightfully his. But I couldn't let him. If they knew about him, they would never let him live. They already killed his father for the money. You have no idea what that family is like."

Waco had a pretty good idea after meeting them. "I can see where you would want to protect him when he was young, but why bring him here?"

"These are my friends. Helen raised Jeremiah. She kept my secret."

"All right, but now he's an adult who can take care of himself. Why not let him claim what you say is rightfully his?"

Stacy narrowed her gaze at him. "I made a lot of mistakes in my life. I suspect you're aware of that and that's why you think I killed Marvin. But since having my son and then my daughter... What do I have to do to prove to you I'm innocent of this crime?"

"Come back with me and get your statement on the record. You do realize the fact that you ran doesn't help your case."

"I had to warn my son. I knew everything was going to come out and that he would be in danger."

"You came up here to do more than warn your son or you wouldn't have brought all your clothes," Ella said, motioning to the suitcases by the door. "You were going to run again."

Stacy's cheeks flushed. "I hoped to talk Jeremiah into leaving the country. I wasn't sure I'd be able to come back."

"You know, it almost sounds as if you don't want your son's DNA tested any more than you did thirty years ago," Waco said. "Because you aren't sure if he is Marvin's son?"

"I told you—"

"Well, I can't let you run. I can't let your son run, either. To get to the bottom of this, I have to know who's lying," he told her.

"I'm not sure my son will go with you," she said quietly without looking at Jeremiah.

"I suggest you change his mind about that," Waco said. "I've already chased you all over Montana. I'm not anxious to do the same thing with him—but I will."

"Stacy, listen to them," Helen said. "You knew that one day this had to end."

Waco looked over at Jeremiah. "I think your mother's right about your life possibly being in jeopardy from Marvin's family until we get this sorted out."

"I'm not leaving my mother," Jeremiah said. "She needs me. I'm going wherever she goes."

"She has a family who'll protect her—just as we always have," Ella said, facing down her brother.

Waco figured she was wondering the same thing he was. How much did Jeremiah know about Ella and their lives on the ranch? He figured Ella still had to be bowled over by the fact that all these years she'd had a brother, one her mother had failed to mention.

"I'm part of the family whether you like it or not," Jeremiah said, his glare locking with her own.

Now that the shock had passed, Ella realized what she had to say, what she had to do. "Then maybe it's time you came back to the ranch, Jeremiah. You'll be safe there. We'll make sure of it." She looked to her mother, but it was Waco who spoke.

"Ella's right. Both your daughter and your son are worried about you. The ranch seems the best place right now for all three of you."

Stacy looked from Jeremiah to Ella and back again. Helen touched her arm. "We're his family here, too, but maybe it's time for Jeremiah to take his rightful place in the Cardwell family."

Ella wondered how much of a shock this would be for the rest of the Cardwells. Dana would open her arms to her nephew. Hud would be concerned about this wild young man who might be too much like his mother—let alone his father.

If there was any good in Jeremiah, the family would bring it out. Her mother stood to hug her friend. Then, with tears in her eyes, she looked at Ella and then Jeremiah. She appeared terrified. Of going back and possibly facing prison? Or of facing the family?

Stacy straightened, lifting her chin as she said to Waco, "I've been running from the mistakes of my past for too many years. I have no choice, do I? I'm finally going to have to face not only the past but also my family."

# *Chapter 18*

It was dawn by the time they all left the cabin. Once back in Hell and Gone, Ella talked Waco into letting her take her mother in her pickup and letting Jeremiah follow in the ranch pickup. "You can follow all of us."

The detective had studied her, a smile in his blue eyes.

"I'm not going to take off with my mother and brother, if that's what you're worried about," she assured him. "Stacy's not under arrest, right?" He nodded. "They're both yours once we reach the ranch. I need this time with my mother." She saw that got to him more than any of her other arguments.

"I'll be right behind you," he said. "Don't make me chase you both down and haul you in. You don't want to be behind bars for interfering any more in my investigation."

She'd smiled, thinking how the man had grown on her. She liked the way he'd handled himself with the situation at the cabin. She liked a lot of things about him, now that she thought about it.

"I definitely don't want to be on your wrong side, Detective," she'd said with a grin.

He'd eyed her as if not quite sure he could trust her. That, too, she liked. He was a little too cocky, as if he thought he knew his way around women. Not this woman, though.

Ella wasn't joking about needing this time with her mother. Once behind the wheel with Hell and Gone in the rearview mirror, she settled in. She was anxious to have her mother alone. She needed answers.

"I need to know the truth, Mom," she said, not looking at her mother as she drove. "It's just you and me. For once, be honest with me."

"I didn't kill Marvin. You have to believe that."

She wished she could. "Then why were you hiding out from the law?"

"It isn't just the law after me. You don't know Marvin's family like I do—and that's the way I've always wanted it. Now...well, we're all in danger. Especially Jeremiah."

"If true, why didn't you go to Hud?"

Her mother's hands were balled in her lap. Out of the corner of her eye, Ella saw her look down at them for a moment. When she raised her head, her eyes flooded with tears. "Hud can't protect me from this. I felt that if I stayed, they might come after you and the rest of the family."

"I can take care of myself," Ella snapped, angry that her mother would use her as an excuse. "Why would they threaten any of us if you had nothing to do with your ex-husband's death?"

Stacy shook her head. "Because Jeremiah is the rightful heir to Marvin's fortune."

Ella snorted. "You've seen his will?"

"I have the will, handwritten and signed and witnessed."

She shot a look at her mother. "I don't even want to know how you pulled that off. But after all these years, do you really think it's still valid? How do you know they haven't already spent the money?"

"They don't know where it is."

"And you do?"

Her mother didn't answer.

"This sounds like an urban legend to me," Ella said. "How do you even know it exists?"

"Marvin wore a key around his neck. He guarded it with his life."

"But now he's dead. Wouldn't the killer have taken it?" When her mother didn't answer, she yelled, "Stacy! Tell me you don't have the key."

"It isn't what you think. I drugged him the night before he disappeared and switched the keys." The words came out short and fast, as if even her mother knew how they would sound.

Ella rubbed a hand across her forehead. "So you have the key." Waco had told her that a key had been found in the well. Wouldn't the killer have taken the key from around Marvin's neck? Unless the killer had known it wasn't the real one.

She said as much to her mother, who seemed surprised to hear that a key had been found with the remains.

"I have no idea why his killer didn't take the key," her mother cried. "Ella, I'm telling you the truth. I didn't kill him."

"Then who did?"

Stacy was silent for a few minutes. "Any one of them could have done it. It would be hard to choose. They all hated him, and with good reason. He was horrible to his family. He was horrible to everyone. To think he wanted to take my son and raise him without me..." She turned away to look out her side window.

Ella heard the hatred and anger in her mother's voice even after all these years. She didn't want to think her capable of murder. She glanced in her rearview mirror and saw Jeremiah behind the wheel of the ranch pickup and, behind him, Waco's patrol SUV. What a caravan they were, she thought, hating to think where they might all end up.

She tried not to think about what would happen when they reached the ranch. Dana would welcome the surly Jeremiah into the family with open arms—as was her nature. But Ella wondered what kind of reception her mother would get. She had put all her siblings through so much when she was younger, and now this.

The one thing Ella knew for sure, though, was that the family would keep both Stacy and Jeremiah safe on the ranch. That was what family did, especially the Cardwell-Savage family.

"As soon as I heard about his remains being found, I had to warn Jeremiah," Stacy was saying. "For years, they've threatened me, believing I took the money."

"You took the key," Ella pointed out. "So they weren't wrong about you having access to the money. Did you dip into it?"

When Stacy spoke, her voice was flat. "I don't know where the money is, and it was hard to search for it on Hanover property under the circumstances."

She thought about the old well where Marvin's remains had been found. "Did you look for it on the old homestead?" Even though she didn't glance at her mother, she could feel her hard stare.

"You still don't believe me."

Ella couldn't deny it, so she stayed silent. Her mind was mulling over everything. Wouldn't Waco have to return the key once the investigation was over? In which case, wouldn't one of the Hanovers know what the key opened? But if they knew where the money was hidden, they wouldn't have let not having a key stop them from opening the door to the money, would they? If the money existed.

Her head hurt. Worse, she was having trouble forgiving her mother. "So when the detective called, you simply took off to warn Jeremiah, taking all your clothing with you and planning to skip the country." Her mother said nothing. "You left without a word to me, leaving me on my own. That means you really weren't that worried about me and any threats against me or the family. Did you know that Mercy accosted me on the street? I remembered the other time she did that when I was just a child."

"I'm sorry. I knew you could take care of yourself and that you had the family," her mother said.

"How could you fail to tell me that I had a half brother all these years?"

Her mother began to cry. "It was all so long ago. I was pregnant, planning my escape from Marvin, when he disappeared. It was a time in my life when I couldn't take care of Jeremiah alone. You know my history. I wasn't getting along with Dana and she had the ranch." Stacy wiped at her tears. "I wasn't welcome there under the circumstances—especially pregnant. I had only one other place to turn. I knew Helen and the family she'd made would take care of him. I would visit as often as I could."

"Yes, those days when you simply disappeared without a word," Ella said. "Is it any wonder that I've always worried about you?"

"I didn't mean to make you worry. I had to hide Jeremiah where the Hanovers wouldn't look for him. That's why I never wanted any of you to know."

Ella shook her head, realizing she, too, was close to tears. Often over the years, she'd felt like the adult and her mother the child. But no more than right now. "Stacy, swear to me on my life that you didn't kill Marvin."

Her mother looked shocked, but slowly nodded. "I swear. I couldn't go home to the ranch. I didn't want to be the one who was always in trouble. I thought I could take care of it myself. But then, when I found myself in trouble again and pregnant with you… I swallowed my pride and went home. I did that for *you*. I wish I had done it for Jeremiah, but I was too young and scared back then."

"Were you surprised when Marvin's remains were found?"

Stacy looked away. "I knew he had to be dead, but I could never take the chance that he wasn't. Or that Lionel or one of the others would learn about Jeremiah. For a while now, Jeremiah has been trying to get me to introduce him to our family. Helen, too."

Ella studied her mother for a moment, realizing that this was why her mother had been different the past year. She'd been getting pressure to tell her secret. So much pressure that she'd planned to run away instead of admit the truth.

Gripping the steering wheel tighter, Ella was silent for a few minutes. Was there anything her mother could say that she would believe? She didn't think so. "You have the key. Do you have the money?"

"No." She seemed to realize that Ella didn't believe her. "Do you really think I would have sat on millions of dollars all these years and not spent any of it?"

"Okay, you have me there."

Ella drove for a few miles before she spoke again. She knew what was at the heart of her hurt. "You should have told me. I'm your *daughter*."

"That is exactly why I didn't tell you," her mother said. "I wish I could have kept everything from my past from you. Ella, when I had you, you're what changed my life. That's why I went back to the ranch. I wanted you to have a family, a better life. It was hard going back, pregnant, the black sheep of the family. But I did it because I would do anything for you."

"Even tell the truth?"

Her mother chuckled. "Even that."

Helen watched them all leave Hell and Gone. Jeremiah had asked her to take care of his Jeep until he returned for it. She wondered if he would ever return. This town was all he'd known. Her and her dysfunctional family.

But she told herself that they'd had some good times. Those memories brought tears to her eyes. Jeremiah had been like a son to her. Her only child, as it had turned out. She'd done the best she could raising him in his mother's absence and in this place.

Not that it hadn't been clear who was his mother. Every time Stacy had shown up, the boy had jumped for joy. Even as a man, he'd looked forward to her visits. He'd never questioned the odd arrangement. He'd turned out fine, given the genes swimming in the soup that was him.

Helen heard Huck come out of the bar. He put his arm around her as he followed her line of sight to the vehicles disappearing on the horizon.

"They're gone?" She nodded. "Are you all right?"

She wasn't. "Yes, but I'm going to have to leave."

"I know," he said and pulled her in tighter. "It won't be

easy, but you're a survivor. Arizona will never be the same once you get there."

She turned her head to look up at him. She didn't have to ask. He really wasn't going to change his mind and go with her. "You'll take care of the bar?"

"You know I will. I'll take care of everything just like you have done all these years. This place won't die."

Helen smiled, liking the idea of some things never changing—even as she didn't believe it. "I'm going to miss you," she said as he kissed her cheek.

"I'll help you pack, because something tells me you're ready to hit the road."

"You know me so well," she said as the taillights on the patrol SUV faded into the horizon and she turned toward the door into the bar.

Waco thought about Ella all the way back to the Cardwell Ranch and mulled over the case. Did he believe Stacy? Did Ella? He felt confused and was glad when Hitch called.

"I wanted to ask how you are, where you are," she said, "but I'm not supposed to be involved in this case."

He chuckled. "I've been to Hell and Gone. Yes, it's a real place in middle-of-nowhere Montana. With her daughter's help, I found Stacy Cardwell. I'm bringing her back for questioning. Heads up—she isn't coming alone, so I would imagine there will be a family meeting at the ranch, and you'll hear all about it."

"So Stacy isn't under arrest? Are you any closer to finding Marvin's murderer?"

"Not really. Once I get back, I plan to pay the Hanover family another visit. Stacy swears she didn't do it, but she has even better motives for wanting him dead than ever."

"You'll figure it out. No hint as to the topic of the Cardwell Ranch family meeting?"

"I thought you'd prefer to be surprised."

"Right. You know how I love surprises." Hitch disconnected, laughing.

Ahead, Waco saw that they were almost to the ranch.

Ella felt exhausted after the drive. Her mother had slept for much of it. She'd stolen glances at Stacy, trying to understand this woman who'd been such a disjointed part of her life. Even from a young age, she'd seen that there was something so different about Stacy compared to her sister, Dana. Stacy kept secrets. Stacy had a past that no one seemed to know anything about. For years, Ella had sensed something dark in that past. That was why she had always worried about her mother.

As she pulled up in front of the main ranch house, her mother stirred awake. Dana came out onto the porch, shielding her eyes from the early-morning sun as she looked first to Ella's pickup and then to the driver of the ranch pickup that had parked next to her. She saw her aunt's frown deepen as cold-case homicide detective Waco Johnson pulled up next to Ella and parked.

Her mother hadn't moved. She seemed frozen on the seat, as if facing death rather than her sister. Ella thought again how different they were. Dana faced things head-on. Stacy ran from anything distasteful.

"You might as well get out," Ella said as she looked over at her mother. "I'll be with you. And so will Jeremiah."

Stacy attempted a smile and reached for Ella's hand. "I don't know what I would have done without you all these years." She squeezed her hand and then let go as she opened the pickup's door.

* * *

Dana had been scared out of her mind for Ella and, of course, for Stacy. She hated the thought of Ella getting involved in one of her mother's problems. Now, as she watched her sister exit Ella's pickup, she felt her heart fill with love rather than anger.

"You're going to have to help Stacy," their mother had said that night on her deathbed. "She isn't like you and me. She's fragile." Dana had silently scoffed at that but nodded. "I'm leaving you the ranch because I know it will be in good hands. That's going to hurt your sister even more than it will your brothers, but it can't be helped. Promise me you'll be there for Stacy, no matter how hard she tries to push you away. She's jealous of you, Dana, and wishes she was more like you. I'm sorry, but you're going to have to be your sister's keeper."

Dana had balked, finding herself at war with her sister over the ranch, and yet her promise had come back to haunt her time and again. Even when Stacy had returned with Ella and seemed to have settled down, she was still sometimes so exasperating, especially when she'd take off for days without a word.

But Dana knew, more than anything, she never wanted to lose her sister again and hoped with all her heart that she wasn't about to. She watched Stacy stop at the bottom of the porch steps before she started up toward her and the ranch house, a house that had withstood all kinds of trouble for more than a hundred years.

Ella stood next to her pickup, watching her mother climb the stairs. As if without a word, she watched Stacy step into her sister's outstretched arms. Ella couldn't help the tears that stung her eyes as she saw the two sisters hugging each other. She wiped hastily at them as Jeremiah stepped up beside her.

"You think you're not like her," he said.

"I'm not," Ella snapped. "I'm nothing like her."

"Just keep telling yourself that."

She was glad when Waco joined them.

"I thought I'd let them have their reunion before taking Stacy in to get her statement," he said.

On the porch, Stacy had stepped out of her sister's arms, and both were now looking at the three of them standing together. Ella watched her aunt's expression as she took in Jeremiah. Stacy quit talking, and for a moment, the two of them seemed suspended there on the house porch.

Dana took the first step down the stairs, then the next, making a beeline for Jeremiah. Ella looked over at him. "Brace yourself," she whispered. "She's going to hug you and welcome you into the family. She'll cry and then she'll take you in the kitchen and feed you. It's just the way Aunt Dana is, so you might as well get used to it."

He looked like a deer caught in headlights as Dana rushed at him, threw her arms around him and cried.

# Chapter 19

"Looks like everything is going to be all right, Ella," Waco commented as the two of them walked toward the creek. He'd noticed Stacy standing alone on the porch, watching her sister and son. There was something about the expression on Stacy's face that made him uneasy. "Did you and your mother have a nice talk on the way here?"

Ella nodded and kept walking. He followed her down to the creek, where she stopped at the edge—out of sight from the family and out of hearing range.

She didn't look at him as she said, "I need to tell you about the key you said was found in the well. My mother said she drugged Marvin and switched the keys the night before she planned to run away. If true, then the one you have is worthless."

He let out a low whistle. He knew he didn't have to tell Ella that this didn't help Stacy look any more innocent. "Your mother has the key but she's never used it?" He couldn't keep the disbelief out of his voice. A woman who would drug her husband...

"According to her, she doesn't know what it opens." Ella finally looked over at him. "But someone in that family has to know."

He caught a gleam in her eye and took a step back as he held up his hands. "Hold on. I don't think I like what you're about to suggest."

Ella looked surprised that he had read her so well. After all, they hardly knew each other. "Have you returned the key found in the well to the family yet?"

He shook his head, suspecting where this was going. "Some of the family is anxious to get the key."

"But maybe not all," she said. "Because one of them already knows the key doesn't work.

"At first," she continued, "when I heard about a key being found in the well, I thought that Marvin had taken the secret—and the key—to his grave. But I couldn't understand why the killer would have let that happen unless Marvin had refused to give up the key, which is why it was found in the bottom of the well with him. But why would the killer have let that happen? It didn't make any sense. Was the key in the well still attached to the chain Marvin Hanover wore around his neck?"

Waco shook his head, making her smile knowingly. "You think the killer took what he or she thought was the original key and tossed one that resembled it into the well so, if the body was ever found, the key would seem to be with the remains."

"I'd wager that is exactly what happened." Ella frowned. "How did you even learn about the remains in the well?"

"An anonymous caller."

There was that gleam again. "So the killer isn't going

to be anxious about getting the key from you because he or she knows it is a fake," she said. "But what if the family finds out that my mother took the original?"

"By the way, where is that key?" he asked. She only smiled. "You do realize that I can have you arrested for not handing it over."

"You keep threatening to put me behind bars," she said, clearly flirting with him. "Is that a fantasy of yours?"

Waco chuckled. "Seriously, Ella. I need that key."

"I didn't have to tell you about it," she said, chewing at her lower lip for a moment. "You want to catch this killer, right?" He narrowed his eyes at her. "I have a plan."

"Forget it."

"You haven't even heard what it is," she said.

"I don't need to. I can tell it involves you putting yourself in danger and interfering with my investigation. I'm not having any of it."

Ella nodded. "My mother has the key. I'm sure she'll give it to you when you take her in for questioning." She started to turn away, but he grabbed her arm, turning her back toward him.

Waco brushed a lock of blond hair from Ella's face. He hated it when he couldn't see her eyes. All that green that seemed to change shades depending on her mood. Right now, they were a dark emerald and slightly narrowed as she took him in.

"Detective?"

"Aren't we at the point that we can use first names?"

"Waco." She seemed to move the letters around in her mouth, tasting them slowly, her tongue coming out to lick her lips. "Waco."

He smiled, loving his name on her lips as he pulled her

closer. "Ella." He cupped her jaw, ran his thumb over her lips and felt her shiver.

"Was there something you wanted to ask me?" he whispered.

Her lips parted. He saw the dart of her tongue as it touched her upper lip. He felt the sensual thrill rocket through his veins.

In no hurry, he slowly dropped his mouth to Ella's. He brushed his lips over hers, felt a quiver that stirred the flames already burning inside him. He touched the tip of his tongue to hers. She let out a long sigh, leaning into him, those eyes locked with his.

It was as if all his senses came alive. He had feared that if he ever kissed Ella, there would be no turning back. He would want her. Want her for keeps.

Pulling her up, he deepened the kiss and felt her melt against him.

"Detective?"

Waco quickly let Ella go and turned to see Stacy standing on the rise over the creek above them. That one word reminded him that he had no business kissing this woman— or, worse, wanting more from her. Not now. He had an old murder to solve.

"You said you wanted a statement from me," Stacy said, looking from him to Ella and back again. "If you're interrogating my daughter…well, I do like your style."

After the kiss, Ella felt almost guilty for what she was about to do as she watched her mother leave with the detective. Her face had flushed to the roots of her hair at being caught kissing Waco. It wasn't the "being caught" part that embarrassed her. It was the fact that she'd never felt anything like that before in just one kiss. She'd seen the way her mother had looked at her. Surprised at first, then a slow, knowing smile, as if she could see herself in Ella.

Ella tried to put that thought out of her head, along with the guilt, as she pulled out her phone and called the Hanover house. An older male answered. Lionel, she assumed.

"My name is Ella Cardwell. I think I might have something you've been looking for." Silence.

"I can't imagine what that might be," he said at last.

*Yeah, right*, she thought. "How about I stop by to discuss it? I'll see you in fifteen minutes."

He started to say something, but seemed to change his mind.

Ella disconnected, knowing she was taking a huge risk.

The first thing she had to find out was how badly one of the Hanovers might want the original key. It was dangerous, but not that much, she assured herself, given she wouldn't be taking the key. So, if they really wanted it, they would be smart not to harm her.

Also, she wondered about the will that left everything to Jeremiah. The will her mother swore was real. Did the family know about it—*if* it existed?

The only person in the family Ella'd ever met had been Mercy Hanover, so she was looking forward to meeting the others. Although she didn't have much time. Waco had taken her mother to the marshal's office to get her statement.

At some point, he would demand the key Stacy had taken from her former husband.

"Let's get right down to it," Waco said once he had the video camera set up and had entered the preliminaries. He looked directly at Stacy Cardwell. "Did you kill Marvin Hanover?"

"No, I did not. Are you leading my daughter on?"

He blinked. "This is not the time to—"

"I want to know what your intentions are toward my daughter, Detective."

Waco swore under his breath. "I'm falling in love with her. Now, can we move on? Tell me how you met Marvin Hanover."

Stacy stared at him for a long moment before she nodded and began to talk.

He'd already heard most of it, but wanted it on the record. He suspected there might have been things she hadn't told her daughter.

"Is that really important?" When he merely waited, she said, "I met him through a friend. I know what you're asking. I married him for security. He had money. We saw each other a few times and one thing led to another." She looked away. "I told him I was pregnant."

"Were you?"

"Not yet," she admitted, looking at him again. "My daughter is nothing like me."

He gave her an impatient look. "When did things go sour between you and your husband?"

She laughed. "The ink wasn't dry on the paper before he told me how things were going to be. He'd made me sign a prenuptial agreement. It promised me ten thousand in cash on the day I came home with proof that I was pregnant with a son."

"But you weren't."

"I kept putting him off, telling him it was too early to know the sex. The rest of his family were telling him that I was lying about being pregnant." She shrugged. "Actually, that worked to my benefit later when I really was pregnant, but I didn't want them to know."

"Eventually, you got pregnant with his son."

Stacy nodded. "I thought I'd gotten lucky. I brought home the sonogram and he forked over the ten thousand. That's when he told me that he was going to keep my son. That I wouldn't be allowed to ruin him, and unless I cooperated, he would divorce me without a cent."

"Sounds like motive for murder."

"Oh, I wanted to kill him, but I had a son growing inside me. *My* son. I knew I had to save my baby from this horrible man. I'd seen how he was with his other offspring. So I planned to leave him."

"Weren't you worried he would come after you?"

"I pretended to lose the baby. He bought it. The rest of the family hadn't believed I was pregnant to begin with, so it worked. I assured him I could get pregnant again with a son and I planned my escape. But before I could leave, he disappeared."

"Didn't you take something before you left?"

She looked confused for a moment. "The key. I might have drugged him and exchanged the keys." Before he could speak, she said, "Okay, I did drug him and exchange the keys."

"Where is the original key?"

She hesitated, but only for a moment before she patted her pocket. "I have it."

Why did this feel too easy? "You kept it all these years. You never used it? How do I know it is the original?"

She sighed. "I never figured out what it fit. While I lived in that house, I looked for something that a key that shape might fit into. I never found anything, and Marvin wasn't about to tell me or his family."

"How do you know he wasn't lying to keep both you and his family under his thumb?"

Stacy nodded. "That would be just like him. That way, he got the last laugh, huh."

"In that case, you would have killed him for nothing, then."

"Detective, I told you. I didn't kill him. I was planning my escape when he disappeared. I woke up one morning, his side of the bed was empty. He didn't show up the next morning or the next. No one in the family seemed that upset. They must have thought, like I did at first, that he'd gone off because he was upset about me losing the baby. Losing his son. He had been hoping to replace all of them with new children, apparently. After a week, I filed for an annulment based on abandonment. I couldn't stand another day in that house and I was worried he would show up before my annulment went through. As it was, I didn't have to worry, huh."

"You do realize that your life is on the line here, don't you?" Waco demanded.

*"I didn't kill Marvin."*

"We only have your word for that. His family thinks you did. Also, before he died, he scratched your name into the rock at the bottom of the well." She looked horrified. "Your name and the word *don't*."

Stacy shook her head. "I have no idea why he would do that. I swear, unless he hoped to incriminate me. It had to be one of his family who killed him. You've met them, right? That's why you have to promise me that my son will be safe."

"As long as he stays on Cardwell Ranch, he will be." Waco knew it was just a matter of time before the Hanovers heard about Jeremiah. They would do the math. Once they realized that he was Marvin's son and the heir to the fortune—

He had to find the killer before that happened. "The only way to protect him is for the two of you to remain on Cardwell Ranch until this is over. Please don't run again. I'll just have to track you down, when I need to be taking care of things at this end. Your family is safe as long as you stay on the ranch."

Stacy shook her head. "You know you won't be able to keep Ella out of this, don't you? So, basically, you will be jeopardizing the lives of both of my children."

"Ella isn't part of the investigation."

She let out a bark of a laugh. "Clearly, you don't know her. Just because you've shared a few kisses—"

He reached over and turned off the recorder. "It was just one kiss."

With a roll of her eyes, Stacy said, "I witnessed the kiss, so don't even try to downplay it to me." He started to deny the impact of the kiss on him, but she waved off any denial. "I know my Ella. You're the first man who's really turned my girl's head. I saw it right away. I should have known it would take someone like you. A *cop*."

"I thought you were going to say it was because I'm a smart, capable, relatively good-looking cowboy, cold-case detective."

"I hope you're smart and capable," she said, clearly not appreciating his attempt at humor. "Save my son and daughter. Please. Because whether you realize it or not, they're both in danger."

He nodded, thinking of Ella, thinking of the kiss. "I need the key," he reminded her and held out his hand.

Stacy reached into her pocket. He saw her feeling around, her movements becoming more frantic, her eyes widening in what could have been surprise.

"You do have it, right?"

"I *did*." She stopped searching her pocket for it.

"What?" he demanded.

"It was in my pocket. Now…it's gone."

He groaned.

"It's the truth, I swear."

"When was the last time you saw it?" he asked.

"I put my hand in my pocket on the way home. It was still there right before I fell asleep for a while. Maybe it's…" Her eyes widened again. "Maybe it's still in Ella's pickup."

"Nice try. Ella has it, doesn't she?" He thought about his and Ella's talk before the kiss. He knew how her mind worked. All the Hanovers needed was the key, because by now at least one of them must know where the money had been hidden. The killer would know that the key found in the well was worthless. But if someone offered them the original key…

# *Chapter 20*

Ella had just started her pickup when the passenger-side door flew open.

"You're taking off in a hurry," Jeremiah said as he climbed in.

She cursed silently. "Get out. Please. I have somewhere I have to go."

He shook his head and buckled his seat belt. "I can't take another moment of your aunt trying to feed me. I heard her on the phone, calling people." He leaned back and closed his eyes. "I don't care if you don't like me. I'd rather be with you right now." He opened his blue eyes and turned his head in her direction, pinning them on her. "Where you're going has something to do with our mother, doesn't it?"

Ella groaned. "You can't go with me, not where I'm going." He didn't move. "Seriously, you have to get out." She was wasting time. "Fine. I'm going over to visit with the Hanovers."

His eyes widened. "Really?" He let out a laugh. "Great. High time I met them."

"They want to *kill* you."

"They don't know me. I can be quite charming when I want to be. Come on—what better way to let them know about me than to show up at their house?" Those eyes narrowed. "So why are you in such a hurry to visit them?" He grinned at her. "Baby sister, what are you up to?"

Her mother would have her head, but as Ella looked at her brother, she made up her mind. She suspected the family would be anxious to get the key. But they would be even more anxious to get it and the money once they met the heir to the fortune. That was assuming Stacy had been telling the truth and Marvin was Jeremiah's biological father and there was a will naming him heir.

"Fine." Putting the pickup in gear, she pulled out. "Maybe it's best for them to meet you, break the ice. But if they stone you to death immediately...well, remember I said this was a bad idea."

He laughed. There was something about the sound that felt familiar. Just like his smile. Ella kept seeing her mother in him. And herself, which really annoyed her.

When they reached the Hanover house, there were several vehicles parked out front, including a motorcycle. Ella cut the engine and looked at her brother. Her *brother*. She would never get used to this. "The smart thing for you to do would be to—"

He opened his door, saying over his shoulder, "I try never to do the smart thing."

"Why does that not surprise me?" she grumbled as she got out and the two of them walked up to the large front door. She braced herself. "I should probably have told you that I'm about to tell a few white lies."

He chuckled without looking at her. "I would expect nothing less."

As soon as Waco returned Stacy to the ranch, he noticed that Ella's pickup was missing. He had a bad feeling about where she might have gone—with the original key to a fortune.

Stacy headed for her cabin, saying she had a headache and needed to lie down. He watched her walk up the mountainside for a moment before he climbed the porch steps and knocked.

Dana answered the door, her usual cheery self.

"I was looking for Ella."

"She and Jeremiah left together in her pickup," she informed him, which made him even more anxious. "I'm sure she's probably just showing him around the ranch."

"I'll catch up with her later, then," Waco said and left, sure Ella wasn't just showing her brother around the ranch.

But where would she go? He felt the weight of the fake key inside the evidence bag tucked in his jacket pocket. He called Ella's cell. It went straight to voice mail.

"Ella, we need to talk. Call me. Please." He disconnected, hating where his thoughts had gone. Had he really admitted on video that he was falling in love with her? He shook his head and grinned, because, damn it, it was true. He knew he should be more upset about that. He was falling for a woman he'd just met? A woman who was almost as strong-willed, independent and determined as he was?

He actually wanted to call Hitch to tell her how wrong she'd been about him. He was capable of falling in love with a woman. He was capable of even thinking about a future with her. He wasn't commitment phobic. He had just never met a woman who made him feel like this.

As much as he wanted to share this news, Waco didn't. He was too worried about Ella because he'd come to know her. He knew where she'd gone. Worse, she'd gone there with Jeremiah.

Unfortunately, he thought he knew that, as well. Swearing, he started his patrol SUV and took off. Once he reached the highway, he turned on his emergency lights and siren and raced toward Gallatin Gateway.

A man in his early sixties opened the door to Ella's knock. "You must be Lionel Hanover," she said.

Looking at her, he raised his nose in the air as if he'd smelled something that upset his finer sensibilities. Then he shifted his gaze to Jeremiah. The man's eyes widened slightly, his unpleasant expression turning even more filled with distaste.

"I'm Ella Cardwell, and, yes, we would love to come in," Ella said, even though Lionel had yet to speak. For a moment, he didn't move, and she wondered if her whole plan was about to fall apart. What if she was wrong? What if coming here, especially with Jeremiah, was the worst thing she could have done?

"Who is it, Lionel?" called a faint female voice from the darkness inside the large space. He didn't answer her.

To Ella's surprise, though, he did step back to allow them entrance. She heard the large door close behind them, afraid she would hear him lock it. She stepped into the lion's den, Jeremiah right behind her.

An elderly woman sat in a threadbare chair near the crackling fire, a lap quilt over her legs. Even though it was summer, the interior of the house felt cold. Ella wondered if the fireplace was the only heat source. Glancing around, she noticed that the entire room seemed threadbare. Was it possible they desperately needed their father's money?

"Who's this?" the woman inquired, squinting at the two of them as they moved deeper into the room and closer to the fire.

"I'm Ella Cardwell," she said. "I thought maybe your brother might have mentioned that I was coming over."

"I didn't want to upset my sister," Lionel said behind them. "Angeline isn't well."

The woman shot him a withering look. "I'm not unwell—I'm dying, you fool. But as long as I'm here, I like to know what's going on." Her gaze returned to Ella. "You're her…"

"Stacy's daughter," Lionel said as the front door slammed open again. Everyone's attention was drawn to it as Mercy came charging in. She stopped short as she saw Ella and Jeremiah. "Welcome to the party," he said sarcastically to Mercy. "I'm assuming Trevor listened in on my call and then reported to you." As if on cue, Ella heard a motorcycle start up out front and take off in a loud roar.

Lionel sighed. "You might as well join us. We were just about to find out why this…meeting has been called." He moved to a chair next to the fire and dropped into it.

Mercy stalked in to stand in front of the fire, her backside to the flames.

"Let's at least offer our guests a seat," Angeline said. "I don't know what has happened to my brother's manners. I apologize on his behalf."

"Thank you, but we won't be staying that long," Ella assured her.

The woman's gaze had shifted to Jeremiah. "And who is this?"

Ella watched Lionel and Mercy out of the corner of her eye. Both seemed suddenly interested in the young man standing next to her. "This is Jeremiah. Your father's and my mother's son."

Hud couldn't believe the news when Dana called to tell him about Stacy's return—with a son in his early thirties. He left the office and drove right home to find Dana in the kitchen. Nothing unusual there.

"Where are they?" he demanded as he walked into the room.

Dana turned from whatever she had cooking on the stove, a spoon in hand. "Ella left with Jeremiah and Stacy went up to her cabin." She started to turn back to her pots, as if this was just a normal, everyday occurrence.

"Dana," he said, "what the hell is going on?"

She sighed. Turned off whatever she was cooking and put down the spoon to turn to look at him. He listened as she filled him in on Ella going to a place called Hell and Gone to find her mother and—surprise—her half brother.

"He's Marvin Hanover's son and, apparently, the heir to a fortune."

Hud shook his head. "Why does this sound like a story Stacy has made up? Do we have any proof that this young man is even her son—let alone Marvin's—and some heir to anything?"

Dana gave him an impatient look. "He's family. That's all I need to know."

"Well, I need to know a whole lot more. Where did you say he and Ella went?"

She shook her head. "Maybe she's showing him around the ranch."

Hud groaned. This man none of them had even heard about before today was with Ella and only God knew where. "I'm going to look for them. If they come back or you hear from them, call me." With that, he thrust his Stetson back on his head and stormed out. Stacy was going to be the death of them all, he thought.

He had to find Ella. He couldn't shake the bad feeling that had settled in his gut that she was in trouble.

After Ella had announced who Jeremiah was, the crackling of the fire was the only sound in the room. Angeline let out a curse, followed by a phlegm-filled cough. "That's not possible," Mercy cried. "Your mother lied about being pregnant. She lied about having a miscarriage. If she was pregnant, we would have known it."

Ella noted that all the color had drained from Lionel's face, but he recovered his composure the quickest.

"What kind of scam are you trying to pull here?" he demanded. "They didn't have a child."

"Sorry, but they did," Jeremiah said. "My mother has kept me a secret all these years to keep me safe. She said my father's family was nothing but a den of vipers."

Ella shot her brother a warning look. "Let's not get into all that. Instead, let's do business. I have what you need to access your father's money."

"The key?" Mercy said on an excited breath. "The detective gave it to *you*? I thought he couldn't give it to us until after the investigation was over?"

She shook her head. "We all know that the key found in the well with your father's remains wasn't the real key." The room again went deathly quiet. "My mother has been in possession of the original key all these years and now I have it."

"I would love to know how she pulled that off," Angeline said with a chuckle.

"You have it?" Lionel asked, something in his tone predatory.

"Not on me." Ella shook her head. "I wouldn't be that stupid as to bring the key with me. First, we need to negotiate a deal." Lionel laughed. "I have the key. I'm betting one of you knows where the money is hidden." She looked around the room, going from Angeline to Mercy to Lionel and back. "I provide the key and I get my cut."

Mercy swore and began to rage.

"Let's cut to the chase. How much do you want?" Lionel asked, waving off Mercy's angry response.

"It's a fortune, right?" Ella said. "Jeremiah and I want fifty percent."

The room exploded with all the Hanovers talking at once. "That's ridiculous," Lionel snapped over the top of Mercy's and Angeline's shocked responses. "Why would you think—if any of what you're saying is true—that we would give you fifty percent?"

"Because we have a copy of your father's *real* last will, leaving all the money to Jeremiah," she said. "Without the key, you have nothing. This way you have half."

"This is highway robbery," Mercy cried. "We aren't going to—"

Lionel rose, silencing his sister with a wave of his hand. "If we agree, I want to see that will."

Ella smiled. "You mean a *copy* of that will. I wasn't born yesterday."

He glared at her. "How long will it take you to get the key?"

"I'll be in touch." With that, she turned to leave, grabbing her brother's sleeve and urging him along with her.

"You just gave away half of my inheritance?" he cried once the door closed behind them.

"I didn't give away anything," she said, "and I think you know it."

He laughed as he climbed into the passenger side of her pickup and Ella slid behind the wheel. "You're running a con. And you thought we didn't have anything other than a mother in common."

Ella shook her head at him as she started the engine and pulled out. They were almost to the main highway when they spotted the flashing lights on the patrol SUV and heard the siren as Waco sped toward them.

# Chapter 21

"This doesn't bode well," Jeremiah said, stating the obvious as Waco pulled them over. A moment later, Ella's uncle came roaring up, as well.

Both Waco and Hud had similar looks on their faces as they got out of their patrol SUVs and approached her pickup. Ella took a breath and put down her window. "You'd better let me do the talking."

Her brother chuckled. "Have at it, little sis," he said and crossed his arms as he leaned back as if readying himself for the show.

"Ella." Waco said her name from between gritted teeth. "Tell me you haven't been to see the Hanovers."

She said nothing for a moment as she looked from the detective's face to her uncle's next to him.

"We should discuss this back at the ranch, don't you think?" she asked, sounding more calm than she felt. Since walking into the lion's den, her heart had been pounding.

But she'd succeeded in doing what she'd set out to do. "I'll tell you all about it there."

With that, she put on her turn signal and swung back onto the highway, headed up the canyon and toward home. She could feel Jeremiah's gaze on her.

"Wow. Got to hand it to you. That was smooth," he said. "Of course, I wouldn't want to be you when you get back to the ranch."

She shot him a look. "As if I put a gun to your head and made you come with me."

"Good point," he said. "Mums will have a fit."

"That's putting it mildly." Ella let out a breath. "In retrospect, maybe I shouldn't have done that."

He laughed. "Are you kidding? You were awesome back there and damn believable. Do you really have the original key?"

"I hope so. You know the woman you call Mums? She often doesn't tell the truth."

"As if that's a bad thing," he said.

Ella shook her head, afraid of how much of her mother had either rubbed off on Jeremiah or was roaring through his veins. Ahead, she spotted the exit into the ranch and slowed to make the turn. Behind her were the two patrol SUVs and two very angry lawmen.

The worst part, Ella knew, would be if they told her that she was acting like her mother. Those were fighting words.

"What were you thinking?" Hud demanded after Ella told him, and the rest of the family gathered in the large living room at the ranch, what had happened with the Hanovers. "And taking Jeremiah with you!"

"To be honest, I didn't give her a choice." Jeremiah spoke up and quickly shut up under his uncle's intense glare.

"Didn't I warn you?" Stacy demanded, pointing a finger at Waco. "I know these two."

"Everyone calm down," Dana said. "Ella and Jeremiah are safe. I'm sure they have now realized how foolish they were."

Hud groaned inwardly. He sincerely doubted that. All of this had hit him hard. It was as if his family had all lost their minds. First, Stacy taking off and then coming back with a son! A son they'd never heard about, let alone laid eyes on. Conceived before her husband had ended up murdered and found at the bottom of an old homestead well.

Dana was sure that Stacy was innocent of the crime. Of course Dana was. As much as he loved his wife, she could often be too accepting and forgiving. But then, that was what he loved about her.

But now Ella was acting like her mother, going off half-cocked. He said as much and instantly regretted it as his niece bristled and shot to her feet.

"I most certainly wasn't half-cocked," she said, confidence in her voice. "I knew exactly what I was doing."

"She's right," Jeremiah interjected. "She was *awesome*. You should have seen her." He seemed to realize everyone was looking at him, and not in a pleased way. He shut up again. He wasn't helping her.

"I won't let you use Ella and Jeremiah as bait," Stacy cried. "Jeremiah is the rightful heir to the money—everything but the houses and businesses. Those went to the family, and they've now sold off most of it and gutted the house of all the antiques so they could continue to live the way they had without working. You can't be sure they won't kill my children, especially when they don't get the key as Ella promised."

"If I might say something—" Hud's voice was drowned out.

"Jeremiah's safe here," Ella argued.

"Easy for you to say," her brother said.

"He's right," Stacy said.

Dana added, "It's too dangerous. There has to be another way."

"I don't believe we've met," Hud said to Waco as he got to his feet. Waco shook hands with the legendary marshal.

"Detective Waco Johnson. Nice to meet you, Marshal."

"You must be Jeremiah." Hud turned to the other person he had yet to be introduced to. "I'm Marshal Hud Savage."

"Another cop," Jeremiah said under his breath.

Hud wondered how long it would take Dana's love to turn this punk around.

It was clear to Hud that no one wanted common sense right now. He looked at Waco. "Detective, what do you suggest we do now?"

The room fell silent.

"I need to speak with Ella alone," Waco said as calmly as he could.

"You can use my den down the hall." Hud rose and reached for his Stetson where he'd hung it by the door. "I need some fresh air."

Waco waited for Ella to rise and follow him. She stepped into the marshal's den and he closed the door behind them.

His emotions were all over the place. Ella had scared him badly because he'd gotten to know how she thought. He'd known belatedly that she would go to the Hanover place. On top of that, her plan had been sound—it was one he would have implemented himself. In fact, he'd been considering something like it. The worst part was that the plan had a better chance of working with it coming from her—something he couldn't allow for a lot of reasons.

"I'd like to turn you over my knee."

She grinned at him. "Maybe when this is over."

"Ella, I'm serious. You scared me."

"I'm sorry." She met his gaze. "I did what I knew had to be done."

"Without telling me." This, he told himself, was why a lawman didn't get involved with anyone he was trying to protect. But it was too late for that. If anything, this had shown him just how emotionally involved he was with Ella.

Still, he couldn't believe she'd taken such a risk. Jeremiah, too.

"Do you have any idea what could have happened to the two of you if one of them turns out to be a murderer?" he asked Ella calmly.

"One of them *is* a murderer," Ella said. "This way, we find out which one."

Waco let out an oath. "That's just it. We don't know who—if any or all of them—is guilty of murder. You have taken a hell of a chance. I can't let you do this."

"You want this case over quickly?" she asked just as calmly. "It's already done. All I have to do is take them the key and a copy of the will."

He shook his head. "I can lock you up if I have to. You're interfering in an ongoing investigation, which is a criminal offense."

She didn't have to speak. He could see the determination in every curve of her amazing body—not to mention in the depths of those green eyes. "The only way you'll stop me is to arrest me." She held out her wrists. "Better pull out those cuffs, Detective. I was hoping we wouldn't use them until all of this was over, but if you insist."

Waco looked at her and shook his head as he closed the distance between them. "You think I won't?" he whispered as he stopped just a breath away from her. Their gazes locked. "I need to go back out there and assure your family that I'm not going to get you killed."

The smile reached her eyes before her lips even curved. "You can do it, Detective. I have faith in you."

He scoffed. "I don't want to lose you."

"You won't. I promise." She rose on tiptoes to brush a kiss across his lips. When she pulled back, she almost looked contrite. "I really am sorry I scared you. But I knew if I told you what I had planned, you would try to stop me."

He nodded. "You're right about that. You've put yourself in danger. You're a civilian out of your league. You have to know that."

"After that kiss by the creek, I figured you'd have my back when the time came. That's why I was waiting for the kiss."

Waco swore under his breath and closed the minimal distance between them. "You knew I was going to kiss you?"

She shrugged. "Why do you think I took you down by the creek so the others couldn't see us? I figured with means, motive and opportunity…"

He felt his blood heat under his skin. "What am I going to do with you?"

Ella grinned. "I'm sure you'll think of something."

"You aren't taking this seriously," he said, his voice hoarse with desire.

"Oh, I am." She wrapped her arms around his neck. "This is all new for me, too."

"I was talking about catching a murderer," he said.

Her grin broadened. "So was I. Waco, you and me…this? It surprises me just as much as it does you. That's why I'm just as afraid for you as you are for me."

He wondered about that, but wasn't about to argue the

point. They had a lot more to argue about. But he wasn't interested in doing either right now. He lowered his mouth to hers, desperately needing to taste her again.

They held each other when the kiss was over, both breathing hard. He could feel that she knew what was at stake by the way she hugged him. The next few days might be the most dangerous of their lives. He couldn't bear the thought of losing her after only just now finding her.

She pulled her head back to look up at him. "We can do this."

He nodded, even though he wasn't sure if they were talking about the plan to catch the murderer or the two of them and where this appeared to be headed.

# Chapter 22

When Waco and Ella returned to the living room, he looked around and cleared his voice. "What we all want is Marvin Hanover's killer caught so we can put this behind us." He saw Hud come in and, having heard, raise an eyebrow. But the marshal was smart and one step ahead already. He'd figured out how this had to go down. He already knew what Waco was going to say.

"The way I see it, we need to flush out the killer and quickly," Waco continued, knowing that none of them was going to want to hear the rest of this.

"I'm not condoning Ella's actions, but the plan was a solid one." He rushed on before the marshal and everyone else in the room could object.

"The Hanovers were going to find out about Jeremiah. Maybe it's better they found out this way. We know that they know. Jeremiah should be safe as long as he stays here on the ranch. Also," he hurried on, "because of the *deal* Ella made with the Hanover family, they want her alive, as well."

"Deal?" Stacy cried. "You can't let her—"

"Let's hear the detective out," Hud interrupted. "Detective Johnson is right. The only way to keep everyone safe is to solve this case. Ella, right or wrong, has set the wheels in motion." The marshal looked to Waco.

"Thank you, Marshal," he said. "None of us likes this. We have to figure out what to do now."

"We draw out the killer and put an end to it," Ella said. "And we do our best to keep my brother alive," she added with a smile for Jeremiah.

"I feel safer already," he muttered sarcastically.

"Let's discuss this in my den," Hud said. "Just the three of us."

"Hey, you're not leaving me out of this. It's my neck on the line," Jeremiah said. "I'm part of this family now."

Waco sighed under his breath.

"Fine. The four of us in my den," Hud said. "As for you, Stacy…"

"Stacy, come into the kitchen with me." Dana quickly cut off whatever the marshal was about to say. "I think we should get dinner started. Don't you?"

Stacy looked as if she might argue, but rose with a glare at the detective as she followed her sister toward the kitchen.

Waco and the others went into the marshal's den.

"Let me say up front that I don't like any of this," Hud said as he closed the door behind them. He waved each to a seat before he looked at Waco.

"Nor do I," Waco said. "If anyone takes the key to them, it should be me."

Ella shook her head. "There is only one way my plan will work. I take the key. And I go alone. And you all know it. Uncle Hud, I know you've used civilians before to bring down crooks. So wire me up and let's do this."

"What about me?" Jeremiah asked, only to have them all glare at him.

R.J. Patterson

it hadn't and I knew you as well enough hardly hurts to bring down again... She looked up and said to me
"I bit about it?" Jeremiah once...only as here that call over to run...

# Chapter 23

After Hud and Jeremiah left them alone in the den, Waco pointed out to Ella all the things that could go wrong. What if someone in the family simply took the key away from her? What if she went into that house and was never seen or heard from again?

But, ultimately, Ella convinced him that the key was the one thing that would flush out the killer. "If the key my mother took from her husband really is the real one, then it will open the door to the family's alleged fortune. If that happens, then the family will more than likely kill each other over it than me. We all know they aren't going to split it with me. They don't have to kill me. They can just tell me to get lost. My mother stole the key. What recourse do I have?"

"Let's not forget that Jeremiah is the legal heir to that money," Waco pointed out.

"Allegedly, but once the money is found and dispersed, they will be the only ones who know how much was there to start with. It will be my word against theirs. Also, you know they can contest the will and drag it all out for years," she said.

"Ella, that's if they don't take the key away from you and you never see what it opens."

She smiled at Waco. "I won't let that happen. They'll be suspicious of the key. It's just that once the key works and they open the hiding place, the fireworks might start. I'll keep my head down until you get there."

He didn't like it, but he told himself he planned to be there *before* the fireworks started.

Ella pulled out her phone and made the call.

Lionel answered.

"I'll come alone but my brother will know where I went—just in case you aren't planning to let me walk away from this." She met Waco's blue eyes. "That's good to hear. See you tonight." She disconnected. "It's all set."

Waco shook his head. "I'd feel better if you were home on the ranch watching out for your brother and mother."

"They've managed just fine for years without my help," she said.

Waco held her gaze. He could see that it still hurt her, her mother's secret. But she'd get over it in time. He'd come to realize that Ella couldn't hold a grudge for long. "I'm serious. I don't want anything to happen to you. You've met these people. They're scary, and I'm afraid that at least one of them is a killer. Maybe more. Promise me you'll do just as we rehearsed."

She couldn't make that promise because she might have to improvise. She stepped up to him so quickly that she caught him off balance. Her plan was simply to kiss him so he wouldn't notice that she hadn't promised. But once her mouth was on his, she couldn't stop herself. It turned into a real kiss, so much so that even if it didn't take his mind off the nonexistent promise, it certainly did hers.

Nor did it help when he pulled her closer, prolonging the kiss. She could honestly say that her body tingled all the way to the toes of her Western boots. She felt as if she were flying. It wasn't until he lowered her to the den floor that she realized it hadn't all been the kiss that had made her feel airborne.

The door opened and Hud came into the room. He glanced at the two of them as Waco was just setting her down. Her uncle merely shook his head, mumbled something under his breath and handed Ella a copy of the written will Stacy had provided.

Ella took it, folded it carefully and shoved it into her pocket.

"Ready?" Hud said to Waco as he turned and left the den.

"I have to go," Waco said, his voice sounding rougher than usual. "Your uncle and I have to get ready. Don't..." He must have realized that he might as well save his breath. "Just be careful. Please." He gave her a quick kiss and hurried out of the house to climb into the marshal's SUV.

Ella watched him go, wondering if she would ever see him again.

"You have the key?" Lionel demanded as he opened the door to her and looked out at the dark street anxiously. He was dressed in tan slacks, leather loafers and what appeared to be a burgundy velvet smoking jacket over a button-up shirt. It was almost as if he'd dressed for the occasion.

With a nod, Ella said, "Of course I have the key. And the will."

He studied the street a moment before he said, "You came alone?"

"Wasn't that the deal?" she asked as she patted her right-hand leather jacket pocket and stepped past him into the house.

"Good evening," she said to the others gathered by the fire. A blaze burned in the huge stone fireplace, and still the large room held a chill. Mercy had been lying on the couch, but now sat up. She wore jeans and a sweatshirt. She must not have gotten the memo from her brother about proper attire for the event. Angeline sat close to the fire in her wheelchair, a shawl around her shoulders and a lap quilt over her legs. She drained the last of her wine and put down the glass, her hand shaking. The only one missing was Mercy's boyfriend. Trevor. Her uncle Hud had told her earlier that he'd been picked up on a local drug raid and was behind bars.

"It's nice of you to make it, Mercy," Ella said. "Of course, I knew you would be here, Angeline."

Behind Ella, Lionel said with growing impatience, "Let's see the key."

"Let's see what it opens first," she said, both hands in her jacket pockets. The key was palmed in one, her cell phone in the other, with Waco listening to the conversation nearby, waiting to make his move.

Ella could feel Lionel's gaze on her. He was suspicious. But if he tried to take the key, Waco would be here in an instant. She couldn't let that happen. She needed Lionel to show her what this key opened. She needed him to show himself for the killer she suspected he was.

"You better not be lying about bringing the key. The *right* key," he said threateningly.

She wondered what would happen if she was lying, but she wasn't sure she wanted to know. "It's the key." As she moved deeper into the living room, she wasn't surprised to see Mercy looking just as anxious as Lionel now appeared.

Behind her, she heard him slam the large front door and lock it soundly. He stepped around her and, turning to face her, said, "The key, please."

Ella took the key from her pocket and held it up—out of his reach. The dim light caught on it for an instant before she repocketed it. "First, I want to see what it opens. Then I'll be happy to hand it over," Ella said. "It's only fair, don't you think? You don't trust me. I don't trust you. So why don't we do this together?"

He seemed to consider that, looking from her to his sisters. "You're assuming that I know what it opens."

Ella laughed. "What is the point of the key if you don't?"

Silence filled the room. They were all looking at Lionel, especially Mercy and Angeline. It appeared that he'd been holding out on them.

Even more interesting, no one had asked to see the will. Because it didn't matter. They were planning to take the money and run—after they killed her?

Waco couldn't remember the last time he'd been this nervous. Ella was doing great—just as he'd known she would. He admired the hell out of her. At the same time, he was terrified that something would go wrong. He'd used civilians before—just as most law enforcement had. Sometimes sending them in with a wire was the only way to get a conviction. While he could hear what was going on through his earbud, he had wanted to wire Ella for sound.

Surprisingly, it had been Hud who'd talked him out of it.

"They might be expecting that," the marshal had said. "If they check her and find a wire..." He didn't have to spell it out. "Supposedly she is acting on her own. Even if they find the phone, she's safer. They'll still think she's alone in this. We have to play it that way. But we'll be right outside."

"Yes," Waco had said with a groan. She'd done this on her own. It was so Ella. So much like the woman he was falling deeper and deeper in love with by the day.

Now he waited to hear Lionel's answer. He could almost feel the tension in that room as they all waited. What if Ella was wrong? What if the key wasn't that important to them because they had no idea what it opened? What if—?

Ella feared for a moment that none of them knew what the key opened—which would blow her theory completely out of the water.

But then Lionel sighed heavily. "I think I might know what the key will open," he finally said, and she breathed again. "Come this way." He began to lead them deeper into the monstrous house. Ella realized that it might be a trap. That he'd get them all back here and—

"This is one long hallway," she said. "How large is this place, anyway?" She hated that her voice broke on the last word. The house was so large that even with the house plans from the county, how would anyone be able to find her?

She tried to concentrate. Now was not the time to have second thoughts about what she was doing. She was pretty sure they were headed to the north wing of the mansion. The other two followed, Angeline bringing up the last of the conga line in her wheelchair, wheels squeaking.

"It would be easy to get turned around in this place, huh," Ella said. "Are we headed east? No, north, right?" But no one answered her question. "North," she said more to herself. She hoped she sounded excited and not scared. But only a fool wouldn't be scared, and she was no fool.

The deeper they ventured, the less confident Ella felt.

Hopefully, Waco was still on the line. That was, if there was cell phone coverage in here. That was, if he could hear her.

The place was massive. Even if he could hear her, he wouldn't be able to get to her in time. She was on her own with just her wits to guide her. But she still had the key, and so far, no one had threatened her. Yet.

Jeremiah had waited until the two cops had left before "borrowing" one of the ranch pickups and heading for the Hanover place. He'd parked a ways down the road and worked his way cautiously to the back of the house. He didn't see Waco or Hud.

Using the glass cutter he'd picked up from the ranch shop—how wonderful that his new family had everything he needed for a break-in—he began to cut open a back window that seemed to enter a guest bedroom. Like so much of the house, it hadn't looked used.

Waco and Hud had ordered him to stay put in the cabin the family had provided for him on the side of the mountain overlooking the ranch. As if he was going to be left out of this.

He smiled to himself as the glass popped out. He caught it and gently laid it on the ground. Then, using his sweatshirt on the sill to keep from cutting himself, he slipped inside the house through the back window. He knew the Hanovers didn't have any kind of security since he'd checked that out when he and Ella had paid their earlier visit.

Jeremiah landed quietly inside what appeared to be a bedroom that hadn't been occupied in a very long time. The old iron bed had been stripped of everything but the mattress, and there was dust everywhere. He moved like a cat across the floor and opened the door to peer out into the long hallway. He had some experience with breaking and entering—but only when called for, as he would have told Helen, who'd done her best to control his criminal behavior. This was definitely called for.

This whole house felt empty. He wondered how he would be able to find Ella. He was wondering how the cops would find her when he heard a floorboard creak behind him.

Waco grabbed him by the back of his collar and hauled him into the bedroom, closing the door. "I told you to stay home," the detective whispered in his face. From the cop's grin, it was clear that he'd known all along what Jeremiah had been up to—and had followed him.

"I have to help my sister."

"The best way you can help her," Waco said as he whipped out his handcuffs, "is to stay put."

Jeremiah heard the familiar *snick* and felt the cold metal of the cuff snap around his wrist. Before he could react, the cop snapped the other end around the ornate iron headboard.

"Say a word and I will hog-tie and gag you," Waco whispered next to his ear. "You don't want to get your sister killed, right?"

Jeremiah nodded and sat on the edge of the bed, giving the cop a *you got me, all right?* look.

Waco nodded. "Stay here." With that, the detective was gone.

Ella was losing track of all the twists and turns Lionel was taking. She couldn't keep a running commentary about each move or one of them was going to get suspicious. "It's like a maze, isn't it? I have no idea where we are." Of course, none of the Hanovers commented.

Finally, at the end of another hallway, he stopped at a large double door. As he pushed the door open wide, she felt a cold gust of stale air. Clearly, the huge room was normally kept closed.

Lionel flipped a switch and the overly ornate fixtures in the room exploded with light.

"Wow!" Ella said, unable to not exclaim at what she was seeing. She knew that a lot of older, large, expensive homes in the area had once had such a room. "A ballroom! It's huge. It makes me want to dance."

Neither Lionel nor Mercy looked in the mood to dance. "I bet you remember dances in here." She looked at Angeline since Lionel and Mercy were ahead of them and not answering.

"When I was small," Angeline said almost wistfully, her weakened voice echoing in the enormous empty space. "My grandfather loved parties and music and dancing. He used to fill this room."

"That must have been something to see." Ella took in the gold leaf, the huge faded spots on the wall—where paintings had once hung?—the heavy burgundy brocade on the walls below the ornate sconces, as Lionel led the way across the parquet floor. He stopped dead center and turned to look at them.

Ella had lagged behind a little. So had Angeline in her wheelchair. Only Mercy had been on Lionel's heels.

She could feel the anticipation in the air as Lionel ordered Mercy to help him with the huge Oriental rug. It appeared to be in better shape than any of the other rugs Ella had seen in the house.

That alone, she realized, was a clue. The rug had to be worth a lot of money and yet it hadn't been sold. It only took a moment to find out why. As Lionel and Mercy strained to roll it back, she saw the irregularity in the flooring.

Mercy stared down at the floor, then up at her brother.

"How long have you known this was here?" she demanded. "How long have you been keeping this to yourself?"

He ignored her as he knelt and pushed on the side of an inlaid handhold in the flooring. It opened enough to allow him to get his fingertips under it. He lifted the trapdoor to expose a wooden staircase.

Ella stepped closer as they all crowded around the opening. The stairs were only a few feet wide and dropped deep into the ground. The air rising up at them was icy cold and smelled of damp earth, as if it had been some time since the trapdoor had been opened.

At the bottom of the dozen steps stood a hulking solid-steel vault set in the wall. She said the words out loud for Waco. "You have to be kidding. An underground vault cut into the earth below the ballroom? Those stairs down look a little...old. Your grandfather did this when he built the house?" It definitely hadn't been on the plans of the house that Hud had procured for them.

Next to her, Angeline rolled closer to stare down at the vault. But it was Mercy who let out the cry of surprise and delight. "That's got to be it!" she exclaimed. "That's got to be where he hid his fortune! You found it!" She was practically clapping.

"The key," Lionel said tersely as he spun to face Ella.

She could almost feel how close he was to the edge of control. He appeared wired, as if he'd been anticipating this moment for far too long. She wondered how long exactly. More than thirty years ago, after he'd killed his father and taken the key he'd been disappointed to find out didn't open the vault? Or long before that?

Heart in her throat, Ella reached into her pocket, her fingers locking around the key. She froze for a moment with sudden doubt. Had Waco heard everything so far? What if Marvin had fooled them all by wearing a key that didn't open the vault? What if he'd hid the real key somewhere else entirely? More to the point, what would happen to her if the key didn't open the vault?

Ella hesitated a few seconds too long.

"Give me the damn key," Lionel demanded as he pulled a gun from his jacket pocket. The look in his eyes told Ella that he would shoot her if she didn't hand it over—and quickly.

"You don't need that gun." It surprised her, how calm she sounded. She pulled the key from her pocket and handed it to him.

That was when she saw his expression darken. He advanced on her so quickly that she didn't have time to move before he grabbed her with his free hand. He opened her jacket and pulled up her shirt before spinning her around to tug at the waist of her jeans, looking for a wire. Her uncle had been right. If she'd been wired for sound, Lionel would have found it.

"Did you really think I would go to the cops?" she demanded indignantly with a laugh and a shake of her head as she stepped away to straighten her clothing.

Lionel trained the gun on her.

She saw his gaze go to her left pocket. "What?"

"Take your hand out very slowly," he ordered. "And it better be empty."

She withdrew her hand and he lunged at her, driving his free hand into her pocket and pulling out her cell phone. The copy of the will had also been in that pocket. It fluttered to the floor.

He stared at the phone for a moment. From the look on his face, he was chastising himself for being so foolish. He hadn't even considered a wire earlier—let alone thought she would have a cell phone.

Fortunately, she'd disconnected the call with Waco when Lionel had first grabbed her. Now he tossed her phone across the room, his gaze boring into her. "How foolish of you to come alone. You didn't even bring your brother with you. But you were right earlier. We should do this together. Then, if the key doesn't work… Come on," he said, motioning with the gun for her to lead the way down the stairs to the vault.

Ella had no desire to go down there, but she didn't see any other option at the moment. She moved to the edge and took a tentative step. The old wood of the first stair creaked under her boot. She took another. Behind her, Lionel's weight on the steps made the entire staircase groan and sag a little.

It was even colder down here, the odor of wet earth strong. She could smell Lionel's nervous sweat, as well, reminding her that he had a gun trained on her back. Before Ella reached the last step, he shoved her aside, and still holding the gun in one hand, he fitted the key into the vault with the other.

His hands, she saw, were shaking. She was shaking for a whole different reason. If that key didn't turn in that lock—

She heard the *click*, saw the key rotate and let out the breath she'd been holding. Relief made her knees go weak as she watched him turn the handle.

The huge steel door swung open.

# *Chapter 24*

As Waco quickly made his way through the maze of hallways, he had a mental image of the original house plans Hud had supplied. But the place was so large, it was taking too much time. He'd heard Lionel search Ella and was thankful he hadn't fitted her with a wire. But she'd had to disconnect the call. Now he had no idea what was happening, and that had him terrified.

All he knew for certain was that he had to get to the ballroom as quickly as possible. It didn't surprise him that it had been Lionel who'd found a trapdoor leading to stairs beneath the floor to an underground vault. Nor did it surprise him that Lionel had a gun.

He knew Ella could handle herself—as long as that key opened the vault. But even if it did, he knew that Lionel had no plan to share the fortune. Not one of them had wanted to see the will. Either because they didn't believe it was real, or because it wouldn't matter after tonight…

That meant that Waco had to reach Ella and fast. He'd suspected Lionel as the killer. It made sense. But he'd also worried that all of them might be in on it, even though Mercy seemed too scatterbrained and Angeline too frail. Not that he didn't think any one of them was capable of killing the others for the money.

Waco just hoped to have made the arrest before that happened, since Ella was at the heart of it. He tried to tell himself this was like every other case he'd ever had. He knew danger. He'd been wounded more times than he wanted to think about since he'd taken this job. That was because he caught the dangerous cases and always had.

But even as he tried not to run through the house and let them know he was coming, he couldn't pretend that this case hadn't taken a turn he'd never expected. He'd fallen in love with one of the civilians. Now she was risking her life to end this.

Ella stared into the vault. When she looked at Lionel, his eyes were as wide as her own. He must have been holding his breath, because he let out a whoosh of sound before he screamed, "It's empty!" He sounded both shocked and furious. His gaze swung to her.

She couldn't believe what she was seeing, either. Her first thought was that her mother had cleaned it out with this key years ago.

"How is this possible?" Mercy called down the stairs, sounding close to hysteria.

Angeline laughed from her wheelchair. "Why are you both so surprised that he *lied*? Our own father. The bastard lied to us our whole lives. There never was any money."

All the color had drained from Lionel's face. He seemed to be at a loss for words. Ella figured his mind was probably whirling like hers. It was only a matter of time before he came to the same conclusion she had.

Ella made a run for the stairs and got up four steps before Lionel grabbed her ankle. He jerked hard, trying to pull her back, but she locked her fingers around the edge of the wooden stairway and hung on.

The gunshot made her start. Her fingers slipped and she slid on her stomach down a couple of stairs. Overhead, she could hear screaming and the crash of Angeline's wheelchair, but all that was drowned out by a second and third gunshot.

Lionel released her ankle. Had he killed both of his sisters? She heard him moan a second before he crashed backward into the steel door of the vault. She looked behind her. His chest bloomed with blood as he slowly slid to the ground.

For a second, Ella couldn't move. She lay sprawled on the stairs, feeling disoriented and confused. She'd been so sure that she'd been hit by one of the bullets. But if Lionel hadn't fired them, who had?

Only an instant lapsed before her brain kicked in and Ella quickly started upward, desperate to get out of this hole.

But after only a couple of steps, what she saw at the top of the stairs stopped her cold. A dark shape loomed over her, the figure holding a gun. The barrel was pointed in her face.

"I'm going to need that key," Angeline said. "Fetch it for me, won't you?"

# Chapter 25

Jeremiah laughed after Waco left the room. With his free hand, he pulled the lock-pick kit from his jacket pocket. It didn't take him more than a few moments to get the handcuff off the bed frame. He worked just as quickly to unlock the one on his wrist. He couldn't have it dangling and making any noise.

The guys at Helen's bar had taught him all kinds of helpful things—even though Helen had threatened them with physical harm if they led him astray. He didn't think of it in that context. He was smart. He'd proved that at the university he'd attended with the falsified papers Helen had gotten him.

The problem was that Jeremiah wasn't sure what he wanted to do with his life. Nothing his university adviser had suggested had appealed to him. He wanted something exciting, and his degree in mechanical engineering, though helpful at times, just didn't cut it.

Once he had his hands free, he shoved the cuffs into his jacket pocket and considered what to do. Staying in the house, knowing that Waco was in here somewhere looking for Ella, now seemed like a bad idea.

But he had a thought. Rather than go through the house, he went back out the window. As he moved along the edge of the house, keeping to the dark shadows, he looked for something he'd seen earlier.

His uncle Hud was somewhere around here. He didn't want to get shot. But he wasn't about to go home, either. That was when he remembered seeing what had looked like the opening into an old root cellar. Now, as he found it, he saw the lock on the door. This time it took a little longer since he didn't want to use his flashlight he'd brought with him.

The lock finally gave and Jeremiah pulled open the door. The moment he did, he noted the stairs that dropped down. Quickly, he stepped inside and closed the door behind him before pulling out his flashlight and shining it ahead of him.

At the bottom of the stairs, he realized he was in a narrow tunnel—and that the tunnel headed in the direction of the house, just as he'd suspected.

He shone his flashlight into the tunnel, the light small and dim. He couldn't tell how far it went—or where it ended.

That was when he heard gunshots.

Waco heard the gunshots—the reports echoing through the house. He realized he'd gotten turned around and had taken the wrong corridor. He rushed down the first hallway and the second. Seeing double doors at the end of the next, he pulled his weapon, rushed to it and shoved the door open at a run. Stumbling into what appeared to be the library, he swore.

There was nothing there but dusty books on miles of

bookshelves. He couldn't believe this. He tried to calm himself, imagining the house plans he'd studied. The ballroom. He couldn't get to it on this floor, he realized.

Swearing, he turned around and hurried back down the hall. He wanted to run, to sprint, but he knew that the echo of his boots on the wood floorboards would warn whoever was wielding that gun that they were no longer alone.

He'd heard…three shots? Or was it four? He couldn't be sure. They'd echoed dully through the old massive house. He could feel time ticking away too quickly.

Waco wanted to scream Ella's name, needing desperately to hear her voice and to know that she was still alive. Soon Hud would be busting down the front door, backup on its way. Waco had to find Ella before that happened.

Ella stared at Angeline. It was as if years of age and ailment had fallen off her as she'd freed herself from that wheelchair. Her hand holding the gun was steady as a rock.

"The key," Angeline repeated with that same frightening smile.

Ella realized that she couldn't hear Mercy. Earlier, she'd thought she'd heard her cry out in pain. Nor had Lionel made a sound since falling back into the vault's door. It appeared that Angeline was a very good shot.

She looked over her shoulder. She did not want to go back down those steps. She especially didn't want to have to step over Lionel to get to the key. "Why do you want—?"

The gunshot so close to her ear was deafening. She heard the bullet bury itself in the dirt next to the vault and quickly eased backward down one step, then another. When she did dare look at Angeline, she saw that the woman was still smiling. Why would she want the key? Or was that just a ruse? Was she going to slam the trapdoor and leave Ella and Lionel down there?

That was better than being shot. Not that being shot was off the table by any means. Once she handed over the key…

She carefully stepped around Lionel, trying not to look at him. His eyes were open and he seemed to be staring up at her. Reaching around the edge of the door, Ella felt for the key. It took a moment to locate it and then attempt to pull it out.

"I'm waiting," Angeline said in a singsong voice.

Finally, Ella worked the key out, stepped over Lionel again and then looked up. What was the woman going to do once she had the key? For a moment, Ella didn't know what her best chance was. But while she'd struggled to remove the key, she'd noticed that there appeared to be a dugout off to her left. How far the tunnel went under the house, she had no idea. But it was definitely deep enough to hide a person.

Ella knew she had to stall for time. Waco would be looking for her. Pretending she was moving to the steps, she pushed past them and ducked into the darkness tunneling under the house.

"What are you doing?" Angeline demanded.

Ella could tell that the older woman was leaning out over the stairs, trying to see her. "Tell me why you want the key."

Silence. Then she heard a sigh from overhead. "Because it is literally the key to the money. So don't make me come down there to get it."

Ella looked at the key in her hand. The light wasn't great down here, but she realized she'd never actually studied the key. It was large and ornate. She ran her fingers along the curved edges and felt tiny numbers stamped on the inside edge of the filigree.

"How long have you known about the vault and that it was empty?" Ella asked.

Angeline chuckled. "My father used to give me grief for always having my face in a book. I loved to read and the others left me alone. No one ever paid any attention to me, but I watched all of them."

"Clearly, you aren't dying."

"Not yet, but I was a sickly child. It was easy to continue to be sickly. Watching them was how I knew about your mother being pregnant. I knew she hadn't lost the baby. My father wasn't fooled by the miscarriage. Neither was Lionel. He knew he had to get to that money before Marvin left all his wealth to Stacy's son. We all knew that our father had already called about having his will changed. We didn't know, though, that he'd made out a handwritten will."

Ella heard the sound of paper being balled up. A moment later, the copy of the will came tumbling down the stairs to land next to Lionel.

She had to keep Angeline talking. "So, Lionel killed him, switched the keys, then found out the one around his father's neck wasn't the right one," Ella said. "How long have you known we were going to find the vault empty?"

"I wasn't sure, but it certainly made sense. My father wasn't a young man and he'd made a lot of enemies—even in his own house. He couldn't trust his wife, and he knew that once he was dead and gone, we would go through our assets unless he could protect them," Angeline said and sighed.

"Eventually you would sell the house," Ella said, seeing where she was headed with this.

The older woman laughed. "He couldn't leave the money in the vault for fear that we were so stupid we'd sell the house and never find the vault—or that one of us would take the key from around his neck when we killed him."

"How did you know the key was really the key to the money?" Ella thought Angeline might not answer.

After a moment, she said, "My father was determined the money would go to his unborn son. He wasn't about to let us get our hands on it. I was surprised when Lionel found the steel vault that he didn't try to blast it open with dynamite. Or at least try to get someone to pick the lock or make a new key."

"But then he would have had to share the wealth," Ella said.

She heard a smile in Angeline's voice. "You forced Lionel into admitting that he knew where it was. Not that he planned to share it, had the money been in there. If I hadn't shot him, my body and Mercy's would already be down there."

"So all you needed was the original key?"

Angeline chuckled. "I had no idea that your mother had taken it. I'd just assumed that when Lionel killed our father, he'd gotten the key. When that proved untrue, all I could do was wait. Then someone made an anonymous phone call from the Gateway bar about the bones in the well."

"Lionel," Ella said.

"That's when I knew for certain that he'd killed our father and somehow hadn't gotten the right key."

"But you would know the right key because it opened the empty vault," Ella said. "I suspect you're more interested in the numbers stamped on the key. Some offshore bank account number?" Ella guessed.

"I could tell you were a smart woman the first time I met you. But enough stalling. I'll make you the same deal you made with Lionel. Bring me the key."

Ella laughed and didn't move. "You must think I'm naive."

"More than naive if you think I won't come down there."

Ella jumped as another gunshot echoed in the closed space, the bullet pinging off the steel vault and thudding into Lionel's body on the ground.

Waco was already headed down the hall, gun drawn, when he heard the shot. He had to get to Ella and now he knew exactly where she was, he thought as he raced to the double doors at the end.

He could hear Hud breaking in somewhere else in the house. Backup would be on the way. But Waco couldn't wait for it. He had to go in. He had to try to save Ella.

As he approached, he noticed a sliver of light coming from between the double doors. He slowed and moved cautiously, his heart in his throat and a mantra playing in his head. *Let Ella be all right.*

At the sound of voices, he eased one of the doors open and peered inside. The first thing he saw was Mercy lying on the floor. She didn't move as he opened the door a little wider and noted the wheelchair lying on its side. No sign of Angeline, though.

Pushing the door even wider, he spotted her. She was standing at the edge of an opening in the floor. Who he didn't see was Ella.

Waco hadn't thought he'd made a sound, but he saw Angeline begin to turn. The gun in her hand caught the dull light an instant before he heard the shot. The bullet carved a wormhole through the wood door frame before lodging itself in the hallway wall next to him.

"Ella!" he yelled, ducking back at the sound of splintering wood off to his right. "Ella!" His voice broke. He was desperate to hear her voice and felt a lunge of relief when he heard her respond from somewhere beneath the floor opening.

He quickly peeked around the corner of the partially open door, his weapon at the ready. Angeline was gone. He did a quick survey of the huge room and, heart dropping, knew where she'd disappeared to so quickly.

Jeremiah moved as quickly as he could through the cramped tunnel. In places, the dirt had caved in and he'd had to force his way through. He could hear voices and felt he was getting closer when he heard more gunshots.

The batteries in his flashlight dimmed. Earlier, he'd been feeling pretty cocky. He had skills. But when he'd heard the gunshots, he'd hesitated for a moment. He was a small-time criminal. At least, that was what everyone in Hell and Gone had always told him. He'd resented it, but now he could see some truth in it.

Maybe the cop was right and he was out of his league and not prepared for this.

Or maybe not.

Now, as he stared ahead into the black hole in the earth, he thought of Ella. Holding his flashlight in front of him, he pushed deeper into the tunnel. His gut told him he had to get to his sister.

Ella heard the creak of the stairs after she'd called out to Waco, followed at once by the gunshot. She knew now that Angeline must have fired the shot and was coming down those stairs still armed.

She hurriedly looked back toward the vault for something to use as a weapon and spotted Lionel's gun lying next to his body. Pocketing the key, she scrambled for the weapon. She'd just wrapped her fingers around the grip when she heard Angeline's sharp bark of a laugh directly above her.

Ella spun around and pointed the gun at the older woman now halfway down the stairs.

"That gun is useless," Angeline said as she continued down the stairs. Her gun aimed at Ella's chest, she was smiling as if she knew something Ella didn't.

Taking aim, Ella pulled the trigger. *Click.* She felt her eyes widen in alarm at the dry sound. She pulled the trigger again. *Click. Click. Click.*

"I took the bullets out of Lionel's gun," the older woman said. "The fool didn't even check." Angeline was almost to her when she kicked the gun out of Ella's hand and then seemed to fly directly at her. She grabbed hold of Ella's long braid and pressed the barrel of her gun to Ella's head.

"Give me the key. Slip it into my pocket *now.*"

Ella didn't hesitate. She could feel Angeline's strength in the hold she had on her hair. But it was the determination in that grip that had her turning over the key. She slipped it into the woman's pocket an instant before Angeline turned them both as Waco appeared above them.

"Throw down your weapon, Detective, or I'll kill her. I've already killed my own family. Do you really think I wouldn't shoot that tramp Stacy's daughter?"

"You're trapped," he said, sounding much calmer than Ella felt. "You can't get away. Let her go. You don't want to make this any worse."

Angeline laughed. "How could it be any worse?"

That was when Ella heard a noise. It had come from the darkness under the house in that tunneled-in space where moments before she'd been hiding. She cut her eyes in that direction and saw something move.

# Chapter 26

Ella could feel Angeline tense. Had she heard something, as well? Or was she reacting to Waco? Either way, Ella could almost sense the woman's trigger finger getting itchy. Angeline had the key, but how did she think she would get away? Ella could hear the sound of sirens and people upstairs in the house. She knew it would be her uncle and backup.

But she feared Angeline planned to end this long before the rest of the law arrived.

Looking up at Waco, Ella knew she had to do something. *Now!*

Angeline had her gaze locked with Waco's in a standoff. Ella knew she would have only one chance. She shifted her body just enough that she could swing her arm back, leading with the elbow. She caught Angeline in the side and doubled her over.

Angeline let go of her braid, the barrel of the gun that

had been at Ella's temple falling away for a moment, giving Waco a clear shot. The gun's report echoed deafeningly through the space around them. Angeline let out a cry, blood oozing from her shoulder as she shoved past Ella, dived into the darkness under the house and disappeared.

Ella didn't have a chance to move before Waco clamored down the steps. He pulled her into his arms, the gun still in his hand. "Are you all right? Ella? Look at me."

She raised her eyes to him, but all she could do was nod. She'd been so sure Angeline was going to kill him or her. Or them both.

Waco quickly released her and stepped in front of her, using his body as a human shield when they both heard movement in the darkness beyond the vault room.

To Ella's surprise, Angeline reappeared, stumbling toward them. Her clothing was covered in mud, as if she'd fallen, and she was no longer carrying her weapon. Behind her, Jeremiah came out, grinning, with her gun.

"Look who I found trying to get away," he said, his grin growing broader. "Hey, sis. Glad to see you're all right. I see the detective here saved you."

"She saved us both," Waco said. "You don't want to underestimate your sister." He put his arm around Ella and pulled her close as the rumble of footfalls could be heard on the floor above them. A few moments later, her uncle filled the opening at the top of the stairs.

She smiled up at him.

Hud shook his head and held out a hand. "Come on. It's time to go home."

# Chapter 27

Two weeks later, Ella looked around the large living room at her family gathered there. The story about the Hanover takedown had hit all the papers, highlighting the gory details—a lot of them provided by Angeline herself. She was promising to write a book about growing up in her dysfunctional family. Said she was playing with the title *The Hanover House of Horrors*. The Hanover matriarch seemed to be enjoying her time in the spotlight, as if almost looking forward to prison.

Mercy and Lionel were dead. Ella knew she could have been, too. She'd taken a dangerous chance. Lionel had killed his father after Marvin had said he was going to replace him with another son. Ella believed more than the money had motivated Lionel, but they would never know for sure.

At least one of the Hanovers had been brought to justice. There wouldn't be a trial, though, Waco was now telling the family, since Angeline had confessed to everything and waived that right.

Jeremiah appeared instantly disappointed. Apparently, he'd hoped to get up on the stand as a witness.

He also seemed to be enjoying his moment in the sun. Even Uncle Hud had grudgingly told Jeremiah that he'd done an okay job catching Angeline before she could get away. True, backup had been waiting outside at the root-cellar opening, so she wouldn't have gotten far. But Hud left that part out.

Uncle Hud had finally retired entirely, walking away from his lifetime's calling. Ella could tell it was one of the hardest things he'd ever done. She'd looked at Waco, knowing that she would soon have the same fears her aunt Dana had had all those years. Waco loved what he did. Like Uncle Hud, he wouldn't quit until he absolutely had to.

"I think I'd like to be a cop," Jeremiah announced to everyone.

Hud groaned.

"My son can be whatever he wants," Stacy declared, daring her brother-in-law to say differently.

"I do have one question," Ella said. "The words carved into the wall at the bottom of the well…"

*"Stacy don't?"* Waco said.

"What do you think he was trying to tell her?"

They all looked at Stacy. "I've thought about that," she said. "I think he was trying to tell me not to get rid of his son. He wanted a part of him to live on that he could be proud of."

Ella thought that was one interpretation. She was just glad that Marvin hadn't been trying to name his killer. If true, then Marvin had been thinking of his unborn son instead of the son who'd knocked him down the well and left him for dead.

"Time to eat!" Dana announced, changing the subject. She had cooked two huge hens with dressing, garden green beans, mashed potatoes and relish she and Stacy had made last fall.

They all ate and talked, the dining room a dull roar of voices and laughter, keeping the conversation light.

Ella looked at Waco and smiled. He fit right in here as he argued with Jeremiah, teased Dana and asked for more of everything.

After dinner, she and Waco walked up to her cabin. They stopped on the porch and leaned on the railing to look out over the ranch, the river and the dark purple mountains against the starry sky.

"Jeremiah wants me to help him get into the police academy," Waco said without looking at her.

"I think he might be good at it, except for the part of following procedure, but then, you'd know more about that than I would," she said with a grin.

Waco shook his head. "It scares me that you could be more like your mother and brother than I know."

"Fear is a good thing," she joked, then sobered. "You have to admit it—my brother came through for us."

"Your brother disobeyed every order I gave him."

She smiled over at him. "So did I." She felt a chill, reminded of how close they had all come to losing their lives that night.

"I was getting to that next," he said softly, the roughness of his voice sending even more shivers over her bared skin.

"Really?" she said, tossing out the challenge as he

opened the front door to her cabin. She stepped through and heard him lock the door behind her. She turned to face him.

"We're going to have to establish some rules, you and I, for the future," he said as he took a step toward her.

"For the future?" she asked innocently.

"Our future. Yours and mine."

She cocked a brow at him. "I can't wait to hear about this future."

He reached out and brushed her hair back from her eyes. "I'm going to be your husband."

"That does sound like it might be interesting."

He moved closer. "You're going to be my wife."

She met his blue-eyed gaze. "Hmm. If you say the word *obey* right now, I won't be responsible for what happens next."

He was so close now that she could breathe in his intoxicating male scent and the great outdoors in the hair curling at his neck.

"I would never waste my breath on the word *obey* anywhere near you. But we do need to discuss boundaries," he said.

Ella reached up and ran her fingertips over the scruff on his strong jaw, imagining what it would feel like on her skin. Desire shot like a flame through her veins. "Sounds serious. Where do you suggest we have this discussion?"

Waco's gaze locked with hers. Another shudder of desire rippled through her and she felt an aching need for this man that she thought could last a lifetime.

"The shower," he said in that low, sexy voice of his.

Ella tried to catch her breath. "The shower? I don't know, Detective. Anything could happen, once we get to…discussing things."

Waco grinned. "I can only hope." With that, he swung

her up into his arms and headed for the bathroom before kicking the door closed behind them.

Waco had never thought about happiness. It wasn't something he'd ever aspired to. Instead, he'd taken strength in knowing that he was capable of doing his job. But once he'd met Ella and her family...

"Everyone in the family?" he said weeks later as he pretended to be terrified as they dressed for the party involving all of the Cardwells and Savages.

Ella laughed and straightened the collar on his shirt. "You are finally going to get to meet the entire family. When my aunt Dana throws an engagement party, she throws a *party*. I just hope you're up to it." She threw that out like a challenge. She knew him so well. He *loved* a challenge.

He pulled her to him. "I've dealt with crooks and thieves and killers. I can handle one of your aunt's engagement parties."

Ella shifted her gaze from his to admire the ring he'd put on her finger. She'd told him afterward that he was making a romantic out of her. She hadn't sounded happy about that, but she had laughed.

It *had* been romantic, down by the river, the sunset making the water flash with brilliant color, the smell of the pines. He'd gotten down on one knee in the sand and looked up at her. Those green eyes... They still made his heart beat a little faster whenever he looked into them.

"Be my wife," he'd said. "Make my world."

Ella had laughed, smiling and nodding, and crying. He'd never seen her cry before, and her emotion had touched him more than she could know.

He'd gotten to his feet to wipe away her tears, and then

he'd kissed her. It had been so sweet, she'd told him that her heart had taken flight, soaring over the scene and imprinting it forever in her memory.

Waco liked the idea that he might have turned her into a romantic. She'd changed him, as well. Changed him forever—the same amount of time he planned to spend with this woman.

* * * * *

# BOOTS AND BULLETS

This book is dedicated to the Malta Quilt Club and all the other wonderful and amazingly talented women who are teaching me to have fun with fabric. Quilting keeps me sane when words fail me. Thanks, ladies!

# Chapter 1

Cyrus Winchester opened his eyes and blinked in confusion. He appeared to be in a hospital room. From down the hall came the sound of a television advertisement for an end-of-season fall sale.

He told himself he must be dreaming. The last thing he remembered was heading to Montana to spend the Fourth of July with the grandmother he hadn't seen in twenty-seven years.

Glancing toward the window, he saw a gap in the drapes. His heart began to pound. The leaves were gone off the trees and several inches of fresh snow covered the ground.

A nurse entered the room, but she didn't look in his direction as she went over to the window and opened the curtains. He closed his eyes again, blinded by the brightness.

As he tried to make sense of this, Cyrus could hear her moving around the room. She came over to the bed, tucking and straightening, humming to herself a tune he didn't recognize. She smelled of citrus, a light, sweet scent that reminded him of summer and driving to Montana with the windows down on his pickup, the radio blaring.

With a start, he realized that wasn't the last thing he remembered!

His hand shot out, grabbing the nurse's wrist. She screamed, drawing back in surprise, eyes widening in shock. What was wrong with her?

He opened his mouth, his lips working, but nothing came out.

"Don't try to talk," she said and pushed the call button with her free hand. "The doctor will be glad to see that you're back with us, cowboy."

*Back with us?*

Cyrus tried again to speak, desperate to tell her what he remembered, but the only sound that came out was a *shh*.

The nurse gently removed her wrist from his grasp to pour him a glass of water. "Here, drink a little of this."

Gratefully he took the cup from her and raised his head enough to take a sip. He couldn't believe how weak he felt or how confused he was. But one thought remained clear and that was what he urgently needed to tell someone.

He took another swallow of water, feeling as if he hadn't had a drink in months.

"Sheriff." The word came out in a hoarse whisper. "Get. The. Sheriff. I saw it. The nurse. Murdered. In the hospital nursery."

# Chapter 2

Cyrus tried to make sense of what his twin brother was telling him. "No, Cordell," he said when his brother finished. "I know what I saw last night."

His brother's earlier relief at seeing him awake had now turned to concern. "Cyrus, you've been in a coma for three months. You just woke up. You wouldn't have seen a murder unless it happened in the last twenty minutes."

"I'm telling you. I saw her. A nurse or a nurse's aide, I don't know, she was wearing a uniform and she was lying on the floor with a bloody scalpel next to her just inside the nursery door." He saw his brother frown. "What?"

"You're in a special rehabilitation center in Denver and have been for the last two months. There is no nursery here."

Cyrus lay back against the pillows, looking past his identical twin to the snow covering the landscape outside. "The hospital was a brick building. Old. The tiles on the floor were worn." Out of the corner of his eye, he caught his brother's surprised expression. "There is such a place, isn't there?"

"You just described the old hospital in Whitehorse, Montana, but you haven't been there for months," Cordell said.

"But I was there, right?"

"Yes, for only one night. They were in the process of moving you to the new hospital the night you were…"

"You're eventually going to have to tell me what happened to me," Cyrus said.

"What's important is that you're conscious. The doctor said everything looks good and there is no reason you shouldn't have a full recovery. As for this other issue, we can sort it out later when—"

"A nurse was *murdered*." Cyrus swallowed, his mouth and throat still dry from lack of use.

"I'm sorry, but it had to have been a dream. You say you got up out of bed that night—"

"I buzzed for the nurse, but no one answered the call button, so I got up and walked out past the nurse's station," Cyrus said, seeing it as clearly as his brother standing before him. "The nurses' station was empty, but I remember looking at the clock. It was two minutes past midnight. I could hear someone down the hall talking in whispers in one of the rooms. I walked in that direction, but as I passed the nursery windows—"

"Cyrus, this is the first time since your accident that you've been conscious," Cordell said gently. "That night in the old Whitehorse hospital, you were hooked up to monitors and IVs. There is no way you got up and walked anywhere. I'm sorry. I know it seemed real to you, whatever you think you saw, but it had to have just been a bad dream."

"Then how do you explain the fact that I can remember exactly how the old tiles felt on my bare feet or the way the place smelled, or that I can describe the hospital to you if I was never awake to see it?"

Cordell shook his head. "I don't know."

"Then you can't be certain that I didn't see exactly what I said I did."

"All I know is that if you had gotten out of bed that night in the old hospital, the alarms on the monitors would have gone off."

"Maybe they did. There were no nurses around to hear them. I'm telling you the place was a morgue and there was no one at the nurses' station."

"Even if that was true, monitors were recording your vital signs. If you disconnected anything and walked down the hall there would be a report of it."

"Maybe there is. Have you seen the records?"

His brother sighed. "You were moved to the new hospital the next morning. Don't you think someone would have noticed you were no longer connected to the IV or monitors?"

"Maybe the nurses covered it up because they were down the hall killing a woman."

"Cyrus—"

"I know what I saw," he said with a shake of his head. What frustrated him even more than not getting anyone to believe him was that after all this time, any evidence of the crime would be gone.

"I'm glad you're the same old Cyrus, stubborn as ever," Cordell said with affection.

"Were there any other patients in the hospital the one night I spent there?" Cyrus asked as a thought occurred to him.

"One of the reasons the ambulance took you to the old

hospital was because there was another patient who couldn't be moved, so the hospital was still staffed for the night."

*Sure it was.* "Another patient? Maybe that patient saw or heard something that would corroborate my story."

"That patient was in his eighties. He died that night."

Cyrus sighed and closed his eyes.

"Listen, the doctor said you shouldn't overdo."

"I want you to call the hospital up there and the sheriff," Cyrus said, opening his eyes. "I'm telling you I saw a murder." He gave his brother a detailed description of the female victim.

"Okay, I'll check into it if it will make you take it easy for a while."

Cyrus lay back against the pillows on the hospital bed, exhausted. How was that possible after sleeping for almost three months?

"Get some rest," Cordell said, clasping his hand. "I can't tell you how good it is to have you back."

"Yeah, same here." He was glad one of the first faces he'd seen after waking had been his twin's. But he couldn't help feeling helpless and frustrated.

He'd seen a murdered woman that night in the hospital and no one believed him. Not even his brother.

Cyrus woke to find his twin beside his bed. Through the open curtains he could see that it was dark outside. How long had he been asleep this time?

Cordell stirred and sat up, seeing that he'd awakened. "How are you feeling?"

"Okay." Had he expected Cyrus to wake up and recant his story about the murdered woman he'd seen? Surely his twin knew him better than that. "What did you find out?"

From Cordell's expression, he'd been hoping, at least.

"I called the hospital in Whitehorse and talked to the administrator. She assured me there was no murder at the old hospital the night you were a patient there."

"Someone moved the body."

"She also assured me that you never left your bed. There were two nurses on duty that night monitoring not only you, but also the elderly gentleman in a room down the hall. One nurse was just outside your room the whole time."

Cyrus knew that wasn't true, but Cordell didn't give him a chance to argue the point.

"I also called the Whitehorse sheriff's department and talked to our cousin McCall, who has since become the sheriff. There was no murder at the old hospital that night. Nor any missing nurse because both nurses who were on duty that night are accounted for. Nor was there a nurse's aide or orderly or anyone else working that night."

*Then she must have just been dressed in a uniform for some reason,* Cyrus thought.

"There was also no missing person report on any woman in the area."

*She must not have been from Whitehorse.*

He saw his brother's expression and knew that Cordell would have thought of all of this and asked the sheriff to run a check in a broader area with the description Cyrus had supplied. He and Cordell were private investigators and identical twins. They could finish each other's sentences. Of course Cordell would have thought of all these things.

"Sheriff McCall Winchester assured me that no unexplained vehicles were found near the old hospital nor has anyone in the area gone missing."

Was it possible everyone was right and that he'd only seen the murdered woman in a coma-induced nightmare?

Cyrus didn't believe that. But then again, he also couldn't believe he'd been in coma for three months.

Within a few weeks, Cyrus was feeling more like his old self. He'd been working out, getting his strength back and was now restless. He hadn't been able to shake the images from the dream. In fact, they seemed stronger than they had the morning he'd awakened in the rehabilitation center.

He still had no memory, though, of what had happened to him in Whitehorse in the hours before the accident that put him in the coma.

Cordell had filled him in, finally. Apparently, he'd driven to Whitehorse in his pickup and stopped that night at the Whitehorse Hotel, an old four-story antique on the edge of town. He'd gone there, he remembered, to see his grandmother Pepper Winchester after receiving a letter from her lawyer giving him the impression that she might be dying.

Even now he couldn't remember why he'd wanted to go see the reclusive grandmother who'd kicked her family off the ranch twenty-seven years ago, never to be heard from again—until now.

In Whitehorse, he'd taken a room on the fourth floor of the hotel, intending to wait until his brother joined him the next morning before going out to the Winchester Ranch.

Apparently he had barely gotten into his room when he'd either heard something outside or happened to look out the window. What he'd seen, Cordell said, was a child molester breaking the only yard light in the hotel parking lot and slashing the rear tire of a VW bug parked there.

Cyrus must have watched as the man went back to the dark-colored van, the engine running, and realized the man was waiting for the owner of the VW to come out.

He'd run downstairs in time to keep the young woman

who owned the VW bug from being run down by the van and killed. While saving her, he'd been hit and suffered a blow to his head that had left him in a coma all these months.

"That's some story," Cyrus said after his brother finished.

It was like hearing a story about someone he didn't know. None of it brought back a single memory. But it did fit in with his dream, since he'd spent a night in the old hospital.

During the weeks he'd spent getting stronger, he hadn't brought up the so-called murder dream with Cordell because it upset him. Cyrus suspected he worried about his twin's mental health. During his last checkup, even the doctor had questioned Cyrus about headaches, strange dreams and hallucinations. Clearly Cordell had talked to the doctor about his brother's inability to let this go.

"I didn't think coma patients dreamed," Cyrus had said to the doctor.

"Actually, they retain non-cognitive function and normal sleep patterns. It's their higher brain functions they lose, other than key functions such as breathing and circulation. You were in a deep-level coma caused by trauma to the brain. I'm sure that explains what you thought you saw."

After his doctor's appointment, Cyrus stopped by Winchester Investigations, unable to put it off any longer. With each passing day, he had more questions—and more suspicions. He knew there was only one way to put his mind at ease.

"Hey," he said after tapping at his brother's open office door.

Cordell looked up and from his expression, he'd been expecting this.

"I have to go back to Whitehorse and check out a few things myself."

"I'll go with you."

"No, you need to stay here and do some work. We both can't be goofing off. When I come back—"

"Yeah, I want to talk to you about that."

"Is there a problem?"

"No, it's just that, well, you've met Raine," Cordell said.

Cyrus smiled. He'd been pleased when his brother had introduced him to the woman he'd been seeing for the last three months. Raine Chandler, he'd been surprised to hear, was the woman he'd saved up in Montana.

"So I brought you two together." Cyrus had never believed in divine intervention. But as eerie as this was, he felt as if it had all happened for a reason. And that reason, he feared, was so he could be at the hospital that night and make sure justice was done.

But that surprise was nothing compared to realizing his brother had fallen head-over-heels in love with the woman. After Cordell's horrible marriage and divorce, no one had expected him ever to consider marriage again—especially his twin.

But when he'd met Raine, he'd seen that she was wearing a gorgeous diamond engagement ring and Cordell was always grinning when he was around her.

"Raine and I made a deal back in Montana," Cordell was saying. He looked uncomfortable. "She said she'd marry me only when you could be my best man."

Cyrus was surprised. "She was taking one hell of a chance I was going to come out of my coma."

"Raine has a lot of faith. I think she knew how much I would need you at my side on my wedding day."

Cyrus laughed. "True enough. Congrats, Cordell, and I'd love to be your best man. So when is the big day?"

"We haven't set it yet. We were waiting to see…"

If Cyrus really was going to be all right. That was the problem with being twins: sometimes you knew exactly what the other one was thinking.

"I'm fine, really. This is just something I need to do. I'm not crazy, no screws loose from the head injury. If you had seen what I did, you'd be doing the same thing. It was that real, Cordell."

His brother nodded. "So go to Montana, do what you have to do and—"

"Set a wedding date. I'll be there for you. This thing in Montana won't take that long, unless you're thinking of getting married right away."

"No, we were considering a New Year's wedding. Did I mention that our cousin McCall is getting married at the ranch at Christmas?" Cordell asked.

"You aren't seriously considering—"

"Raine and Grandmother hit it off." Cordell shrugged. "Grandmother thinks we should move our investigative business to Montana. I know," he said quickly, putting up a hand. "I told her you'd never go for that."

Cyrus had to laugh. Cordell was the one who had wanted nothing to do with his grandmother. He'd tried to talk Cyrus out of even going to Montana in the first place. Now he was actually considering another wedding at the ranch after Christmas?

"Hey," he said, "whatever you and Raine decide. Count me in." He hugged his brother and headed for the door.

"Call me when you get there and keep in touch," his brother called after him. "If you need me, I'll be there in a heartbeat. Or if I don't hear from you."

Cyrus stopped at the door to look back at him and laughed. "Stop worrying about me. I'll probably be back within the week. By the way, thanks for taking care of my pickup."

"Sure."

Cyrus got the feeling there was something his brother wasn't telling him. "You didn't let your girlfriend drive my pickup, did you?"

"The way Raine drives? Are you kidding?"

He started to step out into the hallway.

"Cyrus!"

Turning, he looked back at his brother and saw more than worry on Cordell's face. "Be careful."

Cyrus felt that bad feeling he'd awakened with rise to the surface again. If the murder had been nothing more than a bad dream, then why did his brother look scared for him?

# Chapter 3

His first morning in Whitehorse, Montana, Cyrus headed straight for the new hospital. The squat, single-level building sat on the east end of the small western town. There was an empty field behind it, the Larb Hills in the distance.

For a moment, he stood outside, hoping the cool October day would sharpen his senses. He felt off balance, confused and a little afraid that the blow to his head had done more damage than anyone suspected—and all because of what he believed he'd seen that night in the old hospital.

The doctor had said he might have some memory lapses, either short-or long-term. He'd been warned that he might not feel like himself for a while.

"There are things you might never get back."

*Like my sanity?*

When he'd reached town last night, he'd returned to the Whitehorse Hotel on the edge of town and taken the same room he had planned to stay in more than three months earlier.

He hadn't slept well and when his brother had called and he'd told him where he was, Cordell threatened to come to Montana. Cyrus had talked him out of it, assuring him he wasn't losing it.

Now, as Cyrus stepped into the new hospital's reception area, he wasn't so sure. Maybe he was wrong. Who saw a murder that never happened?

It wasn't just that no one believed him. They all made it sound as if it would have been impossible for anything he said to have actually happened. All of them couldn't be wrong, could they?

Of course, his first thought was conspiracy. But did he believe that even his cousin was in on it?

The hospital was smaller than most, but then Whitehorse wasn't exactly booming. Like a lot of small Montana towns, its population was dropping each year as young people moved away for college and better-paying jobs.

"May I help you?" The receptionist was in her early twenties with straight blond hair and a recently applied sheen of lip gloss. He stared at her name tag, not registering her name as he suddenly had a flash of his so-called murder dream. The woman lying dead in the nursery hadn't been wearing a name tag. So maybe he was right and she wasn't a nurse. Or maybe she'd lost her name tag in the struggle.

"Sir?"

Cyrus stirred, blinking the receptionist back into focus. He removed his Stetson. "I need to speak with your hospital administrator." He realized he should have made an appointment. Had he been afraid the person wouldn't see him once he recognized the name and knew what this was about?

"Your name?"

"Cyrus Winchester."

The receptionist picked up the phone. "Let me see…oh, here she is now."

A woman in her sixties with short gray hair walked toward them. She was dressed in a suit and had an air of authority about her.

"This man needs to see you," the receptionist said.

The hospital administrator gave him only a brief glance. "Why don't you come back to my office."

Cyrus followed her into a small, brightly lit room. The light hurt his eyes. Another side effect of the coma, this sensitivity to light?

"Would you like me to close the blinds?" She was already closing them, dimming the room a little.

"I'm Cyrus Winchester."

"What can I do for you, Mr. Winchester?" She didn't introduce herself but the plaque on her desk read *Roberta Warren*.

"Were you also the administrator at the old hospital?" he asked.

"Yes. I've been the administrator for the last thirty-four years." She clasped her hands together on her desk and seemed to wait patiently, although her demeanor said she had a lot to do and little time.

He kneaded the brim of his hat in his lap, surprised he was nervous. "You know who I am."

"Yes."

"Then you probably know why I'm here." He realized he was nervous because he was sitting in front of a health care specialist who was looking at him as if he might be nuts.

"Your brother called us about an incident you thought

you'd seen while at the old hospital the night you were there."

"That *incident* was a woman murdered in the nursery."

She shook her head. "There was no murder at the hospital."

Another chunk of memory fell as if from the sky. "There were two babies in bassinets," he said as he saw the nursery clearly in his memory. Why hadn't he recalled that earlier? Because it hadn't registered? Or because it hadn't mattered when there was a dead woman lying just inside the nursery?

Now, though, he thought the fact that the two babies were there did matter for some reason. He tried to remember, but that only made his head ache and the memory slip farther away from him.

Roberta Warren was still shaking her head. "There were no babies in the nursery that last night the old hospital was still open. I'm afraid you're mistaken about that, as well."

He tried another tactic. "Do you know a woman with long auburn hair, greenish-blue eyes, tall, slim, maybe in her late twenties or early thirties?"

"As I told your brother, there is no one employed at the hospital who matches that description."

"Do you know anyone in town who matches that description?"

She raised a brow. "I thought you said it was a nurse who you thought you saw murdered."

"She wasn't wearing a name tag when I found her. Maybe she was only pretending to be a nurse."

The administrator looked at her watch pointedly. "I'm sure you've spoken with the sheriff. Had there been a murder—"

"I'd like to speak to the two nurses on duty that night," he said.

"I won't allow that."

"Why not?" he asked, thinking he might be on to something.

"I've questioned both of them at length, Mr. Winchester. One was always at the desk that night. The sheriff also questioned them as well and looked at the monitor readings. You never left your bed that night. If you decide to pursue this, it will have to be with a subpoena and just cause." Her tone said *good luck getting either.* "I won't have you accusing my nurses of something that never happened."

He rose to his feet. He wasn't going to get anything from this woman. "Thank you for your time."

She sighed and gave him a sympathetic look. "I'm sure your doctor explained to you that what you thought you experienced was a coma-induced hallucination of some kind, perhaps stemming from your line of work. There is no cover-up, no murder, no reason for you to waste your time or anyone else's. I would think you would be glad to be alive and have better things to do with your time."

"I am glad to be alive. Unfortunately, the woman I saw lying in a pool of blood in the old hospital nursery isn't and for some reason no one cares."

He saw that his words finally hit home because she had paled. But that gave him little satisfaction. He turned and walked out of her office and reception area into the bright October morning.

He was shaking inside. Where had that come from about the babies? But now that he thought about it, he was certain there'd been two babies in the nursery.

Just as he was certain there'd been a murder. Now all he had to do was prove it—against all odds, because his instincts told him he was right. If that woman was ever going to get justice, it would be up to him.

* * *

The moment the office door closed, Roberta Warren let out the breath she'd been holding. Her hands were trembling as she reached into the drawer for the small bottle of vodka she kept there disguised in a water bottle.

Taking a sip, she told herself that there was no reason she should be so upset. But when Cordell Winchester had called questioning whether or not there had been a murder more than three months ago at the hospital, she hadn't thought anything of it.

That was because he hadn't mentioned that the murder his brother thought he'd seen had been in the hospital nursery. Or that the woman had been found in a pool of her own blood. Or that there had been two babies in bassinets in the nursery the night of the murder.

Roberta Warren took another sip of the vodka and quickly put the lid back on the water bottle. Her hands were a little steadier, but her heart was still pounding. The man couldn't have possibly dreamed any of this. Who dreamed a murder in such detail? But was he just fishing or did he know something?

She took a mint from her drawer and chewed it, debating how to handle this. The best thing was to ignore it. Cyrus Winchester would tire soon since he would keep running into dead ends, and he would eventually go back to Denver.

But then again, she hadn't expected him to come all the way to Whitehorse to chase a nightmare. She'd heard the determination in his voice. The fool really thought he was going to get justice for the dead woman.

Calmer, Roberta picked up the phone and almost dialed the number she hadn't called in thirty years. She put the phone down. She was overreacting. That was probably what he hoped she would do. But still she worried that this would get all over town, hell, all over the county, if he continued to ask questions.

If he didn't give up soon, she would have to come up with a way to dissuade him.

She stood, smoothed her hands over her skirt and walked to the window, half expecting to see Cyrus Winchester standing outside her office, staring in as if he thought he could make her feel guilty enough to panic.

Well, he didn't know her, she thought, but she was glad to see him drive off anyway.

The October day was sunny and blustery. Golden leaves showered down from the trees and formed piles in the gutters. The air smelled of fall with just a hint of the snowy winter days that weren't far off.

He was driving down a wide, tree-lined street when he saw the single-level brick building. Even with the sign removed, Cyrus recognized the old hospital. The realization gave him a chill.

As he pulled to the curb, he saw that apparently the movers hadn't completed the job of removing the furnishings, because there was a large panel truck parked out front and both front doors of the building were propped open.

Getting out of his pickup, Cyrus walked along the sidewalk past the truck. The back was open, a ramp leading into the cavernous, dark interior. He glanced in and saw a dozen old wooden chairs, some equally old end tables and several library tables.

As he passed, he saw that on the side of the truck were painted the words *Second Hand Kate's*. Under that in smaller print, *Used Furnishings Emporium*.

"Hello?" he called as he stepped through the open front doors of the old hospital. The interior still had that familiar clinical smell and that empty, cold feeling he remembered. He reminded himself that it had been empty now for more than three months.

"Hello?"

No answer.

He walked down the hallway, his boot heels echoing on the discolored worn tile. He hadn't realized where he was going until he reached the nursery windows.

His breath caught in his throat as he shoved back his Stetson and, cupping his hands, looked through the blank glass. The cribs and furnishings were gone, the room bare, but he could see it as the nursery had been in his memory.

A half dozen bassinets, but only two babies. Both boys with little blue blankets and ribbons on the bassinets, he recalled with surprise.

He touched his fingers to the pane, then quickly pulled them away as a memory moved through him like a spasm. With a jolt, he remembered seeing the murdered woman right *before* she was killed.

He had stood in this very spot and watched her switch the babies in the bassinets.

"Cyrus, do you realize what you're saying?"

He'd had to go outside to get cell phone service.

"I saw her purposely switch the babies. Cordell, she stood there for a long moment as if making up her mind."

He could almost hear his twin's disbelief.

"I know how crazy it sounds, but when I saw this place as I was driving by, even without the sign, I knew it was the old hospital because I recognized it. Cordell, I walked straight to the nursery. When I touched the glass—" He shuddered at the memory. "I felt something so strong, I can't explain it."

"Okay, let's say you saw this woman who was later murdered after switching the babies," his brother said finally. "It should be easy enough to find out if there were two baby boys in the nursery while you were there."

He sighed. "I already asked the hospital administrator. She swears there were no babies in the nursery that night."

"So you think she's lying? The whole town is lying? Why would they do that?"

Cyrus had no idea. He was more concerned with how he was going to prove it. "The hospital administrator won't let me talk to the nurses who were on duty that night without a subpoena." He heard his brother sigh. "I have to go see the room I was in. I'll call you later. Stop worrying about me. I know what I'm doing."

He disconnected and walked back into the hospital. He felt scared as he entered the long corridor of worn tile. He'd heard the fear in his twin's voice. Maybe he couldn't trust his own judgment. Or maybe it was just that no one else trusted it.

Cyrus heard someone singing from one of the maze-like hallways deep in the building. At least that was real, he thought. The woman had a good voice and he recognized the country-western song. It was one of his favorites.

Past the nursery, he walked down to what he was certain had been his room. It was right beside what had been the nurses' station. Didn't this prove that he had regained consciousness at some point while still in this hospital that night?

He started to step into the room when he saw her. She came out of a doorway at the end of the hall and started toward him, a pair of iPod buds in her ears. She was singing along with the song, completely lost in the music.

As she came closer, Cyrus felt all the air rush out of him.

It was her!

The woman he'd seen switch the babies in the hospital nursery. The woman he'd found murdered right here in this old hospital more than three months ago.

# Chapter 4

Cyrus stared at the woman as if she were an apparition. Everyone was right. He *was* losing his mind. Fear turned his skin clammy. He told himself he was seeing things, imagining her the same way he had the murdered woman.

As the young woman looked up then and saw him, she appeared startled. She slowed, looked unsure. He half expected her to vanish before his eyes.

"Can I help you?" she asked, frowning, as she walked toward him. Was it possible she recognized him? Or was she just surprised, thinking she was alone in the building?

As she drew closer, he saw that either his memory was in error or this wasn't the woman. But she looked enough like the murder victim to be her sister. Her hair was more copper than auburn, her eyes emerald rather than aquamarine and she was shorter than the murdered woman, although about the same age.

She had a small wooden nightstand in one hand and

a slat-back wooden chair in the other and she wore blue denim overalls over a white T-shirt, sneakers on her feet. The logo on the overalls read *Second Hand Kate*.

"Are you all right?" she asked as she plucked out the earbuds.

He knew he must have lost all color. While he'd been getting stronger every day, the shock of seeing her had left him feeling weak and shaky.

He realized how bad he must look when she asked, "You know the hospital moved, right? Do you need someone to drive you up to the new one?"

He could hear the murmur of the music coming from the iPod in her overalls pocket. He shook his head and finally found his voice. "Sorry, I called out as I came in…"

She smiled. It seemed to light up the old building and the sweet innocence in the gesture tugged at his heart. This wasn't the woman he'd seen murdered in the nursery, but she had to be a relative. Wasn't it possible she'd seen him at the hospital?

"Do you know me?" he asked.

She looked at him as if he might be joking. "Should I?"

He shoved back his Stetson and smiled sheepishly. "You look familiar. I thought… You don't happen to have a sister, do you?"

"Sorry." She was smiling again as if she thought this was a bad pick-up line.

She was definitely not the woman he'd seen. This woman, while the spitting image of the murder victim, lacked the darkness he'd felt in the dead woman. This woman was all sunshine and rainbows.

"Is this for the secondhand shop?" he asked, motioning to the furniture and then to the logo on her overalls, desperately needing to say something that didn't come out stupid.

She nodded, clearly pleased with the items. "They don't make furniture like this anymore. I can't wait to refinish some of these pieces," she said, her enthusiasm bubbling out.

"So you must be Kate." Not a nurse. Or even a nurse's aide here at the hospital.

"The Kate in Second Hand Kate's." She set down the chair and wiped her free hand on her overalls and held it out to him. "You aren't interested in used furniture, are you?"

"I might be," he said, realizing he was flirting with her. He held out his hand. "Cyrus Winchester."

"*Winchester?* You're not related to—"

"The sheriff is my cousin and Pepper is my grand-mother."

"Oh." She chuckled. "I see."

"You know them?" he asked.

She shook her head. "I just moved here, but I've heard stories. Your grandmother is pretty famous around here. I've always wanted to meet her."

"Infamous, you mean." The Winchesters had always pro-vided fodder for good gossip. His grandmother had been a recluse for the past twenty-seven years, his grandfather had ridden off on a horse one day forty years ago and never been seen again—until recently—and one of his uncles had only turned up after a gully washer had washed up his remains.

She turned her smile on him again. "Kate Landon."

Cyrus felt a gentle shock run through him at her warm, strong touch.

"So you just happened to stop by the hospital to…"

"Return to the scene of the crime." She laughed and he added quickly, "So to speak. I was brought in a few months ago by ambulance and spent a night here. I don't remember much about it. They tell me I was in a coma."

She instantly sobered. "Oh, I'm so sorry."

"I'm fine now." *Sure you are. You thought this woman had been murdered just down the hall in the nursery. Or at least her sister had. Except she doesn't have a sister.* "I'm just going to take a look around, if that's okay."

"Sure. Just do me a favor, if you don't mind. This is my last load. Close the doors when you leave? There's a chain with a padlock on the outside that loops through the door handles."

He'd forgotten how trusting people were in small towns. "I'd be happy to lock it on my way out."

"Thanks." She seemed to hesitate, her green eyes darkening. "Take care of yourself."

Cyrus knew he was being paranoid, but her words seemed to echo in the still, empty hallway like an omen.


Kate carried the end table and chair out to the truck, put it in the back with the last of the furniture, pushed in the ramp and slammed the rear doors, smiling to herself.

It had been a while since a man had openly flirted with her—let alone a very handsome cowboy. At the memory of the man she'd met inside, her gaze felt pulled back to the old hospital. The interior was deep in shadow, but she thought for a moment she saw movement in the darkness behind the open double doors.

Her friend Jasmine, a Whitehorse native, had kidded her about watching out for ghosts at the hospital. "Seriously, the nurses used to tell stories of feeling something in that old hospital when they worked the night shift and this one nurse swore she saw the ghost of this woman coming down the hall toward her."

Kate had laughed, figuring Jasmine was just fooling with her. She'd felt a little creepy in the old building alone earlier, but had just turned up her music. Now though, she would have sworn she saw a figure just beyond the doorway.

But when she'd turned to look down the long side of the building, she'd seen a set of white metal blinds flash open at a window in a far room.

Cyrus Winchester peered out for a moment, then closed the blinds again.

She felt a chill, remembering the feeling that someone had been watching her from just inside the hospital doors. It couldn't have been Cyrus. Had someone else been in there?

"It's the ghost of that woman," Jasmine would have said.

Fortunately Jasmine wasn't with her.

*You're just imagining things.* But she decided she would swing by later and make sure no one had gotten locked inside the old building.

As she climbed behind the wheel of her truck, she forgot all about ghosts. It was Cyrus Winchester she couldn't get off her mind. He had startled her earlier when she'd looked up and seen him standing in the hallway. Blame Jasmine for her darned ghost stories.

Cyrus Winchester had looked nothing like the legendary ghost woman standing there so tall, dark and exceedingly handsome.

Yet there had been something haunting in his eyes…

She shivered at the thought, remembering that when he'd seen her he'd looked as if he was the one who'd seen the ghost. Probably just recovering from his injuries. Still, it was odd, him wanting to return to the scene of the crime, as he'd said. Who visited his old hospital room?

She looked again at the windows where he'd peered out just minutes ago. With the blinds closed, she could see nothing but white metal.

Turning the key, she started the engine and a Christmas song came on the radio. It was too early to be thinking about Christmas. She was still gearing up for her annual Halloween haunted house. She turned the radio dial until she found country and western and turned her thoughts to Halloween.

She planned to transform the basement of Second Hand Kate's into a haunted house. She'd only been in town for a few months and it was her way of welcoming the community into her new store. The basement of the old two-story, once-a-library building with all its nooks and crannies was the perfect place for chills and thrills.

Fortunately, she'd managed to make a couple of friends who'd offered to help her. Jasmine was sewing some of the costumes and backdrops while Andi preferred working with the blood and guts, turning perfectly normal food into something gross and frightening.

Kate couldn't wait to hear the children's shrieks and screams, giggles and gags. She hoped for a good turnout Halloween night. But she still had a lot of work to do and was glad she'd finally gotten the last of the furniture out of the old hospital. There had been no hurry, but she hated leaving anything undone.

As she drove away, her cell phone rang.

"I found the most perfect fabric for the ghost in the pit of horror," Jasmine said, making her laugh.

"Of course you did. I was just thinking of you." She'd met Jasmine soon after she'd come to town at where else? A garage sale. The two had realized how much they had in common when they'd both tried to buy the same ugly chair.

"Oh, yeah?"

"I was just leaving the old hospital with the last of the furniture."

"You saw the ghost." Jasmine sounded excited. "Didn't I tell you?"

"What I saw was no ghost. I just ran into Cyrus Winchester."

"Who?"

"Pepper Winchester's grandson. You've never met him?"

"No. So what is he like?"

"Gorgeous." She almost added, "and a little strange," but chastised herself for even thinking it. The man had just come out of a coma.

"Sounds like a Winchester. Black hair and eyes?"

"Uh-huh. Tall with broad shoulders and slim hips that look great in Wrangler jeans." Kate remembered how good-looking he'd been standing there in his Stetson and boots. Even now she couldn't put her finger on what it was about him that had left her feeling afraid for him.

"Wait a minute, is he the one who was in the hospital with the coma?" Jasmine and Andi always knew more of what was going on than Kate ever did. Jasmine worked at City Hall so she heard all the good stuff and Andi was the local newspaper reporter.

"Uh-huh."

"He and his brother are private investigators in Denver. I heard he's *drop-dead* gorgeous and that he and his brother are identical twins," Jasmine said.

"Really?" She felt a chill at discovering Cyrus was a private investigator, but tried to hide her reaction from her friend. She'd never told anyone in Whitehorse about her past.

"What was he doing at the old hospital?" Andi asked.

"He stopped by to visit his room."

"Seriously? Don't you think that is a little macabre? Maybe he died there, you know, went toward the light but was pulled back and now he's trying to call up the other side."

"Or maybe you've been spending too much time planning the haunted house," Kate suggested.

Her friend laughed. "Swing by and I'll show you the fabric. I also have some old white curtains I can use for the ghosts, but I want your opinion first."

Kate was tired and dirty from hauling dusty old furniture, but she agreed. "See you in a minute." She hung up and on impulse, circled around the block and made a point of driving back past the hospital.

The pickup with the Colorado plates that had been parked behind her truck was still there, which meant Cyrus Winchester was still inside the hospital.

What *was* he doing in there?

The hospital room was exactly as he remembered it. Cyrus had quit asking himself how he knew that. Obviously he hadn't been unconscious the entire time.

When he'd opened the blinds, he'd seen Kate Landon sitting in her truck. Was she worried he wouldn't lock up? She couldn't be worried that he'd steal anything, since clearly there was nothing left in the building to steal.

He'd dropped the blinds and searched the room, not sure what he was hoping to find. Of course there was nothing either in the room or the bathroom but dust. How quickly the building was falling into disrepair.

When he peeked out the window again, the Second Hand Kate's truck was gone. He had wanted to question her further, but had warned himself not to ask too many questions that would scare her.

She looked too much like the murder victim not to have

some connection. He would have to find out what he could about the Landon family.

Leaving his former hospital room, he walked down the hall, his boot heels echoing. The place had taken on an eerie feel. He stopped to listen as if he thought he could tap into the building's history, feel all the lives that had traveled through here from birth to death and all the broken bones and illnesses in between.

But of course he couldn't. He wasn't psychic. He'd seen someone switch two baby boys in the nursery and then become a murder victim. That was a far cry from being able to tell the future.

He thought about calling Cordell and telling him about Kate Landon. But he knew his brother would try to come up with some reason Kate looked so much like the murder victim.

"You must have seen her before you were attacked, before the coma, and unconsciously put her in your dream," Cordell would say.

Unfortunately, everything that had happened between his last memory of driving to Montana and waking up was lost. Except for what had happened that one night in the old hospital. He knew that alone should be proof the murder was just a bad dream.

At the nursery, he paused. It was just inside there that he'd found the dead woman. He walked a few feet down the hall, found the door into the nursery and stepped in.

Fortunately the power company hadn't turned off the electricity yet. He snapped on the light and studied the room, trying to picture where the bassinets and other equipment had been in this room that night.

At the back of his mind, a thought nagged at him. Why was the equipment still here that night? Why were there two babies still here if most everything had been moved to the new hospital?

He shoved the thought away. It didn't make any sense, but then again none of it did.

Cyrus moved to within feet of the spot where he believed the body had been sprawled. The woman had put up a struggle. In the semi-soundproof nursery and the near-empty hospital, it was no wonder no one had heard it.

Crouching down, he studied the worn tile. There were scuff marks, dust, some dirt and a scrape where something heavy had been dragged out. He wondered if the blood would show up in the thin cracks between the tiles with the luminol crime labs used?

Unfortunately, there was little chance of getting the crime lab involved, since the sheriff's department wasn't even investigating the murder.

*Because there was no murder. No switching of babies in the nursery. No way you could have seen a dead woman because you were in a coma tethered to your bed by tubes and monitors. All this was just a coma-induced bad dream.*

Sometimes he wished he had dreamed all of it so he could just quit this. As he started to push himself to his feet, he was blinded by another flash of memory. The woman lying in a pool of blood, him leaning over her, something on her wrist.

A string of tiny silver sleigh bells. A bracelet. One of the bells had come off and lay on its side in the blood next to her clutched fingers. The woman had put up a fight.

Head aching and even more mystified, Cyrus left the old hospital and drove down to the main drag. He parked in front of the *Milk River Examiner,* the local weekly newspaper, and climbed out, breathing in the crisp Montana air.

The detailed images that kept flashing through his memory were starting to worry him.

Why hadn't he remembered all of it the moment he'd awakened? Why did it keep coming to him, little pieces that were so clear.... He shoved his worry away and entered the newspaper office.

It was small and sold paper supplies as well as putting out a weekly edition.

He took a current newspaper—and one from three months ago that would have come out the week he was taken to the hospital and the week after that. From the young clerk behind the counter, he also borrowed the phone book long enough to look up the last name Landon.

The nearby towns along the Hi-Line were all small enough that they'd been put into the same phone book. There was only one Landon in the entire the directory. Kate. What had he been thinking? If she had any female relatives here, they could be married and have different last names.

Returning the phone book to the clerk, he paid for his newspapers and stepped outside. Across the street was a small park next to the railroad tracks. He sat down at one of the picnic tables and opened the first newspaper.

The paper had a lot of local news about who was in town visiting and who had a birthday or anniversary. He paused on an ad for Second Hand Kate's, complete with an address and news about her recent opening—and her first annual haunted house to be held there Halloween night.

Cyrus realized Halloween was only a few days away.

There wasn't anything else in the paper that caught his eye, so he picked up one from three months ago. Under the sheriff's department reports he found the incident that had put him in a coma. It was brief, only a few words about a deputy responding to a call at the Whitehorse Hotel where a man had been attacked and taken to the hospital. The suspect was still at large.

He scanned through the rest of the four-page paper and found the obituary for the man who had died in the hospital the same night Cyrus was there. The man's name was Wally Ingram.

On impulse Cyrus called 411 on his cell and was put through to Wally Ingram's home number. He was surprised when it rang. He'd been half expecting to hear the line had been disconnected following the man's death.

"Hello?" The woman sounded young.

Cyrus quickly explained that he'd been in the hospital the same night as Mr. Ingram and wondered if any of the family had also been there.

"My mother stayed with Grandpa that night."

He felt his pulse quicken. "I'd like to talk to your mother if possible. Is she around?"

"Martha's gone to Great Falls and won't be back until late tonight, but you could probably catch her tomorrow morning."

He left a message to have Martha Ingram call him and hung up, feeling hopeful. Someone else had been in the hospital that night, someone not connected to the staff.

The answer was in this town, Cyrus thought, and felt a strange sense of apprehension. Little scared him, but he knew at the back of his mind, he was beginning to question his own sanity.

Cyrus checked the newspaper from a week after his accident and read about his brother and another private investigator from California, Raine Chandler, catching some child molesters, one of them responsible for putting him in the hospital.

As he walked back to his car, he felt antsy. The air had cooled down some, the day not quite as beautiful as it had been. He wondered if a storm was coming in.

Sliding behind the wheel of his pickup, he didn't kid himself about where he was going or why as he drove down the street to the address that had been listed in the newspaper for Second Hand Kate's. He was relieved to see the *Open* sign in the window.

Getting out, he climbed the steps of the large, old brick building. Over the door, he could make out the faded letters of the word *Library.* She'd put her shop in an old library building.

The door opened, a bell tinkled and he caught the scent of orange and cinnamon. He breathed in the sweet, rich smell, glad of the warmth inside the shop as the door closed behind him.

He'd expected piles of old furniture—not this decorated, attractive shop.

"Be right with you!" Kate called from somewhere above him. He noticed a beautiful, wide stairway that climbed to the second floor. There was a small sign that read *Private.*

As he walked around the lower floor, he saw that each room had its own setting, each unique and charming. It felt almost magical, the lighting, the tapestries, the overstuffed chairs, the colors and textures, trinkets and curios. He remembered what she'd said about refinishing the furniture she'd gotten from the old hospital and could see her handiwork throughout her shop.

He could well imagine the condition many of the old items had been in before she'd worked her magic. It surprised him what wonders she'd achieved with a collection of what most people would have discarded as worthless. He could feel Kate's energy in every room. It was like walking into the woman's home rather than a shop.

At a rustling sound, he turned to see Kate Landon come down the wide flight of stairs. She'd showered and changed since he'd seen her at the old hospital and now wore a colorful skirt and top with black ballet slippers.

Her hair was still damp and hung around her shoulders, a coppery wave that framed her face and set off her wide green eyes. She was so stunning he stared, completely enchanted with this woman who could turn trash into treasure. As he stared at her, he realized that before, all he'd seen was her resemblance to the dead woman, now...

"Hello," she said in a lyrical tone. She seemed amused to see him again.

"After meeting you, I decided I'd better see your shop," he admitted honestly.

She smiled, opening her arms to take in the expansive rooms. "It's still a work in progress. I haven't been open all that long. I bought the building at an auction four months ago."

So she had been in town before his coma. Which meant he could have seen her, just as his brother would have suggested, and that was how she became part of his nightmare.

"Your shop is amazing. You've done wonders with it," he said glancing around although all he really wanted to do was look at her.

"Halloween night the basement is being turned into a haunted house," she said. "You should come. If you're still in town."

"I just might do that." His gaze locked with hers. "Do you have plans for dinner tonight?" The invitation came out of nowhere, surprising them both.

Her eyebrows shot up.

"I realize we just met and you know nothing about me."

She smiled. "In a town this size? Are you kidding? Everyone in town knows your life history by now."

He returned her smile. "I hope what you heard wasn't all bad."

"Not *all* of it," she teased. "I'd love to have dinner with you, but I'm afraid I have other plans tonight."

Of course she would have a date, a woman like this.

"I have to help my friend Jasmine sew some props for the haunted house. She sews, I help by providing the food and moral support. But I am planning on stopping by the Fall Festival later this evening. Maybe I'll see you there if you're going. There's going to be frybread. I never pass up frybread."

"Great." Cyrus wondered if this woman was why he was supposed to come back to Whitehorse. Maybe it hadn't been about a murder at all. Maybe he'd been destined to return to meet this woman. He liked the idea much better than the alternative.

It made more sense than any other explanation he could come up with. Which would mean there was no murdered woman in the nursery. No switching of babies. No wandering down an empty hospital hallway. None of that had happened.

Instead Kate Landon had happened. He smiled to himself, desperately wanting to believe she was the reason he was in Whitehorse as he shoved off the doubts that had plagued him, the things that made no sense.

He told that nagging little voice demanding a logical explanation for everything to shut up. It didn't matter why he'd walked right to the old hospital nursery earlier today, why he'd been able to find his room, why he knew how the tile felt on his bare feet, or the big one, why Kate Landon looked so much like the murdered woman that he'd thought she was the victim's younger sister.

Couldn't it be possible that he'd had the dream just to get him back here to meet Kate?

Cyrus felt as if a weight had been lifted off his shoulders. He was freer than he'd felt since he'd awakened from his coma. He told himself that he could let it go.

Those months would always be lost, but he had come out of the coma with apparently no long-lasting side effects. He'd been lucky. He was alive. It was time he started enjoying that fact. Just as Roberta Warren, the hospital administrator, had told him.

But as he turned to leave, Cyrus saw something in a glass cabinet that changed everything.

# *Chapter 5*

"Do you like the bracelet?" Kate asked as she joined him at the glass case.

For a moment, Cyrus couldn't find his voice. He told himself there had to be hundreds, thousands of bracelets just like this one. But even as he thought it, he could see that this wasn't costume jewelry.

"It looks old," he said as he stared down at the delicate string of tiny silver sleigh bells and tried to still his thundering heart. He saw that it had been made by a jeweler with an eye for detail. "It's incredible workmanship."

Kate beamed. "My grandfather was a silversmith. He made the bracelet for my mother's sixteenth birthday."

"Your mother?" he asked, his voice sounding strained to his ears.

When she didn't say anything, he said carefully, "There's no price on it."

She laughed softly. "Because it's *priceless,*" she said as

she unlocked the case and gingerly lifted out the bracelet. The bells tinkled softly, sending a chill through him. He'd heard that sound before. A memory, unfocused and distant, tried to surface.

"The items in this case aren't for sale. I just like them where I can see them," Kate said, pulling him out of the memory. "It makes me feel closer to my mother. I can't bring myself to wear the bracelet. I like that she was the last person to wear it. Silly, I know."

"No," he said, looking over at her and thinking he couldn't be more enchanted by this woman.

"It's really quite heavy," she said, surprising him as she laid the bracelet in his palm.

The silver felt cold against his flesh and sent a memory of another palm clutching this bracelet ripping through his mind. He quickly handed it back to her and started to ask more about her mother when the front door jangled open and three women came in with a gust of cold air. Wind whirled golden leaves around the steps before the door closed again.

"Good afternoon," Kate said with a smile as she greeted the shoppers. Cyrus watched her quickly put the bracelet back in the case and lock it. "Maybe I'll see you later at the Fall Festival," she whispered as she passed him to go offer the women a cup of hot spiced cider.

He stood for a moment, staring at the bracelet, before he noticed the women glancing back at him with obvious curiosity.

As he left his mind was awhirl.

The bracelet he'd seen in his dream was real. That had to mean that the woman wearing it had also been real—and murdered in the hospital nursery just like he'd known from the moment he'd awakened from his coma.

If the bracelet had belonged to Kate's mother, then she had to be the woman he'd seen in the nursery. The same woman who'd switched the babies.

When they'd been interrupted by the three local women entering the shop, Kate had felt as if Cyrus had wanted to ask her something more.

As she gave the women a tour, she was again struck with that uneasy feeling she'd had when she'd met Cyrus at the old hospital. He hadn't just stopped by her shop out of curiosity. He wanted something from her and she suspected it was more than a date.

As more women entered the shop, Kate replayed the moment when Cyrus had seen her mother's bracelet in the glass case by the door. At first she'd thought he was taken with it. But now that she thought about it, he'd seemed shocked to see it, almost as if he'd recognized it.

Her heart began to beat a little faster. Was it possible he knew something about her mother?

Now she wished she didn't have to work on the haunted house tonight. She would make sure she saw Cyrus Winchester again. Unfortunately, she had no idea where he was staying or how to reach him. She would have to make a point of catching up with him at the festival tonight—if he went.

Kate thought he would go and be watching for her. Apparently he was as anxious to see her as she was him.

Another group came through the door, then a handful of singles. Kate was busy showing them around her shop when she heard the bell over the front door ring again. She turned, half expecting to see Cyrus coming back through the door because she'd been thinking about him.

But it was her friend Andi Blake Jackson.

"What is going on?" Andi asked as she stepped in out of the cold. Andi was the local reporter for the *Milk River Examiner,* the only newspaper for miles. She used to be a famous television newscaster in Texas, but she'd moved to Montana and fallen in love and as they say, the rest was history. Andi had become a permanent Whitehorse resident when she'd gotten hitched to Cade Jackson, who ran the local bait shop and raised horses on a place out by Nelson Reservoir. His family went way back in Whitehorse.

Kate and Andi had met when Andi did a story on Kate's purchase of the old library building and her plans to open Second Hand Kate's. They'd become fast friends.

"I was down the street and I couldn't help but notice people coming and going in the shop. I thought 'what is she selling?' And then I found out. You know why business has been so brisk, don't you?" She didn't give Kate a chance to guess. "Cyrus Winchester. The talk around town is that he stopped by your shop. Everyone is dying to know what he bought."

Kate had to smile. Andi had been born to be a reporter, with her natural curiosity and ability to ferret out news.

"Is that the man's name?" Kate asked, pretending to play dumb.

Andi cocked a brow at her suspiciously. "Give it up. Jasmine already told me that you met him at the old hospital earlier. What was he doing here?"

She shrugged. "I think he was just looking." Looking for what, though? Cyrus's interest had been less in Second Hand Kate's and more in Kate herself. Had it not been for his interest in the bracelet, she would have been flattered at the attention. It had been a while since she'd taken an interest in anything but getting her business going. Cyrus Winchester interested her. Now more than ever.

"He didn't buy anything?"

"Nope." Kate stepped behind the counter to sort through some new stock she'd purchased at one of the last of the season's garage sales.

"Then why…"

Kate had shared only the basics of her past with her new friends in Whitehorse. There were some things she'd never told anyone. But she knew Andi and knew she would keep digging if she thought there was something going on. "Cyrus asked me out to dinner."

Andi narrowed her gaze. "Get out of here. You do know what he's doing in town, don't you? He's been asking a lot of questions about a murder."

Kate checked her expression before she looked up from her garage-sale finds. "Murder?"

"This is where it gets really weird," Andi said, looking around to make sure no one was within earshot. "There *wasn't* a murder. The night he spent in the old hospital he thinks he walked down to the nursery and found a nurse murdered there, but he couldn't have because he was in a coma the entire time and never left his bed."

"So he dreamed it?"

"He doesn't think so."

"How do you know this for a fact?" Kate demanded, not liking that this was what everyone in town was talking about.

"I have a source at the hospital," Andi whispered. "Her office is just outside the administrator's and she hears everything."

"So who did he think he saw murdered?" Kate asked, hating being part of the gossip and yet wanting to know more about Cyrus. Feeling as if she needed to know more about him and why he might be interested in her—and her mother's bracelet.

Andi shrugged. "All he said was that it was a nurse who worked at the hospital. And get this, he thinks there were two babies in the nursery that night."

"But there weren't any babies in the nursery."

Andi's eyes widened. "How do you know that?"

"Because I was there that night. Martha Ingram's father, Wally, was in the hospital and at her suggestion I stopped by to discuss buying some of the furnishings. You know she's on the hospital board. I think she thought talking about that would keep her mind off the fact that her father was dying."

"So did you see or hear anything?"

Kate shook her head.

"You didn't see Cyrus Winchester?"

"No. Martha and I talked out in the hallway. I saw the nurses behind the desk down the hall. Now that I think about it, I saw one of them go into the room next to the nurses' station to check on the only other patient." With a start she realized that had to have been Cyrus Winchester. "I just remember it was kind of weird with the hospital being so empty that night."

"Creepy," Andi said. "What if there really was a murder there that night?"

"I thought you said there wasn't?"

Andi shrugged. "Still, you have to admit, it's interesting that he is so determined there was a murder that he came all this way to check it out for himself. Clearly he's mistaken, since there was no murder victim found and no babies in the nursery that night."

Kate nodded, remembering the empty nursery she'd passed as she'd left that night three months before. Interesting? Or very odd? "I wonder why he's so convinced?"

"Maybe he's got a screw loose after being hit in the head or he just imagined it. You know he spent three months in a coma and only recently came out of it."

He was in a coma that long? Kate thought about how pale he'd looked when she'd seen him in the old hospital hallway earlier. He hadn't looked well. She was reminded that she'd thought then that he'd looked as if he'd seen a ghost.

"Well, I would imagine he will give up and go back to wherever he's from soon," she said.

"Denver. He's a private investigator in Denver with his twin brother, Cordell. They're the grandsons of Pepper Winchester, a recluse who lives on a ranch forty miles south of here. He's never been married."

Kate laughed, thinking now she really did have his life history. "You left out his shoe size and that he's quite handsome."

"You noticed? I thought you didn't have time for men?"

Andi had tried to set her up with several eligible bachelors when she'd first come to town, but Kate hadn't been interested. "So are you going out to dinner with him?"

"I'm busy tonight, but I might if he asks again." Kate realized that something had drawn her to Cyrus Winchester, something more than his good looks, as if they had some… connection—even before she'd seen his strange reaction to her mother's bracelet. As Andi had put it, creepy.

"I'm not sure you should go out with him," Andi said. "What if he *is* crazy? Jasmine said when you met him earlier at the old hospital he was looking for his room?"

"I was loading up the last of the furniture I bought at the auction. He said he wanted to see the room where he'd stayed that one night." But he hadn't been searching for his room. She got the feeling he'd gone straight to it.

"He came back to the scene of the crime?"

Kate realized that was probably exactly what he'd been doing. In fact, he'd said something to that effect. She shivered now at the memory.

Another group of women entered the shop on a fresh blast of cold air and autumn leaves. "I wonder if there ever have been any murders at the old hospital?" Kate whispered as the women disappeared into the back of the shop.

"None that I know of," Andi said, thoughtfully.

Kate knew her friend. If anyone could track it down, it was Andi. "Let me know what you find out."

A country-western band played on a flatbed trailer parked along the main drag. Fall Festival was in full swing by the time Cyrus got there. He hadn't seen Kate Landon, wasn't even sure she'd show up.

Seeing that silver bracelet in her shop had thrown him for a loop. Then when she'd told him it had belonged to her mother...

He'd gone back to his hotel room and spent most of the afternoon trying to make sense of it, as if any of this made any sense. Maybe seeing Kate and the bracelet was just a coincidence. Just like the murder had been nothing more than his overactive imagination at work.

His head hurt and he tried to put all of it out of his mind as he walked along the crowded streets clustered with booths offering everything from crafts and home-grown pumpkins to Christmas-tree ornaments and baked goods.

A mixture of alluring scents floated along the street: burgers, chocolate, coffee, hot apple cider, barbecue, cotton candy. But one scent in particular drew him until he found the booth where women were making frybread.

He breathed in the delicious aroma, remembering another fall when he was five and his father brought him and Cordell into town for the Fall Festival.

"Two?" the woman behind the counter asked.

Cyrus started. Did he look as if he needed two frybreads? That's when he noticed Kate had come up beside him and was doing the same thing he'd done, breathing in the wonderful aroma.

Her eyes were closed as she breathed in the scent of the frying bread, her expression one of unmitigated pleasure. He smiled to himself, guessing he'd had the same look on his face just moments before.

"Two," he confirmed as Kate Landon opened her beautiful green eyes. He couldn't believe how happy he was to see her and that happiness had nothing to do with his reason for coming to Whitehorse. "I take it you like frybread," he said with a grin.

"I *love* frybread. This is why I wasn't about to miss the Fall Festival or miss seeing you again." She seemed to blush as her last words came out. As he handed her one of the confections covered with sugar and cinnamon, she said, "Thank you, but you didn't have to buy mine."

"My pleasure," he said, taking his own and motioning to one of the picnic tables in the small park by the railroad line that still took passengers as far as Seattle or Chicago and all points beyond.

"How is the haunted house coming along?" Cyrus asked as he took a seat across from her.

"Slowly but surely. I've been so busy with getting all the furnishings out of the old hospital and opening my shop that I'm behind." She took a bite of her frybread, emitting a soft satisfying groan.

He watched her, smiling as she licked the sugar and cinnamon from her lips, making it hard for him to concentrate on the questions he wanted to ask her.

"So are you a Whitehorse native?"

She opened her eyes and shook her head. "West Yellowstone."

"That's quite a change, from a tourist town surrounded by mountains to a prairie town on the Hi-Line just miles from Canada. How did you end up here?" he asked. It was an odd place for a single woman to open a business—unless she came with a husband or a lover, or had family here, he thought.

She chewed for a moment. "You know how some people spin the globe, close their eyes and pick a spot at random?"

He nodded. "I understand that's how a lot of towns along the Hi-Line got their names—Malta, Zurich, Glasgow."

"Well, it wasn't quite that impulsive, but close."

"So you don't have any family here?"

"I didn't know a soul when I arrived four months ago, but people are friendly here and I've settled in fairly well."

"You must like it if you started a business."

"Now *that* was impulsive," she admitted with a laugh. "I just happened to hit town during an auction. As you might guess, I'm a sucker for auctions and garage sales. When I saw that old library building was being auctioned off, it was love at first sight and the price was dirt cheap. Of course it needs work…." She shrugged, her cheeks dimpling as she smiled.

He thought she couldn't look cuter with a few grains of sugar and cinnamon at the corner of her mouth, her emerald eyes sparkling and that smile on her lips.

"How about you? Other than visiting your former hospital room, what brings you to Whitehorse?" she asked.

He realized she'd just been waiting for her turn to ask

him questions. He figured she hadn't been kidding earlier about knowing his life history and wondered what in particular she wanted to know. "Originally, it was because of my grandmother. She'd been a recluse for twenty-seven years so I haven't seen her since I was seven. I got a letter from her lawyer, saying she wanted to see me and the rest of her family." He shrugged. "Pepper Winchester is...well, there is no one like her. She'd make a great wicked witch for your haunted house."

Kate laughed, a wonderful, light sound that made the night feel even more magical. "Was she really that bad when you saw her?"

"I haven't seen her yet. I got waylaid in June when I drove up to see her."

"The coma," Kate said, sobering. "What happened?"

He gave her an abbreviated version of what he'd been told by his brother and had read in the local paper. He got the feeling she might have already heard some of it. What he didn't tell her was that he now knew why his grandmother had asked him and the rest of the family to come back to Winchester Ranch.

It had to do with his uncle, Trace Winchester. Trace was the youngest son of Pepper and Call Winchester and Pepper's favorite. Just recently it was discovered that Trace was murdered twenty-seven years ago.

Before that he was believed to have taken off, running from a pregnant wife and a poaching charge.

Cyrus's grandmother, it seemed, believed that a member of the family might have been involved in Trace's murder. She was getting everyone back to the ranch to question them.

She particularly wanted to question her grandsons after discovering they might have witnessed something from a third-floor room at the ranch—a forbidden room that had once been used as punishment.

"It sounds like trouble has a way of finding you," she said, studying him. "My instincts tell me to give you a wide berth. Tell me I'm wrong about that."

"I'd listen to your instincts," Cyrus said, sounding and looking serious.

Kate wished she could. But her instincts also told her that this man knew something about her mother.

Not just that. She'd noticed when he told about how he'd ended up in a coma, that he'd left out the part about how he'd saved Raine Chandler's life.

After helping Jasmine finish the ghost costumes, Kate had made a point of reading the article about Cyrus her friend Andi had been kind enough to print out for her. She'd remembered most of the articles about the child molesters from several months ago, but hadn't put the names together.

Cyrus had almost lost his life. As it was he'd lost three months. The man was a hero, an honor she saw he didn't wear comfortably.

Was that why she feared—even though the odds were against it—that he really had seen a murder at the hospital? But how could that have anything to do with her mother or her bracelet?

She finished her frybread, wiped her fingers on the napkin and dabbed at her mouth. She knew she was taking time to screw up her courage and it wasn't like her. She thought of herself as being fearless—at least most of the time.

"I need you to tell me why you reacted the way you did earlier when you saw my mother's bracelet," she said bluntly.

Just as she'd expected, she caught him flat-footed. He didn't seem to know what to say.

"I know you think you saw a murder at the old hospital the night you were a patient there," she continued quickly. She'd heard concern in his voice, and when she looked into his dark eyes now she saw worry for her there. There was a connection, just as she'd feared.

"It has something to do with me, doesn't it?" she said. "That's why you looked as if you'd seen a ghost when you saw me at the old hospital, why you came by the shop and why you were so upset when you saw my mother's silver bracelet."

He stared at her in surprise and maybe a little awe and she knew she'd connected the dots correctly. Her heart hammered in her chest. She'd hoped he'd ask her what the devil she was talking about. Or at least try to convince her she had gotten it all wrong.

"Are you sure you want to hear about it?" he asked quietly.

Her pulse thundered in her ears at the gravity in his voice. "Yes." She'd gotten this far in life by meeting obstacles head-on. She couldn't stop now. Taking a breath, she asked the one question she feared the most. "Does this have something to do with my mother?"

"Why would you think what I have to tell you might involve your mother?"

She shook her head. As far back as she could remember, she'd had a feeling that her mother hadn't died the way her grandmother had told her.

"I have my reasons," she said.

He just looked at her. She could tell he didn't want this to be about her mother any more than she did.

"Do you have a picture of her?" he asked finally.

"Back at the shop." As she pushed to her feet, her legs felt weak as water. After all these years, was she finally going to find out what really had happened to her mother? Or was it just as her grandmother had told her and everything else was nothing but a child's overactive imagination?

She hated questioning the stories her grandmother had told. Would she be questioning her mother's death now if it wasn't for that postcard she'd found in her grandmother's jewelry box?

On the walk back, Cyrus asked about her mother and the bracelet.

"My grandmother told me she died of pneumonia just after I was born."

"You don't believe that?"

She shook her head, clearly not wanting to get into her reasons.

"What about your father?"

"He was in the military, killed before I was born in some training exercise that went wrong. They were to be married when he came home on leave. He didn't even know my mother was pregnant with me when he died."

She'd never known either of her parents? Cyrus thought about his own mother, who'd hung in with his father just long enough to give birth to her twin boys before she'd split. He'd never gone looking for her, though sometimes he thought about it.

"My grandmother, Dimple, raised me."

"Dimple?"

She laughed. "A nickname. She had these wonderful deep dimples when she smiled and she smiled a lot." Her own smile faded. "She passed away four months ago."

Four months. Right before Kate had come to Whitehorse.

"So Landon was your mother's name as well as yours."

He could see that talking was taking her mind off the reason they were walking back to her shop.

"Yes."

Cyrus was as nervous as she was about seeing photographs of her mother. Kate's resemblance to the woman he'd seen murdered was too much of a coincidence, then throw in the bracelet... Still, he reminded himself that everyone in town swore there had never been a murder. But for his own sanity, he desperately needed to know why he'd dreamed all of this.

They had almost reached Second Hand Kate's when Cyrus asked, "How old were you when your grandmother gave you your mother's bracelet?"

"She didn't." Kate still felt the betrayal. Why hadn't her grandmother given it to her? "I found the bracelet after my grandmother died. It was hidden in the back of her jewelry box." Along with the postcard.

"Hidden?"

"I don't think my grandmother could bear seeing it." Or didn't want Kate to see it for some reason, she thought. Just like the hidden postcard.

They stopped at the bottom of the wide concrete stairs that led up to the front door of the shop. Suddenly Kate was afraid to go inside. All these years she'd told herself she wanted to know the truth. But did she? What if her mother had simply run off and her grandmother's story was only to protect her?

"I don't see what any of this has to do with the bracelet or my mother. She couldn't be the woman you saw in your dream. How would that be possible?"

"I'm sure you're right."

So why was she so frightened? She knew the reason. "The woman you saw in your dream resembled me, didn't she?"

"Yes."

She took that news like a blow even though she'd suspected as much given his reaction to her at the hospital. She looked into his handsome face and saw real concern for her. He was as scared as she was that somehow the murder he'd seen involved her.

"Let's get this over with." Kate pulled out her keys, her fingers trembling as she tried to get the key into the front-door lock.

Cyrus gently took the key ring from her and opened the door.

"Thank you." He handed the keys back. She stepped past him to turn on a light and heard him close and lock the door behind them. A car went by with a burst of teenagers' laughter. In the distance, Kate could hear the low hum of activity at the festival, but the deeper they moved into the old library building, the more deafening the quiet became.

"If you'll wait here, I'll go up and get the photograph album," she said and hurried up the stairs. She hadn't invited him up because she needed a moment to herself. At the top, she had to stop and catch her breath. The weight of what was about to happen sat like a boulder on her chest.

The album was where she'd put it in the hall closet. Taking it down carefully, she hugged it to her. These were the only photographs she had of her mother and like the bracelet, they were priceless to her.

When she felt a little steadier, she headed back downstairs. She told herself that Cyrus Winchester's dream couldn't possibly be about her mother. Because her mother hadn't been in Whitehorse three months ago. Because in her heart, she knew her mother was dead. But what scared her was that she also knew her mother hadn't died the way her grandmother had told her.

As she came down the stairs, she found him waiting where she'd left him. She motioned to a Victorian velvet couch and carried the album over to it to sit down.

Cyrus joined her. He looked as nervous as she felt as she opened the album to the photographs of her mother taken thirty years ago.

"This is Elizabeth, my mother." Carefully, she slid the album over to him and held her breath.

Cyrus glanced down at the young woman in the snapshot. She was holding a baby in her arms and smiling at the camera. She had auburn hair and wide green eyes and her resemblance to Kate was disturbing—Elizabeth Landon had looked just like her at about the same age.

He could practically hear Kate holding her breath next to him. "She's not the woman I saw murdered."

Her breath came out on a sob. She stumbled to her feet and stood with her back to him for a moment. He thought about going to her, trying to offer her some comfort, but feared it would not be welcome. He was the one who'd put her through this pain. And for what?

Cyrus looked down at the photo album in his lap, studying the woman and baby for a long moment before turning his attention to the other photographs.

He felt his heart drop to the pit of his stomach and must have made a sound because Kate turned to look at him.

"Who is this woman?" His voice sounded odd even to him.

Kate made a swipe at her tears as she looked from him to the album in his lap. His tone must have warned her because she stepped almost cautiously back to the couch and stood looking down at the open photo album.

"What woman?" she asked in a desolate voice.

"That one." He pointed to another young woman. In the photograph she sat in a corner chair holding a baby. Kate, he assumed. What was haunting was that her features were nearly identical to Elizabeth Landon's, but he had known at a glance that they were not the same woman.

Her hair wasn't auburn but bleached blond. The wide blue-green eyes were unmistakable, although there was a sadness in them as well as in her expression.

"That's Aunt Katherine, my mother's older sister," she said in barely a whisper. "I was named after her. People used to say they looked so much alike they could have been twins." Kate raised her gaze as she said it. She bit her lip, her eyes flooding with tears as she lowered herself to the couch. "Aunt Katherine is the woman you saw."

He hadn't had to answer. She'd seen his expression and was already shaking her head. "That's not possible. Katherine's been dead for thirty years. She died just before I was six months old. She'd always had a weak heart..."

Cyrus stared down at Aunt Katherine's photo, wondering what in the hell was going on. This was the woman he'd seen lying in a pool of blood in the old hospital nursery. This was the woman who'd switched the babies just moments before her death and what had weakened this woman's heart was the scalpel that had stabbed her in the chest.

# Chapter 6

Kate couldn't catch her breath.

"Look, everyone keeps telling me it was just a bad dream and obviously it must be," Cyrus said. "I don't understand any of this, like why I dreamed about this woman or that bracelet or why when I saw you and realized how much you looked like..." His eyes widened in alarm as he seemed to realize how much distress she was in. "Kate, I'm so sorry. I—"

"Please," she managed to say as she stumbled to her feet again. "I need you to leave."

"Kate—"

"I just need to be alone."

He shot to his feet. "Of course. I'm sorry. I should never..." For a moment, he looked as if he might reach for her to try to comfort her.

She took a step back. She knew that if he took her in his arms she would break down completely.

"I'm staying at the Whitehorse Hotel, room 412. If you need to get hold of me just to talk or…"

Kate could see how sorry he was for upsetting her, but right now she couldn't deal with any of it. She felt as if her world was crumbling around her. She ushered him out, then stood with her back against the locked door, shaking so hard she had to hug herself to keep from falling apart.

She'd thought she wanted to know the truth. But she'd been so sure he would say he didn't recognize her mother. And he had. She'd been so relieved.

Until he'd asked about her aunt Katherine, the woman she'd been named for. She'd never dreamed the woman he'd thought he'd seen murdered would be her aunt.

All the doubts she'd had her whole life shot to the surface. Kate had lived on the stories her grandmother had told about her mother and her aunt. Even as a child, she'd known her grandmother had exaggerated many of the stories.

For some time now, she had suspected it had been more than Dimple just not being truthful with her.

If her grandmother had lied about the way Aunt Katherine died, then didn't it follow that she'd lied about Kate's mother's death, as well?

So what had really happened to them?

She quickly reminded herself that Cyrus Winchester's coma dream might be just that, nothing more than a weird nightmare. But like him, she was having a hard time believing that, given that he'd identified her aunt as the murder victim in his dream—a woman who'd been dead for almost as many years as Cyrus had been alive.

According to Cyrus, Katherine had been murdered in the Whitehorse hospital nursery. Kate thought of the postcard from her mother that she'd found hidden in her grandmother's jewelry box—and the postmark on it. The card had been dated thirty years ago this December—several years after her grandmother had sworn both daughters had died.

The postcard from her mother made it clear that both her aunt and mother had been in Whitehorse. Wasn't it possible that Cyrus Winchester's dream was the missing piece of the puzzle she'd been searching for?

Suddenly, Kate felt a chill. What if the reason no one believed Cyrus's story was because the murder hadn't happened three months ago—it had happened thirty years ago?

Cyrus mentally kicked himself as he'd stepped out into the cold fall evening air and heard Kate lock the shop door behind him. She was afraid of him, probably thought he was a psychopath or at the very least a sadist.

He should have realized that the only reason she'd shown him the photograph of her mother was that she wanted him to tell her the murdered woman wasn't her mother.

He'd been shocked when he'd recognized the aunt's photograph. That was definitely the woman he'd seen. But how was that possible? Kate said her aunt had died of a weak heart more than thirty years ago—she hadn't been murdered in the hospital after switching two baby boys in the nursery. What was wrong with him going to Kate with all this?

Because he'd hoped that she held the answers.

Now all he had was more questions. Still he was reeling from what she had told him. Both her mother and aunt had died thirty years ago when Kate was only a baby?

And neither had been murdered?

All he'd done was bring up bad memories for her. He wished to hell he'd never had the dream. But then he would never have met Kate. Yeah? Well, he should have just left it alone. Because Kate didn't want anything to do with him now. Not that he could blame her.

Cyrus drove to the Whitehorse Hotel and sat for a while in his pickup, unable to face the desolate room, cursing himself and trying to make sense of all this. Since he'd awakened from his coma he hadn't thought about anything else. All it had done, though, was give him a headache.

He'd been so sure Kate was the reason he'd been drawn back to Whitehorse.

Now he didn't know what to think.

Shaking his head, he climbed out of the pickup behind the old brick hotel. He had no memory of this place, but it was here in this very poorly lit parking lot that he'd almost lost his life.

The night was cold and clear, trillions of stars flickering over his head and a moon as large and golden as any he'd ever seen. He stopped for a moment to find the Big Dipper, just as he had done as a kid, and then went inside to climb the stairs to his fourth-floor room.

What he hated the most was that he couldn't get the mess out of his mind. If Katherine Landon had died from a weak heart thirty years ago, then how could he have seen her lying in a pool of blood in the old hospital nursery? And what about the babies he swore he saw her switch? What had become of them—if they ever existed?

As much as he hated upsetting Kate, he still felt as if the damned dream was real and that not only was the answer here in Whitehorse, but Kate was the key.

Kate paced the floor after Cyrus left, too shaken to sit still. Her mind was racing. None of this was true. It had just been a dream. Dreams meant nothing.

So why was she so upset?

Because she hadn't told him everything.

She stopped pacing. Standing in the middle of her shop, she tried to talk herself out of what she was about to do, but it was useless. Retrieving the envelope from the safe behind the counter, she grabbed her jacket and purse, locked up the shop and headed for her van.

Wisps of clouds drifted across the harvest moon that seemed to hang over Whitehorse. An omen? She laughed at that. She'd already seen the future—and the past, she thought as she parked behind the Whitehorse Hotel.

At room 412, she almost changed her mind.

Cyrus opened the door to her quiet knock. He seemed surprised—and pleased—to see her standing there and maybe a little wary. "Kate," was all he said as he held the door open.

She entered and heard him close the door behind her. Out of habit and no doubt to keep her mind off the real reason she was here, her gaze went to the furnishings. A couple of pieces in the room she wouldn't mind having for her shop—after she'd refinished them.

"I'm not sure why I came here," she said, turning to look at him.

"It doesn't matter, I'm just glad you're here. Would you like something to drink? I can get us a cold soda from down the hall."

"That sounds good." After he left, she walked to the window, glanced out at the darkness and told herself she had to be honest with him. She knew how hard it had been for him to tell her about his dream.

And more than ever she believed that they'd both ended up here in Whitehorse for a reason.

Kate turned as he came back. She took the icy-cold can of diet cola he handed her, glad to have something to do with her hands, and opened it to take a sip. It felt good going down. She met his gaze and was strengthened by the kind look on his face.

"I thought we should talk," she said.

Cyrus sat down on the edge of the bed, motioning for her to take the only chair in the room. It was a straight-back wooden chair much like the ones she'd purchased from the old hospital.

"The reason I got so upset earlier was that I've never understood why my mother would leave me when I was just a baby," she said after taking a seat. "The truth is I don't know what really happened to my mother or my aunt. But I know my mother didn't die of pneumonia. My grand-mother—"

"Dimple."

Kate smiled. "Yes, Dimple. She used to tell me stories about my mother and aunt and what they were like grow-ing up. I'm not sure anything she told me was the truth. I know my mother, Elizabeth Landon, left me when I was six months old. This I know from a postcard I found in my grandmother's jewelry box after her death. It was post-marked Whitehorse, Montana."

"That's why you came here," Cyrus said.

She nodded. "It was the last place I knew my mother had been. But once I got here, I couldn't find any evidence of that. Whitehorse was the end of the trail."

"In more ways than one," he said.

Kate nodded. "Not everyone appreciates Whitehorse. From the moment I arrived here, I just felt that the answer was in this town." She caught his change of expression. "You believe that, too, don't you?"

He did, but he wasn't ready to admit it. Any more than he was ready to admit that any of this made any sense at this point. "You don't know why your mother was in Whitehorse?"

She shook her head. "All the postcard said was that she was sorry she had to leave when she did and was grateful to my grandmother for taking good care of me and that she would be home soon. She said she was bringing my aunt Katherine home with her."

"You don't know if that was the last time your grandmother heard from her?"

"No. The date on the postcard was months after my grandmother said both my mother and aunt had died. I'd always thought it peculiar that my aunt and mother would die within weeks of each other. But Dimple said she thought it was because they had been so close and loved each other so much."

"You have reason to believe that isn't true?"

Kate knew what he was asking. Did she have reason other than just her intuition? "My grandmother saved everything. All her important papers, like my birth certificate, were in her safe-deposit box. There were no death certificates other than my grandfather's in the box."

Cyrus shook his head as if he wasn't sure what she was saying. "Maybe she never put them in the safe-deposit box at the bank."

"There are no death certificates for either my aunt or my mother. She made up the stories because she didn't know what happened to them."

"Surely your grandmother would have notified the authorities," Cyrus said. "She would have had someone out looking for her daughters."

"Unless they vanished. Or appeared to."

He got up and moved to the window to gaze out. "There has to be a logical explanation."

"I'm sure there is. I think you saw what really happened to my aunt in your dream—not three months ago, but thirty years ago."

Cyrus laughed as he turned back to her. "You can't believe that."

Kate pulled out the envelope she'd taken from her safe. "When I first came to town, I asked around about my mother. I knew she'd at least passed through town because of the postcard. Whitehorse was the only lead I had."

"I take it you didn't learn anything?"

"No one had heard of her and I couldn't find any evidence she was here."

"I'm sorry."

"But my efforts weren't wasted. After a few weeks of asking around, I received this." She handed him the envelope.

There was nothing written on the envelope but Cyrus could see that it had been dusted for fingerprints. He opened it and pulled out the brief note inside. The printing was childlike, almost a scrawl.

*Unless you want to end up like your mother, stop looking for her.*

He glanced up at Kate. "You took this to the sheriff?" he asked even though he knew she had because of the fingerprint dust.

Kate nodded. "It was a different sheriff than the one we have now. He checked it for fingerprints but said the person must have used latex gloves, which right there made me suspicious, since the only prints on the envelope or note were mine."

"But he didn't take the threat seriously," Cyrus guessed.

Kate shook her head. "He said there wasn't anything more he could do, but that I was to come to him if there were any further threats."

"And there weren't."

"No. The sheriff was convinced it was just someone fooling around, maybe even a kid."

"A kid who was smart enough to use latex gloves?"

"Exactly. That's why I think something happened to my mother here in Whitehorse to keep her from returning home. She wouldn't have just abandoned me or my grandmother."

He heard the plea in her voice. She wanted desperately to believe that. "There hasn't been any sign of your mother since the postcard was sent from Whitehorse?"

She shook her head. "None. As I said, it's as if she simply vanished."

"If your aunt and mother simply disappeared, then how did your grandmother get your aunt's bracelet and where is your mother's?"

Kate shook her head. "My grandmother didn't have a memorial service for my aunt or mother until I was almost a year old. She told her friends that she wanted to wait until the weather was nicer. She said there was no rush since both my aunt and mother had been cremated."

"Did your grandmother say where they died?" he asked.

"Not in West Yellowstone, that's for sure," she said. "You see why I got so upset when you said it was my aunt you saw murdered here in Whitehorse."

He put the note back into the envelope. The handwriting was *childish*, but he assumed that it been on purpose. Whoever had written it had expected her to take it to the sheriff.

"You didn't do any more investigating on your own?"

Kate shook her head. "I'd hit a wall. The note made me believe I was on to something, but I didn't know what else to do. I ran my mother's photo in the newspaper. No one ever came forward."

Cyrus saw her hesitate. He watched her take a drink of her soda, then put it down on the desk before she said, "There's more. I've never told anyone, but I used to have a recurring nightmare when I was little. My mother was calling to me, trying to reach me, but something was keeping her from coming to me." She shivered as if the nightmare still gave her chills. "I could hear her voice so clearly. I never doubted it was her."

"I'm sorry. I know how real a dream can be."

She looked toward the window, hugging herself as if against the cold. "What made the nightmare so frightening for me was when my mother was calling to me I could hear something in the background..." Kate turned to look at him. "It was the sound of a baby crying. There were babies in the nursery in your dream that night, weren't there?"

"Two baby boys." He didn't mention that he saw the woman he believed was her aunt switch the babies just minutes before she was killed. "But, Kate, I dreamed it was three months ago—not thirty years. How could I have seen something while I was comatose that happened thirty years ago?"

"I don't know, but I believe you did. How else do you explain all of this?"

He couldn't explain any of it. And maybe worse, a part of him believed it.

Kate let out a sigh. "You wouldn't have come all this way and chanced looking like a fool if you didn't believe that what you saw in that dream was real."

"Right now I'm questioning my own sanity." Did he really believe dreams could reveal the future or the past? He'd come to Whitehorse because he was convinced he *hadn't* dreamed the murdered woman.

"What if it was just a bad dream, Kate, and all of this can be explained rationally?"

"You mean like explaining how it was that you recognized my aunt?" she challenged. "How old were you thirty years ago?"

"Four."

"Are you going to tell me you just happened to see her and that's how she ended up in your dream?"

"Maybe." He knew his brother, Cordell, would use that as an argument. "I was in Whitehorse thirty years ago. Maybe I saw her at the Fall Festival."

"Maybe you did. Maybe that's why the dream was so real for you, because you had seen her before."

He felt a chill snake up his spine. Was it possible that he'd remembered her all these years for some reason? *This reason,* he thought, looking at Kate.

"Cyrus, I know my mother mailed a postcard from this town thirty years ago saying she and my aunt would be coming home. My aunt was in this town. I have no idea what she was doing here or why my mother was here."

He shook his head. "I have not been able to prove one thing about my dream was true. That is why I'm so sorry that I involved you in it."

Kate smiled as she touched his arm, her gaze locking with his. "Haven't you figured it out yet? Your dream brought you here to me because together we're going to find out the truth."

He smiled back because he wanted to believe they were destined to meet. But to find a murderer? "Are you sure you want to know the truth?" he asked quietly, fearing Kate Landon didn't have any idea what she was getting into. Worse, how dangerous it might get.

"Yes, with your help," she said with a determined lift of her chin.

Cyrus appreciated her faith in him and told her as much. "The problem is that it's been thirty years. There's more than a good chance that you might never learn the truth—especially if foul play was involved. The killer has had years to cover his or her tracks."

"But there has never been a hotshot cowboy investigator looking for the truth before," she said, grinning at him.

Cyrus was flattered, but they needed hard evidence. He knew there was little chance of solving this and he'd never been the kind of man who chased rainbows—not until he'd had that damned dream.

He was reminded of the weight of the dream when he'd awakened from his coma. He'd felt such a need to tell someone. If a woman had been killed in the hospital nursery, why had he felt he had to tell anyone about it? She would have been found. It wasn't as if he'd seen the killer.

That feeling that he was meant to come here, meant to meet this woman, overwhelmed him. The answer *was* in this town, but so was the danger.

"If your aunt and mother were in Whitehorse thirty years ago, there would be some evidence of that."

"I couldn't find any," Kate said. "But from the first day I drove into town, I felt a connection to Whitehorse."

Just as he felt a connection to this woman standing before him. He could smell the sweet scent of her soap. He hoped she couldn't hear the erratic beat of his heart just at having her this near.

As she looked at him, something changed in all the emerald-green. He glimpsed a flicker of desire there, saw her slim throat work and wondered if she had been holding her breath as he had.

"It's late," he heard himself say.

She nodded. "I should go."

He nodded, knowing that if she continued to stand there looking at him like that he was going to kiss her. "We don't want the whole town talking about you and that crazy cowboy who has coma murder dreams."

"Wouldn't want that."

Cyrus walked her down to her vehicle even though she told him she would be fine. He was worried about her and not just because of his damned dream. She was putting her faith in him. He couldn't let her down. And he feared that if he kissed her, it wouldn't stop there. One day soon he had to get back to Denver and the investigations firm he ran with his brother.

He couldn't make Kate Landon any promises, and she was the kind of girl who deserved promises from a man.

"I'm glad you came to Whitehorse," she said when they reached her van.

"I hope you always feel that way," he said.

"Admit it, you believe there's a reason we both ended up here now."

He nodded, wishing the reason had only to do with the way he felt about her and not a murder—or two.

# Chapter 7

After getting very little sleep, Kate found herself going over what Cyrus had told her the night before. She had no idea how any of the pieces fit together. Babies, the hospital nursery, her mother, the postcard.

The only thing that made any sense was that Cyrus was supposed to help her find her aunt's murderer and figure out what had happened to her mother.

Kate didn't question that. She'd always believed there were things going on outside the realm of human understanding. If Cyrus had seen her aunt murdered in a dream, then Kate believed it was a message from the past.

And the fact that the dream had brought cowboy P.I. Cyrus Winchester to her meant they were to work together to solve this. She had faith that if anyone could find out the answers she so desperately needed, it was Cyrus.

At noon she put a *Closed* sign on the shop door to make preparations for the haunted house that coming weekend.

But something kept nagging at her.

As she passed the glass case with her mother's bracelet in it, she had a sudden urge to take it out and look at it.

Her grandmother had told her that when her grandfather made the bracelets, he'd wanted a way that the girls could tell them apart. That was why he'd put eleven bells on one and twelve on the other. Her mother's, she recalled, had eleven on it.

With trembling fingers, she used the key to open the glass cabinet and carefully took the bracelet. It felt cool to the touch. How many times had she held this, watching the silver play in the light, and wondered about her mother?

More times than she could remember.

Kate counted the bells. Eleven. It was her mother's, then. Had her mother left it behind? Is that how her grandmother happened to have it? What other explanation could there be?

She frowned, wondering if that was what had been nagging at her, or was there something else about the bracelet? Cyrus hadn't told her why he recognized it. Had her aunt been wearing hers when he'd seen her in the dream?

Her mother and Aunt Katherine had left a hole in her life that her grandmother Dimple had done everything humanly possible to fill. And she'd always known there was more to the story than her mother's early death.

With a sigh, she put the bracelet back, closed the case and hurried downstairs. She had too much work to do on the haunted house to think about this right now.

But as she headed for the basement, Kate wondered where her aunt's bracelet was. Her grandmother, who never threw anything away, would have kept it, of course.

So why hadn't it been in the jewelry box with her mother's?

Because her grandmother had never gotten it back.

* * *

Cyrus didn't have any trouble finding the Ingram place north of town, although he wasn't sure why he still felt he needed to talk to Martha Ingram about that night in the old hospital.

The Ingrams lived in a newer-model home on what appeared to be a few acres.

As he got out of his pickup, he spotted an older house behind it and wondered if that was where the now deceased Wally Ingram had lived.

Martha Ingram answered his knock and welcomed him inside. She was a tall, slender woman with a head of salt-and-pepper hair and crinkles around her eyes when she smiled.

The house smelled of pumpkin bread and he was reminded again of how many months he'd lost as he let her lead him into the warm living room. Outside it was one of those cold, crisp autumn days he was familiar with in Colorado.

"You said you wanted to ask about my father?" Martha asked once they were seated and he was holding a hot cup of coffee and had tried the pumpkin bread. It was delicious.

Cyrus couldn't help feeling he was wasting this woman's time and his own. But like Kate, he couldn't understand why he'd dreamed of her aunt if there wasn't something more to it. He explained that he'd been in the hospital that night.

Martha Ingram nodded. "I remember."

"You saw me?"

"I couldn't sleep so I walked down the hall to the nurses' station. I passed your room and saw you lying there. I hope you don't mind, I asked about your condition and was told by the nurses on duty that you were in a coma from a head injury. I'm so glad that you've obviously recovered so well."

"I heard I was hooked up to a lot of equipment."

"Oh, yes. The nurses were monitoring you. My father was only on a morphine drip to make him comfortable. We knew he would be passing soon, given his declining condition. It really was a godsend."

"I'm sorry for your loss."

She shook her head. "Don't be. My father had a wonderful life. He would have said as much himself."

Cyrus liked her attitude. "Your father must have been very special."

"He was," she said, her voice breaking. "I will always miss him."

He hesitated. Why was he bothering this woman so soon after her father's death when he already knew there was no possible way he'd seen a murder that night?

Because he felt he owed it to Kate to at least try to figure this out. "Did you hear anything when you were in your father's room or on one of your walks?"

"Like what?"

"Let me be honest with you. I thought there was a murder the night I spent in the old hospital."

"A *murder?*" She looked appalled.

"Did you ever see the nurses leave their station?"

"No. There was always at least one sitting there. As I said, they were closely monitoring you."

He saw something change in her expression. "You remembered something?"

"Well, yes, but I'm not sure if I should tell you this. I suppose it's all right. I had gone for another walk down the hall when I heard one of your monitors go off."

"Do you remember what time that was, by any chance?"

"No—wait, you know, I do. I remember looking up at the clock and being surprised at the time. It was a couple minutes after midnight. I remember thinking it felt later than that."

A couple minutes after midnight. The same time Cyrus had been convinced he'd gotten out of bed and walked down to the nursery to see the nurse's aide switch the babies— and end up murdered.


Kate was in the basement working on preparations for her haunted house when she felt a gust of cold air blow in from outside.

"Cyrus?" He'd called earlier to tell her about his plans to talk to Martha Ingram. She'd made him promise to stop by afterward to tell her how it went and had told him where she kept the spare key. "I'm down here. Cyrus?"

She listened, didn't hear anything and thought she must have imagined someone coming in one of the doors. Still, she felt a little spooked and that surprised her. Nothing about this building had ever given her any qualms. It had been love at first sight, which just showed how rattled she was, she thought now with a smile.

The basement under the old library building was dark and dank, a warren of spooky space that she'd known the moment she saw it would make a great haunted house. There were stairways on four sides that went up to the shop level. In the center was a labyrinth of wooden structures lined with bookshelves, making the basement a maze that would allow participants to come in one way and leave by another exit.

Kate had turned on the lights but they did little to illuminate the dark corners. Over the last few weeks, Andi and Jasmine had helped her turn the basement into something that would definitely be spooky come Halloween night.

Jasmine's latest creations, a trio of ghosts, now floated

on a cable above Kate's head. On Halloween they would float out of the darkness, promising to scare even the most cynical trick-or-treaters.

There were other monsters throughout the basement, including vampires, werewolves and the devil himself, who would pop up at the very end from a smoldering pit of fiery brimstone. Andi and Jasmine had gathered volunteers to man the stations and make sure everyone got through the maze safely.

Andi had come up with little alcoves with gruesome things to touch and smell, including what appeared to be a bowl of eyeballs, a dissected brain and a boiling caldron of witch's brew straight out of *Macbeth*.

As Kate worked to make sure everything was ready and in working order, she had trouble keeping her mind on the job at hand. Her thoughts kept going to Cyrus. Last night in his hotel room there'd been that awkward moment when she'd thought he was going to kiss her.

Kissing her had probably been the last thing on his mind. She sighed. Just as Cyrus probably didn't feel what she could only describe as chemistry between them. At least on her side.

She was so involved in thought that at first she wasn't sure she heard the sound. A stair to the basement creaked.

Then she heard it again. She froze, listening. Footsteps? Hadn't she thought just moments before that she'd felt a door open? Both Andi and Jasmine had keys and Cyrus would use the spare key she'd told him about. No one else had a key and she'd made sure all the doors were locked.

With a start, she realized how asinine that was. She hadn't had the locks replaced on the outside doors to the basement because of the expense. Who knew how many keys to this place were loose in Whitehorse from when it had been a library?

That thought did nothing for her growing anxiety. Some-one was slowly coming down the basement steps.

"Hello?" she called again, still sure it had to be someone she knew just trying to scare her in her own haunted house.

She couldn't see anything from where she stood next to the soon-to-be-writhing tub of hideous-looking rubber snakes that Andi had tagged the Viper Pit.

She heard another groan, but realized it wasn't com-ing from the stairs. It was coming from the short landing at the top of the steps, where all the electrical boxes were kept for the building.

Kate barely had the thought when the lights went out.


Cyrus felt his heart kick up several beats at the news Martha Ingram had given him. "What did the nurses do when my monitor went off?"

"They rushed into your room," Martha Ingram said. "I heard one of them say your eyes were open and you were... very agitated. But the monitor went back to its normal beep-ing and the nurses came out looking relieved. I asked if you were all right and they said you were. That you'd had some kind of weird episode."

A weird episode. His heart was in his throat. "But you're sure I didn't leave my bed."

"Oh, no. I can't see how you could have in your condition and with everything that was attached to you," she said. "I stood there and talked to the nurses for probably another twenty minutes after that and you didn't move an inch. The nurses seemed worried about you and kept checking the monitors and going into your room after that to make sure you were all right." She looked chagrined. "I hope I'm not speaking out of school here. I wouldn't want to get the nurses in trouble. They were so wonderful to my father and me and so worried about you."

Cyrus nodded. "Thank you. I think this does clear things up for me."

"So was there a murder that night?" she asked with a shiver.

"No. I guess it really was nothing more than a bad dream."

Martha smiled, clearly relieved, and offered him more coffee and pumpkin bread.

"Thank you, but I should be going. I appreciate you talking with me about this."

"Well, if I've relieved your mind, then I'm glad."

On the drive back into Whitehorse, he called Cordell after finding half a dozen messages from his brother.

"Is everything all right?" Cyrus asked, afraid something had happened to his brother. Most of the investigative cases they took weren't dangerous, but you never knew when one could turn that way.

"Everything is fine here," Cordell snapped. "I've been worried sick about you. Why haven't you returned my calls?"

"I met someone."

His twin let out a laugh of relief. "So you're feeling like your old self?"

Cyrus wasn't about to tell him how he'd met Kate or what the initial attraction had been. "I'm going to stay a few more days." He listened to the silence, knowing what his brother was waiting for. "You were right. It turns out there was no murder at the hospital the night I was there, just like you and everyone else said."

"Then I'm glad you went up there to check it out," Cordell said, sounding even more relieved.

"I'm going to a haunted house on Halloween. This woman I met, Kate Landon, is putting it on."

"A haunted house? This woman sounds perfect for you."

Cyrus laughed. "We do seem to have a lot in common." Cordell didn't know the half of it, he thought as he hung up.

Pitched into total blackness, Kate grabbed hold of the tub of rubber snakes, cringing as her fingers brushed one of the vipers. "This isn't funny!" she called out, her words echoing through the cavernous space. "I'm serious. Turn the lights back on. *Now.*"

On the far side of the basement she could make out a faint glow. Whoever it was had a small flashlight. She listened for a moment, feeling as if she could hear the person breathing. Her heart began to pound harder as she heard another creak of a wooden stair. Was the person leaving? Or coming down the steps toward her?

She fumbled for her cell phone, panic rising even as she told herself that no one would want to harm her. It was just a mistake. It had to be someone she knew thinking this was an amusing joke to play on her. Scare her in her own haunted house.

But at the thought of Cyrus and his murder dream, she quit kidding herself. Whoever this was— She dropped her cell phone. It fell into the huge tub of writhing snakes.

Hurriedly she felt around for it, searching frantically in all that cold rubber. No phone.

Suddenly the person stopped moving. She froze, listening to the chilling silence.

Then she heard another sound. What was that? She

couldn't place it. A squeaking noise that sent fear racing up her spine.

A moment later, a loud snap filled the air, then a hissing noise.

Kate sensed something coming at her through the dark and ducked—just not soon enough. She let out a cry as she was struck so hard it knocked her to the floor. Before she could move, feeling dazed and in pain, something fell over her, covering her like a blanket. She beat at the fabric, fighting for breath, until she realized it was only the cloth ghosts that had fallen on her.

With that realization came another on its heels. The person had cut the overhead cable that held some of the props. She touched her forehead, felt a scrape where the cable had struck her.

She heard footfalls on the stairs, then the side door to the basement banged closed, then open again if the cold air that came in was any indication. In the silence that followed, she decided whoever had cut the cable was gone. She tried to get to her feet in the blinding darkness and banged into something heavy, sending stars shooting across her vision.

"Kate? Kate!"

"Down here." Something in her voice sounded all wrong to Cyrus.

"What are you doing down there in the dark?" He felt his apprehension mounting when she didn't answer. He felt around for the light switch to the basement. He'd been concerned the moment he'd seen the side door to the basement standing wide open.

This late in October, the temperature often dropped down into the teens at night and barely got up to fifty during the day. Today had been particularly chilly because of the wind. He couldn't imagine why Kate would leave the door open when she'd told him where she kept the spare key.

He'd tried to call her at the shop and hadn't been able to reach her. That had sent up red flags, since she'd said she would be working on the haunted house and had been anxious to hear how his meeting had gone with Martha Ingram. But maybe she couldn't hear the phone in the basement and hadn't taken her cell phone down with her since it went straight to voice mail.

When he'd swung by the shop he'd seen the side door standing open.

"Kate?" Cyrus called again as he found the light switch and the lights came on.

She made an angry sound, a cross between a sob and a curse.

"Kate?" He hurried down the stairs. Had she fallen? Had the power gone off? Had—

He spotted her fighting off three ghosts as she tried to get to her feet. Lying next to her along with the discarded ghosts was a thick cable coiled on the concrete floor. "What happened?"

She looked up at him and he saw where the cable had struck her forehead and realized that it must have snapped. A deep-seated fear rushed at Cyrus. He remembered the first time he'd seen her coming down the hall at the old hospital. What if his damned dream was a premonition that something was going to happen to Kate?

"Are you all right?" he asked, hurrying to her. She was trembling as he helped her to her feet and surveyed her injury. There was a bright-red scrape where the cable had hit her, bloody to the touch, but other than that, she seemed to be all right.

"Don't worry, I can fix the cable and I'll make sure this

time it doesn't come undone again," he said as he looked into her beautiful green eyes.

"It didn't come undone. Someone cut it. I heard them come in and…" She waved a hand through the air. "I pulled out my cell phone just before the person turned off the lights and cut the cable—and dropped it into the tub with the snakes."

"Here, let me," he said and felt around in the snakes until he located the phone. He handed it to her.

"I guess someone doesn't like haunted houses," she said as she turned on her phone. "I must have turned it off when I was trying to call 911."

"I guess." Cyrus felt sick. This had nothing to do with the haunted house and she damn well knew it. If he'd had any doubt that his dream meant something, he didn't anymore.

# Chapter 8

"Go ahead and say it," Kate said holding Cyrus's dark gaze. "I'm right. Or are you going to try to convince me whoever did this really doesn't like haunted houses?"

"You could have been killed," he said, sounding angry, although it was fear and concern for her behind the anger.

She'd never met anyone like this man.

"If we keep digging into this—"

"So you're just willing to drop it?" she demanded.

"Kate—"

"You know it wasn't just a dream. You've always known. You knew the moment you saw my mother's bracelet, don't deny it. You saw the bracelet in your dream, didn't you?"

He nodded slowly, reluctantly. "It was lying beside her. One of the bells had fallen off."

Kate felt her heart stop. "What?" Suddenly she felt faint again. "Are you sure?"

"What's wrong?"

"My grandfather made the bracelets a little different so my mother and aunt could tell them apart. My mother's had only eleven bells. My aunt's had twelve. The one upstairs has eleven. What if it isn't my mother's?"

He shook his head. She could tell he was as confused as she was.

"But if it's my aunt's, then how did my grandmother get it? And where is my mother's bracelet?"

"Kate, you don't want to do this," he said, lowering his voice to what felt like a caress. "I can't bear to see you hurt. Or worse."

She looked into his dark, bottomless gaze and wondered if they were still talking about the murder—or about what was happening between them. "Is that it or is it some kind of cowboy code?"

He looked confused for a moment, then realized she wasn't talking about murder. "I don't want to hurt you."

"I can take care of myself."

He dragged his Stetson from his head and raked a hand through his dark, thick hair. "Someone just tried to hurt you."

"Which proves I'm right." Kate closed the distance between them. Her palm cupped his wonderfully handsome face. She had to go up on her tiptoes to reach his mouth. Her lips brushed over his.

She could feel Cyrus's chivalrous cowboy code trying to intervene.

But she won him over as she kissed him again.

His arm looped around her waist and he dragged her to him with a groan, deepening the kiss as if, like her, he'd been wanting to do this almost since the first time he'd laid eyes on her.

A live wire of current shot through her veins, settling

at her center. She felt a jolt of desire so strong it made her toes curl.

Who knows what would have happened if her cell phone hadn't rung.

Cyrus drew back, looking shaken by the kiss and the desire he couldn't hide in his gaze. "You'd better answer that," he said, sounding breathless.

She glanced at the caller ID. It was Andi and it was marked urgent.

Cyrus watched Kate take the call, both relieved and sorry for the interruption. He knew instinctively that Kate wasn't the kind of woman who took making love with a man lightly. And because of that he couldn't possibly let it happen. After Halloween he had to get back to Denver, get back to work, get back to his life.

But the thought came with a strange feeling of regret. After coming out of the coma, he'd been anxious to get to Montana and find out the truth about his murder dream. But then he'd always known he would go back to Winchester Investigations. He enjoyed his work and normally would be champing at the bit to get back to it.

However, nothing had been normal since he'd seen Kate in the old hospital hallway. He had a feeling nothing would be normal again.

Still, as she hung up the phone, he reminded himself of all the reasons kissing Kate again would be a very bad idea. Because he knew that what he wanted more than anything was to make love to this woman and one more kiss...

As she stuck the cell phone into her jacket pocket, she said, "That was my friend Andi. She's a reporter for the *Milk River Examiner,* our local weekly newspaper, and she just found what she believes is the only murder ever committed at the old hospital."

"Kate—" Cyrus wasn't even sure what he'd planned to say. No doubt an apology for kissing her the way he had. But she didn't give him a chance.

"Don't you see what this means?" she demanded, waving an arm to encompass the basement. For a moment he thought she was talking about the kiss, about the passion that had sparked between them. "Whoever cut that cable doesn't want us finding out what really happened to my aunt and my mother. This proves it and now Andi has found an old murder she said she thinks we'll be interested in."

He couldn't believe this. She was just going to ignore the kiss, ignore what had just happened between them? He knew damn well she'd felt it, too. Or, like him, was she afraid to look too closely at whatever was developing between them? If anything?

Kate was looking at him as if she couldn't understand why he was still standing there, why he wasn't excited about this news. She obviously was.

He stared at her. "This doesn't prove anything," he said, finding himself wanting to grab her and kiss some sense into her. "Except that, because of me, someone wants to hurt you."

"They must think I know something."

"But you don't know anything and neither do I. Except that there wasn't a murder the night I spent in the old hospital."

Her green gaze locked with his. She grinned at him, completely disarming him. "Don't look so upset," Kate said, brushing a lock of his hair back from his forehead. The tips of her fingers grazed his skin, shattering his senses.

"This is good news. It proves you aren't crazy. Take some encouragement in that."

He shook his head, unable to resist her. "I have never met anyone like you, Kate Landon."

"Trust me, you're my first psychic cowboy."

"If I were psychic I'd have seen that someone was going to cut the cable that hit you." *And I'd know what was going to happen with the two of us,* he thought, wishing for the first time that he was psychic. Then he would know if Kate was going to be safe.

"Let me say this again," he said. "Someone just tried to hurt you, possibly even kill you. If it really was about your aunt's death and your mother's disappearance, then us digging around in it could get you killed. I can't let that happen."

She smiled. "But you also can't stop me."

"Kate—"

"I need to get over to the newspaper. Are you coming or not?"

He looked into her eyes and knew that he would follow her anywhere, anytime. They were in this together. At least until he found out who had tried to hurt her. He had a bad feeling he already knew why.

Andi lifted a brow and mouthed "Hottie!" when Kate came into the newspaper office with Cyrus Winchester. Andi's expression changed, though, the moment she saw where the cable had connected with Kate's forehead. "What happened to you?"

"A little accident in the basement while she was finishing up the haunted house," Cyrus said. "I don't believe we've met." He held out his hand. "Kate has told me all about you."

Andi arched a brow as she shook his hand. "I've heard a lot about you, as well."

"I'll bet you have," Cyrus said and laughed. It was deep and throaty and Kate loved the sound. She looked over at him as he shoved back his Stetson. The man really was gorgeous. And boy, could he kiss. Her toes curled at the memory of being in his arms.

"I thought you might be interested in the only documented murder I could find at the old hospital," Andi said and led them back to the archives at the back of the small newspaper office.

Since the paper had gone out the day before, the office was nearly deserted except for a young woman doing billing.

The headline on the newspaper article Andi had found jumped out at Kate, making her heart begin to pound.

Nurse Found Murdered in Hospital

Her gaze flew to the date. Dec. 19, 1980. Thirty years ago. She gripped the back of the chair in front of the microfiche. Then her gaze focused on the victim's name: Candace Porter.

She frowned. The name meant nothing to her.

As Andi moved the microfiche so they could see the rest of the story, a photograph of a dark-haired woman came up.

Kate almost didn't recognize her aunt. Katherine looked so different from the photographs she'd seen of her when she'd had blond hair. But there was no doubt. Candace Porter and Katherine Landon were the same woman.

The same murdered woman—straight from Cyrus Winchester's dream, only thirty years ago, just as she'd feared.

Suddenly her legs seemed to give out. She felt Cyrus's large, warm hands grab her and ease her down into a spare chair behind Andi. He'd seen the photograph of the murdered nurse. He'd recognized her aunt.

"It doesn't say how the woman was killed," Andi was saying, unaware of the drama going on behind her. "In fact there is little information. There's a follow-up story, but apparently the woman wasn't from around here. There's no apparent next of kin. No wonder I'd never heard of this."

Her aunt had been murdered at the hospital one night—just like in Cyrus's dream. But she hadn't been going by her real name. Was it possible her grandmother hadn't known the truth of what had happened to Katherine and that was why she'd made up the story about the weak heart?

"What about the killer?" Cyrus asked Andi.

"Apparently never caught," Andi said. "The only other story I found about the murder was a follow-up twenty years ago on the tenth anniversary of the woman's death. The murderer was still at large."

"Can you make me a copy of the stories?" Cyrus asked.

"Sure," Andi said. "So is this exactly like your dream?" Cyrus didn't answer and Andi looked back at Kate. "Are you all right?"

Kate could only nod. She knew eventually she would tell Andi everything, but not now. Not when she was too upset to discuss it.

"Kate's still a little dazed from being hit by the cable," Cyrus said.

Kate could tell that Andi was bursting at the seams to ask more questions.

"I should get you home," Cyrus said to Kate. "She took a pretty good hit on the head," he told Andi.

Andi nodded. "I can't believe that cable would break. Maybe we should use something else."

"Don't worry," Cyrus said. "I'll fix it so there is no chance it will fall on anyone again."

"So do you think this is the murder you thought you saw?" Andi asked Cyrus again as she walked them to the door.

He shrugged. "I think it's a coincidence, but kind of interesting," he said, playing it down.

"That would be wild if you dreamed a murder that took place thirty years ago," Andi said. "If that turns out to be the case—"

"You'll be the first to get the story," Cyrus said as he folded the copies of the articles and put them in his jacket pocket.

Kate felt Andi's gaze on her. "Maybe you should swing by the hospital and have a doctor check you out."

It wasn't until she and Cyrus were outside in the brisk fall air that she felt she could breathe. "I don't understand."

"Me neither, but then I've been confused about this since the beginning. Let's talk about it back at the shop."

She shivered as she saw him glance around as if he thought someone might be watching them. He put his arm around her and they started back toward Second Hand Kate's.

The main drag had been decorated with cornstalks and pumpkins and, while there were Halloween decorations in most of the windows, Christmas music played from a few of the stores they passed.

Kate found herself watching the people who drove past them in a way she'd never noticed anyone before. She tried not to think about what this all meant. Her head ached but she still noticed that Cyrus seemed even more worried about her than he had earlier.

Her aunt had been *murdered.*

Why had that come as a shock to either of them? Cyrus had seen her aunt dead in the hospital nursery. And all her life Kate had felt there was more to the story. Still, seeing it in print...

"Is there any reason the front door of your shop would be open?" Cyrus asked, jerking her from her thoughts.

Kate turned to look. The door was ajar. "My friend Jasmine might—"

"Stay here," Cyrus ordered as he pulled a gun from a shoulder holster under his jacket and ran toward her open shop door. Had he been wearing the gun since he'd come to town? Or had he only put it on after the cable incident? He'd gone to his pickup while she'd changed clothes...

Kate had never been good at doing what she was told. She was right behind him when he eased the front door all the way open, and she saw the broken glass sparkling on the rich patina of the old wooden floor—and Jasmine.

Cyrus raced toward the dark-haired young woman standing in the middle of the room with a fireplace poker gripped in both hands. The woman lowered the poker the moment she saw Kate behind him and burst into tears.

"I scared him away," the woman said through her sobs.

"Oh, Jasmine," Kate said, pushing past him to hug her friend.

"Him?" Cyrus asked after Jasmine calmed down a little. He'd surveyed the damage and found that the only thing that looked as if it had been broken into was the glass case that held Kate's mementos.

The silver bracelet was still where it had been. Apparently Jasmine had scared the robber away before he could get what he'd come for. Assuming, of course, he'd been after the bracelet.

It made little sense to steal the bracelet. There wouldn't be any evidence on it after thirty years. That was also assuming there was something to his dream and Candace Porter, aka Katherine Landon, had actually been wearing the bracelet when she died.

So far, the only details he could verify from his "dream" were that the woman he'd seen actually had died in the old hospital nursery—but it just happened to be thirty years ago on December 19, 1980.

That and, as Kate had pointed out, asking about the old murder had someone in town apparently stirred up enough to attack her—and break into her shop.

"You said 'him.' You're sure it was definitely a man you saw?" Cyrus asked Jasmine again.

By now they were all sitting around Kate's red-checked 1950s table upstairs, Jasmine cupping a mug of hot chocolate. While red-eyed, she seemed to have pulled herself together.

Kate had insisted they come upstairs while they waited for the sheriff to arrive so she could make hot chocolate as she said her grandmother always did when she was sad or upset.

She handed Cyrus a cup and took a seat across from him at the table she said she'd found at a farm auction north of town. There was something so cozy and serene about the upstairs apartment—in vivid contrast to the tension in the room.

He watched Kate close her eyes and take a sip of the hot chocolate, a large melting marshmallow floating on top. It reminded him of last night at the frybread stand.

She'd made the top floor into a three-bedroom apartment. There was plenty of room in the high-ceilinged space and it was clear she'd let herself go, decorating it with some of her favorite finds.

He had removed his Stetson and held the large mug of hot chocolate with both hands now. Like Jasmine, he felt he needed the warmth.

"Why don't you start at the beginning," Kate suggested to Jasmine as she shot Cyrus a look to be patient.

Jasmine took a shuddering breath and let it out slowly. "I let myself in with the key you gave me. I didn't turn on a light because I didn't want anyone to think the shop was open. As I headed for the basement…" She took a sip of the hot chocolate. "This is really good," she said to Kate, who beamed and said, "Thank you."

"So you came in and headed for the basement," Cyrus nudged gently. "In the dark?"

Jasmine blinked. "It wasn't dark. I remember now. There was a light on upstairs."

He glanced over at Kate. She shook her head that she hadn't left a light on.

"Then what happened?"

"I glanced upstairs, but didn't hear anything, so I assumed you had just left a light on for when you came home. Then I opened the basement door and started to go down the steps." She paused to put down her mug. "I was about halfway down when I heard someone upstairs. I thought it was you." She smiled over at Kate. "So I went back downstairs feeling weird, you know. That's when I heard the sound of breaking glass."

"The intruder must not have heard you come in," Kate said and reached across the table to cover her friend's hand with her own. "I'm so sorry you had to go through this."

"So then what did you do?" Cyrus asked.

"I called to Kate from the basement stairs where I

had stopped again, asking if she was all right. I just assumed she'd come home and dropped something." Jasmine shrugged apologetically. "When she didn't answer and it got real quiet, I had a bad feeling. I came upstairs. I was just passing the room with the wonderful old fireplace… did Kate tell you that I helped her strip off all the old paint on the mantel?"

"We hadn't gotten to that yet," Cyrus said, feeling Kate's imploring gaze on him, asking him again to be patient with her friend. "That's where you found the poker, right?"

Jasmine nodded. "I grabbed it and came out to the main room to find the front door open and glass all over the floor."

"You scared him away before he could do any more damage, apparently," Cyrus said. "You said him, but you never saw the person?"

Jasmine shook her head. "I just assumed it was a man. A woman would not break the glass on that beautiful case."

Cyrus smiled to himself, thinking of the investigations he'd been involved in where a woman had done much more than break a little glass.

Kate got up to get her friend more hot chocolate.

"I'd like you to look around and make sure nothing else was taken before the sheriff gets here," Cyrus said to Kate.

He could tell she was shaken by the break-in and her friend's near run-in with a burglar. But he suspected it was nothing after what they'd seen at the newspaper—the picture of a murder victim who Kate had been told had died from a weak heart.

At Cyrus's insistence, Kate went through the shop and her apartment upstairs, looking for anything out of place or missing. She was more upset than she'd let on. Angry and scared. Not just angry and upset. She hadn't wanted to fall apart when Jasmine needed her to hold it together. Nor did she want Cyrus to see how upset she really was after what she'd seen in the newspaper.

When she'd seen her friend standing there with a poker in her hands... Kate was just thankful that Jasmine hadn't confronted the burglar.

She felt violated just knowing that someone had gone through her things and at the same time thankful for her friend and Cyrus. He was downstairs now, inspecting the locks and windows to see if he could find out how the intruder had gotten in.

"With all the wonderful things you have sitting around, I'm surprised he didn't take anything," Jasmine said, frowning at her from across the room. They'd gone through the shop and found nothing missing. Not even from the broken case.

Now, back upstairs, Kate spotted the first thing she'd found out of place in her apartment, even though it was clear whoever had broken in had been looking for something.

"What is it?" Jasmine asked, seeing her reaction.

"My photos," Kate said in a voice that broke. She rushed to it but stopped herself from snatching up the album. "Fingerprints. There could be fingerprints," she said to herself out loud.

Going in the kitchen she pulled a wooden spoon from the canister by the stove and returned to the album the burglar had left out.

Using the handle of the spoon, she carefully opened it. Her heart thudded in her chest. Hadn't she known what would be missing the moment she saw that the intruder had pulled down the photos?

"What's going on?" Cyrus asked as he came into the room.

"I think the burglar took some of Kate's photographs," Jasmine said. "Why would he break in to take photos and try to steal something out of your memento case? That doesn't make a whole lot of sense."

It did to Kate. She looked at Cyrus as she let the album fall open on the page with the missing photographs of her aunt and mother and saw that it made sense to him, as well.

# Chapter 9

Sheriff McCall Winchester had known it was just a matter of time before she met her cousin Cyrus. She'd heard he was in town asking a lot of crazy questions. Some of the same questions she'd already answered for his brother when he'd called from Denver asking about a murder.

Rumors were flying and Cyrus Winchester was now the talk of the town.

Given all that, she hadn't been that surprised to get a call from him about a break-in at Second Hand Kate's. Since meeting his twin, Cordell, she'd come to expect wherever the Winchester men went, trouble was never far behind.

"It's nice to finally meet you," McCall said as she shook Cyrus's hand upon arriving at the shop. One of her deputies was busy shooting the scene and checking for prints. "I visited you a few times in the hospital, but I'm sure you don't remember."

"No, sorry." He had the Winchester dark eyes and hair

just like her. She saw him studying her, no doubt seeing the Winchester resemblance, and had to smile. Fortunately she looked like their grandmother, but it had taken Pepper's acceptance to make people quit questioning her birthright. "You're Uncle Trace's daughter?"

She smiled. "Not all the stories about my mother turned out to be true."

He seemed to relax. "I was sorry to hear about your father."

McCall nodded. Finding out that her father hadn't abandoned her mother and her before she was born had been a double-edged sword. Trace Winchester hadn't run off—he had gotten himself murdered. Either way, she'd never known her father.

"Why don't I start with Jasmine and Kate, if you don't mind hanging around until I'm finished with them," McCall said.

"I'll be right here."

She smiled, sensing that protectiveness she'd seen in his brother and wondering how it was that he and Kate had met. All in good time, she thought as she went upstairs to where the other two were waiting.

"Why don't you step in here, Cyrus," McCall suggested a while later. She motioned to one of the small rooms in the shop that had been decorated as a parlor, much like the real one at her grandmother's lodge on the Winchester Ranch.

"I've heard Jasmine's and Kate's stories as to the break-in," McCall continued. "I can't wait to hear yours, since Kate tells me it has to do with her aunt and mother and some dream you had while in the coma."

"We don't know that for a fact," he hedged, but at her prodding recounted his dream.

She listened as he told her about what he'd thought he'd

seen at the hospital and how the woman had been wearing the silver bracelet he'd seen in the glass cabinet—the same cabinet someone had broken into but either hadn't been after the bracelet or had gotten scared away before taking it. A bracelet that could have belonged to Kate's aunt rather than her mother.

McCall raised a brow when he told her about the newspaper article. The woman named Candace Porter had been murdered just like in his dream—and she had turned out to be Kate's aunt, Katherine Landon, only she was going by an assumed name.

"Kate and I both recognized her," Cyrus said.

"And it was her photo and Kate's mother's photographs that were taken from the album upstairs." McCall got the feeling he was leaving something out and wondered why. Perhaps to protect Kate? There was definitely something going on between Cyrus and Kate.

"How exactly did you meet Kate?" she asked and could have sworn he blushed. She listened as he told her about seeing her at the hospital and thinking she was the woman from his dream, only to realize she had to be a relative of the dead woman.

McCall couldn't miss the way he talked about Kate. *These Winchester men,* she thought with no small amount of amusement, since her father had broken more than a few hearts, including her mother's.

"Wow, that was some dream," she said when Cyrus finished. "So you've been asking a bunch of questions around town about a murder and now you think the murderer broke in here, took some photographs and tried to take the bracelet."

"Believe me, I wish it had been nothing more than a bad

dream. There was a point where I was starting to believe it was—even against all odds."

"Until you found Kate in the basement after someone cut the cable and Andi found the newspaper article about a thirty-year-old murder at the hospital, and now this break-in." McCall studied him. "Nothing else was taken besides some family photographs?"

He shook his head. "Apparently not."

"This silver bell bracelet that you saw in your dream, is it the same one in the case that was broken?"

"It looks pretty similar. Apparently there were two bracelets. Kate's grandfather made them for his daughters. Whoever broke in must have seen the bracelet, recognized it and thought…" He hesitated. "Who knows what he—or she—thought."

"Or *she?*"

"Jasmine didn't see the person. I wouldn't rule out that it might have been a woman. Whoever cut the cable wasn't particularly strong. When I inspected the cable just before you arrived, I noticed that it had taken several attempts to cut it."

"Interesting." McCall had heard Cyrus and Cordell were damned good private investigators in Denver. She'd gotten the chance to work with his brother in June and could attest to how devoted they were. Both had almost gotten killed. "So what's your theory?"

"I just got over thinking I was crazy. I was hoping you'd look into the Candace Porter murder. She was apparently killed in the nursery at the old hospital. She was a nurse, according to the story, but Kate says she's sure her aunt never went to nursing school. Unfortunately, we don't have any photographs of her—other than the one in the newspaper article. Whoever broke in took them."

"But you and Kate are sure Candace Porter was her aunt, Katherine Landon?"

"Yes. The same woman I dreamed about while in my coma. Don't ask me to explain it."

"Very strange," McCall agreed, thinking this could be the strangest investigation she'd come across yet. "I'll see what I can find out."

As Cyrus walked McCall to the door, she asked the one question he'd been dreading. "Have you been out to see Grandmother?" He must have raised a brow, because she laughed.

"Yeah, it still seems odd calling her *Grandmother,* but she's accepted that I'm one of you," McCall said. "Not sure that's a good thing, but she seems to be trying to make up for the past."

"You think that's why she invited my brother and me back here?"

"No," she said with a laugh. "From what I can gather it has something to do with my father's murder. I don't believe she's happy with the outcome of the investigation. Which is probably how I became acting sheriff—until the election, at least. Not that she isn't above interfering with the election to get what she wants."

He had to smile at her honesty. "Doesn't sound like Pepper can put much over on you."

"Our grandmother gets whatever she wants one way or another, but I probably don't have to tell you that."

"No," he admitted. "I heard from Cordell that she seems to think someone in the family was involved in your father's death." He saw from McCall's expression that there might be something to that and felt sick inside at the thought. He knew his father, Brand, wasn't involved, but wouldn't put anything past his Aunt Virginia.

"These things have a way of coming out in time," Mc-Call said.

"Didn't I hear you're getting married in December at Winchester Ranch?"

She laughed. "That's probably when Grandmother will drop her bombshell, huh? I've thought of that. But doesn't every bride want a wedding she will never forget? You should go see her. Maybe I'm wrong, but I think she isn't as uncaring as she pretends to be."

"I might before I leave."

"So you'll be staying around for a while?"

"For a while," he said noncommittally. He couldn't leave now because of Kate and whatever was going on, even if he wanted to.

At the back of his mind a part of him still worried that the dream wasn't about getting justice in a thirty-year-old murder case. It was a premonition that Kate was the real victim he'd come to Whitehorse to save—or die trying.

"You told the sheriff about your dream?" Kate asked Cyrus, still feeling shaken. She'd cleaned up the broken glass after Jasmine, the sheriff and her deputy had left.

Cyrus had gone around the house making sure the place was locked up for the night. He'd composed a list of locks that needed to be changed and security measures to be added.

"She's going to see what she can find out about Candace Porter. I'm sorry, Kate."

She nodded. Growing up, she'd believed she could handle most anything. She'd already lost her mother and aunt all those years ago, and recently her grandmother.

But it had been one thing to believe there was merit to Cyrus's dream and another to find out that her aunt had really been murdered, then right on the heels of that to find her shop broken into, her treasured photographs taken and the bracelet nearly gone, as well.

Not to mention that whoever was involved might still be in Whitehorse after thirty years—and knew not only who she was, but that she and Cyrus were looking into her aunt's murder.

"They were looking for something, weren't they?"

"That's my thought, but what? Whoever it was recognized the bracelet. I think that is why they decided to take it as they were leaving. I remember my reaction when I noticed it on my way out the first time. The killer must have been shocked to see it, as well."

"Which means my aunt's killer is still in town," Kate said.

"It would seem so."

"What could the person have been looking for?"

"I would imagine the killer thinks we must have some kind of evidence. Otherwise, how could I know the things I do?"

"Your dream," she said with a nod. "The killer thinks you made that part up."

"I wish."

"Maybe there is evidence," she said suddenly. "I need to go to West Yellowstone to my grandmother's cabin. After she died I couldn't go through all her things. I started, but the woman was a pack rat. I doubt she ever threw anything away. It was just too overwhelming. But now, I can't help but wonder what else she kept from me."

"Well, I'm going with you. I'm not letting you out of my sight until this is over."

She liked the sound of that. Except for the "until this is over" part.

"I probably should mention that West Yellowstone is seven hours from here. If we leave now we'll get there late but we can stay over, if you don't mind."

"Sure." Cyrus looked worried and she wondered if, like her, he was thinking about the two of them alone in a cabin in the woods and that kiss.

Or maybe that was the last thing on his mind.

"Thank you for going with me," she said. In truth, she wasn't sure she could have faced this alone.

As she quickly packed to leave, she couldn't get out of her head that her aunt had lived and worked in Whitehorse. No wonder her mother had sent the postcard from here. But why would her aunt have been using another name? And how was it that her aunt was working as a nurse? Kate was almost certain Katherine had never been to nursing school.

Kate suddenly remembered one of Dimple's friends telling her about her aunt once at a wedding, after her grandmother's friend had had too much champagne. "Katherine was your grandmother's wild child," the friend said in confidence. "Your mother made up for it. Elizabeth was the perfect child. Do you know what she did? When she was little she would take the blame for things her sister did, just to protect Katherine."

Is that why her mother had left her so soon after she was born to come to Whitehorse? Had Katherine been in trouble? Kate could only assume so, given that Katherine hadn't been using her real name.

What else would Kate discover about her aunt and her mother once they got to West Yellowstone?

Whatever trouble her aunt had gotten into thirty years ago, it apparently was still in town, Kate thought as she glanced toward her broken glass case. She'd taken her mementos out for safekeeping. The bracelet was now in her purse.

The photographs of her aunt and mother were gone and it broke her heart. But she thought the person responsible had left them a clue.

"The burglar took both my mother's and my aunt's photographs," she said to Cyrus. "Why would he take both?"

"Maybe he couldn't tell them apart."

"Or maybe he knew my mother." She just hoped the answer was somewhere in her grandmother's cabin.

McCall couldn't believe all the things she was supposed to do just to get married, and said as much to her fiancé, Luke, later that afternoon.

"We could elope," he suggested.

She looked at him to see if he was serious, because at that moment she would have taken him up on it.

He quickly shook his head as if he knew her too well. "It's going to be a beautiful wedding that we will remember the rest of our lives."

She laughed. "That's what I'm afraid of."

He pulled her into his arms. "You deserve this wedding."

"Still scaring me. I know you're worried about what my grandmother might be up to as much as I am."

"Honey," he said after kissing her. "We're getting married at the Winchester Ranch. It's what your father would have wanted, and if you don't go through with it, your mother will never forgive you."

That convinced her. Ruby *would* never forgive her. "You're right."

"Not to mention your grandmother seems more excited

about your wedding than anyone—even us. I really think she wants to welcome you to the family."

"I went to pick out flowers. Luke, there are too many decisions to make without some help."

He looked panicked, as if he was worried she would ask him to go along. "How about your mother?"

"Ruby?" McCall cried. "She'd want plastic flowers, large, bright ones."

"You need to give your mother more credit."

"You think? The other day she suggested that she thought it would be cool if she and I had a double wedding at the ranch."

"Are she and Red to that point?"

McCall shrugged. Her mother had been dating Red for a few months, longer than most of her boyfriends lasted. "Can you imagine what my grandmother would have to say about Ruby getting married at the ranch? It's going to be nerve-racking enough just having Ruby and Pepper in the same room for our wedding."

"They both want you to be happy. Neither would dream of spoiling the wedding."

She wished she shared his optimism.

"I heard there was a break-in at Second Hand Kate's."

She told him about it and about her cousin Cyrus's dream—and the murdered nurse going by the name of Candace Porter.

"Are you telling me he saw a murder that happened thirty years ago while he was in a coma?" Luke asked, looking as skeptical as she'd first felt.

"A woman was murdered who, according to her niece, looks exactly like her aunt," McCall said. "But that isn't the worst part of all this. I suspect there is something Cyrus is holding back. I think it might be the killer's motive."

* * *

Cyrus watched the landscape change from the rolling prairie where thousands of buffalo once roamed to mountain ranges, dark green with pines. The wind howled across the open spaces, bending over the tall yellowed grasses as antelope dotted the hillsides and eagles soared on the thermals.

The two-lane highway dropped southward, the majestic Beartooth mountain range coming up out of the horizon like a mirage. They turned at the Crazy Mountains, caught Interstate 90 and headed west toward Bozeman as the sun sank. As other mountain ranges came into view, all were dusted with snow, another sign that winter wasn't far off.

They stopped in Bozeman for lunch and were just heading for the Gallatin Canyon, which would take them to West Yellowstone, when his cell phone rang.

"Cyrus?" He recognized the sheriff's voice and glanced over at Kate. McCall had found out something or she wouldn't be calling. "Where are you?"

"On our way to Kate's grandmother's cabin in West Yellowstone. She thinks the answers might be there."

"I tracked down Candace Porter, the *real* Candace Porter," the sheriff said. "She used to be a nurse at a hospital in Missoula, Montana. Her purse was stolen the day of her going-away party. She was headed for Paris, where her fiancé was living. The two of them were planning to travel around Europe before settling down."

"Let me guess. Katherine Landon worked at the same hospital."

"Bingo. She was a nurse's aide before she miraculously became a nurse by the name of Candace Porter."

Cyrus had suspected it might be something like this. "Was Candace Porter's family ever contacted after the murder?"

"No next of kin could be found. She was buried here in Whitehorse."

"Thanks for letting me know. We'll be back tomorrow, probably late."

"Don't worry. We're keeping an eye on the shop, but if you're right about what the burglar was after, then I doubt there will be another break-in."

He agreed. For a moment he thought about telling Mc-Call what else he'd seen that night in his dream—Katherine Landon switching the two baby boys in bassinets in the hospital nursery, but he didn't want to do it on the phone. "Thanks" was all he said before he hung up.

Cyrus realized it felt like a betrayal to say anything to the sheriff about the babies until they had some evidence that the babies had even existed. He realized the ramifications if the babies had been switched as they had been in his dream. Both of the boys would be thirty now. What a time to find out that the parents you'd known all your life weren't really your parents. He'd heard of a case or two like that. He couldn't imagine how it would affect not only the parents, but also the young men.

He couldn't, however, keep what McCall had told him from Kate, even though he knew she wasn't going to like hearing it.

"I suspected as much given that she wasn't using her real name," Kate said after he told her. He could see she was taking the news much worse than she let on. "I wonder if my mother knew about her sister stealing another person's identity, pretending to be a nurse?"

"I suspect it might be why she left you to go to Whitehorse. Clearly your aunt was in over her head. Kate, there is something I haven't told you that I saw in my dream. I saw her switch the babies in the bassinets."

Kate stared at him in disbelief. "Why would she do that?" He shook his head. "Did you tell the sheriff?"

"I'll have to if we find any evidence that it really happened."

Kate was silent for a few minutes, as if taking it in. "You think that's what got her killed. Someone put her up to the baby switch. But why would they turn around and kill her?"

Because they didn't want a witness who could come forward years later, he was about to suggest.

"But what if she was switching the babies back, what if she'd changed her mind?" Kate said. She had a point.

"I suppose, depending on the deal that was made, that could have gotten her killed," he said.

"Maybe my mother talked her out of it."

He could see that's what she wanted to believe.

"And it got them both killed."

Cyrus thought she could be right. He just hoped they would find what they needed in West Yellowstone.

The drive down the narrow Gallatin Canyon through the mountains in October was beautiful. The highway followed the Gallatin River, with its crystal-clear water rushing over large granite rocks. The trees had turned to an array of golds, reds and rusts, and now the breeze showered the cold river with the colorful leaves. Caught in the current, they floated quickly downstream.

During the drive, Kate talked about what it had been like growing up in West Yellowstone with her grandmother. "I loved living in a tourist town when I was a kid. Summers were wild and crazy with the town packed with people. They used to have street dances in front of the old Texaco gas station and one of the bars used to pipe the music from the bands out onto the street."

Beside the highway, a few fly-fishermen braved the chilly day to cast long, sleek lines out over the deep, cold green of the river.

"I would imagine winters were quite different there," he said as they passed Big Sky, the snow-capped Lone Peak spectacular against the clear blue sky.

"It wasn't like now, but snowmobiles definitely changed things," she said. "It was how we got around town. There were trails on top of the huge drifts where the snow had been plowed." Kate smiled in memory. "We used to run all over at night in the cold, snowy darkness. It really was a wonderland."

"I'm surprised you didn't go back after college," Cyrus said.

"The town changed for me. Or maybe I was the one who changed. I guess that's why I love Whitehorse. I like the small-town feel."

"Whitehorse suits you."

She laughed. "Thanks. I agree." Then she sobered. "No matter what we find out, I won't be leaving Whitehorse."

Yes, he thought, he'd known that when he'd seen her shop. She'd found herself a home. He knew she would hate Denver.

The canyon opened at the top of Fir Ridge for a view of Hebgen Lake, the surface golden, in the distance. Then the road ran through the dense pines into town.

West, as the locals called it, was a small tourist town on the edge of Yellowstone Park. It sat among tall pines, a mix of old log cabins and new motels and businesses. Once a town that boarded up and closed all but a few businesses in winter, it was now a mecca for snowmobilers who wanted to see Yellowstone in its frosty-white season. This time of the year, though, things were pretty quiet as everyone waited for snow.

* * *

Kate's grandmother's cabin sat back in the tall pines, rustic and rambling, on one of the lots at the edge of town. Past the property the trees and land ran east to hit the boundary of Yellowstone Park.

"My grandmother left the place to me," Kate said as she opened the door. "I don't get down here much, but I can't part with it. I grew up here. It's a part of me."

"I envy you," Cyrus said. "This cabin is wonderful. There is no place that I could really call home—not since my grandmother kicked us all off the ranch."

"I'm sorry," she said, studying him for a moment. "Everyone needs a place to call home."

"We moved a lot when I was growing up," he said as he brought in their bags and set them down in the living room. "My father worked on different ranches across the west. So I got used to things being temporary."

"Not even Denver feels like home?"

He chuckled. "Maybe especially Denver."

Kate looked around the cabin. Now that she was here, she didn't know what to do.

"You said your grandmother saved everything," Cyrus commented. "You weren't kidding."

"Because of that I have no idea where to start." She couldn't help sounding discouraged. It had been a long drive. She was tired. But probably more than anything she was afraid of what they were going to find here.

"We don't have to do this tonight," he said. "We could wait until the morning if you want."

She shook her head. "There is so much to go through— it is still early enough."

"Okay. How about those files?" he said, pointing to three

metal file cabinets next to a desk in what appeared to be a small office.

She put down her purse but didn't move.

"You sure you want to do this?" he asked as she only stared at the filing cabinets.

"Yes." She gave herself a push and stepped to the first cabinet and pulled open the top drawer. "Oh, this is not going to be easy."

"You take one drawer and I'll take one," he suggested. "Anything from thirty years ago."

She nodded as he carried the top drawer to the kitchen table. Kate sat next to the drawer he'd put there for her and pulled out the first manila file folder.

Cyrus went for the next drawer, bringing it back to sit down across from her. It was like searching for a needle in a haystack, but she didn't know what else to do.

It was a little after 10:00 p.m. when Kate found the letters. She froze, her fingers trembling as she read the name the letter was addressed to: Elizabeth Landon. The postmark was Whitehorse, Montana, dated Dec. 12, 1980.

"Cyrus." That was all she could get out.

He came to her at once. She handed him the envelope, he glanced at it, then started to hand it back.

She shook her head. "Would you read it, please?"

He nodded, pulled the letter from the envelope, unfolded it and quickly read through it before he handed it to her.

Kate didn't look at it, just at him. "Tell me."

"Your aunt said she needed her sister. Just for a little while. She wanted her to come to Whitehorse. She'd done something and she feared this time she was in real trouble. She said she'd exaggerated on her employment application and her boss had found out. But it was more complicated than that."

Even though Kate had known this must have been what happened, she still had trouble believing it. "Didn't my aunt realize that I was just a baby? She'd gotten herself into this mess and she drags my mother into it?"

Kate shoved back from the table and stormed into the living room, only to stop because there was no place to run from this. Angry tears burned her eyes.

"I can't believe my mother would go," she said, fighting to keep from crying. She heard Cyrus rise from the table and come up behind her.

"I can," he said softly. "If my brother was in trouble, I'd be there tomorrow. He'd do the same for me."

"But to bail out a sister like Katherine? I'd heard she was always in trouble. Lying about being a nurse..." Kate shook her head. "Couldn't she have gone to jail over that?"

"Possibly," he said, putting his large, warm hands on her shoulders and turning her around to face him. "Sometimes with siblings it's a love-hate relationship, but when push comes to shove, especially if that sibling is in some serious trouble, then you're going to be there. Your mother had to make a difficult choice, but she knew you would be fine with your grandmother."

Kate nodded and made a swipe at her tears. "I envy that kind of relationship."

"Your grandmother was like that with you. She hid the truth from you to protect you."

"I know."

He bent down a little to look into her face. "We can stop this right now."

"No," Kate said. "We can't. My aunt said in that letter that her boss had found out about her not being a nurse, and yet she was still working at the hospital?"

* * *

Cyrus had thought the same thing. If Katherine had been caught then she should have been fired immediately. Why hadn't she been?

He couldn't wait to get back to Whitehorse and ask the hospital administrator, Roberta Warren.

Kate took the letter from him. He watched her read through it. He could tell she was exhausted. "It's late," he said.

She nodded. "I think I will call it a night. Take any bedroom you want. I made up the beds with clean sheets the last time I was here." She glanced toward the table. "There are more letters…"

"I can take a look at them and see if there is anything in them," he offered.

Her emerald gaze filmed over with tears again. "Thank you."

Kate looked into his handsome face and lost a little piece of her heart to Cyrus Winchester. He was so kind and caring and she didn't know what she would have done without him being here with her.

She thought about the first time she'd seen him standing in the old hospital hallway. Cyrus Winchester in his jeans and boots, western shirt and Stetson. She hadn't been able to get that image out of her mind, or shake the feeling then that he was in some kind of trouble.

Is this the way her mother had felt about her sister? Is this why she had to leave Kate to go to Katherine?

"Cyrus…" Words failed her as she was filled with love for this man and understood how feeling like this would make a person drop everything to go to the one they loved.

She searched the depths of his dark eyes and lost herself.

The kiss seemed the most natural thing in the world. Her mouth brushed over his, sending sparks flying. She could feel the struggle going on inside him, him and his darned cowboy code. He was afraid he would end up hurting her.

Kate pulled back, realizing how easy it would be, just the two of them alone in the cabin, to end up doing something they might regret. An image of the two of them beneath one of the thick quilts flashed before her, her lying naked in his arms. She shivered at the thought.

Cyrus hadn't moved. She looked into his eyes and saw something close to pain. He wanted her as much as she wanted him. But his life was in Denver. Hers was in Whitehorse. This was impossible. And yet it would be so easy to throw caution to the wind.

She knew it would change everything between them. So did he.

"Good night," she mumbled and hurried into one of the bedrooms, closing the door behind her.

Cyrus listened to Kate getting ready for bed in an adjacent room. He groaned, still feeling the effects of her kiss. Damn that woman, she was going to be the death of him. He stood for a long time, staring at her closed door, wanting desperately to go after her, needing her in his arms.

Just the thought of making love to Kate… He moved to the closed bedroom door and pressed his fingers against the cool wood. Listening, he heard nothing beyond the door. Maybe Kate had already fallen asleep.

Or maybe she was lying awake, waiting for him to come to her. He groaned inwardly. He cared too much for her to have casual sex. That thought made him laugh to himself. There would be nothing casual about it.

Growling to himself at the thought, he moved away from

the door to go back to the table. He picked up the stack of letters Kate had found and tried not to think about her, just in the next room in one of those tall iron beds he'd glimpsed through the doorway.

There was one more letter from Katherine to her sister, more urgent than the other one, pleading with Elizabeth to help her.

Cyrus sat down and tried to put Kate out of his mind. But it had been impossible since the day he'd met her.

Hours later, after going through files and boxes filled with every birthday card, Christmas card, note or letter Jenny "Dimple" Landon had ever received in her long life, he found the box with the bank statement in it.

His gaze shot to the return address and he felt his heart drop to his feet. The return address was a bank in White-horse.

The statement was under both Katherine Landon's and her mother, Jenny Landon's names. Katherine had apparently had her bank statements sent home to her mother in West Yellowstone.

The statements were filed by date. He pulled out one from the end of December, 1980.

Then he saw the balance and did a double take.

Katherine had deposited five thousand dollars into a savings account that had previously only had seventeen dollars in it.

Cyrus found the next—and last—statement. Thirty years ago Dimple had closed the savings account and had the money transferred into a local savings account in Kate's name.

As he glanced through the financial papers, he surmised that Dimple had saved the money to make a nice nest egg for her granddaughter.

So that was what Kate had used to buy the old library in Whitehorse and start her shop. He had a feeling that Kate had no idea where the money had come from. Had her grandmother?

He closed the folder, wondering what Dimple had thought when she'd found out that her daughter had put the money in a joint savings account with her as beneficiary. Had she known it might get her killed?

And what had Dimple made of all this? She had to wonder where Katherine had gotten the money. Her daughter had been working as a nurse's aide before assuming a nurse's identity. Still, she hadn't been making much money in Whitehorse.

And suddenly, on Dec. 19, she'd come into five grand. Five thousand dollars on the same day she'd switched the babies in the nursery and gotten herself killed.

Cyrus sighed and turned out the light before heading to one of the bedrooms Kate had pointed out to him.

The bed had a great iron frame. He climbed up on top of it without even removing his clothes and shut his eyes.

He'd expected his thoughts to be on all the paperwork he'd gone through or the unexplained five grand.

But as he closed his eyes, his only thought was of Kate and the kiss. It hadn't been the first time she'd kissed him. He wanted her. So what was holding him back? Could he really walk away from her when all of this was over?

Hours later, after having trouble getting to sleep, he'd just drifted off when he felt someone touch his shoulder. Cyrus opened his eyes to find Kate standing over him. She was wearing a long white nightgown with what looked like moose on it, but for just an instant he thought she was an apparition straight from his dreams.

"What's wrong?" he asked, sitting up quickly.

She shook her head. "I had a bad dream." She sounded scared and he could see that she was shivering. The temperature had dropped during the night up here at over six thousand feet above sea level.

He reached for the heavy quilt at the end of the bed and she slid in beside him. Covering her, he wrapped an arm around her and pulled her close.

"It was just a bad dream," he whispered into her hair.

"And we all know there is nothing to our dreams."

"Well, you're safe now," he whispered back.

Kate snuggled against him in answer and a few moments later, she was asleep. It took him a lot longer to fall back to sleep with her lying in his arms.

# Chapter 10

Kate woke to the smell of coffee. It was heavenly. She lay in bed for a few moments breathing in the scent before she remembered last night and realized she wasn't in her own bed.

She groaned. She really had to quit kissing Cyrus. She was playing with fire and she knew it. And yet as she climbed into the shower she found herself grinning. Last night she'd had the most wonderful dream while sleeping in his arms.

As she toweled dry and dressed, she remembered the letter she'd found the night before. Now she knew why her mother had left her and gone to Whitehorse. Not that it made it any easier in the daylight.

"Coffee?" Cyrus handed her a mug as she came into the kitchen.

"Am I going to need this?" she asked, seeing the papers he had laid out on the table.

His expression confirmed her fears. She took a sip of the

coffee. It was good. She said as much, then asked, "Okay, what did you find?"

She had to sit down as he told her about the five thousand dollars and how her grandmother had invested it for her.

"That was the money she left me." Her voice broke. "You know where that five thousand came from. Now we know why she switched the babies. Someone paid her to do it."

"Kate, I've had some time to think about this," Cyrus said quickly. "Maybe your aunt did agree to switch the babies and apparently she did take the money, but I believe she got your mother to Whitehorse to talk her out of it. I think you were right about her switching the babies back and that's what got her killed."

She looked into his face. Could she love this man any more? It didn't seem possible, and yet she did. "But she still took the money."

"We know she was already in a bind over her job. For some reason, she hadn't been fired. We also don't know why someone wanted the babies switched. Maybe there was a reason that made it easier for your aunt to go along with the deal," he suggested.

She couldn't help smiling at him. "Thank you."

They both jumped at the knock on the front door of the cabin.

"Kate, it's just me, May," came an elderly female voice.

"It's my grandmother's neighbor and good friend," Kate said to Cyrus before going to answer the door. She hugged May and invited her inside, introducing her to Cyrus.

"Land sakes, what are you two doing?" May said when she spied the mess.

"Going through Grandmother's things," Kate told her and saw the older woman's worried frown. "I know about Aunt Katherine and my mother."

May looked surprised, then wary. "Know what, dear?"

"I know they aren't buried up at Fir Ridge Cemetery. You could save me a lot of trouble by telling me what you know. Please," Kate said, pulling out a chair. "Have a seat."

"I'll get you a cup of coffee," Cyrus suggested.

May looked trapped, but took the chair she was offered. "Oh, dear," she said as Cyrus slid a cup of coffee in front of her. She waved off the offer of sugar and cream. "I don't know that much. Honestly."

"But you know they didn't die the way my grandmother said," Kate prodded.

"Yes." May glanced guiltily at her. "You have to understand. It was such a terrible time for your grandmother. Katherine was always a worry. Elizabeth had just given birth to you. Dimple had seen the letters from Katherine. She tried to talk your mother out of going, but Elizabeth was a strong, confident woman and she loved her sister so much."

"My mother went to help Katherine." Kate had already figured that much out herself. "Did Dimple know what kind of trouble Katherine was in?"

May sighed. "With Katherine it was either money or men. Or both. But Dimple never mentioned exactly what it was. I'm not sure she knew."

"So my mother went. I found a postcard from her to Grandmother saying she was coming home and bringing Katherine with her."

May nodded. "But they never made it."

"Grandmother must have known that something happened to them."

"Of course. That's why she hired the private investigator," May said. She nodded at their surprise. "It wasn't like Dimple to take such a step."

"She didn't call the sheriff?" Cyrus asked.

"No," May said. "She was afraid she would get Katherine in more trouble. Best to handle it privately."

Cyrus glanced at Kate. "And the private investigator?"

"Couldn't find a sign of either of them."

"What about their cars? Those should have turned up," Cyrus said.

May shook her head. "Kate, your mama had taken the bus to see her sister and who knows if Katherine even had a car that ran at that point. When she didn't hear from them, Dimple didn't know what to think. She waited, thinking one or the other or both would turn up. They couldn't have just disappeared."

"She just waited?" Kate asked.

"I remember those days when Elizabeth didn't come home." May took a sip of her coffee. "I saw the change in your grandmother. She knew something had happened to them and it wasn't good. Elizabeth would have moved heaven and earth to get back to you, sweetie," the elderly woman said, patting Kate's hand.

"So she just accepted that they were dead?" Kate demanded.

May bristled at her tone. "Your grandmother had a baby to raise. She did what she had to do for you. Her life became all about protecting you. The last thing she wanted was to have whatever trouble your aunt had gotten into put you in any danger."

"So she came up with the story about Katherine's weak heart and Elizabeth falling ill with pneumonia," Cyrus said.

"That's right," May said.

"And people believed that?" Kate said.

"Everyone loved your grandmother. If Dimple said the sky was falling, then everyone would have run for cover,"

May said, clearly in awe of her old friend. "I went to your mother's and aunt's funerals up at Fir Ridge. They were beautiful ceremonies. Everyone in town turned out. After that, your grandmother dedicated her life to you, Kate. She never looked back and neither should you."

Kate looked at Cyrus, frustrated and close to tears. "If only she had contacted the sheriff in Whitehorse right away."

"She knew her daughters were gone the moment she found the bracelet on her doorstep."

"What?" Kate cried.

May looked down at her hands, then back up at Kate. "She found one of the silver bracelets your grandfather made on her doorstep that spring. It was just lying there with one of the bells off lying next to it."

Kate's gaze shot to Cyrus. So the bracelet she had was her aunt's? Just as Cyrus had seen in his dream with the broken bell lying next to it on the nursery floor.

She shot to her feet and rushed into her grandmother's room to her jewelry box. The single bell lay under a nest of costume jewelry. She hadn't noticed it the day she'd found the bracelet—and the postcard that had sent her to Whitehorse.

As she came back into the room, she opened her fist to show Cyrus the tiny sleigh bell lying in her palm.

"When she found the bracelet, she took it as a sign," May said. "You have to understand your grandmother. Dimple Landon was all about living. She was the strongest, most courageous woman I knew, and she did a fine job of raising you. She has always been so proud of you."

"What about justice?" Kate asked. "Wouldn't she have wanted justice?"

May smiled sadly. "I would imagine that she knew justice would be served. All in good time."

Roberta Warren felt her heart drop as she replaced the phone. The sheriff was coming over to see her. She hadn't asked what it was about. She'd known.

It had started with Kate Landon moving to Whitehorse. The moment Roberta had laid eyes on her, she'd known. The young woman had asked a lot of questions, had even run a photograph in the newspaper.

*If you know anything about Katherine or Elizabeth Landon, please call,* the ad had said.

Roberta had held her breath, but nothing had come of it. After all, it had been thirty years, and no one knew Elizabeth Landon or would have recognized her from that grainy black-and-white photograph in the ad.

Then Cordell Winchester had called about a murder at the hospital. She'd thought she'd put out that fire, but then his twin, Cyrus, had shown up at the hospital asking not only about the murder and the woman he'd alleged he'd seen in a dream—but about babies in the nursery.

Thirty years ago and now it had all come back to haunt her. Roberta thought of the blood on the nursery floor, the woman lying in it, and felt a shudder of fear move through her. She'd never believed in karma. She didn't want to start now.

But she knew Cyrus Winchester couldn't have dreamed any of this. So where was he getting his information? Who was he getting it from? Someone who wanted to hurt her, the hospital and the town and destroy her career.

Roberta ran a hand through her short hair and tried to still her anger. She'd had a chance to retire and leave this town, but she'd passed it up because she wanted to come to a new, modern hospital for the last years of her career.

She'd made a name for herself in this community despite growing up poor on a dirt farm south of town. Now all of that could be taken away with one fell swoop. She felt all the blood drain from her face at the thought.

Well, she wasn't going down alone. Nor was she going down broke. She'd sworn she would never be poor again.

She reached for the phone, then hesitated. She knew there would be no going back once she made this call.

*To hell with that,* she thought and, picking up the phone, dialed the local number. "You said not to worry when that woman moved to town, but now this man shows up swearing he saw a woman murdered in the old hospital nursery," she said, keeping her voice down.

"What man?"

"Cyrus Winchester," she said and reached over to turn on her radio. The woman in the next office was a terrible gossip and the walls were thin. Roberta thought maybe she shouldn't have called from here. "He's a *private investigator.* And that isn't all, he's asking about the two babies that were in the nursery the night of the murder."

She heard surprise on the other end of the line.

"He knows. I thought you said—"

"He doesn't know *anything.*"

"What if he's found some evidence…"

"I'll take care of it."

"You said that last time." She took a breath. "I'm going to need more money."

Silence, then, "You were already paid."

"You said it was over, that no one would ever know."

"And no one does. I'll take care of this."

"I want more money."

The silence lasted longer this time. "Fine, but don't call me again. I'll contact you." The line disconnected.

Roberta slammed down the phone, her hand shaking. A sliver of worry wedged itself just under her skin like a splinter. She hoped calling hadn't been a mistake.

Now that he and Kate knew what they were looking for, it didn't take them long to find the canceled check and the report from the private investigator.

Cyrus glanced at the report, then handed it to Kate.

"He came up with nothing?" Just as May had said.

"The P.I. couldn't find your aunt or your mother. Your aunt was going under an assumed name and your mother..." Cyrus shrugged. "With neither of them driving a car, it would have been very hard to track either of them down."

Kate shook her head.

"Unfortunately, the investigation firm she hired in Bozeman has gone out of business. Not that the investigator could help anyway, since he came up empty thirty years ago." Cyrus could see how disappointed she was.

Kate had been quiet since May had left, but somehow she looked more peaceful. Her grandmother had done what she thought was right. Dimple's focus had been on the baby left in her care. And she had done a great job, Cyrus thought. Kate was wonderful.

They dug through more boxes in the attic and some in a shed out back, but they found nothing else of interest.

After breakfast at a diner in West Yellowstone, they drove the ninety miles to Bozeman. On the ride there, Kate was quiet. Cyrus lost himself in his own thoughts.

Main Street Bozeman was bustling, unlike Whitehorse.

"Too much traffic," Kate complained as they drove

through. "I forget how noisy and crazy it is being in a larger town."

Cyrus laughed at that. "You really are a small-town girl at heart. You should come to Denver."

"Maybe I will sometime," she said without looking at him. "By the way, thank you for last night."

"Do you want to talk about your nightmare?"

Kate shook her head. "I don't even remember it."

Cyrus glanced over at her and saw her face. With a jolt, he realized this was the first time she'd ever lied to him.

Roberta Warren looked up in surprise as the sheriff appeared in her office doorway.

"Do you have a minute?" McCall asked and watched as Roberta glanced at her clean desk as if searching for a reason to be too busy.

After a moment, the hospital administrator rose behind her desk. "Come in."

McCall stepped into the office, closing the door behind her and making Roberta lift a brow.

"Is this official business?" she asked, instantly looking nervous.

McCall took a seat. "I'm here investigating a nurse who worked at the hospital thirty years ago. Candace Porter?"

Roberta shook her head. "The name doesn't ring a bell." But McCall had already caught her expression. Roberta Warren was a horrible liar.

"Really? She was murdered in your hospital thirty years ago. I would think you would have remembered that name, since I believe she was the only person to be murdered there."

Roberta's cheeks flamed with embarrassment. "I guess

I have tried to forget such a tragic incident. And it has been thirty years, as you say."

McCall nodded. "You still have a file on her, though."

The older woman looked as if she might deny it, but seemed to change her mind. "I'm sure we do."

"I'd like to see it. For some reason it wasn't with the police report."

"Now?" Roberta said, clearly caught off guard.

"Now."

"I'm not sure—"

"I'll be happy to help you look for it."

Roberta didn't looked pleased to hear that. "The file would be in our storage facility across town."

McCall got to her feet. "Good thing Whitehorse is such a small town. We should be able to get the file before lunch. Well?" she asked when the hospital administrator hadn't moved.

"I was just thinking that I would probably need a judge to—"

"Roberta," the sheriff said patiently, "I can get a warrant to go through all your records. I'll just have the storage facility sealed until I get access. The file should have been in the original police report. I can't help but wonder why it isn't in there."

The hospital administrator slowly got to her feet. Her face was pinched as she reached into her top drawer, took out a key and opened another drawer in her desk. From there she took another key, this one on a large key ring. She straightened.

"I really don't need you to come with—"

"I'm tagging along," McCall said. "Did I mention there is no statute of limitations on murder? Or the offense for obstructing justice?"

"You don't need to take that tone with me," Roberta said, bristling.

"Let me be honest with you," the sheriff said. "You've made me suspicious enough just in the last few minutes. If you try to cover anything up—"

Anger flared in Roberta's eyes, her breath suddenly ragged. "I most certainly—"

"Let's just get this over with, shall we? Oh, and I'd also like to get the names of the babies that were in the hospital nursery the night Candace Porter was murdered."

All the color washed from the hospital administrator's face. "That will definitely take a subpoena to release that information. Hospital privacy laws—"

"Yes, I'm familiar with those," McCall said, gratified. She didn't have the names, but she did have something she'd come for. Roberta Warren was scared. McCall had been in law enforcement long enough to know what that meant.

The question was, how deeply involved had Roberta been in this mess?

By the time Cyrus drove them through Big Timber, dark clouds hung over the Crazy Mountains. At Harlowton to the north, snowflakes began to fall and by the time they reached Judith Gap, the snow was blowing horizontally and spinning the impressive blades of the wind farm on both sides of the two-lane highway.

"Thirty years ago, five thousand dollars was a lot of money," Kate said when they stopped in Lewistown at a Chinese-food place. They'd both been quiet most of the trip so far, both clearly lost in their own thoughts. "Who in Whitehorse had that kind of money?"

Cyrus shrugged. "There's money there, you just don't see it like you do in Bozeman or some place where people are moving to Montana and building huge homes. Some of the ranchers do all right, I've heard. They run big spreads. I would imagine any number of them could have raised the five grand."

"I guess we won't know until we get the names of the parents of the babies in the nursery that night," she said with a sigh.

"McCall is working on it. Hopefully, by the time we get home—" His cell phone rang. He smiled. "McCall," he said. "We were just talking about you."

Kate listened to his side of the conversation, filling in the blanks.

"We're on our way back now," Cyrus said. "Lewistown. Sure, we can do that. You'll be at the office? You can't tell me over the phone what you've found out? What about the babies? Yeah, I expected that. Any chance of getting a judge to sign a subpoena? Yeah." He looked over at Kate. "Sure, I understand. Okay, see you in a couple of hours."

"No luck getting the names from the hospital administrator, I take it?" she asked when he hung up.

He shook his head. "But she did say she got Candace Porter's job application. Apparently there isn't much on it. She wants us to stop by."

Kate didn't know what she was feeling. One moment she was depressed, the next hopeful. "We need the names of those babies. There has to be a way."

"We'll get them. Meanwhile, we can check out the application. There might be something there that will help."

She figured if there had been, McCall would have told him about it. But still, now she was anxious to get home as she finished her sesame chicken.

"I just had a thought," Cyrus said and pulled out his phone. "McCall," he said. "I was just wondering. Whitehorse only had one doctor thirty years ago, right? Oh, dead, huh?" He looked disappointed. "Was he also the coroner on the Candace Porter murder case?"

As Cyrus waited he looked across the table at her, a re-assuring look on his face. He waited and Kate guessed that McCall was checking.

"What's that?" he asked, sitting up a little straighter. "How about that? No, great, yeah, that is real interestin'." He snapped his phone shut. "Want to guess who the coroner was on the case?"

Kate shook her head, but she couldn't help smiling since Cyrus looked so pleased.

"Roberta Warren, the hospital administrator. She was filling in because the regular coroner had been hospitalized after an accident."

"How convenient," Kate said.

"My thought exactly."

Cyrus parked in front of the sheriff's department. Twilight had settled over the small town. It had taken them longer to drive from Lewistown to Whitehorse than he'd expected because of the snowstorm and all the deer on the highway. Something about the late October day had brought them all out.

McCall was the only one still in the office. She ushered them in, closing the door behind them. Once seated behind her desk, she said, "You were right. The real Candace Porter has been living in Ireland the past thirty years."

"How can we prove that the woman who was murdered was my aunt?" Kate asked.

"The body will have to be exhumed," McCall said.

"She's buried here in town?" Kate asked.

"According to what I've been able to find out, the local

mortician donated his services when no next of kin was found."

Cyrus reached over and took Kate's hand. She looked pale, but strong and determined. He hoped once everything was out, this would bring her some relief.

"You said they had been unable to find any next of kin," Cyrus said.

"Apparently the real Candace Porter couldn't be found back then, and, as you can see, there is nothing written on her employment application under *In case of emergency.*"

He glanced down the single sheet of paper she handed him, taking in the local address before his gaze lit on the line McCall drew his attention to. He looked closer. There had been a number there, but apparently it had been whited out.

"Wouldn't a hospital especially require an emergency number from an employee?" he asked. "It appears there was a number here but it was covered up," he said, handing the paper to Kate, who looked at it before handing it over to the sheriff.

"I saw that," McCall said. "I'll send it to the crime lab to see if they can recover the number, but I'm betting it was Katherine Landon's mother's number."

"Do we know who hired her?" Cyrus asked.

"Roberta Warren."

He swore under his breath. "If an employee is murdered at the hospital, then wouldn't the next of kin be notified?"

The sheriff nodded. "But apparently your grandmother was never called because Roberta didn't know who Candace really was."

"But she did know," Kate cried, pulling out the letter they'd found from her aunt to her mother. "Her boss knew she wasn't Candace Porter."

McCall took the letter from her. "Okay, your grand-mother was never told, but your mother was in town."

Cyrus nodded. "We think she heard about the murder."

"She would have gone straight to the hospital..." Kate's voice broke.

"Where she would have talked to Roberta."

"Or the sheriff," McCall said. "Okay, what aren't you telling me?"

Cyrus shot Kate a look before he told McCall about the baby switch he'd seen in the dream. "Roberta knew Candace was Katherine. She was her boss. She had to be involved in the baby switch."

"You have no proof Roberta was involved," McCall pointed out. "So far it's all conjecture."

"That's why we have to get the names of those babies," Kate said, sitting forward in her chair. "It's all tied to those babies and why someone hired my aunt to switch them."

McCall lifted a brow. "Hired her?"

Cyrus had brought the paperwork they'd found at Kate's grandmother's cabin. He glanced over at Kate. She nodded and he handed McCall the manila envelope. "Everything we found is in there. It looks like someone paid Katherine Landon, aka Candace Porter, to switch the babies."

"Five thousand dollars?" McCall said as she thumbed through the papers. She stopped on the private investigator's report, her gaze going to Kate. "Your grandmother suspected foul play? But I never saw anything in the file about her contacting the sheriff."

"We suspect she didn't," Kate said. "She hired a private investigator. When he didn't come up with anything..."

"Kate was a baby," Cyrus added. "Her grandmother had her to raise. She symbolically buried her daughters and turned all of her attention to raising Kate."

McCall sat back. "If you're right, someone paid Candace to switch the babies. Why kill her?"

"To cover up the crime," Cyrus said. "Or," he glanced at Kate again, "as Kate has suggested, maybe her mother talked her sister out of it and at the last minute, Katherine switched the babies back and double-crossed the killer."

"You saw all this in your...dream? So now you're saying you could have seen her switching the babies back," McCall said and shook her head. "I can't see Roberta killing anyone in the hospital. The hospital is her little kingdom."

Cyrus agreed. "Roberta is involved, though. She had access to the employment application. She would have been the one to make the call about her murdered employee. Roberta knew Katherine wasn't Candace Porter and yet she didn't fire her. When she found out about Katherine's sister, she would have called someone. She couldn't take the chance that Candace had confided in her sister. Clearly Roberta couldn't trust Candace, since she wasn't even who she said she was and she'd possibly double-crossed whoever was behind the baby switch. Someone would have to take care of the sister quickly."

"Cyrus, we don't know for a fact that when Katherine mentioned in the letter that her boss had found out that she meant Roberta or even that she was telling the truth," McCall pointed out.

He knew he was doing what he'd told Kate not to—jumping to conclusions. "You're right."

"But there is one thing I do know," Kate said, voice breaking. "If my mother had gotten the chance, she would have called my grandmother about Katherine's death. She never got the chance because someone tipped off the killer."

* * *

Roberta had tried to talk herself out of it all day. She knew she couldn't chance making the call again from her office. At least not while everyone was around. But she was so shaken by the sheriff's visit.

She'd been told not to call again. What was she supposed to do? Just take all this heat alone?

She grabbed her purse and cell phone and started for the door. Her plan was to go out to her car, pretend to run an errand and make the call so she could be assured that no one would overhear her.

She was almost to the door when she realized that calls made on her cell would show up on the bill. Now more than ever, she had to start covering her tracks.

Closing her office door, she forced herself to go back to her desk. If she called from her office, there could be all kinds of explanations for such a call.

She knew that phone calls were broken down by department and even by office. That was how she kept track of anyone using a phone for personal calls. Her determination to run a tight ship now had it where her line could be monitored, as well.

She had little choice. She couldn't use her cell or her home phone and it would be impossible to find a pay phone in Whitehorse where she knew no one would overhear—or wonder what she was doing.

She'd been forced to wait all day after turning over a copy of Candace Porter's employee file to the sheriff. She flushed at the memory of what the sheriff had said to her. She was a suspect in Candace Porter's murder.

Correct that. Katherine Landon's murder.

And that was only the beginning, Roberta thought. Once

the truth came out about that murder, the rest of it would start falling like dominoes.

She checked the clock. Everyone in administration had gone home for the day. All the lights were out but the ones in her office, the hallway dark in this part of the hospital.

Roberta had always loved this time of the day, when she would have the place to herself. She often worked late, so no one had questioned her staying tonight.

She got up and went to her door to look out. She listened for a moment. The only light came from under the double doors that led to the hallway and the nurses' station.

She stepped back into her office, closed the door and picked up the phone with trembling fingers. *Don't call me again. I'll contact you.*

Roberta hesitated, but only for a moment. She shouldn't have to bear the brunt of this alone. She dialed angrily, thinking she would demand more money to keep her mouth shut. She deserved it.

"The sheriff knows," she said without preamble. She hurriedly detailed the sheriff's questions about Candace Porter and the request for not just the employee application but the names of the babies in the nursery.

"You're panicking unnecessarily. They don't know anything and as long as you keep your cool, they never will. I told you, they don't have any evidence. If they did, they would already have a subpoena for the babies' names."

Roberta had heard about the break-in at Second Hand Kate's. Maybe there wasn't any evidence. "But if you'd heard the way the sheriff talked to me... She demanded Candace Porter's file. I had to give it to her. I thought this was over. If it comes out about the babies—"

"Get ahold of yourself. I told you I would take care of everything. You just do your part and relax. This will blow over. Whatever you do, don't call me again." The phone was slammed down.

Roberta replaced her receiver, shaking all over. She didn't know what upset her the most, the way she'd just been treated or the feeling that her neck alone was on the chopping block. Of course she would be a suspect. She'd been the hospital administrator at the time of the murder. She'd hired Candace Porter.

Her heart began to pound. Everything would come out.

She groaned at the memory of what she'd done—and why. Her reputation would be destroyed. She would deny it all, but she knew it would come down to her word against— With a shock, she realized that *she* was the one who wouldn't be believed. She was the one who would end up in prison.

Her hand went to the phone again. Maybe if she told the sheriff everything…

She pulled back.

It hadn't reached that point yet. She was panicking and it wasn't like her.

Roberta straightened her skirt, brushed a piece of lint from the sleeve of her jacket and tried to calm down.

They didn't know anything. They wouldn't find anything. The worst that could happen was that the truth might come out about who Candace Porter was.

Roberta told herself that she would pretend to be as shocked about that news as anyone. She would weather this storm and in a few months she would retire and take her money and move to someplace warm, far from Whitehorse, Montana.

But, she thought, she was going to need a lot more money for being forced to go through this alone. And she would damn sure call when the time came.

# Chapter 11

"I know it's a long shot," Cyrus said as they left the sheriff's department. "But I thought we should check out the address your aunt put on her employment application."

Kate had been thinking the same thing. She felt a little shell-shocked after everything they'd found out. She hugged herself. It had gotten dark while they were inside. The wind had come up and now kicked up dust from the street. There was a chill in the air as she climbed into Cyrus's pickup and they drove the four blocks across town.

The apartment house was large and rambling, once an old farmhouse that had sat alone before the town encroached on it. As they walked to the door, piles of dried fallen leaves blew around their feet.

Inside the front door was a list of names of people who lived there. Most of the slots were empty. Apartment three was marked "manager" and the name Harkin.

At Cyrus's knock, an elderly gentleman with a shock

of white hair and a small wrinkled face like one of those apple dolls answered.

"Hello, Mr. Harkin?" Kate asked. "We'd like to talk to you about one of your renters."

"Candace Porter." He laughed at her surprise. "The sheriff called earlier." He opened the door wider. "Come on in. And call me Harry. Everyone does."

"The sheriff already called?" Cyrus asked.

"Wanted to know if I remember renting to the woman. I said, 'What do you think, that I'm losing my mind?' Ha, I'm as sharp as a tack." He smiled and ushered them in, winking at both her and Cyrus.

Once inside, the old man eyed Kate, then Cyrus. "Newlyweds? I've got a nice two-bedroom on the second floor."

"We're not looking for an apartment," Cyrus said. "Kate owns Second Hand Kate's downtown and lives over the shop. I'm just here visiting from Colorado."

That about sized it up, Kate thought. Once this was over Cyrus would be going back to his life in Colorado. She knew she'd needed that reminder, but it still depressed her. She was going to miss him terribly. She'd come to depend on Cyrus and that, she realized, was a mistake.

Was there a woman waiting for him back in Denver? If that was true, wouldn't the woman have come to Montana with him? Kate would have. She wouldn't have let him come up here alone, not when he'd just come out of a coma.

"So you remember Candace Porter living here thirty years ago?" Cyrus asked.

"Sure do. She was a looker," Harkin said and grinned over at Kate. "Kinda looked like you, now that I think about it."

"I'm Candace's niece."

"Oh." He sobered. "Sorry. What would you like to know?"

"Anything you can tell us," Kate said.

"I'll tell you what I told the sheriff. Candace lived here for four months."

"You can remember that after thirty years?" Cyrus asked, sounding skeptical.

"I'm good, but I'm not that good," Harkin said with a laugh. "I looked up her file. I keep files on all my renters. But I remember Candace. She was a loner. She just went to work, worked nights, and never made any noise. I felt kind of sorry for her. If I'd been younger..." He let the thought die off. "I was shocked when she was murdered."

"Did the sheriff question you about the murder at the time?" Cyrus asked.

"Sure did. I told him what I told you. He looked through her apartment. She didn't have much and that was that. Never did catch the bastard. Excuse my language," he said to Kate. "I just made some coffee. Sit down." He disappeared into the kitchen before they could decline his offer.

Kate shrugged and they looked around for a place to sit.

The apartment was filled from top to bottom. No flat surface wasn't covered. Under the scent of fresh-perked coffee was dust, mildew and old age.

Cyrus made a place for them to sit on the old chesterfield couch as Harkin returned with a small tray and three cups filled with coffee. He shoved a stack of newspapers to the floor and set down the tray on a corner of the coffee table.

"Don't get many visitors. Live alone since the wife died," he said.

Cyrus handed Kate a cup of coffee, then took one for himself. Kate took a tentative sip. The coffee was strong and bitter.

"I'm surprised you keep records that long," Cyrus said.

"Got records from longer back than that," Harkin said

with a laugh and pointed to a small alcove. It was filled with filing cabinets, an assortment of papers piled high on top of each.

He put down his coffee to go into the alcove and open one of the filing cabinets. Amazingly he, came out with a folder. "Candace Porter." He smiled and tapped the discolored folder with his finger before handing it to Cyrus.

He opened it so Kate could see. The application for the apartment was sketchy at best, most of the lines left empty. Her aunt had paid one hundred and forty dollars a month with a fifty-dollar cleaning deposit. She'd apparently stayed just over four months.

"What did you do with her belongings?" Kate asked, even though she was sure that he'd tossed them out or the sheriff had taken them.

The old man pointed at the file folder. "Says right in there at the bottom of the application that if anyone leaves anything it will be held for thirty days, then discarded or sold at my discretion."

"So whatever she left is gone." Kate couldn't hide her disappointment. Thirty years was a long time and she'd guess this place had been through a lot of renters and their leftover stuff in that time.

"Actually, there wasn't enough to worry about. I just boxed it up and forgot about it. When the sheriff called, I told her I was sure I'd gotten rid of the box. But then I got to thinking...." He got up and went to a box sitting just inside the door, which Kate hadn't noticed until now. "I got it out of my shed out back."

Printed on the side of the box were the name *C. Porter* and the date: Dec. 24, 1980. He set it down in front of them on the floor.

"I figured her sister might have wanted what she left behind," Harkin said.

"Sister?" Kate said, her voice breaking.

"Her sister was here visiting her. Only visitor I ever saw her have except for that other nurse, now that I think about it. Sarah. Sarah Welch Barnes now. I heard she's visiting her sister down in Old Town." He seemed to shake himself. "Where was I? Oh, her sister. She was staying here but left after… I thought she'd come by for Candace's things, but she never did. I'm afraid that's all she left behind," he said in conclusion.

They thanked him, promised to stop by sometime and left. Cyrus put the box in the back of the truck as Kate climbed in. As Cyrus joined her, his cell phone rang.

Cyrus was surprised to see that the call was from his grandmother. He shouldn't have been. Whitehorse was a small town. Of course she would have heard that he was back and out of his coma. He felt guilty for not calling her.

"I was hoping you'd come out to the ranch," Pepper Winchester said. "I would love to see you. Bring your friend."

"My friend?" he asked as he glanced over at Kate.

A slight chuckle, then, "Kate Landon. You didn't really think I hadn't heard about the two of you, did you? My ranch is remote. It's not on another planet. Maybe you could come out for dinner. Your aunt Virginia is here."

Aunt Virginia. He remembered her only too well as being mean when he was boy.

"Tomorrow would be good. I'll have Enid make something special."

He was still amazed that his grandmother's housekeeper and cook was still alive. "I'll have to get back to you on that."

"I really do need to see you, Cyrus."

He felt a stab of guilt. Three months ago he'd been on his way to see her before he'd been put into a coma. "All right."

"Bring Kate." It sounded like an order as she hung up.

"That was my grandmother," Cyrus said, snapping his phone shut. "She wants us to come out to dinner. Tomorrow night."

"Us?" Kate asked in surprise.

"Apparently the Whitehorse grapevine is in fine working order. Do you mind?"

"No, I told you I've been wanting to meet her." She smiled over at him. "I've kept you from seeing her and I'm sorry. My problems have taken over your life."

He shook his head. "You've been the best thing about all this."

The Welch Ranch was outside of Old Town Whitehorse, the original settlement back when Whitehorse had been nearer to the Missouri River. But when the railroad came through, the town migrated ten miles north, taking the name with it. Old Town Whitehorse was now little more than a ghost town, except for a handful of ranches and a few of the original buildings.

A woman in her sixties opened the door, wearing an apron and a smile. Kate could hear country-western music playing in the background and the scent of chocolate-chip cookies baking wafted out the open door into the crisp fall air.

"We're looking for Sarah Welch Barnes," Cyrus said.

"You've found her and you're just in time," she said. "The cookies are still warm." She ushered them into the kitchen and introduced the slightly older woman scooping dough onto a baking sheet as her sister Mary. "What would you like to drink? I have some apple cider." She looked at each of them, smiling, as she opened the refrigerator and took out a gallon jug of cider. "This came from our trees."

"Sarah, we're here about someone you used to work with at the hospital," Cyrus said. "I'm—"

"I know. You're Cyrus, a private investigator from Denver, and you're Kate, you own a shop in Whitehorse that everyone is talking about." She smiled. "Agnes Palmer stopped by this morning. She *sees* things. She told me you would be stopping by so I told Mary we should bake some cookies." She handed each of them a glass of cider. "Sit. Help yourself to some cookies." She motioned to the cookies cooling on the racks on the table. "I'm not sure what I can tell you about Candace, though."

Kate shot Cyrus a glance. "I'm sorry, you said a woman told you we would be stopping by?"

"Agnes Palmer. It's the darnedest thing," Mary said. "She's psychic. Seriously, she just knows things. I don't think she likes it, but she says it must be God's will since it all started last year when she was struck by lightning out in her garden trying to save her tomatoes. She grows the most beautiful tomatoes." Sarah smiled. "But you want to know about your aunt."

As Kate sat down at the table, she realized she hadn't mentioned Candace was her aunt.

"I liked Candace. I befriended her, I guess you would say. I felt a little sorry for her. She just seemed so…lost." She slid a rack of cookies toward them as Cyrus pulled out a chair and joined Kate. "You really should try them while they are still warm."

Kate took a cookie, as did Cyrus. "What do you mean… lost?"

"I just had a feeling that she'd had a hard life. We weren't close friends. I worked her shift sometimes for her when she didn't feel well."

"Was she ill?" Kate asked, alarmed.

"More like depressed. I got the feeling that she'd struggled. I know she didn't have much money. She didn't own a car and the one time I stopped by her apartment, it was clear she didn't have much."

"Any idea who might have wanted to harm her?" Cyrus asked.

Sarah shook her head. "And it's sad because I had the feeling that her life was just starting to turn around. She just seemed…happier."

Kate wondered if that had to do with Elizabeth being there.

"She was even dating."

"Dating?" Cyrus asked.

"Well, I should say, she'd been out a couple of times."

"Do you know who the man was?" Kate asked.

"Audie. Audie Dennison. They met at the hospital." She smiled. "Audie is the nicest man you'd ever want to meet. His older sister Marie raised him after their parents died. She's a lot older than Audie." She sobered. "I heard she isn't well. I'm sure Audie is looking after her the way she looked after him when they were kids."

"Was he a patient when he met Candace?" Cyrus asked.

"No, his sister, Marie, was. She had a rough pregnancy because of her age, so she was in the hospital for the last few weeks before her son was born."

Kate shot Cyrus a look.

"She gave birth to a son?"

Sarah smiled. "Jace. A beautiful boy."

Cyrus took a cookie. "Was Jace born before Candace

was killed?" He took a bite of the cookie. "Umm, these are wonderful."

Sarah beamed. "Thank you. Jace was born that night. I remember because it was just crazy around the hospital. Marie had some complications. We were all so afraid all during her pregnancy that she would lose the baby. Then in the labor room, the baby was breech." Her smiled brightened. "But he turned and was finally born. Well, it was nothing but a miracle, since Marie never thought she'd have a baby and she'd wanted one so badly. She would have done anything to have a baby and then to have Jace…"

"Was that the only baby born that night?" Cyrus asked.

Sarah laughed. "No, that was what made that night so crazy. The other mother in labor was…well, she was a screamer, demanding, nothing like Marie, and what made it so hard was that she gave birth within minutes of Marie. We really could have used more help."

"Do you remember the name of the other mother?" Kate asked.

Sarah rolled her eyes. "I sure do. I still feel guilty about it because I gave her to your aunt, who ended up delivering the baby since the doctor was busy with Marie. I think it was Candace's first birthing. I remember the way she looked at that baby boy. It was heartbreaking. I really think she would have liked a baby of her own and maybe she would have had one with Audie, if things had been different."

"You said you remember the name of the woman who gave birth to the second boy that day?" Cyrus asked again.

Sarah hesitated. "Agnes warned me it had to do with the night Candace was killed and those two babies. I suppose it's all right to tell you. After all, it's been thirty years. I mean, this can't be about a lawsuit, because I can tell you that Candace did nothing wrong. That baby was as healthy as could be when he was born."

"Are you saying the second baby died?" Kate asked, her heart in her throat.

"I thought you knew," Sarah said, looking confused. "Sudden infant death. We still don't know what causes it. There wasn't an autopsy done, but maybe the baby had a weak heart. With all the confusion, the doctor didn't get to take a good look at the babies before Candace took them down to the nursery."

Kate couldn't speak. Had her aunt known that the baby wasn't well? Is that why she'd agreed to switch the babies?

"Sarah," Cyrus said. "We're just trying to find out who killed Candace and why."

"I am sorry, dear."

"Thank you," Kate said. "I was wondering. Did Candace ever wear a silver bracelet?"

"With tiny bells on it," the woman said, brightening. "Wore it all the time. The patients loved it. That little tinkling sound. They could always tell when she was around. Oh, I am so glad this isn't about Virginia. It would be just like her to be looking for someone to blame for the death of her baby, even after all these years."

"Virginia?" Cyrus said and Kate heard something break in his voice.

"Virginia Winchester." Sarah must have seen his expression. "She had the other baby that night. Do you know her?"

"Virginia Winchester is my aunt," Cyrus told Kate the moment they were in his pickup headed back to town.

"Did you know she had a baby?"

"No. As far as I know she was never married or even dated, for that matter."

"That's terrible about the baby dying," Kate said. "But what if the baby that wasn't well was the other woman's and my aunt knew it?"

Cyrus had thought of that. Given what Sarah Barnes had said about Marie Dennison, her advanced age, her desire for a baby and the problems she had giving birth, he could see how anyone would want to see her leave the hospital with a healthy baby boy—especially if Virginia was unwed and, well, Virginia. She had a way of rubbing people the wrong way.

She'd certainly made a negative impression on Sarah Welch. He could well imagine she hadn't been popular with Candace, either. For all he knew, Virginia could have been planning to give the baby up, which would have made it even easier for Kate's aunt to agree to switch the babies.

"Do you think Jace Dennison is your cousin?" Kate asked.

"I have no idea. I've never seen him. We left here when I was seven, and as far as I know my family didn't even know the Dennisons."

He'd never imagined that this would hit so close to home. But given that he'd dreamed it while in a coma, he knew he shouldn't have been surprised.

"What are you going to do?" Kate asked.

Cyrus looked over at her. Her concern touched him. "I'm going to make sure you're safe. Do you mind if we swing by my hotel and pick up the rest of my things? I'd like to stay with you at the shop."

She nodded and he quickly added, "I thought I could sleep in one of those bedrooms you have made up in the shop, if that's okay."

"Sure. Thank you. I have to admit I feel a little spooked knowing there is a killer still out there."

She wasn't the only one.

Cyrus ran into the hotel, leaving the truck running and Kate waiting. It only took him a few moments to get the rest of his belongings. He wondered why he hadn't checked out before they went to West Yellowstone. Hadn't he known he was going to stay with Kate until this was over?

In his room, he noticed something he hadn't before. The place had been searched—just as Kate's place had been gone through. He'd had so little to search, he hadn't paid any attention when he'd stopped by here on the way to West Yellowstone.

As far as he could tell, nothing had been taken because, he suspected, the intruder hadn't found what he or she had been looking for.

He made an inquiry at the desk, but of course he was told that no one had asked for him and no one had let anyone into his room.

But clearly someone was worried that he and Kate knew more than they did.


Kate hadn't been able to hide her relief when Cyrus asked to stay with her. She really hadn't been looking forward to spending the night alone—not after the nightmare she'd had last night.

She'd told Cyrus she didn't remember it. She hadn't wanted to worry him. But she did: in the dream, someone had tried to kill her. She feared telling Cyrus about the dream would only make him more determined to keep her out of this investigation.

Once they reached her shop and apartment, Cyrus had checked to make sure no one had been there. He'd changed the locks before they'd left, but he said he wanted to make sure there hadn't been another break-in.

There hadn't.

"I need to check the basement," he said.

"Thanks." She could tell he was upset about what they'd learned and probably just wanted to keep busy. That and he wanted to keep his distance from her.

"Would you mind fixing that cable down there?" she asked. "Halloween is day after tomorrow and the haunted house opens at five o'clock, right after I close the shop."

He looked like he might argue that she should cancel the haunted house. She didn't give him a chance and hurried off to get a shower. From upstairs she could hear him working. It was a comforting sound.

She'd always felt she could take care of herself. Now, though, she felt uneasy. Knowing there was a killer still on the loose—a killer who she feared had been in her shop and apartment—had her feeling vulnerable. She hated the feeling and was determined to go back to loving this place and her life here.

But even as she thought it, Kate knew that it was more than just catching the killer and finding out the truth. It was Cyrus. This place would never feel the same once he was gone.

It was late by the time he finished. Cyrus showered while she made them a snack. She wore a skirt, knit top and ballet shoes, and it felt good to be home, especially with him here.

"I baked cupcakes," she said when he came out of the bathroom. "But if you're hungrier than that, I could make us an omelet." He smelled heavenly and his damp hair curled at the nape of his neck.

She hardly ever saw him when he wasn't wearing his Stetson. She'd thought he couldn't look any sexier than in it, but she'd been wrong.

Standing there, freshly showered in a T-shirt and jeans,

he was the sexiest man she'd ever seen. He looked almost shy as he thanked her, but passed, saying he wasn't hungry.

"Are you afraid of my cooking?" she asked, only half joking. She had a pretty good idea that it wasn't the cupcakes he was passing on. She sensed he was anxious to call it a night.

She tried to hide her disappointment. She'd hoped they would sit around and talk for a while.

"Kate—"

"Not to worry. The cupcakes will keep until tomorrow."

"I'm leaving after this is over."

His words hit her hard, even though she'd been expecting them. "I know."

"I can't leave my brother to take care of our business forever," he said.

"No, of course not. I realize that I've kept you from your work in Denver, your life—"

"That's not what I'm talking about," he said, taking a step toward her. "Kate," he said taking her shoulders in his hands.

"Thank you for staying as long as you have," she said quickly, afraid of what he was going to say.

"I care about you," he said, his voice rough. "Too much. Being with you…" He shook his head and let go of her. "I can't do this."

She told herself this would be worse if they'd made love and felt her eyes burn with tears from the lie. "It's late," she said pointedly and started to step past him.

Cyrus grabbed her arm, stopping her.

Desire spread through her, centering at her core, making her ache for him. "Please," she said, pleading, but not for what he thought.

He quickly let go of her. "I'll see you in the morning." He strode out of the room and down the stairs.

She stood, fighting the need to call him back, knowing how much harder it would be for him if she did.

It was dark by the time Roberta reached her house. She'd bought a place up on the hill overlooking Whitehorse. It was the part of Whitehorse people moved up to when they had enough money.

The way the house was situated she had a lot of privacy, something else she liked. She'd planted a hedge along each side and trees formed a shelter at the front and back.

She knew her neighbors, but she made a point of not being too friendly. When she came home, she wanted to be alone and unwind.

Roberta knew that people in town talked about her. The problem with Whitehorse was that everyone knew your business and most people had been around long enough to know everything about you from the time you were that poor little Roberta Thompson.

Marrying Mark Warren had been the smartest thing she'd ever done. He had been sixteen years older. She'd married him for his money and for what he could give her and he'd never tried to renege on their agreement. She liked being married in name only, liked being Mrs. Roberta Warren.

She'd wanted an education. He'd seen that she got it. What she hadn't told him was that she planned to leave Whitehorse in the dust once she was finished with her schooling.

But it hadn't turned out that way. Mark had gotten sick and she had to come back to take care of him. She'd gone to work at the hospital when she'd found out that her husband didn't have any money and had mortgaged the ranch to the hilt to pay the bills. He had a gambling habit she hadn't known about and had borrowed against the ranch.

Now, as she pulled up into her driveway and turned off the engine and lights, Roberta recalled that awful feeling in the pit of her stomach the day she'd learned that Mark was broke. *They* were broke.

Fortunately, she'd had her job at the hospital. But his medical bills in the years before he died had kept her from leaving Whitehorse.

"Water under the bridge," she said to herself and was startled how much she sounded like her mother. But unlike her mother, she had a plan. Soon she would leave and see the world.

Opening her car door, she grabbed her purse and stepped out. As the dome light went out in her car, she realized just how dark it was.

Wind whirled the fallen leaves around the bottom of the trees in the front yard. She'd heard a storm was blowing in. Always did this time of year.

Roberta caught movement out of the corner of her eye and froze. Was that someone standing alongside the hedge by the garage?

She stared until her eyes ached but saw nothing. Just her imagination. But she still stood listening, though, her skin prickling with unease even as she told herself she was just being silly. There was no one there.

Relieved and feeling foolish, she hurried forward through the breezeway toward the side door. It was even darker back here. She wished she'd remembered to leave the outside lights on. But then she hadn't known she was going to be this late when she'd left that morning.

She fumbled with her key, suddenly nervous again. Her

imagination seemed to be going wild. She felt as if some-one was standing right behind—

A hand dropped onto her shoulder. She jumped, letting out a cry and spun around, her heart in her throat. Relief washed over her. "Oh, it's just you. What are you doing here?"

# *Chapter 12*

Cyrus mentally kicked himself as he went downstairs. What the hell was wrong with him? He wanted Kate, that's what was wrong with him. Then why was he holding back?

Because he was going to have to leave here soon. He had to get back to his business. He couldn't leave Cordell handling all of it alone.

But just the thought of leaving Kate was killing him.

He knew that if he made love with her, he would never get over her. He wasn't even sure he would now.

Cyrus thought he would never get to sleep, his body aching for the woman lying upstairs and his mind awhirl with Kate and this case.

He woke to the clamor of footfalls on the stairs. He shot up in bed as Kate came running into the room. One look at her face and his pulse took off.

"What is it?" he cried, leaping from the bed. He'd gone to sleep as he had in West Yellowstone, wearing only his jeans.

Her green eyes were huge with fear and she was shaking. "Didn't you hear it?"

All he'd heard was her coming down the stairs. Was someone breaking in again? He looked past her, uncomprehending, and reached for the gun hanging in his shoulder holster next to the bed.

Then he heard it.

A chill rippled over his flesh and his heart began to pound, his mouth going dry.

Somewhere close by there was the sound of a baby crying.

"What the hell?" he said under his breath as another chill snaked up his spine. He stepped past her following the sound, Kate at his heels.

Outside the trees thrashed in the wind. A storm had blown in during the night. Shadows played on the old hardwood floors. He moved through them as the wail of the crying baby filled the old building.

The baby quit crying.

He stopped. He could hear his heart pounding and feel Kate gripping his free hand. There was nothing but the wind at the windowpanes.

The crying started up again. Cyrus realized where the sound was coming from. The display room Kate had decorated as a baby's nursery.

At the doorway, he looked in. Faint light bled through the window from the streetlamp outside. He could see the crib. It was full of dolls of all sizes and colors. He snapped on the overhead light and stared into the mass of tiny faces, looking for the real baby.

Kate let go of his hand and stepped to the crib. She leaned over and picked up one. It stopped crying as she turned with it in her arms. "It's just a doll," she said, her relief audible.

Something fell from the doll to the floor. A scrap of paper. Cyrus reached for it, sure that whoever had left it hadn't left fingerprints. Still, he was careful to pick it up by the edge. The handwriting was the same as the other note Kate had received. Written in childish scrawl were the words *Don't make me warn you again.*

The baby doll began to cry again.

Cyrus dropped the note into the crib and took the doll from her arms. "It's remote-controlled," he said as he found the batteries at the doll's back and dumped them into the crib as well.

The doll stopped crying. The room fell eerily silent.

He laid the doll back into the crib and looked at Kate. She wore a long white-cotton nightgown. Her hair was loose and hung around her shoulders in a rich wave of copper. Her eyes, so wide and beautiful, looked even greener than he remembered. The desire came like a punch to the chest.

"I should make some hot chocolate," she said and started to step away.

This time when he touched her, he felt her quiver as if an electrical current had run through her body.

"No hot chocolate," he said, his voice sounding hoarse even to him. He told himself all the reasons that this was a mistake as he pulled her to him, his mouth dropping to hers. She emitted a small cry of pleasure as he drew her closer, deepening the kiss.

He'd never wanted anyone as much as he wanted Kate. All thought left him as he felt her full breasts press against his bare chest, felt his heart take off like a wild stallion. He swept her up into his arms and carried her back to his room.

As he gently set her down on the bed, she looped her

arms around his neck, her gaze locking with his. He looked into her beautiful emerald eyes and was lost.

Kate's skin felt alive, her heart a thunder in her chest, her pulse thrumming in her ears as she looked into Cyrus's dark eyes.

"Kate, oh, Kate," he whispered, his voice hoarse with the desire she saw in the dark depths of his gaze.

She smiled as she felt him surrender to it. They'd been racing toward this moment from that first day they'd met. Cyrus slowly began to unbutton the front of her gown, his expression daring her to stop him.

His fingertips brushed the tender flesh of her breast, making her shiver with expectation. He kissed her, cupping one full breast in the palm of his hand, then trailed kisses from her neck down to the slope of her breast to the rock-hard nipple.

She arched into him, her palms against his hard chest. Her fingers followed the dark line of hair from his chest to the V at the top of his jeans. She worked at the buttons, freeing him of the rest of his clothing.

He stood over her for a moment, just looking down at her. His gaze made her feel like the most beautiful woman in the world.

As he pulled the nightgown up over her head, she drew him to her, desperately needing to feel his naked flesh against hers.

Their lovemaking became a blur of caresses and kisses, his hot mouth on hers before moving down her body, leaving a trail of fire over aching nipples to her center. With the wind howling outside, they were enveloped in a storm of their own.

When Cyrus entered her, she cried out and gripped

the iron headboard, her body glazed with sweat, her heart swelling as he took her with him to the peak of pleasure.

Later, lying in each other's arms, they heard the wind die down and looked out to see that it was snowing. Huge, lacy flakes drifted down to make the world outside into a fairyland of white.

They made love again, slowly, tenderly, and then slept, wrapped in each other's arms. It was there that Kate woke hours later.

Cyrus came awake slowly, as if from a dream. At first he thought it was daylight out, the snow was so bright. But when he looked at the clock he saw that it was only a little after three in the morning.

He realized at once what had woken him.

Kate was gone.

He sat up, listening for her, then quickly threw his legs over the side of the bed to pull on his jeans. Padding barefoot across the wood floor, he heard a sound coming from upstairs and smelled hot chocolate.

As he topped the stairs, he saw her sitting in the middle of the floor wearing a pink chenille robe. She had a cup of hot chocolate next to her and the box from her aunt's apartment in front of her. He watched her cut the tape on the box with a paring knife, then hesitate.

She saw him then and smiled. "I woke up and couldn't get back to sleep. There's extra hot chocolate." She motioned toward the stove.

He smiled, kissing her on the top of her head as he went to the stove to pour himself a cup. He dropped three large marshmallows into the cup on his way back to her.

Kate hadn't moved.

"You don't have to open the box," he said, seeing her hesitation.

"Yes, I do," Kate said. She grabbed the cardboard flaps and pulled them apart. He watched her, thinking how strong and determined she was. Thinking also that he had fallen for this remarkable woman.

He got a glimpse of the contents of the box. Clothes, just as he'd thought. She pulled out one item of clothing after another, tossing them aside. At the bottom of the box were a few toiletries. She held up the hairbrush.

With a jolt, he saw that there was still hair in the brush. "Kate—"

"DNA," she said with a knowing nod as she handed him the brush.

Suddenly she seemed to freeze before reaching into the box again. She brought out what he recognized at once as a small address book.

Her gaze swung up to meet his, then she opened the book and quickly leafed through the pages.

Even from where he was sitting he could see that the address book was nearly empty.

He saw her disappointment as she handed it to him. Starting at the As he went through each page. Under D was Dimple's name and phone number and a post office box in West Yellowstone.

He found a Sarah with a Whitehorse number. Sarah Welch, he figured. There was also a number for the hospital. Under Harkin was a number, the same one as the apartment house where Katherine had lived.

Cyrus stopped on the Js, sensing a change in Kate. He looked up to see her flipping through a handful of photographs. She stilled on the last one, tears filling her green eyes. "Kate?"

Soundlessly she handed him a photograph of her mother and aunt. They were standing outside next to a huge old pine. He recognized the tree as the one in front of the Whitehorse apartment house where Katherine had been living as Candace Porter. There was snow on the ground, and both women wore coats and gloves, but their heads were uncovered. Katherine's hair was pulled up in a ponytail. Elizabeth's was down around her shoulders.

They were both smiling at the camera, but the smiles didn't seem to reach their eyes.

He glanced at the date stamped on the back of the photograph: December 18, 1980. The day before Katherine was murdered.

"It proves my mother was here just the day before," Kate said.

"The sheriff will want to see this. Did you find anything interesting in the other photographs?"

Kate picked them up from her lap and handed them to him.

There were several of Katherine in her nurse's aide uniform at the hospital. One with another nurse, a much younger Sarah Welch.

As Kate began to put everything back into the box, he went through the rest of the address book. But there were no more names under the alphabetized sections.

Cyrus was about to close the book when he saw a phone number written small and in pencil at the very back of the book. The number had a local prefix, but no name.

He frowned, realizing it looked familiar. Curious, he took out his cell phone and dialed it.

After four rings, an elderly voice picked up. The moment he recognized the voice he realized why the number had been so familiar.

Still, he had to ask. "Who is this?"

"You've reached Winchester Ranch. Who were you calling?"

He hung up and looked over at Kate who was watching him now with interest. His mind spun like a top. Why would Katherine Landon have his grandmother's number?

Kate couldn't help but feel anxious about meeting Cyrus's grandmother, especially after he'd found her number in Aunt Katherine's address book.

"Why would your grandmother be involved in this?" she asked when they stopped by the sheriff's department to tell McCall what they'd learned from Sarah Welch—and Katherine's address book.

Both McCall and Cyrus had laughed.

"Pepper Winchester manipulate one of her children's lives?" Cyrus said with a groan. "You have no idea."

"Our grandmother always has an agenda," McCall said.

"But aren't you having your wedding out there at Christmas?" Kate asked.

"She caught me at a weak moment," the sheriff said. "Don't think I'm not worried. But my fiancé, Luke, assures me it will be fine no matter what."

"I just can't believe a mother would have any part of switching her own daughter's baby with another one and letting her daughter believe all these years that her son died," Kate said.

"I'm sure Pepper had her reasons," Cyrus said and looked to McCall, who shrugged.

"I never knew Virginia had a baby," McCall said. "They must have kept it pretty hush-hush. Any idea who the father of the baby might have been?"

"I was only four at the time," Cyrus said. "It was news

to me. But we're having dinner at Grandmother's tonight. I intend to ask her."

McCall raised a brow. "Grandmother invited me, as well. I was planning to go, but now…" she joked. "Truthfully, the crying doll, the notes, that isn't the way our grandmother operates. She's much more direct."

"Well, between the two of us tonight, maybe we can get the truth out of her," Cyrus said as they rose to leave.

"Thanks for the information about the babies," McCall said. "I put in a call to Roberta Warren, but apparently she called in sick." The sheriff smiled and nodded. "I'm sure she's avoiding me. I'll try to get hold of Jace Dennison. We'll need a DNA test to clear this up. I'm hoping he'll cooperate. His mother is real sick, I heard. He is probably headed home. I'm sure his uncle, Audie, let him know. That's interesting that Candace Porter, aka Katherine Landon, dated him."

"You think he talked her into switching the babies when she told him that his sister's baby wasn't well?" Kate asked.

"Or maybe the deal was already planned," Cyrus said. "Katherine could have confided in him, not about the money part. They could have both believed that Marie deserved the healthy baby. Virginia wasn't married and wasn't likeable."

"She was also young," McCall said. "She could have had more babies, while it sounds as if this was Marie's last chance. If Katherine changed her mind… Well, Audie idolized his older sister. Everyone's always said he would do anything for her."

"Even kill?" Cyrus asked.

McCall shrugged. "I guess we'll find out."

Just after lunch, McCall drove out to the Dennison place, a small, old homestead and ranch north of town. Audie lived in the old homestead house up the road from his sister and pretty much ran the small ranch they had shared since Jace left.

On this chilly fall day, McCall found him out behind the house chopping wood. He swung the axe, bringing it down on a log, wood chips flying into the air, as she walked over to him.

He stopped, breathing hard and looked at her. McCall feared that the rumors in the town had reached him. Any talk of the woman he'd dated would have him wary if he had any part in her murder.

"Sheriff," he said and set another log on the chopping block.

She stepped back as he brought the axe down. Half the log flew off in her direction. She side-stepped it, the chunk barely missing her leg.

"Need a moment of your time," she said.

"Yeah?"

He started to pick up another log to split.

"We can talk here or down at my office," she said. In truth, he didn't have to talk to her at all and she suspected he knew it.

She'd never liked Audie. He was a short, stocky man with an attitude problem, one of those men who seemed to think he'd gotten short shrift in life and wasn't happy about it.

In his late fifties, he was still physically fit. He'd never married and the only person he seemed to give a damn about was his sister. Only when he was around Marie and Jace did he soften enough to be almost likeable.

"What's it going to be, Audie?" McCall asked. "You have a permit for that wood you cut up in the Little Rockies?"

"You can't prove that's where I got it."

"But it would give me the right to take you in for questioning."

He slowly put down the axe and crossed his arms over his barrel chest.

"I'm sure you've heard I'm looking into Candace Porter's murder." When he said nothing, she added, "She was the nurse who was—"

"I remember Candace."

"You dated her, I understand."

"We went out a few times."

"What was she like?"

He shrugged. "Quiet."

"I'm going to cut to the chase, Audie. I have reason to believe she might have been paid to switch your sister's baby with the Winchester baby."

He let out a colorful curse. "Who the hell came up with that? That guy from Colorado *dream* that?"

McCall felt something give inside her at his response. It felt rehearsed and without the kind of fury she would have expected. "So you're saying there's no chance that happened?"

His gaze narrowed as he took a step toward her. "Jace is Marie's son and I won't have you—"

"Easy," she said, her hand slipping to her sidearm.

He stopped moving toward her. "You want to know who killed Candace? Why don't you ask your grandmother? That's right. She didn't want her daughter having that baby."

"Why is that?" McCall asked, even though she knew her grandmother would have had her reasons.

"Are you serious? Don't you know who that baby's daddy was?" He let out a bark of a laugh. "And you're the sheriff?"

"Who was the father?" she asked, disliking Audie all the more.

"Jordan McCormick."

She studied him, trying to decide if he was telling the truth or not, her heart pounding. Her grandmother would have been livid at even the thought of Virginia with Jordan McCormick. There'd been a feud between the two ranching families as far back as she could remember. Rumor had it the feud started when Pepper Winchester had an affair with Joanna McCormick's husband, Hunt.

"Did you know someone paid Candace to switch the babies?" McCall asked.

"She wouldn't have done it," Audie said. "Candace didn't have it in her."

McCall tried to tell if Audie found that a good quality about the woman or a tragic flaw. "Did you ever meet her sister?"

Audie seemed surprised. "I didn't even know she had a sister."

Again, McCall wasn't sure she believed him. "Did you have anything to do with Candace's murder?"

"Her name was Katherine Landon, not Candace Porter." He smiled at her surprise. "I was in love with her. I would have married her. In fact…" His voice broke. He turned and picked up the axe.

"You must have been devastated when she was killed, then."

"I looked for her killer," he said as he picked up a log from the pile and set it down on the chopping block. His gaze locked on hers. "I even went to the sheriff and told him that I thought Pepper Winchester had done it. He laughed me out of his office."

He raised the axe and brought it down on the log. The fall air cracked as the log split in a burst of wood chips. McCall breathed in the sweet scent of the pine, studying him. "You were the one who paid to have her buried in the cemetery," she said with sudden insight. It hadn't been the local mortuary after all.

Audie didn't deny it as he continued to chop wood.

As she drove away, McCall wasn't sure what she believed. Because sure as hell her grandmother was involved.

Cyrus wasn't sure what kind of reception he and Kate would get at the Winchester Ranch. Clearly his grandmother knew about all the questions he and Kate had been asking in Whitehorse.

They were just leaving for the ranch when his cell phone rang. It was McCall. She filled him in on what she'd found out from talking to Audie Dennison.

"I'm trying to locate Jace Dennison," she said.

"What do you mean, trying to locate?" Cyrus asked.

"Apparently he has a job where he is out of the country a lot," she said.

"I thought I heard he was a rodeo cowboy?"

"Was. Since college he kind of fell off the radar," McCall said.

Cyrus raised a brow. "Are you talking some kind of intelligence job like with the government?"

"Quite possibly, since I can't seem to get a line on him. But Marie is apparently getting worse. The hospice people said Jace usually contacts Marie every few weeks. They've promised to let me know when he calls."

"Hospice?"

"She's dying, that's why I'm sure once he hears, he'll return to Whitehorse at once."

"So there is little chance of getting his DNA," Cyrus said. "That means—"

"Aunt Virginia," McCall said. "She needs to be told there

is a chance the baby she buried isn't hers. I don't have to tell you the kind of fireworks this is about to set off."

*No,* Cyrus thought, thinking of his grandmother. "If Pepper is involved she'll do her damnedest to stop you from exhuming that baby's remains."

"I'm more concerned how Virginia is going to take it," McCall said. "Losing that baby..." She shook her head. "Who knows how different Virginia's life might have been. She could have actually been happy."

Cyrus was still holding out hope that his grandmother had had nothing to do with this. He didn't want to believe that Pepper Winchester could be that heartless, that cold and calculating, and yet he suspected when it came to manipulating her family, the woman was capable of anything.

"We're headed for the ranch now," Cyrus said and heard a phone ring in the background.

"I'll meet you there," McCall said but she sounded distracted. "Cyrus? It doesn't look like I'm going to make it to dinner. We just got a call. Roberta Warren was found dead at her home."

# Chapter 13

As she and Cyrus drove out to the Winchester Ranch through the rolling prairie, Kate felt a sense of calm she hadn't expected. She and Cyrus had been so upset to hear about Roberta Warren. Cyrus had quizzed McCall, but she hadn't had any more information.

Now, Kate realized the reason for her sense of calm was this land. The wide-openness, the grass pale yellow against the darker brush that lined the coulees and the Little Rockies an even darker smudge of color against the horizon. The land was washed with a rich patina that shone in the sunlight.

A chinook had blown in this morning, quickly melting last night's snowfall. The way temperatures changed up in this part of the world still amazed her.

"Wait until winter," she'd been told. "One minute it will be thirty below zero, the next it will be thirty above."

Her life felt like the wild Montana weather, she thought,

glancing over at Cyrus. She hadn't known what to expect this morning when she'd woken up in his arms after their lovemaking and middle-of-the-night hot chocolate.

She'd half expected him to pull away, but he hadn't. He seemed to have quit fighting this chemistry between them, this act of fate that had brought them together. But she didn't kid herself that being lovers was anything other than temporary. She knew he had to go back to his life in Denver and she to hers here in Whitehorse.

After breakfast they'd gone over to the cemetery and found her aunt's grave. She would have the headstone changed, but she had no intention of moving her aunt. As they were leaving, Kate noticed there was an empty plot next to her aunt's. Her heart had stopped for a moment as she realized that was where her mother should have been.

"Are you all right?" Cyrus asked as he slowed the pickup.

She nodded as she saw the wooden arch that read *Winchester Ranch*. She was finally going to meet Pepper Winchester. She didn't know what to expect and she had a feeling Cyrus was just as uneasy about this dinner.

It was impossible for her to imagine a mother who could let her daughter believe that her baby had died because the father of the baby was from a family she hated.

But then again, Pepper might be worse than a domineering, controlling mother. She could be a murderer.

Cyrus turned the pickup under the arch. A quarter mile down the narrow road, she spotted the lodge. It was a sprawling log structure that she realized resembled the Old Faithful Lodge in Yellowstone Park.

She'd heard about the place with its several wings and numerous levels, but she hadn't been quite prepared for this. Cyrus had said his brother told him that the inside had all the original furnishings when he'd left here twenty-seven years ago.

Kate just hoped they were all still there. She itched to see what was inside. If it really hadn't been touched for years.

For just a moment in her enthusiasm as a collector of furnishings from the past, she forgot why they were here. Instantly she sobered at the thought. She was about to meet Cyrus's grandmother and aunt Virginia.

"Pepper and Virginia are the most bitter, unhappy women I know," he said as he drove toward the lodge. "The only meaner woman I know is my grandmother's housekeeper, Enid. Now all three of them are living here." He shook his head as if unable to imagine that.

"Maybe they have good reason to be the way they are, at least in Virginia's case," she said.

"Maybe."

He parked out front. As they got out of the pickup, an old dog growled but didn't get up from the shade of what appeared to be a large log garage.

The front door opened. A tall woman appeared.

"Grandmother," Cyrus said under his breath.

Pepper Winchester was an intimidating figure in her black clothing. Her hair was plaited in a long braid of salt and pepper. Kate could see the Winchester resemblance in her dark eyes. She had once been a beauty. No wonder she'd produced such beautiful grandchildren.

"Cyrus," his grandmother said. "I am so glad you're better." She sounded sincere.

"You might change your mind about that," he said. "We need to talk."

"After dinner," she said. "Whatever it is we have to say to each other shouldn't spoil our appetites. Then again, with

Enid's cooking..." She turned her attention to Kate. "This must be your...friend. Kate Landon."

"You are well-informed," Cyrus said.

Pepper took Kate's hand in both of hers. "Please come in," she said, not looking the least bit worried about what Cyrus wanted to talk to her about.

"I understand you have a charming shop in town," Pepper said as they entered the house.

"Thank you." Kate was surprised by the woman's warmth and her relaxed demeanor. Kate had expected her to be cold and uncaring. Even Cyrus seemed a little off-balance by his grandmother's warm welcome.

Pepper, using her cane, led them inside. "Let's go on down to the dining room. Virginia, as usual, is champing at the bit to eat and Enid gets so perturbed if dinner is a minute late. We can visit before she serves. Do you drink wine, Kate?"

"On occasion."

"Well, I'd say this was an occasion, wouldn't you?" Pepper said cheerfully. "It isn't every day that my grandson comes out of a coma and returns to the ranch."

Just as Pepper had said, Virginia was waiting in the dining room. She turned, a glass of wine in her hand, her expression softening a little at the sight of them. Kate saw at once the strong resemblance to Pepper.

But where Pepper could seem warm and charming, Kate sensed Virginia could not. Somewhere in her early fifties, she could have passed for a woman much older. Her face had deep frown lines. She looked like a woman who'd had a hard life. Kate's heart went out to her, knowing what she'd been through—and might have to face again if they were right about the babies being switched.

"Please sit down," Pepper said.

A skinny, elderly woman with wiry gray hair and a scowl appeared.

"Enid, why don't you get us another bottle of wine," Pepper said.

The woman shot her employer a sour look, but did as she was told.

Kate's head was still spinning at all the wonderful Western antiques in every room they'd passed on the way to the dining room. The dining room was no exception.

"You like what you see?" Pepper asked, smiling.

"Your home is beautifully furnished, so true to the era," Kate said, then realized that might not have sounded like a compliment. "I'm sorry."

Pepper waved her apology away as she handed her a glass of wine, then one to her grandson. For a moment the older woman's gaze seemed to study Cyrus. "I was never able to tell you and your brother apart."

"You never tried," Virginia said and downed her wine.

Her mother merely smiled. "My daughter doesn't approve of me. But then again, few members of my family do. Please, let's sit down. Virginia is much more forgiving after she's eaten."

Kate thought this evening might prove to be the exception to the rule.

The food was ghastly, the conversation stilted and the tension so thick it would have taken an axe to cut it. Pepper looked disappointed. Clearly she'd hoped it would be more enjoyable. Kate almost felt sorry for her.

Virginia was somewhat more agreeable after dinner, although obviously tipsy after all the wine she'd consumed.

"Kate and Cyrus want to have a word with me," Pepper said to Virginia after dinner. "I believe we will go down to the parlor. It is the warmest room in the house. Perhaps you'd like to join us later, Virginia."

She took the snub by snatching up the last of the second bottle of wine and stalked out of the dining room.

Cyrus closed the door behind him once he, Kate and Pepper were all in the parlor. He remembered from when he was a boy what a horrible eavesdropper Enid had been. According to his brother, she'd only gotten worse.

A small fire burned in the grate. Pepper waved Kate into one of the leather chairs. Cyrus declined the other one, going to sit on the hearth as his grandmother lowered herself into the chair, her cane leaning against the chair's arm.

Pepper looked to Cyrus expectantly. "Don't be shy. You never have been, but may I ask you something first? I'm sure your brother, Cordell, already told you what I asked him."

"About the third-floor room and what we might have seen that day," Cyrus said, expecting this was the main reason they'd been invited to dinner. "I'm sure he told you I didn't see anything. He would have known."

His grandmother nodded. "But you weren't alone up there." Before he could answer, she said, "I know Jack was there, but I want to know about the other children there that day."

Cordell had already warned him that their grandmother knew they hadn't been alone, something about some party hats she'd found in the room. The third-floor room had been off-limits. It had been used as punishment when his father was a child.

"What did Jack and Cordell tell you?" he asked.

Pepper made a disgruntled sound. "I already have my

suspicions, but I want to hear it from you, Cyrus. Of the bunch, I trust you to tell me the truth."

It had been twenty-seven years. They'd all kept the secret because they'd known better than to be in that room. They also knew better than to allow anyone else in there, especially anyone from the McCormick Ranch.

But now he realized that all of the pieces of this puzzle seemed to fit together. He suddenly understood a lot more about the past.

"The McCormick girls were with us."

"They used to sneak over from their ranch all the time," Cyrus said. "I thought it was because they saw it as an adventure, knowing what would happen if they got caught. I used to wonder why they always left little things behind, hair ribbons and barrettes, paper dolls and grape bubble gum. But now I know that they came over here to taunt you and Virginia."

Pepper sighed. He'd expected her to lie or at least argue that he was wrong. She did neither. "So you know about Virginia and Jordan and the baby."

"You must have been incensed when you found out."

His grandmother smiled at that. "I could have killed Virginia."

"Instead you made sure her baby died by paying to have her baby switched with Marie Dennison's."

Pepper met his gaze and slowly shook her head. "Is that what you think I did?"

"Someone paid Candace Porter five thousand dollars to switch the babies, then killed her."

"Oh, so now you think I not only let Virginia believe her baby had died, I also killed someone?" Pepper asked.

"You have to admit, you don't have the best record when it comes to people dying around you," he pointed out, referring to her husband, Call, who'd allegedly ridden off on horseback one day, never to return.

Pepper turned to stare into the fire. Cyrus wondered if she was contemplating burning in hell. "I have done a lot of things in my life that I'm ashamed of, but that isn't one of them."

"That doesn't answer the question," Cyrus said. "I'm sure it was justified in your warped mind. McCall is going to be paying you an official visit soon. She is getting proof that the babies were switched. Once she traces that money back to you..." He shook his head.

"Candace Porter was my aunt," Kate said. "My mother was visiting her. I'm not sure what happened to her, but we believe whoever killed Candace Porter and my mother did it to cover up the crime."

Pepper turned to meet her gaze, held it for a moment, then looked away. "I'm sorry for your loss, but I didn't kill anyone and I'm sorry, but I know nothing about your mother."

"I hope not, for your sake and your family's," Kate said quietly.

"Virginia needs to be told that Jace Dennison could be her son," Cyrus said.

His grandmother slowly turned to look at him. Her eyes were dark as caverns. "Did you ever consider that Virginia might have been the one who paid the nurse to switch the babies? Jordan McCormick dropped her like a hot piece of pipe when she told him she was pregnant. He never would have married Virginia and she knew it. Her baby dying let her save face."

"I believe her," Kate said as they walked out to his truck. This time the dog, an old blue heeler, didn't even lift his head.

Cyrus glanced over at Kate as if she'd lost her mind. "My grandmother is guilty as hell."

"Probably. But I don't believe she had anyone killed. If she had the babies switched, it was for her daughter."

Cyrus slid behind the wheel, slammed his palm against the steering wheel and swore before reaching for the key in the ignition where he'd left it.

Kate looked up to see his grandmother standing in the doorway. She was leaning on her cane, looking all of her seventy-two years.

"Her number was in Katherine's address book," Cyrus reminded Kate. "Don't let her frailty fool you. My grandmother has always been a force to be reckoned with." He shoved his hat back and started the pickup.

Kate noticed that Pepper was still standing in the doorway watching them leave, an expression of terrible sadness on her face. "I feel sorry for her."

Cyrus swore as he looked over at her. "Don't. I have a feeling she is finally going to get what she deserves."

"She lost her husband and youngest son, Trace?" Kate asked. "I can't imagine what it must be like to lose the man you love, let alone a child."

"Believe me, she didn't miss my grandfather. I doubt she ever loved him. As for Trace, well, him she idolized, but in the end she turned him against her, too. Trace was McCall's father. My grandmother did everything she could to break up Trace's marriage to McCall's mother, Ruby."

"Is that what happened to your father's marriage to your mother?" Kate asked quietly.

"No woman was ever good enough for Pepper's sons. Or man for her daughter. Now my grandmother is obsessed with finding out if someone in the family was a co-conspirator in Trace's death. That's why she was asking about the third-floor room."

Kate listened as he explained this room Call Winchester had used to punish his children. "It sounds horrible. Your grandmother believes one of you saw Trace's murder?"

"Or at least who else was involved. I have to admit, it is strange that Trace was killed within sight of the ranch. You see now what a screwed-up family I have?"

"Is that why you were afraid of getting involved with me?"

Cyrus shot her a look, then turned quickly back to his driving. "It doesn't matter my reasons. I *am* involved." He didn't sound happy about it.

"So your grandmother locked herself away in that ranch lodge for the past twenty-seven years." She feared Cyrus had locked himself away, at least emotionally, as well. As they drove under the Winchester Ranch sign, Kate realized something.

"Your grandmother wasn't the only one who would have been unhappy about Virginia and Jordan McCormick," she said. "If the rumor was true about Pepper and Hunt McCormick…"

Cyrus swore. "Joanna McCormick hates my grandmother with a passion, so I would imagine there is something to the rumors about Pepper and Hunt."

"So what is this Joanna McCormick like?" she asked.

He hit the brakes, surprising her. "The McCormick Ranch is just back down the road. I say we pay her a visit."

Cyrus hated that his visit to his grandmother had upset him more than he wanted to admit. Being back on the ranch had brought back so many memories. Good memories of when they'd all been a family.

"You never mention your mother," Kate said as if reading his mind.

He chuckled. "That's because she left when I was little. She wasn't strong enough to stand up to my grandmother, so she hit the road. I've heard she remarried and has four sons."

"I'm sorry." She squeezed his arm and let go.

He was sorry to lose her touch. When he glanced over at her, she had tears in her eyes. She quickly wiped at them. "Hey, it wasn't all bad. I was just thinking of all the great memories I had at the ranch. It was a wonderful place to grow up. Cordell and I learned to ride when we were two. We used to ride every day. We literally had the run of the ranch by the time we were seven."

"But then you were exiled," she said. "It's so sad. You have this big family and yet…"

"There's the McCormick Ranch," he said, as if needing to change the subject. "You up to this?"

She nodded. "Does Jordan still live here?"

"He was killed in a hay-baling accident about a year after Virginia gave birth."

Kate shot him a shocked look. "How horrible."

Cyrus nodded. "Joanna has two daughters, both much younger than Jordan. I haven't seen them for the past twenty-seven years and have no idea what happened to them."

As he turned into the McCormick Ranch, he thought about the bad blood between the two families and wondered what kind of reception they would get.

He also wondered what his grandmother would do with the information he'd given her about the two McCormick girls being in the third-floor room the day Trace Winchester was murdered within sight of the ranch.

That day he and his brother had had a small pair of binoculars they'd been arguing over. The last thing he remembered was Cordell letting the girls look through them. They had looked out toward the distant ridge.

What if one of them had seen the murder?

But if one of them had, why wouldn't they have said something—especially if they'd seen more than one Winchester on that ridge that day?

As Cyrus drove into the McCormick Ranch, Kate saw a man shoeing a horse over by an old barn. He looked up, watching them drive by.

She looked away from his intense gaze, suspecting they weren't going to get a warm welcome anywhere on this ranch.

Cyrus parked in front of the large ranch house. As Kate got out, she looked back toward the old barn. The man was still watching her and Cyrus with interest.

"Looks like everyone is over by the corral," Cyrus said and they walked over to see what was going on.

Kate knew at once that the older woman sitting on the corral fence was Joanna McCormick. At sixty-eight, Joanna was a tall, athletic-looking woman with short brown hair and a weathered face that told of many hours spent outdoors.

She was watching intently as a trainer worked with a horse in the ring. Several cowboys sat a little farther down the fence, also watching.

Kate had heard that Joanna McCormick was known for the quarter horses she raised. Cyrus said he'd seen her once years ago at a quarter-horse sale outside of Laramie, Wyoming, on a ranch where his father had been working at the time.

Her husband, Hunt, had been with her. Cyrus had described Hunt as a large, gentle-looking man with a kind face. Not handsome like Call Winchester had been. Cyrus had wondered at the time what his grandmother had seen in Hunt. And, if it was true that his grandmother had had an affair with him, why Hunt hadn't left his tightly wound, brittle wife for Pepper.

Joanna gave them only a glance from under her Western straw hat as they joined her on the corral fence. "Do I know you?" she said without looking at them.

"I'm Cyrus Winchester." Her brows shot up as she turned to give him a hard look. "And this is Kate Landon."

"What do you want?" Joanna said, turning back to what was going on in the corral.

"We need to talk to you about Jordan and Virginia," Cyrus said.

The older woman acted as if she hadn't heard him as she called to the trainer to keep the horse's head up.

"If you prefer to talk to the sheriff…" Cyrus said.

"My son is dead and I could give a damn about Virginia Winchester," Joanna replied. "So I can't imagine why the sheriff would want to talk to me."

"So you didn't pay Candace Porter to switch the babies so it appeared Virginia's had died?" Cyrus asked.

The cowboys down the fence weren't looking in their direction, but they were clearly listening.

Joanna McCormick swung her legs over and dropped off the corral fence, her face crimson with anger. "How dare you—"

"Candace Porter was my aunt," Kate said, keeping her voice low. "The other woman who disappeared at the same time was my mother. We believe whoever paid to have those babies switched killed both women to keep the secret that Jace Dennison is really your grandson."

Without a word, Joanna started for the house. Cyrus shot Kate a what-the-hell look and they followed her.

The McCormick ranch house was a sprawling two-story. Like the Winchester Ranch, it had many of the same amenities, including the western décor, Native American rugs and antler lamps and fixtures. A huge wagon wheel hung down from the ceiling in the massive living room, lights glittering from it.

A fire in the massive fireplace had died to only glowing embers.

Joanna McCormick walked to it, picked up the poker and stabbed angrily at the coals. "Isn't it enough that your grandmother tried to take my husband?" she demanded, turning to glare at them. "Now you want to try to take another woman's son?"

"You don't seem all that surprised," Cyrus said. "I think you knew all about the baby switch."

"I know nothing of the kind," she snapped. "Why would I let someone else raise my grandson?"

"Because you couldn't bear the alternative. I think you were afraid Jordan would marry Virginia."

"He would never have married her."

"Was that his idea or yours?" Cyrus asked.

"I told him that if he married her, he was off the ranch. That was all I had to do."

"Didn't you care that Virginia's baby was your flesh and blood?" Kate asked.

"Was it?" Joanna asked pointedly. "Even Jordan wasn't sure of that."

Cyrus laughed. "You remind me so much of my grandmother. You know, I wouldn't put it past the two of you to have come up with the baby switch together. You both had motive for switching the babies. Coming up with the five thousand dollars to pay off the nurse wouldn't have been that hard, even though that was a lot of money thirty years ago. You could have split it. Would be easier to cover up."

Joanna looked at him, aghast. "Your grandmother and I? We can't be in the same room together."

"Unless you had a common goal. My grandmother wasn't about to let your son marry into the Winchester family."

Joanna raised a brow at that. "Why? *She* tried to marry into the McCormick family."

"That was years ago," he pointed out.

"I have a good memory," she said. "Do you really believe Jace would have been better off being raised by Virginia?"

"You stole her baby and any chance she might have had for happiness with your son," Cyrus said. "So I guess we'll never know how different she might be today."

Kate knew Cyrus was winging it, hoping for a reaction, but Joanna McCormick, other than being furious, wasn't giving him much.

"The only thing I'm not sure about is which one of you killed Candace Porter and her sister, who was in town because she knew about the switch," Cyrus continued. "It's a toss-up which of you is more cold-blooded."

"I've heard enough," Joanna said. "If you had any evidence, the sheriff would be here, not you two. Now get out. If you don't leave I am going to call the sheriff."

"You won't have to bother calling Sheriff McCall Winchester," Cyrus said. "She'll be paying you a visit soon enough."

Joanna made an angry sound. "Too many damn Winchesters around here."

"More Winchesters than you want to admit," he said.

Some of the steel seemed to leave Joanna's spine. "What is the point of ruining Jace Dennison's life if somehow the babies did get switched? I watched him grow up, saw him at every rodeo. He's a fine young man and Marie is a wonderful mother. Are you really going to take that away from them when you aren't even certain the babies were switched?"

She looked to Kate as if hoping to find sympathy with her. "Maybe your aunt getting killed had nothing to do with either of the babies."

"Or are you worried about Jace Dennison?" Cyrus asked. "Or what's going to happen to you and the McCormick Ranch when you go to prison for murder? Maybe my grandmother will come after your husband again."

"Get out!" Joanna screeched.

Cyrus turned to leave, Kate leading the way.

"If I ever see you on my land again, I'll shoot first and ask questions later," Joanna McCormick yelled after them. Behind them they heard something break. Neither looked back.

But as they were leaving, Kate saw the man she'd seen watching them earlier. He was standing just outside and she got the impression he'd been listening to their conversation.

As Cyrus slid behind the wheel, she asked, "Who is that man?"

"What man?" he asked as he started the pickup.

"The one standing by the side of the house," Kate said. "He was watching us earlier and I think he was eavesdropping on our conversation with Joanna McCormick."

Cyrus glanced up, but when Kate followed his gaze, the man was gone.

# Chapter 14

"Boy, have you been stirring the pot," McCall said when she got Cyrus on his cell the next morning. "Joanna McCormick called. She is hotter than a pistol and it sounds like with good reason."

"I know I probably shouldn't have gone by there. It was a spur-of-the-moment decision," Cyrus said.

"She said you accused her of baby switching and murder and taunted her with our grandmother coming after her husband—once Joanna was behind bars." McCall laughed. "Tell me you didn't."

"I couldn't help it. Damn, she is just like Pepper. Only I swear I think she's meaner," he said.

"She wants me to arrest you for everything from trespassing to slander. I calmed her down a little. She did make it clear that if I run for sheriff again, she won't vote for me. As if she did this time."

"Sorry about that."

"Yeah, that was a real heartbreaker."

"I wouldn't be surprised if she paid to have the babies switched. As for the murder or possible murder... I don't know. She's mean enough."

"Cyrus, I didn't call you just about Joanna," McCall said, her tone suddenly serious.

He knew at once. "Roberta."

"We found a suicide note. She confessed to paying Candace Porter to switch the babies. She also confessed to killing Candace when she saw her switch the babies back."

Cyrus shot Kate a look. Moments earlier they'd been sitting at the kitchen table having cinnamon rolls and coffee. Kate had stopped what she'd been doing and was now staring at him.

"She confessed to killing Kate's mother, as well."

He was trying to get his mind around this. He'd known Roberta was involved but he hadn't expected this. "How did she kill herself?"

"Pills."

"Did she say anything else?" he asked.

"No. The confession was handwritten, the writing deteriorating pretty quickly as the pills must have taken effect."

So they might never know what she'd done with Kate's mother's body.

"Would you like me to tell Kate?" McCall asked.

"No, I'll do it." He hung up and looked at Kate. Before he could say anything, she stepped into his arms.

Kate felt as if she was in shock. Roberta Warren had confessed? She'd known the hospital administrator was involved, but she'd suspected the person who'd paid her aunt to switch the babies would be Pepper Winchester or Joanna McCormick or Audie Dennison.

She'd thought there would be more.

"I'm sorry," Cyrus said. "That's all Roberta said in the suicide note."

Kate knew she should have been relieved. She'd been right about her aunt changing her mind and switching the babies back. She'd also been right that whoever had killed her aunt had also killed her mother.

She even knew why Roberta had done it.

Cyrus had said he thought a woman had cut the cable in the basement because it had taken her several tries. The crying baby doll was also something a woman was more likely to use as a threat, rather than a man.

It all added up.

So why didn't she feel some relief at knowing the truth? Instead, she just felt empty inside. She was disappointed that she wasn't going to get to bury her mother beside Katherine in the cemetery. But did she really want to know what Roberta had done to her?

She looked at Cyrus and felt the full extent of this news. It was more than an end to their search. Cyrus would be going back to Denver now. There would be no reason for him to stay any longer. The threat was over.

"Do you want me to make some hot chocolate?" Cyrus asked.

She smiled, her eyes filling with tears at his kindness, but she shook her head. Not even hot chocolate with marshmallows would work this time.

"McCall is tracing Roberta's bank statements to see if she can find the five thousand dollars," Cyrus was saying.

It took her a moment before she shot him a look of surprise. "If Roberta confessed…"

"McCall is just covering all the bases." He hesitated. "Kate, maybe you should cancel the haunted house."

"Why?" she asked studying him intently. "You don't think she acted alone?"

"Until McCall can verify Roberta's story, I would just feel better—"

"No." They'd both put their lives on hold during all this. Cyrus especially. "As far as I'm concerned, it's over. There really isn't any reason you need to—"

"I'm staying to help with the haunted house," he said, almost seeming hurt that she would try to get him to leave sooner.

A line had already formed outside Second Hand Kate's before Kate signaled for Cyrus to open the door. All the volunteers were in place. Kate couldn't have been happier with the results.

She'd gone around making last-minute changes, knowing she was only making them to keep her mind off everything that had happened. She'd also been avoiding Cyrus. He'd worked tirelessly all afternoon in the basement, changing all the locks, not only on the doors, but also the windows.

If she hadn't known he would be leaving, his effort to make her safe was a sure sign.

There was an air of excitement as the door opened and she got her first glimpse of the children and their parents pouring in. Kate told herself that Whitehorse was her home. She could handle whatever life threw at her after this.

*No regrets,* she thought as she took her place at the exit door. Jasmine had sewn her a devil costume. It was huge and allowed her to step into it, disappearing in the darkness by the door until it was time to give everyone one last fright.

No, she would never regret this time spent with Cyrus. Eventually she would get over him, she told herself, even though she feared she was lying.

She wondered where Cyrus was and half feared that he might have already left. He'd told her he hated goodbyes because of all the places he'd had to leave due to his father's work when he was growing up.

Maybe it would be easier if, when the haunted house closed its doors at 10:00 p.m., she would find him gone. The thought broke her heart. She couldn't imagine never seeing him again.

She brushed at the sudden tears that welled in her eyes. She could hear someone moving quickly through the maze and got ready to play her part.

Cyrus had tried to station himself where he could see Kate, but the moment she stepped back into the huge devil costume, she disappeared into the darkness from sight. The basement had quickly filled with screams of terror and excitement. It echoed through the cavernous room.

Kate and her friends had done a wonderful job. He'd been amazed how many people had been waiting outside the door and since he'd taken his position, the line had not stopped for a minute.

Kate must be so proud.

Just the thought of her tore at his heart. Maybe it would have been easier on both of them if he'd left this morning. After her successful haunted house, she would have her friends and all the volunteers to celebrate with.

He'd originally planned to leave in the morning, but he realized now that leaving tonight would be better. Kate knew he hated goodbyes. She'd understand.

The roar of the basement increased. He tried to see Kate in the darkness of the devil's cape by the back door. There was only the faint exit light glowing on the wall nearby, but every once in a while the cape moved.

He tried to relax. McCall had called earlier to tell him that they'd gotten a fingerprint off the batteries from the doll he and Kate had found in the shop crib. The print had matched Roberta's.

Cyrus still believed that someone had come up with the money to pay Candace Porter, aka Katherine Landon, to switch the babies. He was sure it had been either his grandmother or Joanna McCormick or both.

Those suspicions were confirmed when McCall called to tell him that she had found in Roberta's files that she'd made a deposit to her account on Dec. 17, 1980 for ten thousand dollars. She'd made a withdrawal for five thousand Dec. 19, 1980.

Roberta Warren must have been the go-between. Her neck must have been on the line to make sure the nurse did as she was told.

They wouldn't know if the babies had actually been switched until McCall located Jace Dennison. McCall had told him that she was having trouble getting Virginia's baby's body exhumed. Not only Pepper and Joanna were fighting it, but Virginia, as well.

Was it possible Virginia had been the one to pay to have the babies switched?

He tried to put it out of his mind. McCall was still investigating. But he had to let it go. All he cared about was that now Kate should be safe.

The devil costume hadn't moved for some time, he realized with a start. Nor had he heard anyone shriek as they exited the building for he wasn't sure how long.

He swung down from his perch and raced along the back of the horror exhibits to the exit, telling himself she was fine. The killer was dead. He had no reason to worry about her.

As he swung around the corner, he saw at once that the huge cape hung empty. Even then, he told himself she must have just stepped out of it for a moment.

Then he saw the note pinned to the fabric.

He snatched it off and stepped out of the way of the costumed revelers. He read the scrawled letters.

I have Kate. If you ever want to see her alive again come to the old hospital alone. We will be waiting.

"Cyrus?"

He jumped at the sound of Jasmine's voice. Hastily, he stuffed the note into his pocket as he turned to face her.

"Is everything all right?" she asked.

He knew he must have looked like hell. "I need you to do something for me," he said, surprised how calm he sounded. "Can you make sure everyone gets out of here and lock up? I've sent Kate to a motel. She wasn't feeling well. I'm going to go check on her now."

If Kate's friend suspected anything, she didn't let on. A part of him wanted to tell her, wanted to tell her to call the sheriff. He knew he might need backup in case things went to hell tonight, but he couldn't take the chance that if he didn't go alone, it would get Kate killed.

He left by the side door and ran the five blocks to the old hospital. It was pitch-black beside the building. He stood for a moment getting his bearings.

The inside of the building was dark, the windowpanes like blank eyes staring out. He couldn't see if someone was watching him. Or waiting just beyond the glass.

The front door was still chained and padlocked. Cyrus walked around the building to a side door. Also locked.

At the back door, he slowed as he saw someone had left it ajar for him.

Away from a window, he reached into his shoulder holster and drew out his weapon. A sliver of fear embedded itself beneath his skin. He had no idea what he was going to find once he stepped inside.

All he could think about was getting to Kate. If whoever took her hurt her…

Cyrus moved to the door, listening, but heard no sound coming from inside the building.

Carefully, he eased the door open, staying to one side, then slipped into the darkness. It took a moment for his eyes to adjust before he could see a faint light coming from down the hall.

He started toward it, his boot heels echoing softly as he approached.

When he reached the corner, he saw where the light was coming from, but then again, he'd already known, hadn't he?

The light was coming from the open door of the nursery.

# Chapter 15

McCall had expected her cousin to go back to Denver once he'd heard about Roberta Warren's confession.

Even though he hadn't said anything, she'd bet he was as suspicious as she was. McCall didn't like it when everything got tied up too neatly. It made her cautious. That was one reason she was determined to get all the evidence together as quickly as possible.

That meant verifying everything in Roberta's confession. McCall had already contacted the president of the bank. She was meeting him there after discovering a safe-deposit box key among Roberta's possessions.

At her knock, he opened the door and led her into the safe-deposit room. Using her key and he using the bank's, she opened the box and carried it to a table.

McCall dumped the contents of the safe-deposit box on the table and began to go through it. She hadn't found anything at Roberta's death scene to indicate it had been anything but a suicide. Of course, McCall had been suspicious nonetheless. If Roberta really had been responsible for everything, then this case was over, all the missing details lost forever.

But what bothered McCall was Roberta's motive. Money? What other motive could she have had?

In her suicide note, Roberta said she'd found out that Candace was really Katherine Landon and had lied about being a registered nurse. So Roberta said she'd blackmailed her into switching the babies because Virginia Winchester had no business raising a baby and Marie Dennison deserved a child. Roberta said she'd known that Marie's baby had a weak heart.

There'd been no mention of the five grand she'd paid Candace/Katherine in the suicide note. That seemed odd to McCall.

The contents of the safe-deposit box included a stack of stocks and bonds, a large amount of cash, Roberta's husband's birth and death certificates and her own birth certificate and an envelope marked *In case of death.*

Carefully McCall opened the envelope and began to read, her heart pounding as she read Roberta Warren's *real* confession. The woman had definitely known too much.

"I'm going to need backup, two units, stat," the sheriff said, getting on the phone.

Kate stared at the gun, then at the masked man pointing it at her.

He'd appeared before the rest of the crowd had reached her, wearing a hideous monster mask. The moment Kate had seen him with the gun, she'd screamed, but the sound had been lost in the ruckus of the haunted-house revelers.

He'd grabbed her arm and shoved the barrel of the gun

into her ribs. "Give me any trouble and I will kill you right here."

She'd believed him as he'd handed her a mask that covered not only her face but her hair.

"Put that on," he'd ordered, then he'd forced her at gunpoint out the side door to where he'd parked his pickup right outside her shop in the alley. Then he drove her to the old hospital.

Now she sat on the floor, her back against the wall, watching him pace. He kept looking at his watch, giving her the impression he was expecting someone. There was something about him that almost seemed familiar, but with that horrible mask covering everything but his eyes and a little slit of mouth, she couldn't place him.

"Who are we waiting for?" she asked, but like the other questions she'd asked him, he hadn't bothered to answer.

So, she sat and listened, waiting, her heart in her throat, afraid she knew exactly who they were waiting for.

As Cyrus walked down the hallway toward the nursery, he thought of the dream that had started all of this. It had brought him to Whitehorse, to Kate. He knew Kate had been in danger since the moment she'd set foot in this town, but it didn't make it any easier. His dream and him showing up had only put her in more jeopardy.

For days he'd been telling himself he had to get back to Denver, back to the life he and Cordell had made for themselves.

It had been fear. He'd seen his twin go through a horrible marriage and an even worse divorce. His own father had been forced to raise his sons alone because he'd married the wrong woman.

Cyrus hadn't realized just how afraid he was of falling in

love until Kate. Love. He loved her. He tried to think of the exact moment it had happened and instead saw a series of moments culminating in him falling head over heels for her.

What was he so afraid of? Marriage to Kate?

Or the fear that somehow marriage would ruin what they had?

But now that he might lose Kate...

He paused to listen. This old hospital seemed even creepier tonight, although this wouldn't be the first time a killer had moved through these halls. He could almost feel the ghosts of those who had walked these halls before him. Kate's aunt, for one. And probably her sister, who had come here to find out what had happened to Katherine.

*Who else?* he wondered as he neared the nursery. Who was waiting for him?

He thought he could smell the person's anxiety, a mixture of fear and anger and regret. But it was thoughts of Kate that had his heart pounding. She had to be all right.

He stopped just before he reached the nursery. He knew that the killer had heard him approaching. He had to know if Kate was okay. "Kate?"

"Cyrus?" He heard both relief and fear in her voice. "Cyrus, don't—"

"Shut up," he heard someone order in a hoarse whisper. "We're waiting for you," said the muffled voice.

Cyrus stepped around the corner and into the old hospital nursery, just as he had that night in his dream.

Only this time he knew the woman on the floor.

"So you're the dreamer," the man in the mask said as he pointed the gun in his hand at Kate's head. "Drop your weapon on the floor and kick it over to me.... Join your girlfriend."

The man wore a monster mask, his voice muffled behind it. Pale blue eyes peered out of the holes. Cyrus could smell the fear coming off the man and see his nerves showing in the way he held the gun.

"Why don't you take off the mask," Cyrus said as he moved over to where Kate was on the floor. He sensed the man was hiding behind the mask, not to conceal his identity, but to distance himself from what he was about to do.

"Sit down next to her," the man ordered, waving the gun.

"What's the point of the mask since you plan to kill us anyway?" Cyrus said. Kill us, then kill himself, would be his guess from the jumpy way the man was acting.

"I told you to sit down."

"Not until you take off the mask and tell me what the hell this is about."

"You are in no position to make demands," the man said angrily, his words losing a lot of their power, muffled as they were behind the mask.

Cyrus could see that the man was trying to prepare himself for what he was about to do. Otherwise he would have shot Cyrus the moment he came through the nursery door.

They stood glaring at each other, the gun shaking in the man's trembling hand. He was no killer, but Cyrus suspected he'd felt forced to kill before—and would again. He'd known the killer had nothing to lose. He realized with a start that was even more true of the man standing before him.

"I know who you are, Audie," Cyrus said. "Audie Dennison."

Audie started, clearly surprised that Cyrus knew who he was. With a furious curse, he ripped the mask from his face.

On the floor next to Cyrus, Kate let out a gasp. "He's the man I saw out at Joanna McCormick's ranch. He was shoeing a horse out there and eavesdropping on our conversation," Kate said as she pushed herself to her feet.

"I told you to stay down," Audie cried, waving the gun at her.

Kate didn't listen. Like Cyrus, Kate had to see that Audie was losing his control over them. She looked scared but unhurt and he couldn't have loved her more than he did at that moment.

"It's going to be all right," he wanted to tell her. But he couldn't be sure about that. "I love you," he said.

She glanced over at him and smiled, tears welling in her eyes. "It's about time you realized that."

"Both of you," Audie ordered, looking scared that he was losing control of this situation, "sit down—"

"Not until you tell us what this is about," Cyrus interrupted. "Don't you owe us that much?"

"Owe *you?*" Audie bellowed. "Do you know how much pain you've caused my sister with your questions and your stupid dream?" His voice broke and tears filled his eyes, but Cyrus knew better than to try to take the gun away from him. At least not yet.

"What happened all those years ago?" Kate asked quietly.

Audie looked at her and Cyrus saw the man weaken. Clearly he wanted to get this over with, and yet the magnitude of what he was about to do had him hesitating.

"You did it for your sister," Kate said, her voice soft, comforting.

"Katherine told you about someone paying her five thousand dollars to switch the babies," Cyrus prodded.

"Five thousand?" Audie was shaking his head as if confused.

So she hadn't told him about the money. "You encouraged her to do it, knowing how much your sister wanted a baby, deserved one, unlike Virginia Winchester," Kate said, still speaking to him in that calm tone.

Audie's confusion seemed to clear as he locked onto her words. "That tramp Virginia had no business with a baby. She wasn't even married."

"But then Katherine changed her mind," Cyrus said. "She betrayed you."

A sadness filled the man's eyes along with a deep anger. "I loved her. I would have done anything for her. She promised. I heard her talking to her sister on the phone by the nurses' station. She'd left the cart with the medical supplies in the hallway. I didn't even realize I'd picked up the scalpel."

"You had no choice but to kill her sister, too," Cyrus said.

"You're the one who left the bracelet on my grandmother's doorstep," Kate said.

"It was a foolish, sentimental thing to do," Audie admitted. "But I couldn't throw it away and I couldn't keep it, either."

Kate began to cry softly.

"I couldn't let it come out about the babies," Audie said angrily. "Marie was so happy. Of course she was sad about Virginia's baby dying. Marie is that kind of woman. I owed her. I had to do whatever it took to make her happy."

"And you did," Cyrus said. "Roberta Warren must have known it was you. Was she threatening you? Is that why you had to stop her?"

Audie blinked. "That old hag at the hospital?"

Cyrus felt his stomach clinch. Audie Dennison hadn't killed Roberta. Nor had he known about the five thousand dollars that had changed hands. "Whose idea was it to switch the babies? Who paid Katherine to do it?"

\* \* \*

It took McCall too long to find Jasmine in the depths of the haunted house. "Where are Kate and Cyrus?"

Jasmine looked surprised and instantly worried. "Cyrus said he sent her to a motel and that he was going to join her. I thought it was odd. No way would Kate have left her haunted house before it even got started good." Her eyes widened in realization.

"You've been right here since the haunted house opened, right?" McCall said. "Who came through at the beginning?"

Jasmine frowned, clearly working to remember. She rattled off a few names of families she remembered. "Wait a minute. The first person who came in didn't even have a kid with him. I thought it was funny, but I figured he must be a volunteer Kate had recruited and he was late and that's why he rushed in the way he did."

"Jasmine, who—"

"Audie Dennison."

Audie frowned. "How would I know who paid her to switch the babies?" he demanded. "I thought she was doing it out of the goodness of her heart. I was going to marry her..." He was waving the gun again, clearly upset. "I was in love." His gaze seemed to focus on the two of them. "Like you." His voice broke.

"Audie," Cyrus said, seeing something in the man's eyes that turned his blood to ice.

"My sister Marie died tonight."

Before Cyrus could move, Audie turned the gun on himself. The loud report echoed through the nursery, a thunder of pain-ending sound.

Cyrus grabbed Kate, sheltering her from the sight as

Audie Dennison dropped to the floor, his gun clattering to the worn tiles. And Cyrus found himself again standing in the old hospital nursery with a body lying in a pool of blood.

As he took Kate in his arms, he heard the sound of sirens in the distance.

# *Epilogue*

Kate heard the racket outside the front door of the shop and hurried to see what was going on. She hadn't seen Cyrus all morning and now when she looked out, she caught a glimpse of him through the thickly falling snow.

As she opened the door, he dragged in a Christmas tree and stood it up for her inspection. "So, what do you think?" Both he and the tree were covered in fresh snow. She breathed in the scent of pine and snow.

What did she think? That she loved this man more than life.

Love had saved them. As corny as it sounded, Kate knew that the love she and Cyrus shared that moment in the old hospital nursery had saved their lives.

She'd seen the change in Audie Dennison. He'd come there to kill them. He'd killed before. She didn't doubt that he would have done anything to spare his sister. But Marie was dead and while Audie had nothing to lose, he couldn't bring himself to kill again. Not two people who anyone could see adored each other.

McCall had arrived moments after the sound of the gunshot died away. She'd come barreling in, weapon drawn, fear that she'd arrived too late in her eyes. Maybe blood *was* thicker than water, because Kate could see that McCall had true affection for her cousin. It would be nice for McCall to have family again. And Cyrus, too.

She knew how relieved he was to find out that his grandmother had had nothing to do with switching Virginia's baby with Marie's. Kate thought maybe Virginia and Pepper's relationship might have a chance to heal and that McCall's Christmas wedding could bring the entire Winchester family back together.

Cyrus was still concerned that his grandmother was up to something and anxious about the wedding. He didn't want anything to go wrong for McCall and Luke. Only time would tell, but Kate, always the optimist, thought this could be the most perfect Christmas ever for all of them.

She was looking forward to the Christmas wedding, which was now only two weeks away.

Whitehorse had been shocked when the news had come out that Joanna McCormick had been arrested for the murder of Roberta Warren. McCall had found proof, not only in Roberta's real confession, but also in phone records, bank accounts and DNA from the scene at Roberta's house.

Faced with all the evidence, Joanna McCormick had confessed it all. She was the one who had paid Roberta ten thousand dollars to switch the babies. Joanna would have done anything to keep her son from Virginia Winchester—including letting him believe his infant son had died.

What Joanna didn't know was that Roberta used blackmail and five thousand dollars to try to coerce Katherine into making the switch.

Joanna had hired Audie to do more than shoe some of her horses. She'd paid him to try to scare off Kate, and when he'd balked, she'd taken the job into her own hands. She'd been the one to cut the cable and put the doll in the nursery. She'd had a key to the old library back when her husband, Hunt, had been on the library board.

After the shock and horror of what had happened, Kate had been filled with a deep sadness, but Cyrus had been there for her. It turned out that Roberta Warren wasn't the only one to leave a detailed true confession of her part in all this. Audie Dennison had left one as well at his house.

That confession had given Kate the greatest peace of mind. He'd told her where he'd buried her mother. She'd been able to have her mother's remains buried properly next to her aunt's at the local cemetery.

The sisters were now buried side by side, with matching headstones and inscriptions with their real names and the dates they had died. Earlier Kate had gone by the cemetery to put Christmas wreaths on her aunt's and mother's graves. It seemed fitting that they were together again.

"I know the tree is a little flat on that one side, but I thought we could put it against the wall," Cyrus said now, looking worried that she didn't like it.

She smiled, still taken aback sometimes at how lucky she'd been to have him come into her life. She liked to think her aunt and mother had had something to do with that.

"I love the tree," Kate said as she stepped toward him. "And look what I have." She held mistletoe over their heads and saw his dark eyes shimmer with love. His kiss made her toes curl and her heart pound.

But it was nothing like his proposal that night under their

first Christmas tree. An odd thing happened when she said yes. She thought she heard the sound of tiny tinkling sleigh bells and glanced toward the glassed-in case where her mother's and her aunt's bracelets now rested side by side.

\* \* \* \* \*

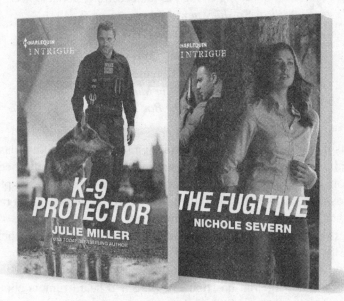

Rising to her feet, Lori peered through the floor-to-ceiling glass
walls into the reception area separating the county's legal offices
from the law enforcement branch. She spotted them by the empty
mosaic-tiled fountain. Two men, one nearly as handsome as the
other, but both equally repugnant to her.

Coulter and his attorney, Simon Wingate, stood with their
heads bent close to one another. Lori's lip curled. There'd been
few sightings of the eccentric millionaire since he'd bought the
massive acreage out on Highway 19. She'd heard rumors about
the man being good-looking but... Lori narrowed her eyes. He
wasn't just handsome; he was gorgeous.

Disgusted with the thought, she shifted her attention to the
man's clothes. What did a man suspected of endangering young
women wear to be questioned by the local prosecutors? Loose
linen pants and a finely woven white shirt. And flip-flops. Not the
cheap dollar-store shower shoes Bella'd been wearing. No, his
had wide straps fashioned in supple leather. He looked like a guy
on vacation.

The sandals were a sharp contrast to the impeccably shined wingtips the man standing next to him wore.

Simon Wingate looked every inch the prep-school-educated politician's son.

Lori clenched her back teeth and focused on the man in the expertly tailored suit. He was the light to his client's dark. The perfect foil. All warm, gold-tipped curls, crinkly blue eyes and sun-kissed skin. Lori was woman enough to admit her mouth sometimes watered when she saw Simon Wingate. Not today, though.

Masters County's newest resident had lawyered up and come to head them off at the pass. No doubt Coulter waved a wad of cash, and city slicker Simon had come a-runnin'. Judging by Coulter's unperturbed expression and the district attorney's abrupt halt to Lori's statement, whatever they'd said had worked. He was about to slither out the doors of Masters County Municipal Center a free man.

*Don't miss*
For the Defense,
*available September 2021 wherever*
*Harlequin Intrigue books and ebooks are sold.*

Harlequin.com

# HARLEQUIN

# INTRIGUE

## SEEK THRILLS. SOLVE CRIMES.
## JUSTICE SERVED.

Save **$1.00**

on the purchase of **ANY**
Harlequin Intrigue book.

Available wherever books are sold,
including most bookstores, supermarkets,
drugstores and discount stores.

---

# Save $1.00

## on the purchase of ANY Harlequin Intrigue book.

Coupon valid until November 22, 2021. Redeemable at participating outlets in the
U.S. and Canada only. Not redeemable at Barnes & Noble stores. Limit one coupon per customer.

52617166

® and ™ are trademarks owned by Harlequin Enterprises ULC.

© 2021 Harlequin Enterprises ULC

BACCOUP40622MAX

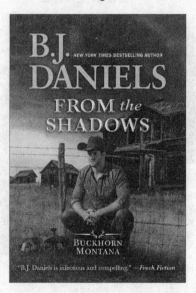

SPECIAL EXCERPT FROM

**◈ HARLEQUIN**

# ROMANTIC SUSPENSE

*Daisy Rambler's new job in small coastal Knoware, Washington,
is a new start for her and her sixteen-year-old daughter, away
from an abusive ex. When her daughter goes missing, local hero
and paramedic Blade Savick comes to the rescue—but more
danger lurks around the corner...*

Read on for a sneak preview of
A Firefighter's Ultimate Duty,
first in Heroes of the Pacific Northwest,
a new series by Beverly Long.

He reached out for her hand. Held it tightly. His hands were warm
from holding his coffee cup. His touch was firm yet gentle.

"You do not have to be afraid," he said. "I will not let him hurt
you or Sophie, or anyone else for that matter. I'm going to stop this
bastard."

That scared her. "He's got no moral compass, Blade. He won't
fight fair."

"I had that pretty much figured out when you told us that he
knocked you out of a chair."

Harsh. The words were harsh. And her body gave an involuntary
flinch.

"He'll never get close enough to you again to do something like
that. You have my word," he said.

Tears came to her eyes. Her grandmother hadn't been there to
tell. Sophie had gotten the sanitized version, and even Jane had

simply gotten bits and pieces. It was the first time she'd ever told anyone the whole ugly truth. Well, almost all the truth.

"There's one more thing," she said. "Nobody knows this. Well, that's not true. The police in Denver know this but nobody else. After he hit me, I made the decision that I was going to leave him. But I didn't do it for a couple weeks. During the interim, I found an opportunity to look at his laptop computer."

"What did the Denver police say?"

"About what I expected. That it wasn't illegal to keep an electronic file of publicly released news articles. Or to look at odd things for purchase. I just wanted it documented somewhere what I had seen. In case."

"In case you disappeared."

"Yes." And damn it, her eyes filled with tears.

"Hey, hey! Don't cry," he said, somewhat pleadingly.

She did not want to. She sniffed and blinked and still a sob escaped.

In one smooth movement, he was out of his chair and kneeling next to her. He gathered her in his arms. And he held her, her head resting against his chest, and he rocked her gently.

*Don't miss*
A Firefighter's Ultimate Duty *by Beverly Long,*
*available September 2021 wherever*
*Harlequin Romantic Suspense*
*books and ebooks are sold.*

Harlequin.com